Isn't It Pretty To Think So?

NICK MILLER

ISN'T IT PRETTY TO THINK SO?

FERNANDO FRENCH PUBLISHING

BERKELEY

2012

PUBLISHED BY FERNANDO FRENCH PUBLISHING

© 2012 by Nick Miller
All rights reserved.

Inspired by Los Angeles.
Written in California.
Printed in the United States of America.
Published 2012.

ISBN: 978-0-983-89611-1

Cover art by Emily Tea.

To my father, who inspired me to read books when I was a child.

To my mother, who lives for my happiness.

"We could have had such a damned good time together."

"Yes," I said. "Isn't it pretty to think so?"

—Ernest Hemingway, *The Sun Also Rises*

It is common for those who have glimpsed something beautiful to express regret at not having been able to photograph it. So successful has been the camera's role in beautifying the world that photographs, rather than the world, have become the standard of the beautiful.

—Susan Sontag, *On Photography*

BOOK I: GENESIS

ONE

Tatiana was a prostitute. I've been living with Tatiana for nearly three months now, and I awoke with her again this morning. After our first night together, I tried to imagine my circumstances from the perspective of myself as a child—the version of me that wore a Catholic school uniform, recited passages from the Bible in class, and regularly attended Sunday mass—and came to the conclusion that I'd become, in the best case, an unsavory someone who could, after a lifelong devotion to prayer, be forgiven by God, but more likely someone damned to hell for irreparable sins.

I attribute my first impression of a prostitute to my first-grade teacher—a frighteningly large, hard-hearted, old nun, named Sister Margaret, who had a perverse fondness for slapping young, fleshy wrists with her old, wooden ruler. One morning, during religion class, Sister Margaret read from the Gospel According to Mark in the *New American Bible*. After she read the line, "Mary Magdalene, out of whom [Jesus] had driven seven demons," one of my more brazen classmates raised his hand and asked why Mary Magdalene had demons in her. Sister Margaret, perhaps too senile to realize how young we were, said that some believed Mary to be a prostitute. The same student, emboldened by curiosity, then asked what a prostitute was, and Sister Margaret coldly snapped, "Quiet down, boy. Never mind that," but sneered condescendingly as though whatever Mary Magdalene had been or had done was so evil, only someone as loving as Jesus could forgive her.

Later that night, when my mother was setting our dining-room table for one of her and my father's dinner parties, I asked her about the meaning of the word prostitute. My mother, preoccupied by the seemingly arduous task of choosing the right color of cloth napkins to complement her place settings, ignored my question and told me to help set the table. But, hours later, after all the guests had gone home, she stumbled into my room to kiss me goodnight, smelling of the mysterious liquid she and her friends were always drinking; and, because I was still awake, she ranted about how my grandfather on my father's side had destroyed his family when he began an affair with another woman. "That other woman …" she whispered, "that's what a prostitute is." Years later, my mother became a full-blown alcoholic (white wine was her drink of choice) when my father began a love affair with a mistress of his own.

As my religious education continued, I was taught that there were two forces in the world, good and evil, always in conflict—every day, all day, while I was sleeping, while I was walking around, while I was socializing with others—and that it was my responsibility to ensure that good would always prevail. I latched onto a literal translation of the message, and, consequently, my world was aswarm with unseen good and evil spirits hovering in the air around me, vying for dominance over each other. And everything I *could* see in the world—people, animals, insects, and even inanimate objects (a pillow resting on a bed, a doorknob, a fork, a car)—was ensouled and either governed by a good spirit or an evil spirit. So, as a young boy, I vowed to be an ambassador for the triumph of good over evil. Every night, while my parents cleaned up in the bathroom, I blessed their bed and each of their pillows, using my hands to encase them with an invisible shield of goodness. I also sneaked around to secretly perform cleanses, with my hands outstretched like a priest's, of rooms or cars soon to be occupied by people I cared about. And whenever I was near a baby in a stroller (babies, to me, were even more defenseless against the bad spirits), I waited until the parents looked away for a second before creating a large, protective shield around the baby with my hands and then darting off in another direction with a smile on my face, knowing I'd saved another soul.

My mission to keep others and myself away from harm did, however, result in my developing many disruptive obsessive-compulsive tendencies. Before doing anything with my hands I considered to be important—taking a math test, writing a paper, playing a game of basketball on the blacktop, throwing a baseball—I made the sign of the cross with my thumb on each of my fingers and then, with my index finger, made one on each of my thumbs, believing the ritual would bring me success. I washed my hands (my tools to repel evil) excessively throughout the day, hoping to keep them pure and good, and held my breath—sometimes until I was blue in the face—whenever I felt the air was too thick with bad spirits. And because I forced myself to find an alternative route when I could sense the evil on a section of the ground I was about to walk on, it would often take me several minutes to travel a short distance, as I tiptoed along a curb or swung from a tree branch or guided myself across a fence toward my destination.

In hindsight, Catholicism was, in my interpretation, the art of self-torture: feeling good about oneself was never allowed unless it was deserved (never), and a true hero in the eyes of God was one who starved himself of his desires rather than indulged in them. A belief system rooted in such principles evoked from within me—as a young, impressionable believer—the very powerful and controlling feeling of guilt. So, naturally, I dealt with the feeling quite often in my early life: when, for example, I was too lazy to cleanse my parents' bed of evil or put a protective shield around a baby in a stroller, I'd feel guilty, as if my inaction were endangering them, and, often in those instances, I feared I'd have to live with that guilt for the rest of my life.

But guilt began to really dominate my life when, during my pre-adolescent years, sex education was introduced into the curriculum. I learned about sex from strict, God-fearing women who'd sworn to live life without it. Their message was clear to me: don't do it; it's a sinful act—unless of course it happened during marriage with the intention of bringing another Catholic baby into the world, which, in that case, made it a good and pure thing. But otherwise it was evil; and, as an ambassador for good, I knew that it was my duty to not only stay away from sex, but also to fight the growing temptation to even think about it—a task that proved to be frustratingly difficult at that age.

I still remember the first time I masturbated. I was eleven or twelve when I stood naked in my parents' bathroom in front of a body-length mirror, and, because of an earthly urge, began to rub myself. I remember it feeling increasingly wonderful, but I also remember detecting an inner voice pleading with me to consider the immorality of doing something that felt so good. I had every intention of stopping. If I stopped, I thought, I could still be saved from some of the impending guilt and have a fighting chance at being normal and good again.

But with every stroke, my willpower to stop dwindled under the weight of my desire to continue, until, in a dramatic fashion, a creamy mystery shot out of me, hitting my chin and chest, the rest dripping into my hand and onto the green rug beneath me. The pleasure was fascinating and full of heat; I could feel it in my thighs and in my toes and deep in my lower back. My head tingled. I took a deep breath, feeling light and dreamy, and struggled to make sense of my spectacular introduction to the orgasm—recognizing at that moment in my young life that I'd known no greater feeling. But when my head started working normally again, all the warmth and wonderfulness slowly receded from me, and the room became harshly cold and judgmental.

My parents' bathroom had one of those old-fashioned heaters built into the wall that, when switched on, emitted heat through a spiraling metal rod. Hoping to replace the heat I'd lost, I flipped the switch. The rod creaked to life, turning a dark, angry red at the top—as if enraged at being stirred from a deep slumber—and then hellishly coiled down in bright orange, like a slowly burning fuse, scolding me with an overbearing heat. I lay close to the heater, curled in a ball, and tried to shield myself from the walls of guilt encroaching on my conscience. I cried and prayed for an hour to the God I thought I knew at that age. Catholic school might be the worst goddamn thing for a young kid.

I wanted to take my innocence back, and, in the nature of self-preservation, I found comfort in memories of an innocent past: watching Disney movies on an early Saturday morning; camping around a fire with my parents in the Sierras; reading Roald Dahl books on the floor of my bedroom; or eating pancakes slathered in butter and drowned in Aunt Jemima's maple syrup and washing them down with two-fisted gulps of cold milk, while my mother listened to Vivaldi's *The Four Seasons* and my father read the newspaper. *Please, God, let me get it back.* But the rosy lens through which I viewed my world was a shade darker. I knew that I'd ruined *something*.

In the shower, I scrubbed myself frantically with a white bar of soap, but being no match for my dirtiness, it got thinner and thinner until it crumbled in half and both pieces shot out from my hand like slimy fish, swirled around in the dirty water at my feet, and then, as though they were trying to escape me, chased each other down the drain. I gave up, got out of the shower, toweled off, and put on my sweats; I tiptoed into my room, slid beneath my covers—my hair still damp from the purge—and surrendered, for the longest night of my young life, to the guilty thoughts that tore through my brain like thousands of tiny, cancerous, razor-sharp claws.

Many years later, during the fall semester of my junior year in college, while studying abroad in Italy, I had to deal with a different, slightly more complex strain of guilt, after losing my virginity to a Swiss girl I met at a bar. She was coquettish, charming, as virginal as I, with a warm, dimple-decorated smile and a pleasantly round face that somehow reminded me of home. I didn't know she was only sixteen when we went home together from the bar, but when I found out the next morning, my depression set in; I hid in my room for a week, and, while the words "pedophile" and "statutory rapist" feasted on my conscience, I researched the punishments on the Internet—both religious and legal—for my actions. When I finally came out of my room, I recoiled in guilt whenever a girl passed me on the street, seeing in her eyes the same innocence I thought I'd destroyed in the Swiss girl.

But later in the week, when I saw the Swiss girl again, at the same bar where we'd first met, I told her how I felt, and she laughed, covered her face with her hand, and laughed again. I wanted to plug her dimples with my fingers, because, to me, they made her sexy, and I didn't want to face that thought ever again.

"First, why does it matter? Also, did you know"—she leaned in close to my face, her dimples emphasizing her words—"sixteen is a legal age in this country? Ha! I've never known someone to worry like you," she said.

I apologized for being upset, and she, still laughing, grabbed my face, kissed me, and said, "You are so strange and think too much. Let's have a drink." And so we ordered rum shots with pear juice and then two bottles of Tuscan red wine. In the morning she returned to Switzerland, and I never saw her again.

Masturbating for the first time and sex with a sixteen-year-old were momentous events in my life. They were not only reminders of the grip my Catholic faith had on me, but also evidence that the life of purity I was hoping to maintain was really just keeping me naive and causing me harm. But as I grew older, guilt made fewer appearances in my life, as if the combination of life experience and self-justification was too much of a numbing force against it. And then, when I went to college at one of the most liberal universities in the nation, I began—free for the first time from the uncompromising doctrines that had ruled my entire life—to think for myself and view life much differently.

After I embraced agnosticism, my guilt and my obsessive-compulsive disorder disappeared—*coincidently?*—and the tiny, razor-sharp claws, forced to adapt, found alternative ways to mutilate my mind; it was then I became aware of the far greater issues worth battling, like, for example, my new fear of death, never an issue before, because there had always been heaven patiently waiting for me. When I was a child, images of the devil or demons often haunted me, but packaged along with the fear of those images was a calming force; for if evil was real, good had to be real, too. So in my pursuit of meaning in a world without the devil or demons, my idea of "good" became nebulous.

Seeing certain things, little things, haunted me—the way people acted towards each other, the way they sought happiness, the way they contradicted themselves, the way they got married, the way they invested in retirement, the way they lied—and I couldn't go on happily or willingly, knowing everything in my life was shrouded in pretense. The newly focused, razor-sharp claws sliced me into a comatose state, and, like a beetle in its final moment of despair after being trapped in a bucket of water and swimming in circles for hours, I made a last attempt to escape my bucket and seek something meaningful—anything. I still tried to guide myself by some sort of moral standard, which at first was, "Don't hurt anyone," and then, unfortunately, evolved into, "Try to avoid everyone." But, in most cases, I tended to play with the lines of reason, tiptoeing at first, then edging closer with one foot slowly venturing in front of the other, until I was sprinting to the next checkpoint.

Now I rent a room with Tatiana in a charming boutique hotel in Los Angeles, tucked away on Fairfax across the street from the Farmers Market. The rooms, built only on the ground level and modeled to look like little farm cottages, encircle a courtyard outfitted with old, pastel-colored lounging chairs, wooden dining tables, several varieties of potted plants, and a garden with flowers and trees and a patch of open grass. It's a place one might visit and say, "When I quit my job, I'll rent a room here and play music or write poetry and drink wine and learn new things and hang out with interesting people and wake up and do it all again and live forever." Our room, in the far back of the hotel, has a window nestled against the drooping branches of a weeping willow, overlooking the garden.

Not long before Tatiana arrived, the inside of my room—refrigerator empty, curtains drawn closed, books unopened, bed cold and desolate—was just a barren fort, shielding me from the outside world, where I tried, unsuccessfully, to sleep or write something new. My problems (self-loathing, depression, insomnia, thanatophobia) seemed fatally serious, as each new day presented a new internal conflict for me, and, in my lowest moments, I considered making it all go away ... forever. But with the addition of Tatiana, the room has come alive with aromas of cooking, the sound of clinking wineglasses and conversation, the feeling on our faces of a warm, California breeze rolling in through an open window, and the warmth of our entwined bodies under the covers. And in knowing what *she's* gone through, my problems have been invariably trivialized.

I awoke this morning to a single ray of sunlight, one that had battled its way through a blockade of stubborn foliage to pour a vintage yellow light into the room—a vision reminiscent of an old Polaroid picture found buried deep in a sock drawer, capturing a smiley, sunny moment on a tropical vacation. As I lay with Tatiana, still asleep and curled up against me, I thought about how light is always more beautiful when it has to fight to be noticed, like sunlight fighting through the clouds after a rainstorm.

As I did again this morning, I often stare at Tatiana while she sleeps, falling in love each time with the shape of her face, the way her dish-water-blond hair falls loosely over her green eyes, the soft slope of her nose down to her pink lips, and the little birthmark on her left cheek. Her skin is fair but with a touch of olive in it, so that, after a day in the Los Angeles sun, she radiates with a magnificent gold. She has a quiet, sleepy smile and a hidden laugh, that, when I find it, reminds me of an innocent childhood love I had during a baseball-filled summer long ago.

I never planned to love her, nor, despite my intense loneliness at the time, use her to fill the emptiness within me; rather, I was interested only in saving her, without any idea of how, from the hellfire that engulfed her. My love for her came later—long after I knew about her passion for learning—in the flash of a summer glance around a table set with two dinner plates and two glasses of wine.

And although Tatiana has seemingly flourished in our time together, she still has episodes that suggest she'll be forever bound by the severity of her psychological scars. Fortunately, we discovered early on that the best way to combat the dark side of her mind is to maintain a healthy lifestyle, and, above all, honor some form of routine. We started with the simple habit of making breakfast every morning, which, after we became comfortable eating together, turned into me helping her to learn English. Soon after, she was reading children's stories to me, and when she was ready, I began reading poetry and novels to her.

Tatiana feels most comfortable in our hotel room, but—though I sometimes believe she would be happier always staying inside—her willingness, one day, to have lunch at the hotel restaurant, which serves a delicious paella, was a sign that she was slowly overcoming her fear of other people. Soon after, she memorized the menu, and, now, as she continues to become more confident with her English, she sometimes converses with the hotel groundskeeper or any of the actor-waiters or singer-waitresses who tend our favorite table in the back of the court-yard.

Our routine continues to evolve. Perhaps the most significant measure of Tatiana's progress was her first step out of the hotel and onto the streets of Los Angeles—an adventure that, each time it happens, makes me apprehensive, because it is when Tatiana is most vulnerable to a setback. But we've also had several rewarding experiences in our time together outside the hotel. One day, we discovered a little tea shop, just outside the hotel, that Tatiana has since come to love. She claimed that, before we knew each other, she was devoted entirely to black tea, and I'd always stuck to green tea, the same flavor every time, but now we adventurously explore several varieties of Chinese teas, Japanese teas, African teas, and English teas.

Despite the break in routine, my favorite days are, selfishly, the ones we decide to let slip away while we're together in bed. On these occasions, with the warmth of the sun on our faces and music in our ears, the bed is our sanctuary; the floor, the bathroom, the kitchen, the outside world are all reminders of a reality we don't want to admit exists. So we stay in bed, our white-sheet island, as long as we can, as if our departure from it would mean we'd lose the magical feeling forever. When we are forced to make trips to the bathroom, we do it in haste and sprint back to the bed; when we become hungry, we hurry to prepare something in the kitchen, so we can bring it back to eat on the bed; and then, after eating, we set the dirty plates on the floor, because once they are there, they don't exist for us anymore.

"Do you feel it?" she says, as we lie together during one of our bed days.

"I do. All over."

"What do you think that is?"

"I can't describe it. I hope it never goes away."

Of course, I try to be attentive to the boundaries that protect me, so that I can continue to protect Tatiana; I quit drinking whiskey and haven't once considered going back to the drugs that dominated my life months ago.

Tatiana believes I saved her. But I've failed to convey to her the grave state of my mind before she came into my life, my inability to write anything other than a few unremarkable short stories and some scribbled thoughts, and the despair that had nearly choked me to death. I remember when I first checked into the hotel room, long before Tatiana, I bought two big bags of white T-shirts and, at one point, wore a new one each day, so that the dirty pile, amassing in the corner of my room, would remind me of the passing time and all the work I'd neglected to do. I hoped, by some form of self-torture, it would inspire me to come alive, but, sadly, it was just a dirty pile that grew clockwise with the long-drawn-out days and the semi-sleepless nights. Because she deserves to know, I hope one day I'll be able to articulate to Tatiana that she is the reason for my new sensibility, and, therefore, the reason I'm able to write these words now.

Drunk on the euphoria from this long night of writing, I've caught myself, a few times, indulging in my own fantasies: one reverie, in particular, involves people, who, after reading my novel, visit the hotel I stay at now to take a tour of my room, touch my desk, and sit on my bed. For lunch, they go to the hotel restaurant where their waiter tells them, "Jake Reed's favorite dish here is the paella," and so they order it. Later they ask if I still come around, and the waiter says, "Of course. He comes here all the time. It's still his favorite place."

The truth, however, would be that I was long gone by that time, that I'd disappeared with Tatiana to a little house in a secluded town out in the country with J. D. Salinger as our neighbor; and, during afternoon walks, Salinger and I would pass each other and nod, until one day he'd say, "I read your book." After we had become friends, he would teach me all the secrets he'd withheld from the literary world, and together we'd write only for ourselves, promising never to publish anything. Tatiana would be the only person allowed to read our work. The three of us would drink wine around a table, and Salinger and I would ask Tatiana what she thought about this character or that sentence.

But J. D. Salinger is dead, and all I have is the start of a story, its meaning still unclear to me.

I think it was mostly truth I was after. I know now that truth is a troubling thing. You can't drink your way to it. You can't snort your way to it. You can't fuck your way to it. You can't cheat your way to it. You can't love your way to it. You can only let it envelop you and try to make sense of it all.

"You are," Tatiana, pausing to yawn, says from our bed, her eyes flashing green in the morning light, "still writing?"

"Couldn't stop."

"What did you write?"

"I think I just started writing the beginning of a novel."

"I want to read it!"

"You'll be the first to read it."

"Your eyes are tired. Maybe you sleep?"

"No, it's time for you now. Let's get the coffee going. I just have to write one more sentence."

I think it's best to start last summer, nearly one year ago, when I lived with Andrew in a lazy, Southern California beach town.

Two

I lay on the couch, sipping the final third of a palm-warmed can of beer and reflecting on, as I'd done countless times, the realization I'd come to many years before that loneliness would forever be a part of me. At some point, I decided to embrace it rather than fight it—that way, I thought, something good might come from my loneliness.

I went through much of high school and college keeping mostly to myself; my friends waited around just long enough to know that it was probably too much work to remain my friend. I concluded, at the time, that people at such a young age just want to be around other people who make their own lives easier. So my understanding of "friend" became someone who makes someone else's life easier, and I thought about how unlikely it was that I would ever make anyone's life easier.

I presumed the theory also applied to a romantic relationship, with the added complication that a girl would want someone who fit into her plan—whatever that was. But girls always seemed to have a plan. I never had a girlfriend in high school, and it wasn't until the middle of my freshman year in college that I met a girl who said she wanted nothing from me other than to teach me things; so the breadth of my carnal knowledge (which still didn't include actual sex) was defined by that girl for quite some time. Later in college I did get to know a few more girls, not girls who thought I fit into their plans, but rather, girls who—at the tail end of relationships with other boys who had once fit into their plans—were seeking some sort of distraction.

I finished my beer, grimacing as I swallowed the last warm mouthful, and wondered what had roused these memories. *Change.* That was it. Lately I'd become increasingly frustrated by my unwillingness to bring change into my own life, and, naturally, I'd turned to my own history for any clues about why I was the way I was.

"Jake, did you fill out those documents I sent you?" Andrew said from the kitchen.

I angled my head back on the armrest of the couch to look at him, and even though my view of Andrew was upside down, I knew what he was doing. I watched him take a piece of bread and smash it down with two hands on top of another piece of bread coated with peanut butter. Andrew prepared peanut butter sandwiches every night for his lunch at work the following day. He made two of them—with no jelly or jam, just cold pieces of bread glued together by cold peanut butter—and placed them in a brown paper bag, which he then set by the door to pick up on his way out in the morning. I enjoyed watching him make his sandwiches every night, because I was fascinated by the way he adhered, without faltering, to his routine.

His appearance never wavered, either. Andrew always had an impeccably shaven face, round-rimmed prescription glasses fixed around his eyes, and bright red hair so tightly combed to his scalp that even wind and rain were powerless against it. He was short but stood proudly, sometimes on the tips of his toes, with a protruding chest and a smile permanently on his face. He once told me that he made the decision, for "greater longevity," as he put it, to quit eating candy and drinking soda at the age of five.

Andrew was a financial analyst. He chose to wear a suit to work every day, and, because he worked so much, I rarely saw him dressed any other way. When we started living together, I imagined that after he woke up in the morning, disheveled from his eight perfect hours of sleep, he'd rush to the bathroom to shave, put on his glasses, and realign his hair. One night, while Andrew was stressing to me the importance of routine in a young man's life, I realized my speculation was frighteningly accurate.

"You'd be surprised at what you can do with an hour and a half of your life, Jake. I'm up every morning at five o'clock. Shower and shave take twenty minutes. Hair takes three minutes, but I allot myself five. Getting dressed: eight minutes. One bowl of oatmeal and one glass of orange juice: twelve minutes. Prepare for daily meetings: fifteen minutes. Then my drive to work takes fifteen minutes, but I allot myself thirty in case of bad traffic. Simple discipline, really." I knew the rest: he worked ten hours, came home, ran two miles in fourteen minutes, and then prepared his peanut butter sandwiches before bed. Rinse. Repeat.

Forever.

Andrew and I had attended the same high school, but had rarely spoken to each other—maybe a few words here and there—and I never saw him throughout our college years. After graduating, I flew home, unable to find a job with my English major, in the middle of a nationwide recession, and moved back in with my parents. But the tranquility of my conservative, suburban neighborhood began to haunt me, especially at night, while I lay in bed, hoping for the noise of a passing car on the street or anything else to disrupt the eerie silence. During the day, when I heard voices outside, I'd peer through my window at two women power walking, or a couple pushing a stroller, or someone talking on the phone while walking a dog—all very simple and normal activities that, for no apparent reason, would confuse the hell out of me. When my parents hosted dinner parties, they loved to introduce me to their guests—usually friends and business associates of my father—and I knew, soon after the nice-to-meet-you niceties, the insufferable topic would be broached.

"What are your plans now that you've graduated, Jake?"

"Oh, well, I'm just trying to figure it out, you know, seeing what's out there," I'd say.

"You'll be fine. A smart kid like you won't have a problem."

"I hope you're right."

"Have you thought about going into real estate?"

"Well, I'd like to try to do something with my English major."

"Law school. I hear they love English majors."

"That's an option," I'd say, hoping that an agreeable conversation would also mean a short one.

"He'd make a wonderful lawyer," my mother would say, drunk and smiling proudly, before refilling her glass with white wine for the third or fourth time.

My grandmother, sensing my unrest on one of my visits to her house, offered to let me stay in her vacant vacation condominium on the beach until I figured out a plan. My move was easy because her place was furnished, and I didn't have many things other than some books, my laptop, an armload of clothes, and a few pairs of shoes.

After I was settled into my new place, I spent my nights alone, sipping beer while reading fiction or watching films, and, occasionally, looking for a job. I loved listening to the ocean in the distance, working relentlessly, creating wave after wave, as if it were nature's fail-safe metronome.

I'd often wake up on the floor in the morning with a book or my laptop open beside me, wondering why I hadn't walked the twenty feet to my bed the night before. I'd already known I wasn't a good sleeper, but I soon discovered that trying to sleep in a bed made it even more difficult for me—something about the planning part of falling asleep ruined it. A bed was, apart from its sexual implications, a symbol for sleep, and once I was aware that I was contributing to some tradition, I'd just lie there for hours, hoping sleep would come, though it hardly ever did. I could feel my body hunkering down into the sheets, worn out, begging sleep to take it, but my mind was far too conniving to comply. And sleep— similar to my experiences with the last scheduled train passing through a Western European town—seemed to elude me when I was the most desperate to catch it; once the fleeting opportunity had escaped me, I knew I had a whole night of restlessness ahead of me.

So the best nights of sleep I ever had were ones resulting from my own trickery; I set up on the floor to read a book or watch a film, and sometimes my subliminal mind would make a mistake and let me fall asleep because I wasn't in a bed. But then my mind would get smarter and recognize my intentions, and I'd have to try the chair on the deck, or the top of my kitchen table, or behind a bush outside. I soon realized the difficulty in outsmarting the suspicious mind, especially when it was my own. Sleep was a battle I was constantly losing.

One night, when the excitement of having my own place had mostly worn off, and I was bored with myself and scared of my thoughts, I decided to meet some old high-school acquaintances at a house party I was invited to on Facebook. My name making it on the list was likely the result of one person's impersonal rampage of invites, as he or she scrolled through hundreds or thousands of Facebook friends. But, nonetheless, the idea of a change in environment and some social interaction seemed appealing.

I overheard Andrew at the party telling a group of people that he was looking for a place to live, that he'd just started a new, intense job and wanted to move out of his parents' house "to start my life," giving me the impression of a rather aspirant and enthusiastic young man. So, later in the night, when we drifted on the party currents to the same corner of the house, I decided—because I felt that I could learn something from him, and that, maybe, being around him would help me focus on my own career—to ask Andrew if he wanted to rent a room in my condo.

"Be your roommate?" he repeated, before awkwardly laughing.

"Yeah, sorry—I overheard you earlier. But I have this great little con-do by the beach, and I live alone right now. I mean, you'd have your own room and everything. I figured I'd at least give you the option."

"You remember me?"

"We went to school together, Andrew."

"I know … but you never said a word to me in high school or ac-knowledged my presence, really."

"I remember that we talked a few times," I said.

"Jake Reed. Damn," he said, laughing again. "I still remember your speech at graduation. People still talk about it. I think the administra-tion hated it, but they probably weren't allowed to like it, especially the priests and nuns. Anyway, sorry, I've had a few beers, and I don't normally drink."

"It's fine. All that was a long time ago, though. Take my number. Call me if you want to check out the place."

"Hey, I will," he said, smiling widely. I gave him my number, and he saved it into his phone. "Appreciate it, Jake."

"See ya."

I had one more beer, drove home, and woke up on the floor the next morning to Andrew's phone call; he came to see my place that night.

"How much is rent?" he asked after the tour.

"Five hundred is fine," I told him.

"Dollars? A month?"

"Yeah, that works."

"What the hell? I can hear the damn ocean!"

"Well, my grandma owns this place, and she doesn't seem to care too much. She told me to charge you a little to, you know, keep it profes-sional."

"Works for me. When can I move in?"

"Whenever you want."

He moved in the next day, and nearly a year later we were still room-mates.

"Jake! The documents?" Andrew said, snatching me back from my memories.

"Andrew, do you ever think about trying something new? Don't you get sick of eating the same sandwiches every day?"

"Ah, come on, Reed. It saves money. Which reminds me: I don't know why you keep your money in a checking account like you do. Don't you realize you're losing money with inflation?"

"Yeah, I know. I just thought … I might spend it on something."

"Spend it on what?"

"I don't know. Something."

"You should be investing in your retirement. I spend a little on groceries and a little on entertainment each month, but the bulk of my paycheck goes straight into a retirement account I can't touch. I don't even know it exists. I should have around $3 million waiting for me when I retire."

"You'll be set," I said wearily.

"Damn straight! Bills to pay. Insurance. Wife and kids someday. All these things are very expensive."

Andrew finished preparing his sandwiches and placed them neatly in a brown paper bag; then he folded the top of the bag over evenly three times and set it by the door for the next morning.

"Jake, once you fill out those documents, I'll set you up with a retirement account. It'll be the best thing you can do. It's amazing how quickly the money grows when you don't touch it for forty years. Just pretend it's not there and then *boom*—one day you have a shitload of it!"

"Yeah, OK. I'll go over the papers tomorrow."

"You'll feel so much better about your future."

"That'll be nice."

Andrew said goodnight, went into his room, and probably brushed his teeth for two and a half minutes, washed his face for thirty seconds, toweled off, neatly untucked his bed, slid into position, double-checked his alarm, and powered down for his eight hours of sleep. *Christ. Forty years? Save money until you're too fucking old to do anything with it?*

I got up from the couch and opened the refrigerator. Only two beers left. I cracked one of them open, took it outside to the deck, and sat in one of the white plastic chairs facing the ocean. My neighbor, Steve Duggins, sat across the way on his own deck and stared solemnly into the night's black nothingness. He didn't notice my arrival. I took a sip of beer, and, as I listened to the waves pounding against the cliff below, leaned my head back on the top part of the chair, took a deep breath of the fresh ocean air, held it in my lungs, and let it out slowly, momentarily putting my mind at ease.

My grandmother's condominium was a short walking distance from the ocean in the small town of Dana Point in Southern California. Sand was permanently in the rug, and anything on the porch, like the barbecue, was tinged with the red hue of rust, because the breeze carried with it some of the sea as it blew in through the homes. The town we lived in was often described by the townspeople as the last undiscovered beach town along the coast. That term, "undiscovered," seemed, in my experience of hearing it, to be rooted in the presentiment of ambitious land developers showing up to build salable multimillion-dollar homes, and, as the neighborhood surfers liked to say, "fucking destroying what's rightfully ours, man."

Dana Point was, essentially, a town perched on the edge of a magnificent cliff, the southern tip of which jutted out into the sea, where cerulean waves beat violently and spectacularly against it to create the purest white, like the snow that blankets the triangular rooftops of log cabins on early winter mornings in the Sierras. Tourists came from all over to stare at the cliff and the waves beating against it, as if the scene had been made famous in a movie. I lived in the row of condos closest to the edge of the cliff, just before it steeply dropped hundreds of feet to several acres of sheer undeveloped coastal land covered in nearly untouched vegetation, except for the skinny man-made trails zigzagging down toward the beach. North of the cliff, the hilly beach ran for a mile along the coast, and the sand, during low tide, stretched as wide as 500 feet between the sea and the vegetation. During the day, from my deck, I had a view of the vast coastline and the tip of the cliff, and, on an especially clear day, Catalina Island in the distance.

Dana Point, the furthest south in a row of three beach towns, was a tightly knit community of story-telling hippies and lazy surfers who'd lived there for their entire lives. Most of the residents had inherited their homes from parents or grandparents who'd bought the land for cheap decades before. Most also worked odd jobs to get by: one of my neighbors was a saxophonist at a local Italian restaurant; one a community dog-walker; another a masseuse who made house calls; and some gave tourists surfing lessons in the summer. Land valuations of coastal property in California had skyrocketed in the past decade, making some of these townies millionaires on paper, while they brought in salaries as low as $20,000 a year. Thus their property was everything to them, and they fought fervently to keep the status quo.

The bordering town to the north, Laguna Beach, was much more in tune with finer culture; art shows, boardwalk activity, fine restaurants, wine tastings, and music festivals were all part of the town's repertoire.

It was tucked away in the rolling hills and sprinkled with tiny, isolated beaches nestled between cliffs, difficult for the tourists to find. Locals hung out in cozy restaurants, lived in little cottages, and walked everywhere. I grew up in Laguna Beach (my parents had never moved out of my childhood home), but for me it had become the tale of the same people doing the same things, rehashing the same stories, and chasing the same old thrills.

Newport Beach, the most northern town in the row of three, had beaches, unlike those of the other two cities, that sat remarkably flat, and instead of rocks jutting out of the sea or little caves hidden in cliffs, they offered wide expanses lined with volleyball nets and plenty of room for other activities: groups of kids playing home run derby, teenage boys playing tackle football, young couples playing beach tennis, or old men tossing bocce balls. Newport also had a large pier, where people shopped, ate, and fished, and little islands that people visited by ferry. Locals drove golf carts or rode bikes to get ice cream on hot summer weekends, and those who owned yachts stored them in the harbor and kept them immaculate for the yearly boat parade that drew wine-drinking, cheese-eating locals close to the water's edge.

The adult male uniform in Newport was khaki shorts, a breezy white-linen shirt, gelled hair, boat shoes without socks, Ray-Ban sunglasses, and a lizard-like, cocky grin. The women had flowing dresses, tanned skin, extravagant jewelry, and a bright twinkle in their eyes that radiated bourgeois confidence. They sauntered, feet pointed slightly out, down streets with their friends—as if they had all the time in the world— pointing at shop windows and, uninterested in anything else, gossiping about town affairs. The kids were freckle-faced, with shaggy, sun-stained hair and mischievous eyes. The teenagers zipped around town in Audis. The young men took real estate jobs and closed deals for their fathers' companies. The young women drank vodka sodas and white wine and dated the young men. Rarely did anyone who grew up in this town associate with outsiders.

The homes, showing a united and powerful front, were proudly marked by bright and bold University of Southern California flags waving victoriously in the breeze. Once, on one of my unaccompanied walks during a work break, I noticed the flag of my alma mater, a dark blue lone warrior, conspicuously out of place among the long line of cardinal and gold. As I stood in front of the house, I considered knocking on the door to meet the people brave enough to hoist a Berkeley flag on enemy soil. I daydreamed that I'd been falsely accused of a heinous crime in some foreign country, and that, after being chased by authorities and angry civilians, I'd stumbled safely within the protective borders of my nation's embassy. If my job hadn't been in Newport, I would have been fine avoiding it altogether.

I took another sip of my beer; it was still cold and fine to drink. Steve, the owner of the undeveloped property in Dana Point, finally noticed me.

"Hey, Jake. Nice night, huh?" he said.

"It really is," I said.

Steve's sole mission in life was fighting the Coastal Commission (as its sole mission was to protect the coast) for the right to develop the overgrown land below us. He'd bought the property decades before, but his dream to develop it had been handicapped by the Commission, which, every year, found a new reason ("destroying the natural environment of the pocket mouse" or "uprooting a rare coastal plant species") to reject his proposal and shut him down. And, naturally, the surfers, who likened Steve to Satan, celebrated with a thirty-pack of Bud Light every time he was defeated.

"Did you hear?" he said.

"No. What happened?"

"I took some of the people on the Commission out to lunch. I think they're gonna budge this year. Things are really looking up."

"That's great, Steve."

"I'll be able to sell the dirt lots, just the dirt lots, with no houses on them, for fifteen million each. Just the damn dirt!" he said, his voice trembling with excitement.

"Jesus, that's a lot of money. How many lots do you have?" I said, trying to appear interested, although it was difficult considering we'd had a similar conversation many times before.

"Well, you know, I could do over a hundred lots if I wanted to, but I want the buyers to have good-sized lots, so I think I'll spread the houses over only fifty lots. I think that's a good compromise. Yeah, about fifty lots."

"That makes sense."

"You have $15 million, Jake? I'll save a lot for you. Hell, I'll give it to you for ten because I like you."

I forced a laugh and said, "Thanks, Steve. I'll start saving now."

"Night, Jake."

Steve, rejuvenated by hope, popped out of his chair and skipped off the deck into his bedroom. I knew that the quicker he got into his bed and fell asleep, the sooner he could dream about his lots. I imagined he'd given each of them endearing names, and that, before going to bed, he would wish all of his lots good night by name, or even read them a bedtime story from his deck, pausing after every page to turn the book around and show them the illustrations.

Each year that Steve's proposal was rejected, he would return home immediately, and, every day until the next hearing, work tirelessly with his lawyers on a new plan. But the Coastal Commission was a very powerful entity, and nothing pleased its members more than stopping a developer from building on coastal land. I thought about how happy Steve would be to finally sell his lots, and how happy Andrew would be to finally collect his retirement money.

I heard a noise below and strained to see with squinted eyes the approaching familiar shape of another one of my neighbors, prompting me to quickly return inside. I wasn't in the mood for any more conversation. I locked the door, retreated into my bedroom, listened to Sigur Rós through my headphones, and tried to get some sleep before work in the morning.

THREE

I was lying in bed, my eyelids sagging low over my eyes, listening to myself breathe, when my morning alarm sounded, reminding me that I needed to get ready for work. I quieted the alarm, and, for the first time all night and into the morning, felt like I could sleep, as if my mind had finally relented, knowing I had no time left. But I seized the opportunity anyway and went to sleep. I woke up thirty minutes later, slowly sat up, rubbed my eyes to get them working properly, then reached for my laptop, which was an arm's length away on the nightstand, and flipped it open to check my email. I scrolled past the daily spam, a few friend requests, and an email from my mother.

"Goddamn it."

Every morning, I felt a little excitement as I checked my email, as if part of me believed there would be an unread message—with a beautiful, boldfaced title—waiting in my inbox that would bring me great news or inject energy into my humdrum routine, or, in the highest of hopes, change the course of my prosaic life. But, since I wasn't doing anything noteworthy with my time, I had no reason to hope for such an email, nor any idea what I even hoped to find—maybe an email from *The New Yorker* informing me that they intended to publish something I'd written. But I'd never written anything I didn't consider a piece of shit, and I definitely had never submitted a piece to *The New Yorker*.

From: <u>Fiction, TNY</u>
To: <u>Jake Reed</u>

Dear Mr. Jake Reed:

Here at *The New Yorker* we believe in the potential of a writer above anything else. Although you have never submitted anything to us before or, for that matter, written anything worth reading, we still believe in your potential. We would like to publish something you will write in the future. Please email us your piece after you write it.

Thank you,
The New Yorker Staff

Ridiculous. I'd begun to grow weary of my constant daydreaming because, as I retreated more often into fantasy, it had become a reminder of my growing discontent with real life. And my thoughts, after very little sleep, seemed to float even further into the realm of the superfluous.

I snapped my computer shut and slid it into my shoulder bag, and, as I rose from the bed, noticed, resting on the floor, my copy of Murakami's *Norwegian Wood*—the novel that, more than any other, had lured me into a state of sentimental attachment, so much so that immediately after I'd finished it I turned to page one and started reading it again. I snatched the book up, smelled the pages, and read the first few paragraphs before tossing it back on the floor. I wished I were Murakami. In college, I had bought a ticket to see him speak on campus, and, in front of an auditorium packed with formally attired fans, he took the stage wearing an old, white T-shirt and tattered khakis (God, I loved him even more for that). I checked my phone: no missed calls, no texts, and it was already past nine. *Late to work again.*

In the bathroom, I took my habitual, relieving, long-lasting morning piss, and then, with my head buried in the sink, splashed cold water onto my face; after patting it dry with a hand towel, I looked at myself in the mirror; my hair had grown down to my eyes, which were puffy and discolored from too many sleepless nights, and the lower half of my face was covered in week-old facial hair. In nearly a year of working for my company, I'd never gone two consecutive days without shaving. My boss loved a clean-shaven face.

On my way into the kitchen, I passed Andrew's room and glanced at his neatly made bed. He'd already been gone for hours. I opened the fridge and considered drinking the last beer for breakfast; instead, I grabbed a nearly empty carton of orange juice and poured the rest of it into a glass, admired the pulpy consistency, and took it all down in one drink. Then I peeled a banana and took small bites, as I stared blankly at the floor. Without showering, I dressed in a wrinkled, white collared shirt and black slacks (the same pair I'd worn the day before), slipped into some dress shoes, grabbed my shoulder bag, and, before walking out the front door, stared into the mirror and searched—tilting my head from side to side—just long enough to find an angle from which my face didn't look so bad.

I always enjoyed the twenty-minute drive along the coast to my office, especially during the summer season when the rhythm of morning activity on the streets seemed to carry along in synchrony with the lively tune of my favorite morning-drive song—"Hair blowing in the hot wind … Smell the leather of your new car"—as I pulled away from my condo, rolled down my windows, and zipped north on Pacific Coast Highway.

With the ocean on my left and the rolling hills on my right, I passed through Dana Point and Laguna Beach, and then, once I was in Newport Beach, drove inland for less than a mile before turning into my office's parking structure in Newport Center, the town's business district. As I rode the elevator up, I enjoyed my last few seconds of freedom before walking through the company doors into a large, square room with sickly off-white walls and unpleasant, headache-inducing fluorescent lighting. Since my tardiness had started to become a daily occurrence, I was usually one of the last ones, if not *the* last one, into the office. Hoping to avert attention from my co-workers or bosses, I always stepped noiselessly and cautiously along the path to my desk, as if I were tiptoeing across a minefield. Unfortunately, I never once made it to my desk without being noticed, and that morning was no exception.

"Good morning, Jake!"

Roger, always the first associate in the office, took pleasure in announcing, to the entire room, the arrival of each employee who showed up to work later than he did—which was, of course, everyone. Because he was several years older than all the other associates, he felt entitled— even though he was no one's boss—to treat everyone on his level superciliously.

"Hey, Roger," I said, without looking at him.

I worked for a real estate consulting firm as the New Media Associate, meaning I curated all the company's social networks and wrote the content for its blog. Many companies, forced to evolve in a new technological landscape, had started creating these new media positions, and Andrew, after hearing from a contact about a new job opening at this company, got me an interview. From the moment I was hired, my bosses emailed me daily reports on the company's new deals or successfully closed deals—"Share this with our followers"—and articles involving the overall real estate industry—"Use this to spin something favorable about our company on the blog." And every day, without fail, one of them reminded me of my goal: "To increase sales by way of generating traffic for the website and bringing more awareness to the company."

When I first started working, I approached the job with the same exuberance I saw from every new hire at the company: I arrived early, proposed ideas, participated in meetings, and ate lunch with the other employees. Eventually realizing, however, that nothing I proposed would ever be approved, that meetings were just long, pointless gatherings where soapbox executives—each one in a love affair with his own voice—incessantly repeated themselves, and that employees just gossiped about other employees at lunch, I became disenchanted with my job, and, consequently, very detached from the office affairs. But my worsening estrangement with the company was probably owed, at least in part, to an incident with Roger, who, one morning—after I'd been with the company for a few months—came over to my desk with a noticeably concerned, almost frantic expression on his face.

"Jake, can I talk to you about something?"

"Yep." I followed him into the kitchen.

"You know that huge deal we just closed?" he whispered.

"Yeah, sure," I said.

"Well, when you blogged about it, you put the wrong client's name in there."

"OK …"

"Well, when you weren't responding to my emails last night, I felt the need to alert the bosses."

"I just posted it yesterday. I would've fixed it this morning," I snapped.

"Well, like I said, you weren't responding, and I felt that our team leaders had a right to know about the situation. You understand, right?"

"Yeah, fine. So what's to come of it?"

"Probably nothing. Don't worry about it."

"OK, Roger," I said, irritation sharpening my voice, as I turned to walk away.

"One more thing."

"What is it?"

"Just so you know, to get everyone up to speed, I also wrote an email explaining the issue and cc'd all the employees in the company. It's important that we handle this misstep as a team."

"Good thinking, Roger," I said sarcastically and walked out of the kitchen.

Back at my desk, I found the mistake Roger had referred to and corrected it in a few seconds. One minute later, one of the bosses called me into his office.

"It's come to my attention that we've made a mistake that has potentially jeopardized our relationship with someone who gives us money," he said in a way that suggested to me that he had no idea what the issue was, just that there was one.

"If you're talking about the error on the blog post, that was my fault, and I've already fixed it," I said.

"Jake, that's *not* the point. The point is that it *happened*, and it may have hurt our relationship with a client," he said, hoping to evoke a stronger reaction from me.

"OK. I understand. I'm wondering if there is something I can do to help resolve the situation—maybe an apology email to the client?"

"No, we'll take it from here," he said. "That's all. Thanks."

Since that meeting, anything I posted on one of the company's social networks was monitored by a content director who, at the end of every day, reported any of his "controversial" findings to my bosses. Sometimes I got called into an office because one of the bosses didn't like how one word or phrase reflected on the company.

"I don't know if this is the right word here."

"Sure, I'll replace it," I'd say.

"You're too edgy here. Remember, we're a conservative company with conservative clients."

"OK. I'll remove that part. And I'll remember to tone it down in the future," I'd say.

Also as a result of my blunder, anything I wrote for the blog was put into a queue for publication the following day so the content director would have ample time to safely review it before it went "out to the world," as they liked to say. Early on, I tried to impress my bosses by injecting a little creativity into the blog—including what I thought to be some funny or clever commentary along with the daily updates—but soon discovered that the more effort I put into being creative, the longer the meetings were to discuss how much I needed to change what I'd written. I responded by embracing a very minimalistic approach, and they responded by saying I needed to be more creative. My bosses often contradicted each other; after one would tell me to be more conserva-tive, another would tell me to liven things up. Eventually I wrote a para-graph which met their approval, and, hoping to eliminate the need for an onslaught of new meetings every day, nearly copied it—just switched the names of the clients—for every subsequent blog post. My strategy worked seamlessly until website traffic decreased, and then I was called into an office again.

"People keep telling me that we need more followers, that we need more 'likes' and more comments, that we need to make something go viral," one of my bosses said to me during a low-traffic week.

Viral. Christ, that word again. "Well, that might require our being a little edgier," I responded.

"Then let's be edgier. We need more traffic. You need to write some-thing that'll bring us a lot of attention. Let's have you put together a proposal," he said.

But not one of my proposals was ever approved—"This is much too edgy"—and, at some point, they stopped asking me to make them. Consequently, my required work each day—write a paragraph promot-ing the latest company deals and a paragraph proving the company's merit on the blog, then share it with everyone on our social networks—became very formulaic, enabling me to get the entire day's set of tasks done in under an hour. I spent the rest of my time pretending to work while listening to music, browsing the web, or working on my own sentences. Sometimes I went down to my car and slept in the backseat for an hour. I enjoyed long lunches and took frequent breaks to walk around town. And because I assumed that my detachment was both no-ticeable and problematic, I walked into the office every morning expect-ing to be fired. But it still hadn't happened, leaving me to waste away in an employed but purposeless purgatory.

Despite my tardiness being blazoned to the entire office by Roger, I made it to my desk that morning without attracting attention from any of my bosses. I quickly opened my work-designated laptop and checked my work email—twenty-eight new messages already (most of them were a result of my inclusion in a never-ending thread of emails having nothing to do with me). I took a deep breath and looked around the room. Except for the private offices in the back awarded to the executive team members, the entire room was set up in the style of the "team-oriented bullpen"—which meant that all the desks were grouped in fours, two facing two—so all the employees could easily see and communicate with each other. Since the "social media guy" never took meetings with clients, I was the only male in the office allowed to dress in business casual, and, in a room filled with suit-and-tie-sporting, cologne-wearing, clean-shaven young men, my presence was largely incongruous with everyone else's.

The girl who sat facing me said, "Morning, Jake," without looking up from her screen. I gave her a quick, perfunctory wave. My co-workers always appeared busy with work—their fingers continuously tap-dancing across keyboards—but were, most of the time, instant-messaging their friends. In college, I'd always been intimidated by the working world and had held in high esteem all those who were a part of it, but it wasn't until after I got a job that I realized what little work people did during the day. Meetings were the exception; people in my company were great at having those.

"Meeting time!" Roger yelled, standing up from his chair.

Every Tuesday, at ten in the morning, all the employees filed into a large boardroom, sat in overpriced chairs around a Last Supper–like table, and waited for the arrival of the CEO (Jesus) and the executive board (Jesus's apostles). All the employees were a bit more put together on Tuesdays—the girls did something different with their hair, and the guys' outfits were complemented with vests or sweaters or fake prescription glasses.

"Jake, you coming to the meeting?" Roger asked, as he walked toward the boardroom.

Without acknowledging him, I rose from my desk, maneuvered through the herd, and walked into the kitchen to pour myself a cup of coffee before the meeting. I reached for the stack of Styrofoam cups next to the coffee pot, unhinged one, and stared at it incredulously. The executive board had, in an effort to feign prudence during a recession, decided to minimize the office amenities, one of which, apparently, was the size of the Styrofoam cups the employees used for coffee. I grabbed the pot and poured myself a shot of coffee, took two sips, and refilled the tiny cup.

I then joined the others in the boardroom, and, after finding a seat at the far end of the room, glanced around a table filled with marketers, financial analysts, research analysts, brokers, assistants, and a few interns. Some anxiously fidgeted in their chairs while shuffling through notes or presentation slides; others nervously cleared their throats while readjusting their clothes or their hair. One of the administrative assistants circled the table while placing a one-sheet agenda—crisp, white paper still warm from the printer—in front of everyone in attendance. The agenda was the same for every meeting, every week.

Fuck. I didn't shave.

After keeping us waiting for fifteen minutes—a habitual tactic—the executives filed into the room, each one looking like an all-American replica of the one before. The CEO walked in last, closed the door behind him, and took his seat at the head of the table.

"OK ..." he said, distracted by his phone. "Let's get started."

Being with the company for nearly a year meant I'd attended almost fifty weekly meetings, and not one had ever differentiated itself from any other; every week, each employee, on his or her turn, updated the others in the room with a short presentation. After several meetings I became convinced that most people were giving the same presentation they'd given the week before, and the executives, too excited for their chance to pontificate to their subordinates, were failing to notice. Unfortunately, my attendance at the weekly meetings was required. To remedy my boredom, I often kept running tallies of the most repeated words or phrases throughout the meeting—money, transaction, huge, tremendous, fantastic, deal, quota, managing expectations, at the end of the day, offline, run rate, ancillary revenue, mindshare—and, when it finally ended, I circled a winner.

"Let's start with new business," the CEO said. "What do we got?"

Someone on the brokerage team, on the other side of the table, began his presentation. I tallied two uses of "tremendous," but, growing weary of my own game, I let my eyes drift toward the wall-to-wall window, which offered a spectacular view of the ocean and the various islands within the harbor, the skyline, and Pacific Coast Highway. After a few minutes of cloud gazing—which somehow lured me into fantasizing about all the places in the world I'd never been—I focused on another office building in the distance, of similar height and design to the one I stared from, as if both structures had been born in the same architectural litter. I counted the windowed levels of the building from bottom to top (forty-two) and then wondered how many companies similar to mine existed within its walls. Somewhere in the middle, I picked one window and studied it, trying hard to detect the outline of a tiny person who, sitting around a boardroom table during his company meeting, was also staring out the window in search of someone else like him.

"Let me make something very clear to the whole team here: we are in the business of *making* money ..." one of the executives said, as I briefly tuned back in to the meeting before drifting out again. *Maybe I could teach English in a developing country. Some place in Africa? Or Asia? Thailand ... Yes, a little island in Southern Thailand. That'd be nice. I'll teach my classes and then, after, read books and drink beer on the beach—every day for the rest of my life. But I don't know how to teach. I'd be a horrible teacher, because I can't speak in front of people—I never know what to say. Maybe I'd be able to just write down everything I want to say and read it to the class. Would they let me do that?*

"*Please*, everyone!" the CEO shouted. "Let's add this under our learnings."

Learnings. I doubted that "learnings" was a word. Curiosity drove me into my pocket to retrieve my phone. With my hands hidden under the table, I opened the dictionary application and typed "learnings." No. Not a word. I slid my phone back into my pocket and took a small sip of my coffee, trying to preserve what little I had for the rest of the meeting. *This tastes like shit.* I stared into my little Styrofoam cup and wondered what it would be like to be a tiny person swimming around in there, trapped in a sea of black coffee. *What an awful way to die, trapped at the bottom of a cup filled with shit-tasting, tepid black coffee.* I hastily took another sip to swallow my imaginary, tiny self and save him from the pain of drowning. *At least I gave him a good death.*

"*Hello?* Jake!" the CEO said, looking at me along with a roomful of others.

"Sorry," I said, feeling the heat of the room on my face.

"What's the new media update ... apart from your new caveman look?"

Everyone laughed. I forced a smile and nodded my head. "Well, no real update from me. Just business as usual: keeping our followers well-informed."

"Well, we have an update for you," he said, as one of the executives handed him a brochure. "There is this social media conference in New Jersey this weekend," he said, pausing, and then, reading from the brochure, "'All the things you need to know about monetizing your business from social media.' We've already booked your flight and hotel."

"OK ..." I said, completely blindsided.

"We expect that you'll come back with some useful learnings, which, next Tuesday during the meeting, you'll present to the team. OK, good. That's all for today, guys."

I stayed in my seat as everyone filed out of the room; and just when I thought I'd have a few minutes alone, I felt the hovering presence of Roger behind my shoulder.

"Jake," Roger said.

"What is it, Roger?"

"Let me shut the door first," he said, walking over to it, waiting for the last person out of the room to walk a few more steps away, and then shutting it. "A social media conference, huh?"

"I guess so."

"Let me ask you something. What do you think about during our meetings?"

"What do you mean?"

"You're always zoned out."

"I have no idea, Roger."

"You look so miserable. Do you hate your job?"

"No," I lied.

"I'm just thankful I have a job during this recession. I would hate to be searching for a job right now."

"Yeah, that would be terrible."

"Well, I just wanted to make sure that everything is OK."

"Everything is fine, Roger. Thanks for the concern."

"You're like family to me."

Everyone in the company—the just-hired to the just-fired, the interns to the executives—was "like family" to Roger.

"I know. Thanks," I said, hoping desperately for the conversation's end.

"All right, Jake."

"Talk soon."

"Jake, one more thing."

"What's up?"

"When the CEO makes a joke, you should laugh. It shows that you care. It's really just an appreciative gesture to the man who gives you a job during a recession. We should all be so thankful to have jobs."

"Yeah, you're right. Thanks," I said, indulging him for the sake of my sanity.

"No problem, brother."

When I returned to my desk, a folded piece of thin yellow paper was resting on my laptop keyboard; the texture and smell of the paper reminded me of my report cards in elementary school. I unfolded it and read, unemotionally, that I'd received a demerit for being "unshaven." I crumpled it into a firm, little yellow ball and tossed it into the wastebasket beneath my desk.

A few minutes later, the CEO's executive assistant approached my desk and said, "The CEO would like to meet with you today. Can you do the end of the day, at five?"

"Sure. No problem."

When she walked away, I put headphones over my ears but didn't play any music; I was just trying to give the impression to the rest of the office that I couldn't hear anything—which, I hoped, would be enough to deter everyone, especially Roger, from casually chatting with me. Over the next hour, I finished my work for the day, answered a few emails, and then, around half past noon, sneaked out of the office to avoid any invitations to lunch.

Outside, I walked around the corner and into a newly opened Greek café—one of those places where the owner also takes the orders at the cash register—and asked for a lamb gyro.

"Anything to drink with that?" said the woman, who looked Greek.

"What kind of beer do you have?" I said.

"Bud, Miller, Coors, Stella ..."

"Do you have any Greek ... or, uh, would it be called Grecian ... beer?"

She laughed and said, "Yes, we have Mythos."

"I'll take one of those," I said, handing her my credit card.

"You're the first non-Greek around here to ask for a Greek beer," she said with a polite smile.

When she handed me the bottle of beer, I smiled back at her and then found a small table in the corner of the café alongside the window facing the street. I raised the cold bottle to my lips, and, although I'd never been to Greece, swallowed down the pleasant feeling of being submerged in glassy, sky-blue water, tanning on white-sand beaches, and living in a white-sculpted home on a cliff during an imaginary summer vacation on one of the Greek Islands. After a few minutes, the woman brought my meal, and I ate it slowly while watching the passersby through the window.

And then I noticed *it* surging my way, sucking up the sidewalk and swallowing whole anyone in its path: The Mob, an indeterminate shape of dark-colored shirts and white collars, ties with thick Windsor knots, suspenders, and big-faced watches. I hunkered down into my chair—my only protection being a thin sheet of window glass—and stared right into the center of it. I knew most of The Mob's members, some from my company, some from high school, and even those I didn't know were still my "friends" on Facebook. Leftover confidence from their fraternity days at USC had spilled into their careers, which had become their new fraternity—the post-graduation "fraternity of real estate in Southern California." The Mob charged forward—its members obnoxiously laughing and playfully shoving each other—and I hoped it would pass by, unaware of me. Because of The Mob's surging momentum, one of its members would often be spit out from its center, and, forced to confront the unfamiliar pressure of individuality, even for just a couple of seconds, he would hurry to rejoin the comfort of the mass. The Mob came up just outside my window, and, through the open door of the Greek café, I could hear conversation emitting from its core.

"Shut the fuck up, pussy."

"I don't even need salary, son. My commission alone is more than your salary plus your commission."

"Fag."

"You're buying lunch then, douche bag."

"Fine by me, nigga."

Finally they disappeared into a popular sushi place, bringing a momentary silence to the street. I finished my meal, and, before leaving, thanked the Greek woman, who smiled and told me to come back again. Since I'd been in the café, the street had come alive with lunch-hour activity—people were crowding the entrances to restaurants, swarming down crosswalks, and sitting on curbside benches to enjoy the summer sun.

Back at my desk, I put on my headphones and listened to music on shuffle play, while I browsed the web. I heard a song from Edward Sharpe and the Magnetic Zeros, and, wanting to know more about them, researched the band's story. I learned that the lead singer decided, after too many drug-filled nights in Los Angeles, to hide from the world in a tiny apartment where, in his seclusion, he thought up the idea of Edward Sharpe, a "messianic figure" who "kept getting distracted by girls and falling in love." I didn't know why, but I felt moved by that story in some way, almost inspired by it.

I took a break from listening to music to watch the trailer for an upcoming Sofia Coppola film, and, because I loved the feeling it gave me, watched it again, then noted its release date in my notebook. I streamed that day's episode of NPR's *Fresh Air* and became enamored, as I always did, with the intelligent, sexy cadence of the host's voice. *Maybe she's my soulmate?* I researched her and found out that she, Terry Gross, was already in her sixties. *Oh well.*

Time for another break. I walked out of the office, got in an elevator, and swiped my keycard to get down to the lobby. When I heard the little beep and watched the light turn green, I remembered how uncomfortable it made me to take the elevator, because every keycard swipe was monitored by the company; every time I left the office and used the elevator, they knew about it. The elevator reached the lobby, the doors opened, and I walked toward a little food stand run by a hard-working Cambodian woman named Veata.

"Hi, Mister Jake," she said, smiling, wearing an apron that read, "Life is Good."

"Hello, Veata."

"For you today?"

"Just one hard-boiled egg," I said, and then, after noticing how big her coffee cups were, "I'll do a cup of coffee, too."

"No sugar or cream, right?"

"Right."

"Three dollar," she said, and I paid her. "Thank you, Mister Jake. See you again tomorrow."

"See you tomorrow."

Outside the office building, I sat on one of the empty benches along the street and took a sip of my coffee, grimacing as it burned my mouth. I took the hard-boiled egg out of the bag, dented it on the corner of the bench, and began peeling away its shell. Two girls from my office sat together in silence on a bench a few feet away from mine and fidgeted with their phones; they had frozen, vacuous expressions—eyes wide open, mouths slightly open—as they ensconced themselves in their high-tech worlds. A man, also staring down at his phone, waited on the corner to cross the street, and, when the light changed, refused to look up from his device as he walked, weaving like a blind man across the crosswalk, guided to the other side only by the automatic chirping from the speakers. I took a bite off the top of my peeled egg—getting a bit of the yolk—and had another sip of coffee, which had cooled enough to enjoy.

Back at my desk for only a few minutes, I got a call from the CEO's executive assistant. "He'll see you now."

I walked the hundred or so paces to the big-and-fancy-offices area, stopped in front of the CEO's door, knocked, and opened the door.

"Take a seat," he said, glancing up at me for a second and then back down to the brand-new iPad he was playing with.

I sat on the couch facing his desk and sunk so low to the ground my knees were almost even with my chest, as if I were sitting on toy furniture made for children. I awkwardly readjusted myself before looking up at the CEO, who was towering above me. *You bastard.* I realized then that the seating arrangements were planned so that he always had the upper hand in every meeting in his territory—whomever he met with would be forced to subserviently peer up at him. He still hadn't looked away from his tablet, and I sat there waiting, looking up at him, as though I were a young boy patiently watching his father in his study. I noticed a large coffee mug on his desk and wondered how many refills of one of the tiny Styrofoam cups it would take to fill his mug with coffee. I guessed fifteen, maybe twenty.

"Technology," he said, finally putting the tablet aside and looking down at me. "I'm still trying to understand ... Anyway, why did I bring you in here ..." he said, shuffling through papers as if he were searching for the one that would tell him why I was in his office. "So ... Jake, I don't think you've risen to your full potential at this company. You've been with us for almost a year now, yes?"

"Yes."

"Perhaps it's our fault for not providing you with enough incentive to excel in this environment. What's your job title?"

"New Media Associate."

"Tomorrow your new title will be New Media Manager. I'll have someone draft a memo announcing your promotion."

"What will change for me?" I said, trying to conceal my bewilderment and deciding that I was terrible at foretelling the future. *I thought he was firing me. First a conference. Now a promotion?*

"Your day-to-day duties will remain the same. However, just having the title of 'Manager' brings you more responsibility, makes your voice more important, and, of course, garners you more respect from your co-workers."

"I see."

"Congratulations."

"Thank you," I said, numbly.

"OK—moving on. What else ... This whole social media thing—I'm not sure we're doing everything the right way. We really have to know this stuff, especially since everyone in our industry is getting into this social space. Make sure that you really take advantage of the conference this weekend. I want you to come home and really start dominating this game."

"OK."

"Remember, our focus is making money. Before making any decision at this company, ask yourself a simple question: 'Will this decision *make money* for the company?' If the answer is yes, then it's the right move. If the answer is no, then it's the wrong move. Do you understand?"

"Yes," I said, nodding, in a daze.

"Lastly, remember, during next Tuesday's meeting, you'll present your learnings. OK, that's all."

I picked up more beer, a twelve-pack of Bohemia, on the way home from work that evening. Andrew, still in his suit, was patiently waiting for me on the couch in a dignified posture, his shoulders arched erectly back and his legs delicately crossed.

"There he is! You ready to go?" he said with a frozen smile.

Andrew allowed himself to go out for dinner once a week; he chose Tuesday because—with Mexican restaurants promoting cheap tacos on "Taco Tuesday" and other restaurants also offering something cheap to stay competitive—it made the most economical sense, and, because many young people in the workforce had the same plan, provided the most entertainment.

"Are you OK?" Andrew asked.

"I had the strangest day at work. But it's fine. Where do you want to go this time?"

"Let's do the Thai place again."

The Thai place Andrew referred to was a few blocks south on Pacific Coast Highway and about a ten-minute walk from the condo. On Tuesdays, the restaurant offered half-priced drinks and appetizers, but since we rarely ordered appetizers and Andrew never liked to drink much, I knew that the real reason he wanted to go, although he'd never admit it, was a Thai waitress named Tamarine. Each time we went to the Thai place, Andrew made sure we sat in her section. If a table wasn't available in Tamarine's section, he always insisted, while attempting to veil his true intentions from me, that we "wait for our favorite table," which was, of course, in her section. The previous Tuesday at the Thai place, I had suggested, after a few beers, that he ask her out to dinner.

"Ha ha! What? I don't see her that way at all, Jake. Anyway, we'd never work. Society wouldn't understand a relationship like that," he said.

I wasn't sure what he meant by "society," but, weary of Andrew's dogmatic life lessons, had decided against pursuing the matter.

"Do you want a drink for the walk over?" I asked, loading the fridge with the beer I'd bought.

"No, thanks. I don't see any value in the risk. South County cops are ruthless."

"OK, let's go," I said, grabbing a bottle of beer for myself, popping the top on an edge of the table, and walking toward the door. Outside we saw Steve Duggins sitting on his deck, watching over his lots. "Hey, Steve," I said.

No response.

A few paces down the road, Andrew said, "I'd be depressed, too, if my entire retirement plan rested on a proposal that'll never get approved."

Once we were seated at Andrew's favorite table in the restaurant, Tamarine skipped over, smiling, and sat in one of the empty chairs next to us. "Hey, Jake. Hey, Andrew," she said.

Tamarine had shiny black hair, pure, unblemished, porcelaneous skin, and glassy black eyes. When she smiled, her eyes sparked, as if they were two pieces of black flint being struck against steel, and a milky dimple formed in her cheek. Tamarine was tall and lean but curvy in the right places. She was unquestionably the most popular waitress at the restaurant, and males, old and young, fawned over her. Aware of her appeal, she flashed smiles all over the restaurant and swung her hips as she walked from table to table. She'd left Thailand, several months before, to stay with the owner of the Thai restaurant in Dana Point. The owner also housed most of the other waitresses in his home, which was conveniently built above the restaurant. Since there were several girls who lived with him in seemingly small quarters, I imagined that all of them, after their shifts ended, jammed into a room stacked with bunk beds to sleep so they would be well rested for work the next day. When we first met Tamarine, she could barely speak English.

"Hey, Tamarine," Andrew said, his face reddening to the color of his hair.

"To drink?" she said.

"Oh, well, OK, sure, I'll have a beer, here," Andrew said, nervously fidgeting with the menu. "How about a Singha?"

"And I'll have a Chang," I said.

"OK, be back soon," Tamarine said.

While we waited for her to bring the beers, Andrew told me about the benefits of using a credit card with rewards—"You get double points for gas and groceries!"—and that, at his spending rate, in ten years he "will have racked up enough points to go around the world for free."

"When are you going to have time, with your schedule, to travel around the world, Andrew?"

"The point is that I'm creating value with my spending, Jake," he said in a serious tone, but still smiling.

Tamarine came over to the table carrying a tray with two beers and two frosted glasses; she placed a glass in front of Andrew, filled it half-way with Singha, placed a glass in front of me, and filled it halfway with Chang. "Ready to order?" she said with a smile, swiveling her hips.

Andrew, embarrassed to try the pronunciation of the Thai words, said, "Number seven," which meant the fried rice with chicken and sausage, and I asked for the Phat Thai with shrimp. As Tamarine turned to walk away with our orders, Andrew called her back and asked for another round of beers, even though we still hadn't tasted the ones in front of us. During my time living with Andrew, there were a few nights when I felt that, because he was so repressed from disciplining himself, he had the potential to really come undone, like dieters who starve themselves for three days to lose weight but then gorge themselves on the fourth day. When he'd impetuously ordered the second round of beers with that rare, desirous pain in his eyes, I worried that it was going to be one of those nights for him.

"Let's ask her to come hang out at the condo," Andrew said after a large drink of his beer.

"What?"

"Tamarine. Do you think she'd come over?"

"I don't know. Maybe. You should ask her."

After we each finished our second beer, Tamarine brought our meals, and we ordered a third round. "You guys thirsty!" she said before skipping off to another table filled with more of her admirers.

"Will you ask her to come over, Jake?"

"Yeah, I'll ask her," I said, recognizing his unease.

We ate in silence until Tamarine came back, a few minutes later, with our third round of beers. "How the food?" she asked.

"Extremely wonderful," Andrew said, awkwardly.

"What?" she said.

"Tamarine, what're you doing tonight?" I said.

"I work."

"Well, after work, what're you doing then?"

"Nothing. Go to bed."

"Do you want to hang out at our place for a little while?"

"What do you guys do?"

"I don't know—maybe have a bonfire on the beach?"

"OK, I maybe come. Take my number. Text me address."

"Cool. I will."

We paid the bill, and, on our way home, I texted her.

"Do you think she'll come?" Andrew asked, slightly swaying on his feet, his voice a pitch higher and his shirt uncharacteristically untucked after his three Thai beers.

"I don't know, but if she wants a drink, we have nothing to give her except beer."

"Let's stop at the liquor store."

Holy shit, Andrew, what's got into you?

After leaving the liquor store, we walked north along the coast, each of us carrying a bottle of wine, as the evening summer breeze rolled off the ocean and dampened our faces. As we ascended the steps to our deck, I caught the scent of marijuana and knew it could only be one person.

"Jake, my man," Robbie said, sitting on one of the white plastic chairs on our deck and smoking a joint. "Hey, Andrew."

Robbie—a never-married, forty-year-old cook at a bar in town—had long, blond, matted hair, almost dreadlocked, with a thin strand dyed pink falling down over his face, and thick yellow facial hair that attached, like a leather strap, from his sideburns to the middle of his chin. He lived in the condo beneath ours, and I'd never seen, in over a year of knowing him, his sober side; he was always stoned or drunk or both, and I often came home to him sitting on my deck in just such a state. In the summer, on days when the waves were small, he taught surf lessons to beginners, usually tourists—a job he could easily manage while intoxicated. He was popular in Dana Point among the night crowds, loved for his mellowness, but mostly known for going to one of the few bars in town every night. Andrew despised him, saying once, "That guy's such a waste. What does he contribute to society? He just sits around all day, gets drunk, and does *those drugs*."

But Robbie was oblivious to Andrew's disdain for him; he simply thought—as easygoing, unsuspicious, imperceptive people tend to do—that everyone either liked or loved him. Andrew slid past Robbie on the deck and went inside.

"How are you, Robbie?" I said.

"All good, my man. You want the last hit?"

"I'm all right."

"Don't mind if I do," he said, sucking in, with puckered lips, the last bit of life from the dying joint. "Did you guys go out for grub?" he said, exhaling.

"Yeah, the little Thai place."

"Oh … man … the Far East babes that work there … You see my girl, Tamarine?"

"Yeah, actually, she might stop by tonight."

"No shit? I had a girl like her once. I've had a few like her."

"You want to come in for a beer?"

"Absolutely not," he said, laughing loudly at his own sarcasm. "Why would I want to come in for a beer?" he said, laughing again.

"Robbie, you're fucking crazy."

Inside, Andrew had neatly stacked a bundle of our leftover wood and some blankets by the door next to his brown paper bag of peanut butter sandwiches, so, if Tamarine decided to come over, he would be ready. I opened three bottles of Bohemia from the refrigerator and brought the guys each one. Andrew, having tucked his shirt back in, grabbed the beer from me and drank half of it in one swig. I pulled him into the kitchen, as Robbie sat on the couch and rolled another joint.

"Are you OK, Andrew?"

"I'm completely fine. I should be in bed though. This is so irresponsible."

"What does it matter for one night?"

"It's very important that I don't go off course."

"Andrew, we never do much of anything. I think it's fine to do something different tonight. Maybe we should change out of our work clothes though, you know, in case we go down to the beach."

"No, I feel more comfortable like this."

"OK."

"Can you ask Robbie to leave? He's going to stink up the house with that stuff. I don't want anyone to think it's coming from our house."

"I'll talk to him."

Just then, Tamarine tapped on our screen door, and I caught the outline of her shapely figure against the dark blue backdrop of the evening.

"Come in," Andrew called out, quickly reaching for his hair to see if it was still in the right place.

"Hey, guys. Oh, hey, Robbie," she said, stepping inside.

"Tamarine, my sweetheart, I never see you outside the restaurant," said a stoned Robbie. "What a wonderful, wonderful, wonderful, wonderful surprise," he said, then laughed loudly again.

"Well, I usually go to bed. I work so much, you know. But ... Jake say maybe we do bonfire on beach."

"Just the kind of night I'm looking for," Robbie said, prompting Andrew, who'd been bouncing on his toes in the far corner, to shoot me the I-don't-want-him-to-come look.

"Tamarine, do you want some beer or wine?" I said.

"It OK. I don't drink."

"All right. I have to talk with Robbie about something for a few minutes. Why don't you two find us a spot on the beach? Get everything set up, and we'll meet you down there," I said, looking back and forth between Andrew and Tamarine.

"OK, we'll pick out a good spot," Andrew said, gathering the wood and blankets and then running his fingers across the fold of his brown lunch bag to tighten it where it had come undone a little.

As they were leaving, Tamarine looked at me with concern and said, "You come—right, Jake?" and I nodded at her reassuringly.

After they'd gone, Robbie lit his newly rolled joint, sucked on it to get the flame going, and said, "You wanted to chat about something?"

"I figured we could have a few more drinks."

"I fucking love drinks," he said, laughing. "Tamarine's ass. Holy fuck. You see that thing? Did I ever tell you about that threesome I had on tour?"

Robbie frequently retold the same stories from a period in his life, twenty years before, when he'd played for a band that had, allegedly, signed a million-dollar contract with a record label the week after they kicked him out.

"I don't think so," I lied.

"Try some of this grass, my man," he said, passing me the joint.

As Robbie told me about the two girls he was with once at the same time in a bathroom stall, I took a tiny drag on the joint, not enough to affect me, and thought about how I was never into drugs during college—smoked pot a few times, sure, but never tried any of the *real* ones. I'd been offered them but had always declined out of the fear that doing them would make me lose my mind. After graduating, I began to think of drugs as just part of a phase people went through during college, and since that time for me had already passed, I really didn't see the point in ever trying them.

"A million-dollar contract one week after … Can you believe that shit? I was that close. *Fuck*, man. I was that close," Robbie said, his eyes glazing over with memories of a better life.

"I feel you, man. But you got further than most," I said.

"How's the weed?"

"It's nice."

"If you ever want some weed, or anything else, come to me, baby."

"I will."

"There's no better person to score drugs from than someone in the restaurant business. *So many* drugs, man. We all hate our fucking jobs, so we need something, you know?"

"Yeah, that makes sense."

"All right, let's go to the bar," he said, already having forgotten about Andrew and Tamarine on the beach.

"I think I'm going to call it a night."

"Really? Shit, Jake. All right, see you soon, then, brother," he said, walking toward the door.

"Later."

At my desk in my room, I opened my laptop and started reading a short story I'd been writing. "This is *fucking crap*," I said after reading through it and realizing that, as with everything I'd ever written, I didn't have a compelling story. *I haven't experienced shit. I need to have some adventures before I can write about anything worth reading. No. That's what an imagination's for. But real writers don't ever come out of Orange County … do they? I should've been born in New York or something.* I deleted the short story, opened a new document, and stared at the blinking cursor on the blank screen until I fell asleep with my head on the desk.

"Jake. Jake. You sleep? *Jake!*"

"What's wrong? Who is it?" I said, confused and unaware of how long I'd been sleeping.

"This Tamarine. Sorry."

"It's fine. What's wrong?"

"We wait for you on beach. You not come."

"Yeah, sorry, I was talking to Robbie and then fell asleep. Where's Andrew?"

"I ran fast here. He coming," Tamarine said, speaking quickly and sounding a bit peculiar.

"Is everything OK?"

"Andrew show me his penis."

"Wait—what? Why'd he do that?"

"Don't know. On the beach he say, 'I show you something.'"

"Oh … uh, well, I'm not sure what he was thinking. You want me to talk to him?"

"No, no, it fine. But I come to see you."

"You need something?" I said, unable to see the expression on her face, as she stood above me in the dark.

"You like me, Jake?"

"Yeah, I like you, Tamarine."

She leaned over and kissed my mouth with her tongue, and I kissed her back at first but quickly pulled away, worried that Andrew might walk in on us.

"You no like me?"

"It's not that—"

"You no want girlfriend?"

"I'm not sure what you're asking me, Tamarine."

"You never marry me, huh, Jake?"

"Sorry—what?"

We heard Andrew come in through the front door, and Tamarine ran out of my room.

FOUR

My company booked me on a red-eye flight going to Newark, New Jersey late Friday night, which meant that I would arrive Saturday morning, just in time for the start of the conference. Because Andrew had gone to bed exceedingly early that night, probably as an act of self-punishment for his Tuesday night escapade, I couldn't ask him to drive me to the airport. Robbie was drunk at a bar. Steve and his lawyers were busy preparing for the yearly hearing with the Coastal Commission scheduled for the following Monday. I didn't want to ask my mother—and by association my father—because I wanted to avert any chance of discussing the email she'd sent me earlier in the week, which included a link to an article that was headlined "Top Lawyers in Orange County Under Forty," followed by her generous offer: "We're more than willing to help you out with law school, should you decide to go. We love you very much."

I drove myself north on the eerily empty 405 freeway and exited at MacArthur Boulevard for the John Wayne Airport. Inside, the airport was spotlessly clean, a characteristic I used to appreciate in the naiveté of my youth, especially while en route to the Hawaiian Islands on the twice-yearly family vacation. But on that particular night, the airport wasn't just clean, it was shiny, like the glass frame of my college diploma hanging on the wall in my mother's living room or the wineglasses set around the table for my father's dinner parties—shiny like the veneers on the housewives who lived in my childhood neighborhood or the Mercedes convertibles my bosses drove. On that night I would've been more comfortable in a dirty airport—a place where canceled flights forced travelers to crowd together on the floor and use their luggage as pillows, their jackets as blankets; a place that pulsated through the entire night with the chatter of whiskey-drinking storytellers, all settling into the cozy dirtiness.

I joined a few others in the security line, and, after a few sleepy employees decided I wasn't a threat to airport safety, found the only open restaurant—a beach-themed place with decorative surfboards everywhere—and sat along the bar, which was simply the top of a long surfboard, as the only working waiter tidied up.

"What can I get you?" he asked.

"I'll do the pale ale."

"Sure."

"Are you still serving food?" I asked, scanning a stray menu.

"Well, for the next five minutes," he said, handing me a glass of beer.

"Can I get the chicken sandwich?"

"Too late to do the chicken."

"A couple of these fish tacos, then," I said, pointing to the menu.

"Out of the fish tacos."

"What *can* you do?"

"We can make you a quesadilla."

"I'll take the quesadilla."

"Be ready in five."

"Can I get it to go?"

"Sure."

I sipped my beer, and, while scrolling through my phone, clicked to read the text Tamarine had sent me earlier—"You come to restaurant tonight we talk about us"—and then texted her back: "On a work trip, talk when I get back."

As I stared out of the restaurant at a coffee-sipping couple softly chatting in the sitting area, and then at a lone employee vacuuming the rug with broad strokes, I wondered at the connection I felt with airports. Fighting through long security lines and hordes of rushing travelers certainly caused me unease, but, once inside the terminal with time to spare, I was seduced by the magic subtleties of a place that not only seemed to expose the rawest and most emotional sides of people, but cultivated a collective camaraderie among them, as well. Strangers complained together about the weather or the price of bottled water or delayed flights, which usually segued into a story—with a newly appreciated perspective—about who or what they were being delayed from. Others joked about the most popular meme of the week or the end of the world coming, or, with a playfully disgusted look, the rise of the latest pop star. Most people, forced into the predicament of waiting, seemed—at least from my vantage point—to embrace the short-lasting, casual nature of the friendships they forged while passing through an airport.

Although I enjoyed sharing a look and a nod with fellow travelers, I preferred to observe them from behind a book or magazine—that way, I could secretly read the stories written in their expressions; sometimes I could detect the imprint on their faces of a loved one left behind or the twinkle in their eyes for the new destination that awaited them. I'd yet to find a better place to learn about people than an airport.

And being in an airport—despite the loud noises, the mix of strange smells, the concrete-like carpet, the uncompromising chairs—seemed to be a temporary remedy for my sleeplessness. *Sleep ... When was the last time I slept overnight in an airport? Rome. That's right. On my way home from my semester abroad in Italy.* Instead of going to a hostel for the night, I had decided just to stay in the airport. *I miss that semester—the best three months of my life.* Memories of my time in Italy flashed in my head: the thrill of waking up every day in a foreign country, the smell of fresh bread wafting through my window, the vision of old, craggy-faced Italian women hanging laundry to dry on clotheslines that colorfully decorated the cobblestone-paved path to my favorite café, where I enjoyed an espresso before class in the morning.

It felt good to be back in an airport.

Once on the plane, I took my aisle seat in an empty row; after takeoff, when the plane had leveled out, I ordered a whiskey from the flight attendant to calm my fear that, at any moment, the plane would explode—something I had never worried about during my childhood or adolescence.

"Jack Daniel's OK?" she asked.

"Fine."

"I have the mini bottles. Do you just want one?"

"Can you bring me a few?"

"Ice in the cup?"

"No, thanks."

I pulled the quesadilla out of the bag, unfolded its wrapping, and eyed the crispy tortilla, cut into several wedges, with melted cheese pouring out all the sides. I finished the whole thing before the flight attendant brought me three shot-sized bottles of whiskey and a clear plastic cup. I poured myself a drink with one of the bottles and took it down quickly, feeling its burn and then its warmth, then filled the cup with the two remaining bottles to sip slowly. I plugged my headphones into my phone, started playing an album from Bon Iver, then removed a notebook from my bag, and, feeling the whiskey, wrote a terrible, uninspired short story with a talking Styrofoam cup as the protagonist. Frustrated with my inability to write one good sentence, I ripped the pages out and crumpled them up. I then thought about using the plane's instant-messaging service to playfully communicate with the young guy sitting alone three rows ahead of me, but, unable to think of anything to send other than, "Are you going to the conference, too?" I decided against it. Instead, I read the fiction piece in the latest *New Yorker*, and then, over the next few hours, drifted in and out of a head-bobbing sleep.

In a compact rental car, I drove away from the noise of the airport, onto the freeway, and, guided by the car's GPS, eventually onto a wide country road, where the extraordinarily lush and verdant greens of summer suffocated my eyes. I continued along the road for a few miles, turned left onto a much smaller, bumpier road, and, not long after passing a sign that read, "Welcome to the unincorporated area of Zarephath, New Jersey," turned right into a hotel parking lot and parked.

"Checking in," I said to the woman at the check-in counter.

"Name please," she said without looking at me.

"Jake Reed."

"Are you here for the conference?"

"Yes."

"OK, Mr. Reed, the conference starts in five minutes. Here's a sheet with the relevant information—directions to the conference room in the hotel, schedule of speakers, meal times, et cetera," she said, handing me the sheet. "And here's your room key. Enjoy your stay."

Toting my travel bag, I rode the elevator up to the level with the conference room. As the elevator doors opened, a woman sitting at a six-foot-long table greeted me, asked for my name, then, after I told her, scribbled something onto her clipboard, handed me a name tag, and said, "Just through those doors. It's going to start very soon."

I walked inside and took a seat in one of the few empty chairs in the back. The fairly small room—carpeted in a terribly dizzying pattern of odd shapes, with a podium and projection screen in front—was pulsating with the murmur of several different conversations happening at once within the dozen or so rows filled with enthusiastic-looking men and women of all ages. Most people had their laptops open, but a few had yellow notepads flipped to a fresh page. The young man sitting next to me stared eagerly toward the front of the room, his fingers poised just above his laptop keys, ready to type, and his phone set to record audio. The people in the room—their well-groomed, perfumed bodies wafting professionalism into the air—seemed to be fizzing with excitement over whatever might happen next, like children on their first day back to school after a long summer vacation.

After a few minutes, a middle-aged woman in a business suit took the podium, and the projector flashed to life with a slide welcoming all in the room to the conference. She introduced herself and then recited a background on each of the "experts" scheduled to speak that day. As the young man next to me started typing notes, I considered leaning over and whispering to him that he should probably take my job, that he would be better for it, that my company would be better off with him in my place.

The first expert speaker—a cheery-eyed, blond, spikey-haired businessman with two purportedly successful companies to his name—took the podium, and, after the applause had settled, began his presentation by saying, "What *is* social media?" as a slide with the same words appeared on the projection screen. I looked at the exit doors, which had been closed at the start of the conference, and wondered how much noise the push-bar handles would make during my exit. The spirit of Andrew appeared before me and said, "No, Jake. You can't leave yet. Only forty more years of conferences similar to these until you can collect your retirement savings. Come on, Jake. Stay focused." But when the speaker began reading a passage from his own book on the "top ten proven ways to get more customers to 'like' your content," I rose quietly from my chair and pushed myself to freedom through the exit doors.

The hotel restaurant, empty when I walked in, had the feel of a classic diner; the room was square with a bar built into the middle of it and a pool table in the far corner. I took a seat on one of the stools around the bar and browsed the menu. A tall, thin waitress with delicate facial features and a boyish haircut appeared from the kitchen and took a seat alongside me at the bar.

"Having breakfast?" she said, smiling softly without showing her teeth.

I ordered coffee and eggs, over medium, with toast and hash browns, and when she came back to pour me a cup of coffee, she asked if I was there for the conference.

"How did you know?" I offered her a half-smile.

She laughed. "Why else would you be here?"

"Ha, well, I'm supposed to be here for the conference. But I'm over it. So now I'm just here on vacation."

"Where are you from?" she asked

"Southern California," I said, bringing alive a soft shimmer behind her eyes.

"No way! I'm moving to Los Angeles one day."

"Really?"

"Yep. Going with a girlfriend as soon as we've saved enough to get started."

"That'll be an adventure."

"They always need more waitresses, right?"

I nodded and smiled.

"So is LA really like it is on the reality TV shows?"

"You know—I actually have no idea. I don't really *know* LA at all. Besides going to a few college football games, I've never really hung out there or anything. I'm from Orange County, an hour or so south of LA, and went to college in Northern California."

"Well, I guess I've never been to New York, and it's not too far from here."

"Why not?"

"I don't know. Maybe for the same reason you don't go to LA. Let me see if your eggs are ready."

A few minutes later she came back with my plate of food, set it in front of me, and took a seat beside me again.

"Why is this place so empty?" I asked her, slicing into my eggs and taking a bite, then taking a sip of coffee.

"It's always empty."

"Are you from here?"

"Unfortunately."

"What's life like in this town?"

"There *is* no life in this town. You have to go to the next town over to get any action. It'll be more fun for you there."

"But I'm interested in *this* town."

"Well ... OK ... so it's this unincorporated and very religious town that, besides these little conferences here and there, has literally *nothing* going on. Everything closes early."

"I love it here."

"Really? It's so boring I want to die. When I'm not working, I'm seriously just on the Internet all day."

I smiled. "I don't think you're alone in doing that. Do you go to school around here?"

"No, I started taking classes at a community college but then decided I wanted to take a year off. Do you think that's stupid?"

"Nope. I think you should do whatever you want."

An elderly couple came into the restaurant and took a seat at one of the tables; when she left to wait on them, I finished my breakfast and left a twenty on the table. On my way out, I asked the waitress for her name.

"Amanda," she said. "Yours?"

"Jake."

"See you around, Jake."

I walked down the hallway toward my room on an old, dusty, yellow carpet and admired the fading, chipped white paint on the walls. *I like the feeling of this place.* I slid the room key into the slot and, in the few seconds I had left before opening the door, enjoyed the familiar sense of excitement and curiosity I felt every time I was about to enter a hotel room, especially a cheap one.

Once inside, it struck me that with the serenity and ease of being alone in a little hotel room with no agenda, I felt invigorated, inspired even, as if, in the absence of all other distractions, the things around me—an old, dusty, boxlike TV; a stiff twin bed covered by a cheap-looking spread; a lone bedside lamp shaded by thin yellowing paper; a small circular table between two tub chairs upholstered in a garish red—had come alive, flourishing with rich character, shining bright with their long-forgotten specialness. What may have been boredom to others was exhilaration to me. For me, boredom was sometimes a room full of people.

Along the back wall, the curtains were drawn shut over a window. I pulled the curtains back and looked at thick, low-hanging clouds over a vast grassland blanketed in bright green, edged by colorful, flowering bushes, and a long stretch of trees with overhanging leaves the size of dinner plates.

I fell back on the bed and, because I felt like hearing the harmonica, played The Decemberists's "June Hymn" from my phone while happily whistling along to the melody. When the song finished, I opened the minibar, said, "Fuck it," and cracked open a late-morning beer to sip while showering. After toweling dry, I flipped through the information folder and read about the hotel pool; I changed into a pair of shorts and gathered two more beers from the minibar, Jonathan Franzen's *Freedom,* and my notebook.

The pool—half-sized, shallow, and filled with pale blue water—was vacant, rekindling my pleasant feeling of being alone in a secluded town. I reclined on one of the lounge chairs along the pool's edge, read some of the Franzen book while sipping my beer, and, after being inspired by some of his sentences, wrote some of my own in my notebook. I took a break, played Bob Dylan's *Blood on the Tracks* from my phone, and dozed off for a few minutes. Later, I took a dip in the pool, swam its length three times before coming up for air, and then decided to explore the town.

As I walked to my car, an unfamiliar, early afternoon humidity closed in around my head, as if two strong hands, placed on each of my temples, were crushing it. I'd already started sweating. Because I was alone in the little parking lot—with patches of weeds sprouting through cracks in the blacktop—I expected a certain quietness to greet me, but such was not the case; the air was vibrating with the numbing drone of unseen buzzing insects and croaking frogs and chirping birds, as well as the higher-pitched, violin-playing mosquitoes circling my ears. *This place is like a damn jungle. A beautiful jungle.* The wet heat of a New Jersey summer was quite different from the much milder, drier heat of the Southern California summers I'd grown used to.

On the road into town, I drove past an undersized fire station paint- ed a bright red with a small, toylike fire truck parked alongside the curb, and then past a charming post office that resembled a little bed-and- breakfast. I imagined that the townies took shifts working at the fire station one weekend and the post office the next weekend.

I parked along the curb in front of a bookstore, walked inside to a pleasantly cool room redolent of timeworn pages between tattered cov- ers, immediately found the fiction section, and, like a child in a room full of unopened gifts on Christmas morning, browsed for a novel to go after first; but I soon became overwhelmed by all the books I hadn't yet read, as their authors hassled me while I ambled along the alphabetical aisles: Margaret Atwood shook her head in disappointment, William Burroughs threw his hands up in disbelief, Willa Cather leered, Michael Chabon screamed, Michel Houellebecq shouted, James Joyce scoffed, D. H. Lawrence glared, Marcel Proust cried out, "*Mais que dites vous?*" Philip Roth angrily shook his fists, and Edith Wharton scoffed, "*Really?*" There were so many books still to read, so many to add to my ever-growing queue.

An employee, organizing one of the shelves, asked me if I needed help finding anything.

"How about something contemporary—something young people are reading?" I said.

"Hmm ... You know what, follow me," he said.

We walked to another aisle and, after he'd skimmed a few sections, he plucked a very thin book from the shelf and handed it to me. "Everyone's reading this."

I flipped through it, rubbed the glossy cover, and asked, "What's so special about it?"

"He writes the whole book like an online-chat session, you know, like, in the style that we instant-message our friends. It's really quite representational."

"OK, I'll give it a read."

After buying the book from him, I found a chair and finished the book entirely within the hour, but, when trying to reflect on the story minutes later, couldn't remember one thing I'd just read. *What the hell just happened? This is what people want to read?* Before leaving the bookstore, I made a peace offering to the writers I'd neglected by promising to read their works soon.

Strolling down the main road, I came upon a little deli and went inside; on my left, two men in white aprons were busy behind the counter dicing and packing food. I was the only customer in the deli. A large-bellied man, who beamed with the confidence of an owner or a manager, looked up at me, still seamlessly dicing, and said, "How are we doing today, young man?"

"Well, thanks," I said. "What's good here?"

"My roasted turkey is very fresh today. I can put it on sourdough with melted jack, lettuce, and tomato for you," he said, pointing to a chalkboard hanging above him that had a written description of the sandwich.

"Let's do that."

"You also get a drink from the fridge," he said, whipping his broad-bladed knife in the direction of the fridge in the back of the deli. "And a side—fruit, chips, or our famous potato salad."

"Sure, I'll do the potato salad."

"You bet. Take a seat, and we'll bring it out to you."

"Thanks."

I walked over to the old-fashioned refrigerator with see-through glass doors and stared at a variety of drinks—milk, soda, tea, beer, water—before grabbing an unsweetened ice tea and taking a seat at a wooden table facing the deli counter to watch the portly man in the white apron prepare my lunch. *I love this simplicity. I don't want to go home. Maybe I should move to a place like this …*

Back in the lobby of the hotel, I weaved, as if I were a car going the wrong way on the freeway, through a herd of chatty, social media enthusiasts, who were presumably at the tail end of their lunch break and heading back to the conference room. Some of them were trading business cards or discussing their job descriptions, and others were going over their notes. In their presence I felt a bit like a disrespectful truant, but, as I hurried past them, I felt more like a relieved escapee. *I made the right decision.* In my room, I lay on the bed, browsed the online lives of people I hadn't spoken with in years, and then watched the first fifteen minutes of Woody Allen's *Manhattan* before fading into an afternoon nap.

I awoke naturally—feeling uncharacteristically refreshed and calm and clearheaded—and wondered hopefully if New Jersey had cured my insomnia. I'd left the curtains open, and the sun, nearly finished with its work for the day, cast a wonderful, soft reddish yellow into the room, imbuing me with the urge to capture it in some way. I excitedly grabbed my notebook, and, like a madman, began writing on a fresh page.

THE PORTRAIT OF THE SUN AS AN ARTIST

Every morning the sun peeks through the horizon with a youthful curiosity. He slowly grows stronger as the morning matures, showing a brighter light. And then, like a budding artist, he realizes his passion to shine his light for all to see and feel; but, in the boastfulness of his high-noon position, he shines his light with such ferocity that the people and the trees and the animals have to shelter themselves from him to avoid burn marks. As the afternoon comes, however, the sun loosens his grip because he learns compassion and a willingness to compromise. And just before sunset, in the calm of the sun's final moments, when he is the wisest but also the weakest, he becomes very generous, and to apologize for his wrongdoing at high noon, he shines the prettiest light upon the land. And in a final appeal for forgiveness, he gives us one more flash of beauty and disappears, as his trail is enveloped by darkness and memories of a brighter day.

As I finished writing, I tuned in to a faint murmur in the distance—a repetitive, eerily harmonious sound with the rhythm of a slowed heartbeat. Guessing where the sound was coming from, I stared fixedly at the window along the back wall, got out of bed, and walked toward the large pane of glass, unnerved by what I might see. Through the window, in the dusk, I saw hundreds of black-robed people moving in a procession around the field, each of them carrying a book and following the leader, who hoisted a large cross high in the air. They seemed to be chanting softly in unison, but I couldn't make out the words.

"What the fuck?" I whispered.

After a few minutes, I lost interest in guessing the meaning of the procession and, hungry for dinner, showered and changed to go down to the hotel restaurant. But before I was able to leave my room, I heard a knock at the door and opened it, expecting to see the hotel's housekeeper.

"Hey, Jake," Amanda said, tucking her short hair behind her ear with one hand and holding a paper bag by the handles with the other.

"Hi, Amanda. Come in," I said, letting her in and closing the door. "I was just leaving to see you at the restaurant."

"I just got off, but I brought food, if you want to hang out."

"Even better."

"And a bottle of gin."

I laughed and said, "*Gin?*"

"Yeah, I stole it from the restaurant. I figured a missing bottle of gin has a better chance of going unnoticed. There's some club soda in your minibar we can use. I brought some slices of lime, too."

"Ha, good thinking. I'll go get some ice from the machine down the hall."

When I came back into the room with the bucket of ice, she'd set up two plates on the table, one with *insalata Caprese,* and the other with several little chicken sandwiches. I made two gin-and-soda drinks, each with a slice of lime, and handed one to her. Amanda said, "Cheers," and we clinked glasses. I tasted the gin drink, and, unlike the gradual body heat I got from a sip of whiskey, felt the heat instantly in my head. We used plastic forks to pluck pieces of fresh mozzarella and tomatoes from the plate and our hands to eat the little sandwiches.

"What goes on out in that field at night?" I asked.

"Oh, a big group of locals get together and pray."

"Every night?"

"Yeah, I think so."

"I didn't know what to make of it at first."

"Pretty normal shit around here."

"I see ..." I said, then after a few seconds of silence, "You want to listen to some music?"

"OK."

"What do you feel like?"

"Hmm ... Do you have any Portugal. The Man?"

"Yep," I said, walking over to my laptop and setting it up to play.

"So you just decided to skip the entire conference, huh?" she asked, covering her mouth with her hand after a bite of her sandwich.

"Yeah. And having an incredible time," I said, rejoining her at the table and reaching for another sandwich.

"*Really?* Doing what?"

"Nothing, really. I just like the way I feel being here."

"Because you're somewhere new?"

"Maybe. I think that when I'm back home I feel lonely when I'm alone because I'm where I'm supposed to be ... but when I'm here, I feel OK alone because no one knows where I am. I don't know—it's kind of weird. Does that make any sense?"

"I think it makes perfect sense. What's it like where you live?"

"It's a really beautiful place on the coast—beaches, cliffs, hills, all that—but it's so expensive to live there that everything is always about money, all the time."

"What do you mean?"

"Well, I guess, those who have a lot of money are worried they're going to lose it, so they obsess over ways to make more of it. And then those who barely have enough money spend their lives trying to change that," I said, and then when I saw that she'd finished her drink, "You want another?"

"Oh yes."

I finished the last of my drink, added some ice to both of our glasses, filled them up mostly with gin, and added a little bit of soda.

"Much stronger this round," she said, sipping her new drink and smiling delicately.

"And real estate is religion where I'm from. It's like," I said, feeling the gin, "these huge businesses are formed around one person transferring land to another person. Nothing really happens, you know? Only land gets transferred, and then all this money is created, and people go fucking crazy over it."

"What does your dad do?"

"Real estate."

"Your mom?"

"Drinks white wine and wishes I'd become a lawyer and find a nice girl from the neighborhood to marry. 'Come on, Jake. A pretty girl. A nice, pretty girl. Why can't you make your mother happy?' She says it just like that," I said, imitating my mother's voice, eliciting laughter from Amanda. "I mean, I know she just wants the best for me. And it's really my fault for whetting her appetite."

"How so?"

"I used to be so straight, you know? Always got straight As, asked my parents to take me to visit colleges when I was thirteen, was the valedictorian of my high school. She thought I was really put together, you know? But at some point after college, I stopped feeling OK, stopped feeling anything, really. She always tells me, 'You can only take care of the one person who matters in this world: yourself.' But that's coming from a person who hosts all these dinner parties for all of her friends. Her mentality just doesn't make any sense to me."

"Have you ever loved a girl?" she asked.

"I don't think so."

"I was in love once ... I didn't think about anything else, and everything seemed to make sense for a while. Maybe you should try that."

"But let's forget about love for a second. How about just a real fucking connection? I don't like the idea of a world where people just worry about taking care of themselves. Sometimes I think I hate people—I really do—but I'm not ready to give up on them yet. I mean, there has to be something, right?"

"Something ... ?"

"I don't know. Something that means something."

"Maybe you should move to this town and find God," she said, playfully.

I laughed. "Maybe I should. Actually, when I believed in God, I used to worry all day about doing something morally wrong. But now I worry that there's no point in doing anything, like there's no point in drinking from this glass or walking around or going to a baseball game or watching a film. I feel like I'm just passing through life. But then there's this voice in my head telling me to do something, to create something, to make something, and I want to listen to it, but I don't know how. I want to be able to say something, but I have nothing to say. I want something extraordinary, but I'm ordinary in every way—I just read books about other people and browse the lives of my Facebook friends all day."

She laughed and said, "That's all I do, too, really."

"Ah ... fuck."

"What?"

"I'm going on a drunken first-world, white-boy-problem rant, aren't I?"

"Yep! No, I like it ... God, my head is hot from this gin."

"Mine, too. It feels good," I said, adding a little more gin to my drink, and then asking her, "You want some?"

"Yeah," she said, and I poured her a little. "So maybe that's it then. Since you like the feeling of being here, you should travel around to places like this and stay in little hotel rooms like this until you figure something out."

"I might just do that. I have a little money saved."

"So that's the plan then. Maybe you should start in Los Angeles, and I'll start in New York, and then we'll each make our way to the opposite coast and write each other if we figure anything out along the way."

"I'm in," I said, standing up and walking over to my laptop. "Let's listen to some classic shit, some Van Morrison or something."

Amanda got up from the table, sat on the bed facing me, and, when I glanced up from my laptop, looked at me suggestively. "Come here," she said.

"Oh my God!" Amanda yelled, as she jumped out of bed the next morning.

I opened my eyes and saw her slide into her pants on the edge of the bed and then gather the rest of her clothes in a hurry. "Are you OK?" I asked.

"Yeah. Sorry. I have to get out of here before the maid comes. I could get into a lot of trouble for … well … you know … fucking a hotel guest," she said with a smile.

"Right," I said, laughing.

"I'll find you on Facebook," she said, scurrying toward the door.

"Sounds good."

"Bye, Jake."

After she'd gone, I drank a glass of water from the bathroom faucet while I looked around my room—at the lamp, the old TV, the untidy sheets, the table with the remnants of last night's dinner and drink—and thought about how the last couple of days had reminded me of how much I loved traveling, whether it be to Europe or to a cheap hotel in some unincorporated, unpeopled town in New Jersey. It was the feeling that was important to me, not the destination. And then, although my head felt heavy from a gin hangover, I felt inspired to write something again. I *needed* to write something. I opened my notebook and wrote down the thoughts in my head, read them over, and rewrote them—losing track of time, losing track of the world—until I was finally satisfied.

TRAVEL

Travel is little beds and cramped bathrooms. It's old television sets and slow Internet connections. Travel is extraordinary conversations with ordinary people. It's waiters, gas station attendants, and housekeepers becoming the most interesting people in the world. It's churches that are compelling enough to enter. It's McDonald's being a luxury. It's the realization that you may have been born in the wrong country. Travel is a smile that leads to a conversation in broken English. It's the epiphany that pretty girls smile the same way all over the world. Travel is tipping 10% and being embraced for it. Travel is the same white T-shirt again tomorrow. Travel is accented sex after good wine and too many unfiltered cigarettes. Travel is flowing in the back of a bus with giggly strangers. It's a street full of bearded backpackers looking down at maps. Travel is wishing for one more bite of whatever that just was. It's the rediscovery of walking somewhere. It's sharing a bottle of liquor on an overnight train with a new friend. Travel is "Maybe I don't have to do it that way when I get back home." It's nostalgia for studying abroad that one semester. Travel is realizing that "age thirty" should be shed of its goddamn stigma.

FIVE

I arrived back at my condo in Dana Point late Sunday night, and the first thing I noticed, walking through the front door, was the neatly folded brown paper bag with Andrew's peanut butter sandwiches, ready to be picked up in the morning. Andrew was asleep. The place was silent. I went straight into my room, lay flat on my bed—rigid with fear—and stared up at the white ceiling. *Oh my God.* An awfulness was deep inside me, and I couldn't fight it; forced into submission and taken hostage by it, I could only just lie there, let it wash over me, and let myself be consumed by it. *If I cooperate, maybe it won't stay too long; maybe it'll let me go free. But if I fight it, it might stay longer just to spite me.* So I decided to let The Feeling inhabit me as long as it desired, while I lay still, cautious not to incite it, secretly hoping it would leave me soon and bother someone else, but, outwardly, pretending to be its gracious host.

The most discouraging element of what I felt was my inability to understand it. Usually when I was filled with an unpleasant feeling, I could make it go away, or at least tame it, by watching a light-hearted film or reading a good book or listening to a feel-good album. But *this* feeling was different. I knew none of those distractions could rid me of it. But I knew nothing else. I couldn't even describe it. *Is this depression? Maybe once you ask someone to describe depression, he can't find the words. Maybe I'm part of the official club now.* I imagined myself in a room full of people where someone in the crowd, also suffering from depression, immediately noticed me—as if he detected the scent of his own kind—walked over, and looked into my eyes. He knew that I had The Feeling inside me because he, too, had The Feeling inside him. He didn't ask me to talk about it, because he understood that our type of suffering was ineffable. He only nodded at me, and I nodded back; and then, during our moment of silence, we both shared a sad smile of recognition, knowing that we only had each other in a room filled with people who would never understand us, because they didn't have The Feeling inside them.

On Monday morning, when I walked into the office, my vision was flooded with the terrible fluorescent lighting that seemed, on that day, especially unbearable. And as I hurried toward my desk, squinting away the light from my eyes, I was intercepted by Roger.

"He's back! How was the conference, Jake? Did you bring us back anything useful?"

"Hello, Roger. Yeah, I hope so."

"Great to hear. I can't wait for your presentation at tomorrow's meeting."

Fuck.

The girl whose desk faced mine said, "Hey, Jake," without looking up, but, on that day, I didn't acknowledge her. I sat down, opened up my laptop, and checked my email: fifty-two unread messages. Then I noticed a wrapped rectangular cardboard box that had been placed on my desk in my absence and opened it to find hundreds of brand-new business cards with my fancy new title: New Media Manager. I massaged my forehead, grimacing at the thought of how long it would take me to hand out so many business cards. I put on my headphones, played the latest album from Beach House, and, over the next hour or so, finished my daily tasks. I spent the rest of the day trying to conjure up, without any success, a passable presentation of my "learnings" for the Tuesday meeting. I stared for hours at the blinking cursor (a longtime enemy with a particular predilection for taunting me), and tried to translate an idea in my head to text on the screen, but couldn't even get my fingers to type a meaningless conjunction.

Between five and six that evening, people packed up their things and left. Turning down the volume on my headphones, I listened to part of a conversation the last two people in the office—one of my bosses and a young intern—were having on their way out.

"Think of the marketing department at our company as the Air Force," my boss told the intern. "Think of the sales department as the infantry. We have to be smart, so before we send out our infantry guys, let's first send out our planes to patrol the battlefield and bomb the shit out of the defense. This way, the defense will be weakened, and then we can send out our infantry to finish the bastards off," he said as the doors shut behind them.

Alone in the office, I got out of my chair, and, thinking a nap might be the remedy for my incapacity to think of any ideas for my presentation, climbed under my desk and lay on the carpet, staring up at the underbelly of my desk.

When I awoke, my head felt heavy, and both my arms were asleep; I got out from under the desk, shook the life back into my arms, and checked the time on my phone: three in the morning. *Christ. Presentation in seven hours with nothing to present.* I decided that I'd splash some water on my face in the bathroom, brew a pot of coffee in the kitchen, and make a final attempt to formulate a presentation before going home. *Maybe I'll call in sick tomorrow ...*

Because the entire floor shared a bathroom, I had to exit the office and walk down a long hallway; on my way out, as I pushed through the sturdy wooden doors, I immediately stumbled into the cleaning crew: a group of four Mexican men—sitting on the floor, next to vacuums and mops, sharing a six-pack of Budweiser—who, when they saw me, frantically scrambled to their feet while trying to hide their beer.

"*Lo siento, lo siento,*" one of the men said to me with fear in his eyes.

"It's OK. I don't care," I said, feeling bad about ruining their few minutes to enjoy conversation and cold beer. "Do you guys speak English?"

"*No,*" one of the men said.

"Wait here. Just wait here. Don't worry," I said, signaling them to wait.

A few weeks before, a bottle of Johnnie Walker King George V had been delivered to the CEO as a gift from a client, and, because I was the only employee in the office not out to lunch when the delivery showed up, I signed for it. Well aware of that particular brand's reputation for quality among Scotch whisky drinkers (in my real estate circles anyway), I hoped, as I walked into my CEO's office, that he'd been saving the bottle for a special occasion that had yet to present itself. *It's still here!* I found the bottle—unopened, extravagantly boxed in brilliant blue—in one of his cabinet drawers, and, without questioning myself, took it with me into the kitchen, where I grabbed five Styrofoam cups, and then back out to the hallway.

"Look. I brought us something," I said, removing the gleaming crystal treasure from the box and showing it to the crew, who had, fortunately, decided to wait for me. "This is a very good Scotch. I brought us some cups, too," I said, tilting the bottle a bit so it caught some of the hallway light and reflected a sparkle on each of their faces.

Each of the men had a partly bemused, partly suspicious expression, but when I opened the bottle, poured Scotch into one of the cups, and handed it to the closest man, they all seemed to lighten up, except for one man, who still stared at me skeptically. Taking a seat on the ground, I squeezed myself into their circle, poured the rest of them each a cup, and, when all of us had a drink, raised my glass and said, "*Salud, amigos.*"

"*Salud,*" all four of them said in unison.

Communicating with smiley nods and hand signals, we drank until we finished the Scotch in our cups, and then I poured us some more. Enjoying myself and feeling comfortable with them, I practiced the few words I knew in Spanish, obscenities I'd learned growing up in Mexico-adjacent Southern California, and my new friends laughed, seemingly entertained by my pronunciation or my word choices or both. And then one of the men, watching me to gauge my reaction, reached into his back pocket and pulled out a page he'd ripped from a magazine; as I watched him unfold the page, I recognized that it was from *Playboy*. With an impish grin, he beckoned me to come closer, and, when I did, showed me a picture of a naked woman. I made a gesture as if to say, "Look at those breasts!" and all the guys laughed uproariously. I couldn't remember the last time I'd seen porn from a tangible magazine.

We'd nearly finished the $600 bottle of Scotch when the man who had been staring at me said something and pointed to his watch, spurring the rest of them into action. I swallowed what was left in the bottle, set it in one of their trash bins, and then held my index finger over my mouth and said, "Shhhh," and we all laughed together one last time.

"*Gracias, compadre,*" one of them said to me.

"*Hasta luego,*" another said to me.

"*Gracias, amigos.* Let's do this again," I said to all of them before walking back into my office.

Roger, the first one into the office at seven in the morning, flipped on the fluorescent lights, and I shielded my eyes with my hand.

"Jake? What are *you* doing in so early?" he asked, in a way that suggested his disappointment in my breaking his long-running streak of being first into the office.

"Just finishing up this presentation," I said.

"Oh, great to hear. Well done, Jake," he said insincerely.

Within the next couple of hours the office had filled with employees, and the quietness I'd come to know during the night had been replaced by the disharmonious tune of phones ringing, printers spitting out presentations, employees clearing their throats, and fingers tapping on laptop keys. One of my bosses came over to my desk.

"I want you to write something about the Steve Duggins deal. I sent you a link to the story. Perhaps we can get him to consider us for some of his business," he said.

"What happened with Steve Duggins?" I asked.

"His hearing with the Commission was yesterday, and his proposal passed. I guess they caved because money is tight, and they needed the deal."

"OK, no problem," I said, holding back a joyous grin. I was excited for Steve, not necessarily proud of his victory in the business sense, but happy about the overwhelming euphoria he must have been feeling. He deserved to feel good. I wondered if I could ever care for something as much as he cared for his lots, and what the feeling would be like for me to realize a lifelong dream.

I opened the email from my boss and clicked on the link to a story with a subhead that read, "Local developer Steve Duggins wins momentous victory to sell coastal property lots to general public, skyrocketing his personal worth to upwards of $300 million and making him one of the county's fifty richest." *Good for him.*

At ten, we all filed into the boardroom and gathered around the large table for the weekly meeting. One of the assistants made a loop around the table, setting the agenda in front of everyone, and, for the first time in my span with the company, I noticed something new had been added to the top of the page: "Jake Reed presents learnings from the social media conference." *Shit.* The bosses came into the room, and the CEO said, "OK, everyone, let's get started." I stared out the window and wondered how many Tuesday meetings there were in forty years— *one per week ... fifty-two weeks per year ... for forty years is about ... two thousand Tuesday meetings.* "Jake Reed, as you all know, was at a social media conference this weekend. We'll start the meeting this morning with a presentation of his learnings. Go ahead, Jake."

As the eyes around the table focused on me, I looked at Roger, who stared back at me while nervously twiddling a pen between his fingers, and smiled at him. In the silence of the room, as Roger's lower lip submitted to an anxious quiver and sweat began to form on his brow, I stood up and cleared my throat.

"Hello, everyone," I said. "As a company, we're currently part of a time when social media is especially crucial to a thriving business. Because it's important that we stay ahead of our competition, I propose that we ..." I paused when I noticed Roger vehemently taking notes, as if he were writing every word I was saying, and then, after having the most lucid few seconds I'd ever had while working for the company, I said, "I can't do this ... I haven't been fair to you all for quite some time. There is no presentation. I think that," I paused again, looking around a room full of faces frozen in fear, "I'll leave now. I quit. I'm sorry."

I left the deadly silence of the boardroom, returned to my desk, gathered my things, and walked through the office doors for the last time. I pushed the button to call the elevator, and, when the doors opened, got inside with two other people from another company, who, upon my entrance, quit their conversation and played with their phones. The elevator stopped on another floor to let in a few more people, and together, in silence, we descended the floors. *Floor* 17, 16, 15 ... I hoped we didn't have to stop for any more people. *Floor* 10, 9, 8 ... Someone coughed. Silence. *Floor* 3, 2, 1 ... The gates finally opened in the lobby, and we charged the open land like freed horses.

A few minutes later, I cruised down Pacific Coast Highway—with my windows rolled down, the sunroof open, and the excitement of being on the road at such an unfamiliar time—under the summer sky sprinkled with high cotton clouds, listening to a song that matched my mood ("There's nothing that the road cannot heal. Washed under the blacktop, gone beneath my wheels. There's nothing that the road cannot heal"), and stealing glances of the bright blue sea on my right.

Back home, I changed into a T-shirt and shorts and, on the way down to the beach, ran into Robbie.

"Jake, my man. You take the day off?"

"I guess so."

"Where you going?"

"To the beach. Want to join?"

"Yes, sir! Let me grab a bottle of something."

"OK."

He ran back into his condo and came out carrying a green bottle.

"Jägermeister?" I asked, playfully.

"It's all I had left. It'll get us where we need to be. Don't you worry."

On our way to the beach, we descended the cliff, through the vegetation on one of the man-made trails, and saw Steve Duggins in a clearing, surrounded by a team of construction workers, holding a clipboard and excitedly shouting instructions.

"Jake! We did it, buddy," he said, running over and embracing me.

"I heard. Congratulations, Steve. You deserve it," I said.

Down on the beach, Robbie and I found a spot on the dry part of the sand, not too far from the water, and he passed me the bottle.

"I quit my job today," I told him after taking a sip and handing the bottle back to him.

"No shit, man? Do you want me to see if there's a job for you at the restaurant?"

"Yeah, maybe," I said, staring at a group of long-beaked sandpipers trying to avoid the waves breaking on the shore as they hastily dug for crabs.

As we shared the bottle, Robbie retold the story about him being a drummer in a band that signed a million-dollar contract the week after they kicked him out. "Almost made it, man. Almost made it," he said as he finished the story.

"I know, man. But you got further than most," I said.

I woke up from an alcohol-induced midday nap on the beach to several missed calls and one long voice mail from my mother. After listening to the message, I solemnly closed my eyes and thought about the time, years before, when I told my grandmother I wanted to be a writer.

"Then be a writer," she had said. "Start writing. Write about anything. If you really want it, you have to work at it every day. I know that much. I always wanted to be a painter, but I never found the time to practice. And then I became a wife and a mother, but that's all I ever was. Start early. Don't stop. Be passionate about it, Jake."

My grandmother had responded in the way I'd hoped she would, especially after the disappointment I felt in hearing my mother's take on the matter: "Jake, creativity is fine enough as a hobby. Do what you must to get it out of your system. But you have far more important things to focus on."

On Thanksgiving Day that year (my senior year in college), my grandmother quietly pulled me away from the dinner table and asked how my writing was going.

"I have nothing to write about," I told her.

"Jake, you have to live and do things and then write about those experiences."

That Christmas she gave me a stack of beautifully bound Moleskine notebooks and a card that read, "Now you have no excuse."

I started to listen to my mother's voice mail again, but then, unwilling to keep listening to the unsettling sounds of her crying, turned off my phone. My grandmother was dead.

Three months before, she was as healthy and lively as I'd ever known her to be—that is, until she was diagnosed with pancreatic cancer and, within a month, had lost nearly half her body weight.

"How the hell is this possible?" I shouted at her doctor, while visiting her in the hospital. "She goes from healthy to deathly ill in less than a month?"

"There are very few symptoms with early pancreatic cancer, and, if there are symptoms, they are often confused with something else. It creeps up on us, and by the time we discover it, it's often in a very advanced stage. I'm very sorry," the doctor said.

At some point, in the final stages of her lucidity, my grandmother had decided that she wanted to leave the hospital and spend her remaining time in the comfort of her own home. So my mother hired a nursing staff, and they set my grandmother up in a light-filled, seaward-windowed room of her home on a cliff in Newport Beach. The last time I saw her was the day I left for the conference in New Jersey; I spent the late afternoon by her side as we stared out the window, where, below, the waves broke against the cliff, the cake-batter white foam churned against the rocks, and the sun sunk into a horizon tinged blue-orange-crimson. But it didn't seem beautiful to me that day.

I was usually able to elicit at least a nod or a smile from her with one of my stories. But not that day. A story, the touch of my hand on hers, the beautiful view of the California coastline, the luxury of her multi-million-dollar home—none of it seemed to matter, none of it meant anything, none of it could help her. She just sat there numbly with a withering, frail body, staring with jaundiced eyes through the window at nothing, and, as my hand rested on top of hers, I could already feel a chill in her blood that foretold the inevitable—and all of it made me very angry.

Three days after my grandmother died, I rode in a black limo with my parents to her vigil at a Catholic church in Newport Beach. As we pulled up along the curb outside the church, I stared at a large group of people dressed in black gathering in front, some of them hugging each other, others crying. I got out of the car and followed my parents toward the group of mourners.

"Hey, Jake," an old man, whom I didn't recognize, said to me. "I'm very sorry for your loss. Your grandmother was a great pillar of this community. Very generous to us all. We'll miss her."

"Very kind words," I said, nodding solemnly. "I appreciate it."

"She was always very proud of you, always talking about your achievements and how smart you are," he said.

"Thank you, sir," I said.

Inside, the smell of the church—the incense, the pages of the hymnals, the old, wooden pews—took my mind back to my childhood days of being an altar boy in church every Sunday. As I approached the front pews designated for immediate family, I realized it was an open-casket vigil. *Why the fuck is there an open casket?* I took a seat and looked at her lying in the casket with makeup on her face and fancy clothes on her body, and the sight of her—lifeless, meaningless, soulless, thoughtless—stirred in me an unfamiliar uneasiness. The feeling began to overwhelm me, and I didn't like where my mind was going; I couldn't get the image of her dead face out of my head even when I looked away at the crucifix or the priest or the little altar boy. She was *dead*. My fingers trembled. My heart palpitated. I tried to settle my nerves by closing my eyes and putting my head into my hands, but my palms were clammy, and the image of my dead grandmother was burned into the inner part of my eyelids. I got up, pushed my way through the pew in a panic, and walked down the side aisle until I was outside, where I remained on a bench with my head buried in my hands for the rest of the vigil.

My parents hosted an after-vigil gathering at their house in Laguna Beach, and I was sitting alone in a side room, hidden behind dark sunglasses, sipping warm whiskey, when someone came in.

"Jake, do you have a few minutes to chat?"

I looked up to see my grandparents' longtime attorney standing above me. "About what?"

"Your grandmother was very adamant that I speak with you before I proceed with the more formal legal matters."

"OK, sure."

He took a seat in one of the cushy chairs next to me and said, "While deaths in the family are difficult for the obvious reasons, they can also be a burden on the family because of the will or trust left behind by the deceased. When finances are involved, it can get messy. Now, you *are* in her will to be the sole beneficiary of her condo in Dana Point, but that's not why I'm speaking with you now. Your grandmother asked that the matter I discuss with you now be kept off the record. She asked me to produce a check in your name for $50,000, which I have now, along with a note from her, in this envelope," he said, reaching into his coat pocket, retrieving a white envelope, and handing it to me. "I'll let you be now. I'm truly sorry for your loss."

When he left the room, I opened the envelope and pulled out the check and a handwritten letter.

My Grandson Jake,

You're a very special boy to me. Sometimes the world gets you down, and I see that. But know this: most people don't do anything about it. It's easier to stay still and just hope things get better. But I know you want more than that. During my later years, I found myself more curious than anything else. Take the money from me, and spend it on something you really love. Search for something beyond what you know. You just might discover something remarkable about the world, but, regardless, you'll surely learn much about yourself on the journey. I love you.

—Grandma

I read her letter three times before I got up from my chair, left the room, and walked toward the front door of my childhood home.

"Jake, where are you going?" my mother said from behind me.

I turned around and looked at her holding a glass of white wine.

"She held you in a very high regard, you know," she said.

"I can't imagine why, really," I said.

"She always thought you'd be something great. She really believed that."

"I wish I shared her confidence."

"Perhaps you should start taking responsibility for your life. Have you thought more seriously about going back to school?"

"Mom."

"Yes, Jake."

I hugged her for a few seconds, pulled away, and, still gripping her shoulders, said, "I love you. I want you to know that. But I'm not going back to school. I really don't know what I'm going to do. Actually ... I think I'm going to go away for a while. I'll speak to you when I know more."

I walked away from her, through the front door, and out of the house. I got into my car, which was parked along the street, and sat for a long while with my head resting on the steering wheel. I read my grandmother's letter one more time, put it down, opened my notebook (one she'd bought me), and wrote:

MY PLAN FOR LIFE

To not die until I've accomplished something worthwhile. To not hurt anyone. To have a few lovers here and there. To write about it. To travel. To buy things for my family. To stop making my mother cry. To eat good, fresh food. To cook well. To have a mentor. To learn. To have barefoot excursions and midnight conversations with pretty-eyed girls. To live in a hotel room with a huge, white bed. To have wine parties with old friends who have wondered where I've been. To have a collection of vinyl records. To be friends with the invisible people in the invisible towns. To have a local wine-shop owner greet me by name as I walk into his store. To watch the sun rise a few times. To watch the sun set every time. To write a perfect sentence. To read all the great books. To dream about what could have been. To see a perfect opportunity for love and walk in the other direction. To find passion. To make people think.

When I finished writing, I started the car and drove off down the street away from everything I knew.

BOOK 2: EXODUS

Six

I drove north on the 405 freeway and watched it change, subtly at first, like the slight differences in a middle-aged man's face from one year to the next. But then, the freeway, newly besmirched with urban grime, began to clearly shed itself, like a snake, of the candy-land naiveté of Orange County until I'd officially crossed into Los Angeles County. I drove in silence, mired in thoughts of my grandmother's death, but also eager for the new experiences that awaited me. I'd decided to take a year off to travel, under the conditions that I try to enlighten myself—soak up books and films and music, learn about interesting people in the world, refine my cooking skills, work on my writing every day—and, equally important, connect with others on a basic human level without ever ensconcing myself in one place for too long.

I took the Rosecrans Avenue exit and headed west toward Manhattan Beach, a small beach town south of Santa Monica I'd chosen as my starting point. I turned left on Highland Avenue and drove south between a cluster of restaurants and bars, and immediately got the feeling that Manhattan Beach was the slightly sullied, weather-beaten, tattooed version of my hometown. I made a right toward the ocean on one of the numbered streets. It was a warm, clear Friday afternoon in summer, and the boardwalk was alive with passing dog walkers, power walkers, joggers, skaters, rollerbladers, bikers, parents or nannies pushing strollers, and flocks of midday, college-aged partiers. I drove slowly along the side streets looking for available places to rent and, on the corner of Rosecrans and Ocean Drive, found something that appealed to me: a little house with a sign on the door that read, "1 bed. 1 bath. Furnished. Kitchen. Living room. Garage w/1spot." I parked near the house and dialed the number.

"Hello, I'm interested in seeing the place," I said.

"Can you meet now?" the voice on the line asked.

"Yeah, I'm parked outside."

"I'll meet you there in a few minutes."

I sat in my car, listening to a musician perform an acoustic cover of a Bob Marley song on the radio, until the garage door under the available house opened, and an old, white Porsche convertible pulled into it. A middle-aged man wearing a Dodgers hat and sunglasses emerged and waited for me out front; I got out of my car and walked toward him.

"You're the one interested in seeing the place?" he asked.

"That's right."

"Come on in."

We walked up a short flight of steps to the front door of the house, and I followed him inside. On my left, there was a tiny, rustic kitchen—white and old-fashioned, with a stove, a sink, and a few cupboards—and, straight ahead of me, a living room with a couch resting against the back wall, a small dining table with two chairs, and a sliding-glass door that opened to a balcony overlooking the ocean.

"OK. So, as you can see, kitchen is here … with pots, pans, cups, utensils, plates, a coffeepot, everything you need, really—even some spices, salt, pepper, and garlic powder in that cabinet there. Do you cook?"

"A little."

"OK, next—living room here with a couch and a table. Sorry, the last tenant bought the TV from me," he said.

"Not a problem. I won't be needing one," I said.

"And this is the balcony," he said, walking over to the glass door and sliding it open, "with a wonderful ocean view, as you can see."

"Very nice."

"Now this way …"

We walked through the living room and down a short hallway into the bedroom, which had a bathroom, a double bed, a closet, and a square window at eye level with another view of the ocean.

"This is the bedroom. Good closet space. Bathroom with a shower. There are a few beach towels in the drawer there for you, as well. And … well … that about does it. Pretty simple but great location. Restaurants are nearby, and it's a minute walk down to the beach."

"How much is the rent?" I asked, as we walked back into the living room.

"Fifteen hundred a month plus utilities—which usually end up being around a hundred extra."

"Can you do a month-to-month lease?"

"Minimum three-month commitment."

"I won't be here that long."

"Unfortunately—"

"There won't be any trouble with me. I can write you a check right now."

"Well ..." he said, pausing to study me. "OK. I guess I can make an exception this time. I'll need a deposit of another month's rent."

"Sure," I said, sitting at the table to write him a check. "I don't see myself being here longer than a month—but I'll let you know."

When I handed him the check, he gave me the house keys, the garage-door opener, the wireless code, his contact information, and told me to enjoy my stay. After he drove off, I pulled my car into the garage, popped the trunk, and looked inside at the three black trash bags filled with books. A fourth trash bag, filled with my clothes, rested on the backseat of my car, along with my shoulder bag carrying my laptop. In two trips, I had all the bags on the living-room floor. I then walked up the street for something to eat.

A few blocks south on Highland Avenue (the town's main north-south street), I found a charming, green-colored café with a few two-seat tables in front; inside, people lined up to order from an exhaustive list of sandwiches—cold, hot, or open-faced—handwritten in chalk on a large, hanging blackboard behind the cash register. I perused the menu while standing in line and, when it was my turn, ordered a beer and the "Big Jim"—turkey on a baguette with mozzarella, tomato, Creole sauce, and bacon topped with two fried eggs.

I sat at one of the available tables outside, sipped my beer, and watched a group of girls in shorts and bikini tops, and guys in board-shorts and tank tops, walk up from the beach—carrying towels, a volleyball, and a Frisbee—and into a bar across the street. Within a few minutes, a short Mexican man—wearing a white T-shirt underneath a greasy, yellowish apron—came out carrying a sandwich on a plate, set it in front of me, and tiredly said, "Big Jim." It was a lovely first meal.

With another hour of daylight left, I walked down onto the boardwalk, which was still, impressively, a cement conveyor belt of activity, and moved safely aside to take in the grandiose view; the beach was very long and flat—a thirty-second sprint from the boardwalk would barely get me to the water's edge—and volleyball nets lined the sand like the wind turbines on the way to Palm Springs.

The beach was also swarming with walking, tanning, and swimming reincarnations of Michelangelo's *David* and Botticelli's *Venus*. Beach activity, for me, had always been entertaining to observe, mostly because certain technology still wasn't allowed in the water; the phones, laptops, e-readers, and computer tablets had to be set aside, even for just a few minutes, and people, while they were in the water, were forced to coexist sans their high-tech tools. I found it refreshing to watch people resort to primitive ways of interacting with each other: a teenage boy and girl flirtatiously splashing each other with water, children doing handstands in the shallows, a girl clinging to her boyfriend's shoulders as he takes her under a wave, an adventurous group of friends treading water in a circle out beyond the breaking waves …

I walked back up the hill and into the town market, a very organized and clean store, with seemingly everything one needed packed into a tiny space. A woman tidied the area behind the cash register, while a man swept the floor. I grabbed a basket and explored the aisles, plucking, along the way, enough groceries to get me through the next week or so. I set the basket down on the counter in front of the cash register, and the woman, with an expressionless gaze, nodded at me; I held up my finger, said, "One second," and went to grab two bottles of cheap red wine from a shelf and a few packs of AleSmith IPA from behind the glass door of the refrigerator. Back at the counter, I said, "How's business?" to the woman, who, surprisingly, loosened her expression.

"Oh, very good now. Summer always good," she said, smiling.

"I'm Jake. Just moved here today."

"I'm Ki. That my husband," she said, pointing to the man sweeping, "Kwan."

I spoke with her for a few minutes and came to know that they were both Korean, that Ki had inherited the business from her father, and that Kwan had quit his other job to help her run the store.

Ki gathered my food items and efficiently packed them into one large, brown paper bag with handles; she then put the bottles of wine into another bag and the beer into a third. After paying and saying good-bye, I left the market—the weight of the bags' handles turning my fingers bright white in the middle and dark red at the tips—and walked back to my place. Inside, I unloaded the groceries and put everything away. I found a corkscrew in one of the drawers, used it to open a bottle of red wine, and poured myself a glass. I sipped it, and, despite the bitterness of a newly opened, cheap bottle, enjoyed the feeling of it going down.

In the living room, I untied the trash bags containing my books and dumped my lifelong collection of literature onto the floor; troubled, brilliant men and women greeted each other from the backs of book covers, and I imagined that I was hosting a literary event in my living room, where talented contemporary writers could mingle with deceased literary greats. I took the final trash bag, filled with my clothes and toiletries, into my room, emptied it on the bed, and put everything away. While pausing to stare through my window at the horizon, where the blue of the ocean rendezvoused with the blue of the sky, I thought about how the faces of my co-workers at my old company were already blurring in my mind; it seemed so long ago that I'd quit my job, a distant memory of cheap Styrofoam coffee cups and superfluously repeated business words.

Back in the living room, I retrieved my glass of wine, took a seat at the table in front of my laptop, and checked my email, but then immediately closed my browser when I saw a message from my mother in the top spot with the subject: "Where Are You???" But out of deeply ingrained habit, I reopened my browser, impulsively loaded Facebook (my digital identity), and mindlessly browsed the photographs and status updates of my "friends," until I was lured into clicking on a video someone had posted—titled "OMG! Baby Monkey Chases Baby Pig! So Funny!"—which, after it was over, baited me, for the next thirty minutes, to click on and watch a succession of kitten, puppy, and baby penguin videos. *What the hell am I doing?*

When I'd finally broken free from the addictive hex of Internet videos, I grabbed my notebook and made a list of contemporary novels I wanted to read. I then researched greatest-novels-of-all-time lists and noted down all the classics I still hadn't read. The books on the living-room floor were ones I'd already read; I carried them with me for inspiration.

Because it was of paramount importance to me to make writing a daily part of my life, and also because I needed an efficient way to monitor my progress, I started a blog with the intention of writing fictional stories inspired by the conversations, observations, and thoughts I might have on my journey. And, in an early act of discipline, for the next few hours I worked on my first piece, about a young man leaving his hometown after a death in the family and settling in Los Angeles; after finishing a draft, I posted it on my blog under the title: "The Tales of a Desert Wanderer: Part One."

Much of the night had escaped me while I wrote, so it was nearly midnight when I preheated the oven, brought out two chicken breasts from the refrigerator, and laid them flat in an ovenproof dish. I poured a bit of olive oil over the breasts, peppered and salted them, and then sprinkled them with garlic powder. While the chicken cooked, I put some asparagus over a low flame on the stove. When the food was ready, after thirty minutes or so, I enjoyed, along with a glass of wine, my first home-cooked meal in my new town.

I awoke, facedown on the floor, at around ten on Saturday morning, with an empty wine bottle pressing painfully into my head and a Fitzgerald masterpiece stuck to my face. After a shower, I had a bowl of cereal topped with banana slices at the living-room table, while I read a new email from Andrew.

From: Andrew Martin
To: Jake Reed
Subject: IMPORTANT!

Jake,

Got the news about your grandmother. I sincerely apologize for your loss. Where did you go? How long will you be gone? Robbie and the other neighbors are asking about you. What should I tell them? Also, I know this isn't the best time to bring it up … but do you think it was a good idea to quit your job? I heard about it from some of the guys. Do you have another job lined up? Are you interviewing at least? I'll see what I can do to help. Remember, we are in a recession!!! It's very important to make prudent financial decisions during this time. Think about your future …

Cordially,
Andrew

From: <u>Jake Reed</u>
To: <u>Andrew Martin</u>
Subject: Re: IMPORTANT!

Thanks for the words about my grandma. I don't know how long I'll
be gone. Don't worry about helping me with a job. Taking some time
to travel. You can tell the neighbors that. Stay in the condo as long
as you want. Just transfer the rent money to my account each month.
Hope you're well. Take care.

--Jake

Carrying my notebook, I walked up the hill and along the main street,
passing groups of late-morning breakfasters sitting at curbside tables,
and, after a few blocks, came up to a hilly park, grassed over in bright
green, with several scattered benches, trees, and one pathway through
the middle that led down to the boardwalk. Saturday loungers were
spread out on the grass, sitting on blankets, enjoying snacks, and watching the great blue ocean in the distance. And then I noticed a group of
girls sharing a blanket—playing music, laughing, and drinking white
wine from paper cups—who beguiled me with their nonchalance, their
carefree enjoyment of life. I paused, then inched closer, and, trying to
be inconspicuous by pretending to admire the ocean, looked at them as
if I were seeing girls for the first time in my life. They had tanned skin
and thick, layered hair, wore large sunglasses and bikini tops and jean
shorts, and were as wild-looking as untamed mares roaming the country,
with their manes dancing in the wind, stopping along the way to drink
from white-wine rivers. I was particularly drawn to one of the girls,
who, between sips of white wine, swayed pleasurably to the music and
smiled, flashing glimpses of her straight white teeth to the world. She
had sleek, shoulder-length, dark hair, shimmering with traces of auburn
in the summer sun and blowing gently in the soft coastal breeze. The
uncovered sides of her round breasts and her shapely legs were the most
sensuous pieces of art I'd ever seen. *My God.* I could feel something in
my lower stomach, as though a heavy lump of coal were forming there.
  Fighting back the urge to stay at the park and watch her, the girl with
the auburn hair and infuriating curves, I continued along the street past
a crowded pancake house that emitted a potent breakfast aroma into

the street for blocks, then stopped on the corner of Manhattan Beach Boulevard to admire the large pier lying out over the ocean like a magnificent, godlike finger. I ordered a coffee from a café on the corner and sipped it while observing the passersby from an outside table. When I finished, I went into a bookstore further up the hill, and, an hour later, came out carrying a bag of books from the list I'd made in my notebook the night before. And then, moved by midday hunger, I used my phone to search for a nearby restaurant, choosing the one with the best rating in the least expensive category—a place about a block down the hill toward the ocean called Simmzy's.

The tiny, hut-like restaurant, painted a rustic red, was nestled between a coffee shop and a clothing store; it had a patio outside with a few tables, and, inside, a small space that was tightly crammed with several more tables. Waiters, carrying trays of food and drink, seemed quite skilled at navigating through the congestion. I took a seat at the only available table, in the corner of the patio, and enjoyed an ahi sandwich with a beer.

Toting my bag of books, I walked along the road back to my house, and, as I passed the park, looked for the wild girls laughing on the blanket; but they were gone, and others—a much less alluring group—had replaced them.

Back inside my house, I thumbed through my new books, smelling their pages, picked one to start reading, changed into lighter clothes, and then walked down the hill toward the beach. I paused at the boardwalk, searching for a good spot on the sand, noticed a less crowded area down the way, and started for it. At the spot, I unfurled my towel, and, just as I tried to set it evenly on the sand, the breeze came in and distorted its shape, but I was fine with it being a little bit crooked. I sat on the towel and watched the waves; everything seemed so simple to me when I was staring at the ocean. I read for the rest of the day—pausing only to write in my notebook, and, once, to take a short nap—and finished my book in time to enjoy the sunset.

I showered, dressed, and, during the first twenty minutes of a Noah Baumbach film streaming from my laptop, ate leftover chicken and asparagus for dinner. Enjoying the tranquility of being alone in a new town but still keen on the idea of meeting new people, I decided that it was in my best interest to spend more time out of my house. *I can't just cook, eat, and read. I'll have nothing to write about.*

The town had livened up with the Saturday-night energy of restaurant-goers, night strollers, and the early appearance of all-night drinkers. I passed an uproarious bar—with sweaty, drunken people spilling out of the entrance to smoke cigarettes—and looked inside through the front window. Because most of the people were wearing tank tops and shorts and hats, I guessed that the party had started long before, sometime during the day, and carried over into the night. As the music blasted into the street, the youthful crowd inside joyously fist-pumped to the beat. One guy, getting bumped from both sides, carried three pitchers through the crowd, as the beer spilled over and down to the floor. A few disheveled girls—hair in their faces, hands in the air—danced on a tabletop. Some guys, taking shots at a table, wore mustaches in such a way that made it difficult for me to discern whether their intentions were to be comical or fashionable; one of them wore a yellow USC T-shirt with the slogan, "First we beat you, then we buy you."

I found another bar down the road, nearly hidden between a quiet restaurant and a shop already closed for the night, and went inside to a much tamer group scattered around tables and along the bar. I took a seat on a stool at the bar, and, when the bartender came over, asked for a Jameson, neat. He poured the drink, set it down in front of me, and I handed him my debit card.

"Keep it open?" he asked.

"Sure."

I got a comfortable feeling from the place, which seemed like a mixture of locals and people who just avoided crowds. Only one person, sitting in the far corner along the bar, looked a bit out of place, probably even more than I did. He had long, dark hair styled so it was slightly parted, with strands that fell over his face and down past his chin; he had thick facial hair, but he wore it in a way that suggested it was strategically unkempt; and he had on a thin, white T-shirt, with a very deep V-neck, and a skinny scarf that coiled around his neck. A black leather jacket hung from his chair. His right arm was tattooed in two places: the outside of his bicep down to his elbow and then again on his inner forearm. And his body was ornamented with a sheen of silver: his hands were decorated with a few thick rings, his wrist had a glistening ID bracelet, and the bare part of his chest showed several pendants hanging from a thin chain around his neck. He was drinking something—judging by the color, it looked like whiskey—in a short glass and, to back it, a beer in a tall, chilled glass. His left elbow was planted on the bar, and he rested his head in his left palm, while, with his right hand, he steadily and slowly raised one of his two drinks to his mouth, pausing every thirty seconds or so to check his phone.

Feeling good from the whiskey and a relaxing day on the beach reading, I ordered another Jameson, opened my notebook to a fresh page, and wrote about the thoughts I'd had during my walks, and about the girls in the park sharing a blanket and drinking white wine. And because I felt comfortable writing in that little bar, I decided I'd go there to have a drink and write every night. After my third consecutive night there, the bartender, perhaps in a gesture of gratitude for my newfound loyalty, started a conversation with me.

"You new in town?" he asked.

"Yeah, staying here for a bit. Just sort of passing through. Never really experienced LA before."

He laughed and said, "You chose Manhattan Beach to learn about LA?"

"I guess so—only been here a few days. Wrong place to start?"

"Samy, by the way," he said.

"Jake," I said, giving him a nod.

"Well, to answer your question, the South Bay—you know, like Redondo, Hermosa, and Manhattan—is fake LA. Especially Manhattan Beach, which is a fucking island divided between volleyball bros and rich families. In the summertime, it's an extended USC frat party on the beach. Beautiful place, sure, but it's really just an expensive beach town," he said, generously pouring more whiskey into my glass without asking me.

"So what is real LA, then?" I asked, curiously.

"Exactly. What is Los Angeles? The million-dollar question. You know, I've got a friend from New York. She says everyone from NYC knows what NYC is. LA, unfortunately, isn't like that. Everything is so sprawled out and different here. I've lived in LA my whole fucking life, and I'm still confused—you know what I'm saying? I mean, on the Westside, I think Playa del Rey is the best kept secret, but Venice is a real fucking city, you know? It's got culture. It's like a good mix of shitty beach shacks and beautiful, modern homes. People bike around town. Cool bars. And in Venice you see some fucking brown people, you know? That's real life. Not like here, the white-only island."

"Right," I said, chuckling.

"Malibu—forget about it. Too far. Too expensive. I don't know, what else ... Culver City—cheaper, up-and-coming, but not as active. Silver Lake is another very cool place—it's like Venice without the beach and with more hipster-artist kids and wannabe-hipster-artist kids. And downtown ... every city has to have a downtown, I guess, but the streets are fucking empty during the weekend. Ghost town. But I hear it's slowly changing ... you know, with the art walk and shit. Some of the hipster kids are moving there now, too, I guess."

"Where would you send me?" I said, enjoying the conversation and baiting him for more of his opinions.

"Shit, man—I don't know ... You know what?" he said, as if enlightened by an original idea. "I'd probably send you to West Hollywood because it's everything and anything. Great food. Great bars. Beautiful girls. Fake tits. Clubs. Bottle service. Wait, are you gay?"

"No," I said, confused by the question.

"Well, it has a huge gay community, too—bunch of gay dudes running around there. Anyway, all that crazy shit everyone hears about LA happens in West Hollywood. But it also has the culture, you know? You can see all the great indie films, go to art shows, poetry readings, comedy shows ... You probably won't find a girl to take home to Mamma, but you'll have the time of your life. I sort of think of WeHo as LA's downtown. But there's one thing you should know about WeHo ..."

"What's that?"

"You need to have a good group of friends to get the real experience. Find some buddies to live with. Not a good place to be alone, you feel me? You won't be able to experience anything."

"I'll remember that. So what's kept you in LA for your whole life?"

"You know, it's really easy to talk shit on LA. Everyone does. But no one wants to leave, because, the truth is, it's so much fucking fun here—the sun in your face all year, the girls, the day-drinking at pools, the house parties, all of it. LA is really what you make of it ... It's much more of a feeling than a place."

During our first conversation, we established a casual rapport that matured during my subsequent visits to the bar—rooted mainly in my asking him questions about Los Angeles—and, although everything he told me was a generalization, I appreciated my time with him because I loved his overall excitement, the blatant bias in his perspective, his quick pontifical responses to everything I asked, and, most important, that I felt I was learning about a new way of life, at least through one local bartender's point of view. I also discovered from our ongoing conversations that I had indeed, if not deliberately, then unconsciously, chosen to live in Manhattan Beach because of its undeniable likeness to my hometown. I'd made the safe choice but, trying to find the positive, I also believed I'd made a choice that would allow me to build confidence, to become more comfortable in foreign territory before moving on.

After I left the bar every night, I stopped for a few tacos at the taco truck along the street near my house. Since I always arrived before the after-hours rush at two in the morning, I was able to have a few words with the potbellied, mustached, mocha-skinned Hector, who owned the taco truck. Hector, in his early thirties, worked the truck every night with his sister, Maria, a shy and timid girl of eighteen or nineteen, who always had her black hair pulled tightly back and tied in a ponytail.

I introduced myself to Hector, who was wearing an oversized LA Lakers T-shirt, the first time I ate tacos at his truck, and, in return, got only a cool and, perhaps, slightly suspicious nod from him. But one night, about a week later, after becoming comfortable with me, Hector, suddenly imbued with a chatty confidence, said, "Look at that fucking restaurant over there," pointing to an exquisite Mexican restaurant across the street with a fancy oak-door entrance. "That shit ain't fucking *Mexicano* food. It's owned by *pinche gringos*—white boys. You pay twenty dollars for an enchilada on fine china with some white-boy sauce on top in squiggly lines, like they trying to be Picasso and shit. Enchilada Picassos! Come on, homie, you know what I'm talking about, right? That shit ain't right."

I'd been laughing during his short, amusing rant, but I caught my breath and said, "And it's always so crowded. What's wrong with people?"

"What's wrong with people? It's simple, *cabrón*. You white boys love to spend money to impress your white girls. Seriously, *cabrón*, you can pay all that money for fake-ass Mexican food, or you can come to my truck and have a real taco for one dollar. Come on, *cabrón*, tell your white-boy friends to use their *cabezas*. Over here, I make you the best taco you've ever had, *güey*. And then after you are done eating that taco, I even give you some cucumber slices to make your mouth fresh before you try another taco, *güey*—I do all this shit for one fucking dollar, *cabrón*," he said excitedly, and then, reaching somewhere underneath him, retrieved a bottle of beer and brought it to his lips for a drink.

I smiled, truly enjoying his company, and said, "I agree, my friend.

But I just moved here, and I have no white-boy friends to convince."

"Just remember, *cabrón*, the best shit is cheap ... made by the bare, brown hands of people like my sister and me, like my mother and my grandmother. We don't use no fucking cookbooks. Our hands already know how much spices to add. *Nacido con las manos en la masa.* We are born with that shit, homie. When I was a little kid—*un pinche mocoso*— my grandmother used to make *menudo* on Sundays. I always ask her—I say, 'Nana, is it ready yet?' and she say, 'I don't know, *mjio*, let me taste it.' Then she taste it with a spoon and say, 'No, *mijo*, it's not ready yet.' After three or maybe four more tastes with that fucking spoon, she says, 'OK, *mijo*, now it's ready.' You see? It's the way the real *Mexicanos* do it, *cabrón*."

"That's awesome. I love that. I promise you, Hector, that I'll never eat at that fake-ass, white-boy Mexican restaurant for the rest of my life."

"Ha ha, OK. Now you're a homie—my only white-boy homie. So try my *carnitas* taco on the house," he said, spooning red salsa into a steaming, little corn-tortilla taco filled with meat and handing it to me.

"Thank you," I said, pausing to take a bite of the taco. "Shit, that's *really* good!"

"My specialty, homie. Hector's famous *carnitas* taco."

"The best seller?"

"Nah, *güey*, cuz the white boys love the *al pastor* tacos. They want to taste the pineapple."

"You should put 'Hector's Famous Carnitas Taco' on your menu board. It might sell more."

"Nah, *güey*, I'm here to give the people what they want, homie. *Un hombre del pueblo.* Like a *pinche* Mexican politician. Just here to please with tacos."

"What's it like when all the white boys come to your truck after the bars close?"

"Fucking crazy, *güey* ... All these drunk, sweaty, big fuckers. But it's good, because when they are wasted they buy more tacos from me. Some of those big-ass white boys, *hijos de putas*, eat twenty fucking tacos, *cabrón*."

"What do they say to you?" I said, after a good laugh.

"Come on, *cabrón*—I pretend I don't speak English good. It's better like that, *güey*. Drunk white boys love to try talking Spanish. They like to show off for their little, drunk, blonde girls. So I act like the stupid Mexican guy, and when they say something Spanish, I smile and laugh

87

to make them feel good, *cabrón*. Ha ha! With their gringo accents—that shit is funny, *güey*. But they love that shit, *cabrón*, and then I pretend I don't hear the racist jokes, and I keep taking their money and tips. It's good business for me."

Hector, the taco-truck owner, had quickly become my favorite person in Los Angeles so far.

SEVEN

Every morning during my first two weeks in Manhattan Beach, I woke up early, between seven and eight, without an alarm, because the day was my own to do the things I wanted to do. I read books. I drank wine. I cooked at least one meal a day. I listened to music and watched independent films. I researched leaders of other countries, singer-song-writers, poets, authors, musicians, how to cook a great steak, how to prepare a fish, the cost of land in Montana, how much money truck drivers make, the best kinds of coffee beans, how to brew beer, and the process of wine fermentation. I walked along the beach and watched the volleyball players. Occasionally, I chatted with the mail carrier on my street, a waiter at one of the restaurants along Highland Avenue, tourists walking the boardwalk, people on the beach, and my neighbors. And each new day, I continued to write down my thoughts, inspired by my experiences around town, and, later, used them to write more stories, the best of which I posted on my blog as sequential parts to "The Tales of a Desert Wanderer."

But, excluding my casual relationship with Ki and Kwan, the Korean couple who owned the town market, Hector, the taco-truck owner, and Samy, the bartender who discussed Los Angeles life with me, I'd been unable to connect with anyone not providing me a service of some sort. So, after two weeks in Manhattan Beach, I felt that I'd absorbed all I could from the place, and that, perhaps, it was time to move on. But, on my third Saturday night in town, when my normal spot along the bar was occupied, I walked around to the other side and sat next to the long-haired, tattooed guy, realizing that despite both of us being in the same place every night, we'd never acknowledged each other.

"What are you writing?" he asked me after I'd nearly finished my first drink.

"What's that?"

"I see you writing in that notebook every night."

"Ah, just practicing writing, playing with ideas—something I sort of promised myself I'd do."

"So you're a writer."

"No, not really ... Well, trying to be, I guess, like everyone else with a notebook and a blog. I'm Jake, by the way."

"Jayson."

Samy, the bartender, came over and asked us if we were OK. Jayson, after glancing at my empty glass and then swallowing the rest of his drink, asked me what I was drinking.

"Jameson," I said.

"It's a recession, man. We should support our economy."

"How so?"

"By drinking bourbon—whiskey made in America," he said, giving me a playful nod and a smile. "Pappy Van Winkle for the two of us," he told Samy.

"Thanks, man," I said to him.

"You must live around here?" he asked.

"Just for another couple of weeks. You?"

"Yeah, I live down the way a bit. So what's your story?"

"Well, taking some time to travel, I guess," I said. "Not quite sure where I'm headed next."

He laughed. "Good shit, man."

"And your story?" I asked.

"On a short break from work. Relaxing in this quiet town," he said before becoming absorbed in his phone for the next minute.

I'd noticed on other nights that he was repeatedly checking his phone, but, being up close to him for the first time, I realized he was checking it because he was continually being called and texted, literally every few seconds.

"Look," he continued, "I have this table at a place down the street. I was supposed to meet some friends, but they can't make it. I know we just met, but you wanna go chill and have some drinks? I don't really want to waste the table, you know?"

"Sounds fine to me."

"Let's stop by my house for a second, then we'll go."

We each finished our bourbon in a single gulp and then went outside. After Jayson paused to light a cigarette, we walked down the hill until we hit the boardwalk and then walked along it for a block or so. "Here," he said, showing me through a little gate that separated his beachfront house from the boardwalk. His house was just a block down the hill from mine.

Inside, the living room had a long leather couch, two leather reclining chairs, three guitars—two electric and one acoustic—hanging on the wall, a complete drum kit in the corner, a flat-screen TV mounted on the wall, a full bar along a side wall, and a floor that was almost entirely paved with unopened, square cardboard boxes.

"Here, wear one of these tonight," he said, sliding one of the boxes toward me with his foot.

Inside the box, I found several neatly folded, long-sleeved, thin flannel shirts in a variety of colors.

I laughed. "Am I underdressed?"

"Just can't wear a T-shirt in the place we're going."

"Got it. Thanks, man."

I grabbed the shirt on top, put it on over my T-shirt, buttoned it up, and ripped away the tag hanging from the side. He plucked a shirt from the same box, one identical in style to mine but a different color, and put it on.

"How about some beers for the walk back up?" Jayson said.

"Sure."

He grabbed two PBRs out of the fridge and handed one to me, as we walked out of his house. "Need to get something out of my car," he said, as I followed him around the side, where he opened his garage door by punching in a code.

Inside the garage, he opened the passenger door of a glistening, black Porsche 911, ducked into the car, and came out wearing a large, beanie-like hat that came tightly over the top of his hairline but then loosened toward the back to accommodate some of his long hair.

We walked back up the hill, sipping our beers, and turned on the main road; a block ahead, a group of girls, dressed up for the night, walked toward us, the contrapuntal melody of their high heels on the pavement—clickety, clickety, clack—growing louder as they approached, drumming pleasantly in my ears, reminding me that it was a Saturday night. That harmonious sound, along with the sight of the girls' long, slender legs on display in the moonlight, awakened in me the desire to make a human connection—a look, the exchange of a passing smile, something. But we had to step aside as they marched quickly past, unaware of us, with each of their heads angled down, their eyes fixed on their phones, and their thumbs dancing erratically on glass screens to a high-tech rhythm.

"Let's finish the beers," Jayson said, as we stopped in front of a trash can, swallowed the last mouthful, and threw them away. "That's the place," he said, pointing to a lounge with a dimly lit entrance and a massive, broad-shouldered, fedora-wearing bouncer in a striped suit standing guard.

The outside of the building was fringed with a twenty-person line—mostly anxious and annoyed guys—but when the bouncer noticed Jayson approaching, he unhooked the rope and let us cut the line. I followed Jayson through a swanky entranceway where we were met by an attractive hostess holding a clipboard; she greeted Jayson by name and walked us through a lavish lounge with blue water dripping, like a calm waterfall, down the side walls, and, in the middle, a blue-lit bar with hundreds of martini glasses hanging across the top. We then followed her into a rectangular alcove, behind open curtains, with a white leather couch that traced the shape of the room, six square wooden tables in the center, and a flat-screen TV mounted in the corner. We took a seat on the couch, which could have easily accommodated twelve people. A waitress, who was just as attractive as the hostess, came over to us, welcomed Jayson back to the lounge, and asked what she could get him.

He looked at me and said, "Can you do vodka now?"

I nodded.

"Let's get a bottle of Goose," he said to the waitress, "and then water, soda, cranberry juice, and some pineapple juice."

"You got it," she said, smiling at him, and then darted across the room toward the bar.

She returned a few minutes later with a silvery, shiny bucket filled with ice and holding a large bottle of Grey Goose, setting it down in front of us. A lip that encircled the base of the bucket held several Old Fashioned glasses, one of which was filled with sliced limes. A tired-looking Mexican man, trailing the waitress, pushed a small cart with all the mixers Jayson had requested; he laid them (they came in tall, slender, pellucid vases) in a straight line on the table next to the bucket of vodka. The combination of the blue hue inside the lounge, the sharp green of the sliced limes, the incandescent red of the cranberry juice, and the sunshiny yellow of the pineapple juice was, when absorbed all at once, an extraordinary exhibition of rich color.

"Dig in, my man," Jayson said.

I grabbed a glass and the bottle of vodka, made myself a drink, with a bit of ice and a touch of soda water, and then tossed a lime into it. Jayson added only a little water to his vodka drink. I looked around and tried to make sense of the apparent energy forming around us. Groups of girls seemed to be pretending to have conversations with each other while staring at Jayson. Guys, with smirks on their faces, gestured combatively in our direction. And then, slowly, the crowd around our table grew thicker: people, mostly girls, sprouted up in front of us like beads of sweat on someone's arm in a sauna. But Jayson, sipping his vodka and checking his phone, appeared oblivious to all the activity.

"What is it that I don't know about you?" I asked him.

He looked incredulously at me for a second, laughed, and then said, "You don't watch shit TV, do you?"

"Well, I haven't watched any TV, lately."

"I'm on a little reality show," he said, seemingly embarrassed. "It's not something I'm proud of. I kind of fell into it a few years ago and just kept telling myself I'd only go another year if the money was right. Well, I guess the money kept being right."

"That's cool, then."

"Not really. I'm a musician, and I figured being on the show would be good for my band. You know?"

"Yeah."

"But it's fucked, man. Every bit of it. They label you. When I perform with my band now, I'm the 'reality douche bag trying to start a music career.' But I had the music the whole damn time. People don't know that. And the fuckers at the network create whatever they want out of you."

"What do you mean?"

"You sign this contract before going on the show that basically gives them complete control. Most people sign it. I signed it, obviously. In the beginning, I did a few scenes, and they edited them into something completely different. Now I'm officially the asshole womanizer who drinks too much. You know … the whole drill."

"And now you're between seasons?"

"Yeah. I have a couple more weeks off before we start filming—a couple more weeks to get drunk."

"They don't let you drink during the season?"

"Nope, against policy."

"But aren't you the alcoholic asshole?"

"Yeah, again, it's all bullshit. During the season, they provide me with a trainer so I look good while being a dick on TV—a dick who doesn't drink actual whiskey, but a dick who drinks apple juice."

I laughed.

"The fucked-up part is that the producers created this persona for me, and now everyone who watches the show thinks I'm that guy. So what did the producers do? They asked me to just start acting like that guy during filming to save them editing time. They gave me a fucking acting coach!"

"Wait ... so you're learning how to act so you can play yourself better on a *reality* show?"

"Ha! Yeah, dude, exactly. But it's not all bad, man. There are a lot of perks. Other than when I'm on set, hardly anyone ever tells me no."

"Damn, that's cool," I said, entertained by my quick reverie of Jayson walking down the street while all the townspeople danced and sang, "Yes! Yes! Yes! Oh, yes, Jayson!" I started to chuckle, but pulled myself together before asking him, "So why did you choose to live in this little town?"

"Because, when I lived in Hollywood, I learned a few things about myself. When I was making music, I never wanted to stop. When I was fucking, I never wanted to stop. When I was doing drugs, I never wanted to stop. And whenever I was doing any of those things, which was all the fucking time, I could never imagine doing anything else. That's the best way I can explain it."

Wait ... what? "I see," I said, not getting it at all.

"There was never an 'off' button. You know, like, how a dog goes away, like hides from people, when he's about to die?"

"Yeah, OK."

"That was me every night after I did too many drugs. I hated the feeling at that point. But then, somehow, I was doing drugs again the next night. But here in this town it's quiet if you want it to be."

"Hi, Jayson ... Can we sit here with you?" said a girl, interrupting him, standing with her friend at the mouth of our alcove.

"Yeah, fine, join us," Jayson said, and when they sat on the couch in the space between us, "This is my friend, Jake. He's a writer."

Both the girls said hello to me; but then the girl nearer to Jayson leaned in close to him, and they started their own conversation.

"So do you write screenplays?" the girl next to me asked while making herself a vodka and pineapple.

"No, I just write in a little notebook."

She giggled and said, "Shut up."

"It's true."

A burlesque show started on a stage at the other side of the lounge, and I couldn't hear anything the girl said to me anymore. But, as we watched the show, I made myself another drink and began to feel the vodka well up inside me, creating a numbing heat that traveled from the top of my head down through the rest of my body and tingled at the tips of my extremities. After the show was over, when everyone could hear each other again, the girls laughed at everything Jayson and I said; so— as a way of rewarding them, I suppose—we kept refilling their glasses with vodka and pineapple until, at some point, they persuaded us to get up and dance with them.

The girl sitting next to me grabbed my hand and yanked me toward the dance floor. *The dance floor* ... I'd dreaded the existence of dance floors since I was in the seventh grade and the principal announced the details of the upcoming school dance over my classroom's loudspeaker. Even though, at the time of the announcement, the dance was still another month away, my body shook under my cheap student desk; I couldn't concentrate in school the rest of the week, until, failing to come up with any other alternative to calm my nerves, I decided that I simply wouldn't go to the dance, which made me feel instantly better.

A few days before the dance, when all the popular kids were bubbling with excitement over who they would kiss during one of the slow dances, I didn't feel excluded by my decision, but rather, safe and protected by it; that is, until I came home from school, went into my room, and noticed a brand-new brown leather jacket resting on my bed. (The thought of wearing it back then embarrassed me, but, interestingly, the jacket seemed to coincide with the latest male fashion on display at the lounge in Manhattan Beach over a decade later.) On top of the jacket was a note from my mother: "I bought this for you to wear at your big dance! Have fun!"

After an argument that lasted the length of dinner, my mother and father decided it was in my best interest to attend the dance, and that I would be going "whether I liked it or not." My father drove me, and we rode in silence all the way to the parking lot of my school's auditorium, where he let me out and said, "Try to enjoy yourself." As I watched him drive away, I suddenly felt the fear of being very alone. For what may have been ten minutes or an hour, I loitered in the parking lot, walking in circles, and hid behind parked cars from my arriving classmates, who giggled and talked loudly in groups. I dreaded my entrance because I imagined the worst scenarios: everyone would stop and stare at me when I walked in, I would trip and fall, or people would make fun of my outfit. I knew that my survival inside the auditorium depended on my ability to quickly find someone to talk to—that way, I could, at the very least, blend in to the crowd and conceal my self-consciousness.

When I finally summoned the courage to enter the auditorium, I was relieved by the dark room and walked immediately to the long, rectangular table covered with bowls of chips and candy and red punch. Trying hard to be invisible and, at the same time, feign confidence, I kept refilling my plate with chips and M&M's and drank several glasses of punch until I had to go to the bathroom—a development I found consolation in because it gave me a reliable excuse to be somewhere else, even for a short while.

I found refuge from the outside world behind the walls of the bathroom and, if others came in, behind the thin, kick-dented plastic door of one of the toilet stalls. I thought I'd be fine if I could hide in there the whole night; my plan worked flawlessly, until the same group of boys entered the bathroom for the second time and, noticing that I was still in there, made jokes to each other loudly enough for me to hear. One of the guys, whom I'd helped study for a math test earlier that week, made a crack about my leather jacket. My bathroom strategy had to be revised.

After they left, I realized that, from the bathroom, I could hear the music coming from the auditorium and discern whether a slow song or a fast song was playing. So my new strategy was born: I would go into the auditorium during the slow songs (there were always people left out during the slow dances), blend in by the rectangular table, and drink several glasses of punch until I had to go to the bathroom again, ideally before a fast song started.

"Hello!" the girl holding my hand yelled in my ear, pulling me back into the present. "What are you thinking about?"

"Sorry, got lost in a memory."

"Let's dance," she said, rubbing up against me.

The dance floor that night seemed far less intimidating: maybe it was having a reality TV star as my wingman; or maybe it was, simply, the vodka. The girl and I danced together through several songs before she disappeared with her friend to use the bathroom. I decided to go, too. As I waited in a ten-person line, I was momentarily amused by the thought that the bathroom, once my place of refuge, was now pulling me away from the dance floor.

Coming back into the main room, I noticed that Jayson was sitting with a new group of girls in our private area. The girls we'd just been dancing with had simply been replaced, as if by leaving Jayson's side they had created an opportunity for other girls, who, always aware of Jayson's location in the room, had been waiting patiently to make a desirable impression on him. I'd never witnessed anything like it before.

I rejoined Jayson on the couch. I was drunk, from the vodka of course, but much drunker from the sweet-smelling scent of the perfumed female bodies; the sight of their tight, colorful dresses, blow-dried hair, exposed shoulders, shiny, freshly shaven legs—firm and tight from high heels—and the sound of their bubbly, Saturday-night laughs. I was intoxicated by it all.

And to amplify my euphoria, just as Jayson ordered another bottle of Grey Goose, I saw *her* at the far end of the lounge. I knew it was the girl—the tanned, auburn-haired, laughing beauty—I'd seen in the park that Saturday, a couple of weeks back, sharing a blanket and a bottle of white wine with her friends. She was with a group of girls, seemingly the same group I'd seen her with at the park, and she had one hand in the air swaying to the beat of the music and another hand wrapped around her drink. She wore a short black dress that tightly hugged the middle of her tanned thighs. When one of her friends leaned in to say something to her, she tossed her head back in laughter and then slipped rhythmically back into dancing. I walked over to her.

"Can I get you a drink?" I said, feeling confident.

"And then what?" she said, as she stopped dancing to look up at me with her indigo-blue eyes, which had been, that day in the park, hidden from me by large sunglasses.

"What?" I said.

"Then what happens if I let you get me a drink?"

"You can drink it."

She laughed and said, "But I have a drink already. Can't you see? Besides, I'm already drunk."

"Come sit with us anyway."

"Who is 'us'? Tell me everything!"

"I'm sitting with a friend in that space over there," I said, pointing to our private alcove. "We have room for you. Bring a friend if you'd like."

"But I'm crazy," she said, snapping a picture of me with her phone. "You should know that about someone before you invite her to sit with you."

Nothing she could have said in that moment would have discouraged me. "I think I'm OK with crazy. So finish your drink and come get a refill," I said, surprised at my newfound self-assurance.

Back on the couch, I made myself another vodka and soda, and then pretended not to notice them, the girl and her friend, walking toward me a few minutes later.

"I didn't get your name," she said, smiling impishly.

In that moment—with her in a tight black dress, hovering above me, smiling down at me—I felt myself recoil in the remembrance of my lifelong history of misinterpreting the intentions of the opposite sex. During the years of my burgeoning romantic curiosity, I identified my problem to be my faith in the simplest (and most romantic) explanation: if, for example, a girl smiled at me, it was because she was interested in learning more about me. Later in my adolescent years, after mulling more seriously on the subject, I decided that my problem could be simplified even further: I fell immediately in love with every girl I fancied who showed me the slightest bit of attention.

During college, I realized I knew nothing about the girls I fantasized about, and that I was only falling in love with the images of them I'd conjured up in my mind. And, even worse, I began misconstruing a passing smile from any girl to mean that she was the one for me, that she was the answer to my loneliness. Whenever I pulled up to a red light in my car, and knew, by my acute peripheral awareness, that a girl was in the car next to me, I delayed looking at her until I'd already imagined her face, the way her hands rested on the steering wheel, the way she would look over at me and smile, and how we would pull over to the side of the road to have a conversation and start a relationship.

My issue was exacerbated when the social networking frenzy took hold of my generation; I could imagine my entire relationship with a girl simply by staring at one of her online photographs. When my fanciful expectations fell short—and they always did—I acknowledged fearfully that I was not only an idealist, but perhaps, even worse, an incurable one. I suspected that I'd always be plagued by my naive perspective (I could label it a selfish one, but I never seemed to have a choice). I never wanted to be *that* type of person (I was much more enamored of the guys who never seemed to care whether a girl smiled at them or not).

After years of battling with my self-image, I finally accepted that I simply *was* who I was—normally an encouraging realization, but, for me, one that spawned self-loathing. Fortunately, during the year after college when I was working, and up to the current moment, I'd seemingly found a way to contain myself, to tame my romantic idealism— that is, until she, the girl from the park, stood above me, smiling.

"Jake," I said, giving her a cool and calculated nod. "And yours?"

"Liz, and this is my friend, Brittany."

"Hi," I said to her friend, then to both of them, "Have a seat."

Jayson was at the far end of the couch talking with a girl, but when I called him over to meet Liz and Brittany, he took one look at them sitting next to me, excused himself from his conversation, and slid down the couch toward us.

"Jayson, meet Liz and Brittany."

"Hi, ladies."

Brittany, who had wavy blonde hair, fawn-like hazel eyes, and a whole lot of womanly curves on display, started a conversation with Jayson, while Liz focused her midnight-blue eyes on me.

"How do you know him?" she asked.

"I don't—met him earlier tonight. Time for a new drink?" I asked, making her a drink anyway.

"Trying to get me drunker than I already am?"

"Trying to be a good host. Some pineapple juice?"

"Just soda," she said and then, leaning closer to me, "Do you believe in having fun, Jake?"

I laughed. "I think so. What do you mean?" I said, handing her the vodka and soda with a lime.

"I just got out of a five-year relationship, and I learned two things from it all."

"Oh yeah? What are they?" I said, playfully.

"My ex-boyfriend is fucking crazy, and the only thing that matters in life is having fun."

"Sounds like a great philosophy to me," I said, trying to ingratiate myself with her.

"You really think so? No ... I don't believe you. You seem much too serious for fun."

I laughed again and said, "Well, then, I'll just have to prove myself."

"Good—because attachments are *just … plain … stupid*, you know? So let's make a promise that for as long as we know each other—ten minutes or eighty years—all we'll ever do is have fun."

"You have a deal."

"Yes!" she cheered, smiling and applauding herself. "So where do you live?"

"In town … but my lease ends in two weeks."

"Interesting …" she said, squinting flirtatiously at me. "Leaving me so soon? Where are you going?"

"I have no idea," I said truthfully, because I didn't have any idea where I was going; but what I had even less of an idea about was the reason this girl seemed so interested in me. I drew the conclusion, fighting the urge to indulge my idealistic side, that because of my association with a guy like Jayson, a girl like Liz would associate with a guy like me. *So this is how it works?*

We took sips of our drinks while we bantered back and forth, playing off each other: she listened to what I said to her, packaged it into her own rendition, and sent it back to me, while time whistled by unnoticed by either of us. We lifted from the ground, like hot-air balloons, and ascended higher into the air with every drink, our view of the world becoming increasingly beautiful. Soon we were touching knees and grazing shoulders in failed attempts to be inconspicuous, and then, after another cocktail each, we were kissing on the couch. When we pulled away, I looked at her and smiled, and she laughed. I felt high from the sweet taste of her mouth and realized then I had no control over the desire and infatuation welling up inside of me, just as a sinking ship has no control over the water flowing into it and sinking it further from the surface. I looked at her hand on my leg. I smelled her perfume. And then I looked at her legs. *Christ. I'm in trouble.*

"You know what I miss most about a relationship?" she said.

"What?"

"Sex."

I laughed.

"Seriously," she said. "I just can't stand not being able to have sex whenever—ugh … it's the worst thing ever."

"I'm sure it wouldn't … you know … be hard for you to make that happen."

"I can't just have sex with someone I'm not into."

"Why's that?"

"Because I have no interest in doing that."

"Fair enough. But that sort of ruins the whole just-have-fun concept, doesn't it?"

"Well, Jake, I guess I'm just going to have to find someone I like, then."

As we continued our repartee, trying our best to be witty and cute and always flashing our most flattering smiles to each other, I was particularly struck by a three-word phrase she repeatedly said to me with such a seductive expression I almost wanted to oblige her right then in the lounge.

"Tell me everything!" she would say. "Tell me everything!"

You say it so wonderfully. Sure, I'll tell you everything. Especially when you say it like that. So when can I start telling you everything? Now? Let's start now. I was flattered, feeling almost giddy, that she wanted *me* to tell her everything. And I hoped, in that moment, I'd get the chance someday to tell her everything.

When last call was announced, Brittany got up from the couch and took Liz with her to the bathroom. The waitress delivered to our table a closed, leather-bound folder, and Jayson, without hesitating or looking at the cost, handed her a credit card.

"How much do I owe you?" I asked Jayson.

"My treat. You can get it next time," he said.

"Very cool of you. Thanks, Jayson."

"No big thing, my man."

The waitress brought back the receipt and Jayson signed it.

"Thank you, Jayson. Hope we'll be seeing you again soon," the waitress said.

The girls returned, bubbly and giggly, as if something they'd discussed in the bathroom had enlivened them, and I think all of our spirits were heightened by the words that came out of Jayson's mouth next: "Let's all go back to my place."

Outside, Liz brought the four of us together and, with her outstretched arm, snapped a photograph with her phone, checked it to see if it met her approval, and then, shifting the angle of her face a bit, took another one.

"Don't fucking post it if it didn't come out good," Brittany said.

"Obviously, slut," Liz said.

"Wait—did you check us in?" Brittany asked Liz.

"Duh."

"No more fucking pictures," Jayson said, and Brittany flirtatiously nudged him.

A small group of drunken, sweaty guys approached us, and, as they passed by, one of them muttered, "Reality TV douche bag," igniting the four of us into a drunken laughter that carried on for a block down the hill until we stopped to breathe; but then we started up again, laughing this time at our own laughter.

Inside Jayson's house, he mixed us more vodka drinks, and we played a board game with teams, using a timer and trivia cards; Liz and I beat Jayson and Brittany, and the defeated couple, deciding the bedroom was a good place to win at something else, disappeared down the hall. Liz and I listened to the fading sounds of their drunken giggles, until Jayson's bedroom door was shut and we were left alone in silence.

"I don't live far," I said.

"Let's go," she said.

After one step inside my house—I hadn't even removed the key from the lock—we were already intermeshed, kissing deeply and strongly, one of us pushing away for a breath but the other pulling back with an impassioned haste, as if we were fighting over each other's faces. Her hands gripped my lower back tightly, and I held the back of her head with one hand, guiding my other hand down her back until I could feel the curves of her ass under her dress. Still kissing her, I then moved my hand down her thigh and pulled her leg up and toward me. She jumped into me, wrapped her legs around my waist, and unbuttoned my shirt, peeling it away, as I held her up by her thighs and carried her into my room. I dropped her onto the bed and crawled over her, kissing her chest and neck and lips, and then, with the weight of my lower body between her thighs, moved heavily against her, as she closed her eyes and exhaled deeply. I paused and looked down at Liz. The straps of her dress had come slightly undone around her shoulders and were hanging loosely down the sides of her arms, revealing the top half of her breasts; the bottom of her dress had been hiked up so tightly around her upper thighs that I had an intoxicating glimpse of what was underneath. She looked up at me, still breathing heavily, and said, "I want you inside me." I moved my hand underneath her black dress, between her thighs, and firmly rubbed her over her panties, feeling the heat of her wetness. I then reached behind her back, unzipped her dress, and pulled it off over her head, kissing both of her breasts and then running my tongue down her stomach and underneath the top of her panties.

"Oh ... my God," she said—her back arching—from some very deep place.

I slid off her panties, kissed each of her calves and her knees and her upper thighs, and then sucked the soft skin just to the side of her pussy; she moaned as her head tilted back and then, grabbing my head and pulling it up, said, "Please stop teasing me and just fuck me." She sat up and, with both of her hands, undid the button of my pants, unzipped them, and pulled my cock out, as I winced from the pain of it being so swollen, almost too hard. I kicked off my pants and—feeling like a goddamn congested volcano or an eager San Andreas Fault or a kamikaze—climbed on top of her, as she guided my cock into her.

"Oh ... *shit*," I said.

"I know," she gasped.

And then it was happening. We found a rhythm, and, because of our drunken confidence, we weren't afraid or embarrassed to try new things. When I was behind her, she turned her head around to watch me fuck her, and—as I looked at her blue eyes, her mouth half-open in ecstasy, her wild, auburn hair, and then at her delicate shoulders and her lower back, all bouncing to our rhythm—I paused to avoid coming too early and tried to relax for a few seconds before turning her over and getting on top of her again. At some point, she pressed her fingers very hard into my back, clenched her legs tightly around the backs of my upper thighs, and said, "Oh ... *fuck*, I'm ... going!" And then, once I could feel her body rising to the feeling occurring within her, I knew I couldn't hold it much longer. Her whole body tightened as her moans escalated, and then she climaxed, and her body loosened, as she languidly sank back into the sheets. When I was just about to come, she pushed me off her—until I stood with my feet on the ground—and, sitting on the edge of the bed, put her mouth around my cock and kept it there until I had nothing left. I fell facedown on the bed, panting heavily, and said, "My *God.*"

It took a few minutes for us to notice the blood everywhere: the sheets were stained with it, and Liz's left hand was covered in it, some dripping down her arm. It took us a few more seconds of exploration to locate my back as the source.

"Oh my God, I scratched the shit out of your back. Oh, shit, I'm so sorry. I hope you don't get scars," she said, covering her mouth with both of her hands, giving me both a concerned and apologetic look.

"It'll be fine," I said. "I don't care. It's probably nothing."

I got out of the bed, walked into the bathroom, and, with my back facing the mirror, turned my head over my shoulder to see the damage. *Oh, wow.* Several bleeding cuts, in claw-like patterns, covered the middle of my back, which was in much worse shape than I thought it would be. But then a strange feeling of satisfaction came over me; I was almost excited for the day when the wounds would make the transformation into scars, because then I'd have proof that my time with the beautiful girl who once sat on a blanket in the park was real—a thought that made me momentarily question my sanity as I stood naked and bloodied in front of the mirror.

"It's fine, really," I said, reassuringly. "Don't worry."

"Are you sure? I'm so sorry," she said, erupting in laughter but still apologizing with her eyes, as if part of her felt guilty, while the other part of her found the situation overwhelmingly amusing.

I walked back over to the edge of the bed with a smile on my face and stared at her, as she tried to control her fit of the giggles, and then—when she looked into my eyes, started giggling even harder, and fell back onto the bed, holding her stomach—I, too, erupted in laughter.

EIGHT

"I've never done that before," Liz said late the next morning, as I opened my eyes to a pile of bloody sheets and her dressing at the edge of my bed.

"Done what?" I said, wearily, feeling hungover.

"Had a one-night stand."

"One hell of a time though—*fun*, right?"

She smiled at me and said, "Do you want to do a Sunday fun-day, then?"

"Sure. But let me try to feel normal again first."

"I know what'll help. I'm going to stop by my house—be back in a bit."

Thirty minutes later, Liz, who had changed into a turquoise bikini and little white shorts, brought me a grilled-cheese sandwich and a beer, and said, "This is the best cure for a hangover. I swear." After I finished the quick meal, and, as she'd promised, felt better, she said, "It's so beautiful out. Let's go."

We rented bicycles from a shop in town and rode south along the boardwalk, pedaling hard on the uphill stretches and letting our legs rest on the downhill stretches; it was then, during the downhill stretches, that we observed the summer activity on the beach: volleyball players practicing, dogs pulling hard at their leashes in pursuit of birds, summer lovers walking along the shoreline, surfers idling in the water, waiting for the perfect wave, and day-drinking–beach-goers staking out plots of sand. Soon we reached the pier, and, using the locks provided by the rental place, attached our bikes to upside-down U-shaped metal poles, and then walked out on the pier to watch a fisherman standing along the railing, ferociously reeling in his line. His pole was bent in the shape of a question mark, and excitement was in his eyes. We watched him do the fisherman's dance—yank back abruptly, throw the pole forward, reel in quickly, yank back abruptly—until, finally, something (definitely not a fish) plopped over the railing and onto the cement floor of the pier. Others gathered around the fisherman and excitedly pointed toward a large, flapping stingray, angry as hell. Liz captured a photograph of the scene, and many others in the crowd, having the same idea, pulled out their phones and got up close to the stingray.

"I can't wait to post this photo and see how many of my friends will 'like' it," a young girl said excitedly.

The fisherman unhooked the stingray and tossed it over the railing; as I watched it glide through the air back into the sea, my attention was redirected to a surfer in a full wetsuit, waiting for a wave dangerously close to the pier's mussel-caked pillars. A teenage boy near me, aware that I was also watching the surfer, declared, "The waves are much better by the pier. That's what a surfer told me." When a set of waves started to roll in, the surfer went for the first one—paddling hard with his head down—and, when he caught it, leaped up on his feet and bent his knees, angling the board to the left and gaining speed down the slope of the wave, until he turned the board to the right, and, zigzagging with intensity, rode back up the wave, as if he were trying to carve his mark permanently into the sea. But when the wave lost its momentum, his carvings disappeared into the white foam of the broken wave, as though chalk were being erased from a board, and he went to try again.

Liz and I walked off the pier, and, when she suggested that we get something to drink, toward a restaurant along the boardwalk that had both an inside-seating area and a large roof-deck with tables facing the sea. As we approached the entrance, I attributed my sudden feeling of nervousness—my throat was drying up and my hands were trembling—to the first and last date I'd ever gone on.

During my freshman year in college, I asked a barista at a local café out to dinner (she said yes) and took her, a week later, to a sushi restaurant on Telegraph Avenue in Berkeley. I met the girl, named Christina, on a street corner a few blocks away from the restaurant (the moment I'd expected to be nervous), and, surprisingly, we had a nice walk with a few laughs and unforced banter. Inside, however, after the host had seated us at a table for two, and during the momentary pause that came while we situated ourselves, I became overwhelmed with anxiety, as if being inside the restaurant and confined to a little table with a girl I hardly knew had made the situation unbearably formal.

I quickly interrupted the waiter, who was hovering annoyingly close to me during his rehearsed introduction, asked for a glass of water, and then nervously ordered too much sushi, more than enough to feed a large, hungry family. With a furrowed brow, the waiter scribbled my order on a little pad and darted off, leaving me alone with Christina again. My knees began to shake, and beads of sweat began to sprout from my forehead. A busboy brought us two glasses of water, and, still not having exchanged a word with my date since our walk to the restaurant, I guzzled mine down in a few swallows, hoping it would fix me. With a look of concern in her eyes, Christina asked, "Are you OK?" (a question I've since dreaded) which, in knowing that my problem was identifiable to her, made me even more nervous.

I told her that I was fine and tried to listen to her tell a story, but my knees began to tremble harder, and my throat completely dried up; without any more water to drink, I began repeatedly adjusting myself in my chair and clearing my throat to prevent myself from gagging. With a trembling hand, I motioned to the waiter for more water, then, after I finished the glass he poured me, immediately asked him for another. At that point, the waiter, staring at me as if I were a crazy person, offered to bring a pitcher of water for the table.

When the sushi came to our table, I quickly plucked a roll (one of the fifty or so), put it in my mouth, and tried to chew it; but my mouth was so dry that I imagined I resembled a dog struggling with a mouthful of peanut butter. I tried swallowing. Wrong choice. The half-chewed sushi roll lodged itself in my throat, and, after choking for a few seconds while sweat streamed down my face, I was finally able to keep it down. But, as a testament to the cogency of Murphy's law, that little sushi roll moved down my esophagus at the uncomfortable pace of a dying snail.

Because of the amount of water I'd consumed, I had to excuse myself several times throughout dinner to use the bathroom. Later, when the nightmarish date was—*finally!*—nearing its end, the waiter brought the bill, and I asked him to box up the remaining sushi (enough to feed a smaller but still hungry family). The waiter brought the Styrofoam containers to our table, and I told Christina, hoping to make amends for putting her through such misery, that she could take them home—"You know, if you get hungry later … or something"—which only seemed to make her more uncomfortable. Outside the restaurant, I walked one way up the street, and she walked the other, awkwardly carrying the stack of containers. I never saw her again.

"Inside or the roof-deck?" the host asked.

"The roof-deck," Liz said.

When the waitress came to our table, we each ordered a Bloody Mary, and then, once we'd finished those, several rounds of mimosas. We were drunk before noon, and my nervousness was a distant problem.

"What do you do?" Liz asked me.

"Nothing right now. I quit my job. You?"

"Absolutely nothing. Who cares. No one works anymore, anyway. We should all just enjoy fun-employment forever."

"Ha, but I have to do something."

"What is it that you must do?"

"I don't know ... I guess I want to be a writer."

"Hmm ... well, maybe you could, like, you know, practice by writing me something?"

"Maybe ..." I said, giving her a quick nod and a smile.

"Let's go down to the beach," she said, with wild, blue eyes.

After I paid the bill, Liz pulled me by the hand out of the restaurant, and, after stopping to get two beach towels from within the basket on her bike, led me out onto the beach. She laid one towel down on the sand, sat down on it, mischievously looked around at all the people near us as she slid out of her white shorts, then flashed a look at me and said, "Let's do it under the towel." With the other towel behind my back, like a cape, I lay down on top of her, as she moved her bikini bottoms to one side.

Back on our bikes, we continued to pedal south along the boardwalk, as the town underwent slight changes in the wideness of the streets and in the architecture of the houses and in the color of the street signs—as if we were watching one of those picture-flip books in our peripheral vision—until it was very obvious that we'd ridden into the next town of Hermosa Beach. We picked a good spot to turn around.

"Now what?" I asked.

"Let's lie on the grass in the park and listen to music," she said, pulling up alongside me and steadying her bike with one hand to snap a photograph of us with her other hand.

"OK. Let's stop at the little market on Highland for a bottle of wine first," I said.

We parked our bikes outside the market, locked them to a sign, and walked in.

"Hi, Jake," Ki said from behind the counter.

"Hey, Ki," I said and then, "Hey, Kwan," when he emerged from the aisle, nodding, with a broom in his hand. "This is Liz."

Ki said hi to Liz, and Kwan nodded at her. She said hello to both of them and then followed me to the wine section at the far end of the market. I searched for a good bottle.

"You *know* them?" Liz asked.

"Just from coming in here."

"I've lived here my entire life, and I don't even know them."

"They're cool people."

"Who would've thought ... Just one bottle?" she said to me, as I walked back toward the counter with one screw-cap bottle of white wine. "Let's get more for your house later."

She met me at the counter with four more bottles of wine—two white and two red—and I paid Ki for them.

We unlocked our bikes outside the market, and Liz rolled hers next to mine, kissed me, and said, "Let me carry the bag."

"It's OK. I'll get it."

"I'm the only one of us with a basket," she said, grabbing the bag from me and putting it in the basket attached to her handlebars.

As we rode toward the park, we came upon a hill, and Liz, with the extra load in her basket, was fine going up the hill. But on the downward slope, trying to slow her bike to avoid ramming into people waiting to use the crosswalk, she lost control, wobbled off the sidewalk into the middle of the street, and—yelling, "Shoooot!" while laughing on the way down—crashed, as the wine bottles shattered all over the street right in front of a parked police car. She stumbled to her feet, uninjured and still laughing, while I, rendered almost useless by the sound of multiple honking horns, drunkenly ran over to help. The police officer got out of his car and started briskly toward us.

"No, no, we're fine," I said, waving him off, partly embarrassed, but mostly thrilled to be involved in the adventure with Liz.

"We're OK, Officer. The bike just has a loose tire," she said, trying to tame her drunken giggles.

The officer just stood there, motionless and expressionless, as if he was unsure how to handle us.

"We'll just pick up these bottles and be out of your way," I said.

"This bottle isn't broken!" Liz said, as if she'd made a great discovery, and then happily put it back into the bag.

We stumbled around, while the officer stood above us, and picked up shards of glass, throwing all the evidence of the crash into a nearby trash can.

As we remounted our bikes, Liz whipped her head over her shoulder toward the police officer, the breeze flourishing her auburn hair, and glibly said, "Take care, Officer."

We pedaled away—laughing and saying, "Holy shit!" and, "What just happened!" and, "I can't believe he didn't arrest us!"—toward the park with the only bottle of wine we were able to salvage from her fall. We laid our towels on the grass, and I unscrewed the bottle of wine, took a sip, and passed it to Liz after she'd started playing mellow rock music from her phone. Lying in the July sun with a white-wine buzz, I couldn't help indulging myself in the pleasant thought that I was in the same grassy park, nearly in the same spot, with the auburn-haired beauty I'd once watched from afar, as she laughed and swayed with her friends without a care in the world besides the pursuit of fun. And now she was doing just that ... with me.

We awoke naked on the couch in my house just as the sun was setting, and Liz, grabbing her phone, ran out to the balcony, snapped a photograph, came back inside, and, showing me the image, said, "Look how pretty this filter made the photo."

I glanced at the photograph nonchalantly at first, but then, as Liz pulled her phone away, said, "Wait a second—let me see that again." When she handed me her phone, I studied the image: the oranges and blues and purples and reds of the sky were intensely enriched, the cottony clouds had a textured look, and the whitecaps in the sea looked as though they'd been painted on the glass screen with the fine tip of a paintbrush. "This is the same sunset ... I mean, this is a photo of the sunset happening just out there, right?"

"Yeah, isn't it cool?" Liz said, proudly. "You should download the app—it gives you all these cool filter options for your photos. It's the new big thing. Where have *you* been?"

"Impressive," I said, staring out at the real horizon and feeling disappointed at how inferior it looked compared to Liz's photograph of it. "Stay for dinner?"

"OK," Liz said, smiling.

I cooked couscous and some vegetables. When it was ready, I grabbed a bowl and, with a large wooden spoon, scooped in a clump of couscous and then put some vegetables on top. I did the same with a second bowl and handed Liz the one that looked better.

"Thank you," she said. "This looks delicious."

"A beer with your meal?" I said.

"Yes, please."

We took it all to the balcony, sat in the chairs with our feet propped up on the wooden railing, and enjoyed dinner in the waning light of dusk.

"Cheers," she said, raising her bottle of beer. "To an incredibly fun weekend."

"Cheers," I said, clinking my bottle on hers. "And to a lot more fun to come."

Before Liz left on Monday morning, she gave me her number and asked me what my last name was.

"Reed," I chuckled. "Why?"

"Just curious."

When I heard the front door close behind her, I started a pot of coffee and took a quick shower. Back in the kitchen, I fried an egg and ate it with a piece of wheat bread and a cup of coffee, while I wondered when I should call Liz; I wanted to call her right then and invite her back over. I checked my email and ignored all the unread messages, except the most recent one from my mother.

> **From**: Mom
> **To**: Jake Reed
> **Subject**: PLEASE RESPOND!!!
>
> Jake,
>
> Where are you?! I've been calling and emailing you nonstop. Where have you been?! Have you forgotten your FAMILY! The people who love you deeply??? Please please please call home. It's VERY IMPORTANT. Your grandmother's funeral was hard on all of us. She loved you very much.
>
> But please don't throw away your future. Do you know how many people dream of the opportunities you've been given? PLEASE REMEMBER WHO YOU ARE. Don't lose sight of the man you could be. I'm your mother. I want what is best for you. I want you to have a

good life. Find a nice girl. Have a great job. Raise a wonderful family. These are things every mother wants for her child. I'm your mother! I'm entitled to my opinion!

Please call home. You have responsibilities, Jake. You're everything to me.

Love,
Mom

I sighed—knowing she would never change—and then clicked reply.

From: <u>Jake Reed</u>
To: <u>Mom</u>
Subject: Re: PLEASE RESPOND!!!

Mom,

Won't be home for a while, still. Sorry. Please allow me a little time to sort some things out. I'm well. Everything is fine. Tell Dad hello.

--Jake

I checked Facebook and felt a rush of excitement when I saw that I already had a friendship request from Liz. *My last name … I get it now.* After accepting, I browsed some of her profile photographs—her lying on the beach wearing big sunglasses, dancing with friends, sipping a glass of white wine on a couch, sitting cross-legged on the grass, lounging on a boat in a bikini, drinking from a red plastic cup at a house party, laughing in the snow holding a snowboard—and realized that they all captured, along with the quotations she'd posted, the essence of her carefree spirit. *The only thing that matters in life is having fun.* As I continued to browse through her photos, I came across several of her with the same guy—cuddling, kissing, holding hands, laughing—on the beach, at restaurants, on dance floors, and on a boat; and, although I was reluctant to acknowledge it, with every photograph I saw of them together, I felt a tiny shock of disappointment, as if her past relationship with him couldn't coexist with the idealistic image of Liz I'd already created in my head.

I wrote her a message, an attempt at being witty and charming and presenting myself as a better option for her than the other guy in her photographs, and then anxiously waited for her response, as if I expected her to start working on a message to me—equally witty and charming—the minute after I sent mine to her. But nothing came the rest of the day. Or the next day. Not even the day after that. I texted her. No response. I called her. No answer.

As a way to distract myself from thoughts of Liz, I immersed myself in my writing—really the only thing that always made me feel alive and well and healthy. I read over the blog entries I'd posted under "The Tales of the Desert Wanderer," and, feeling inspired, worked tirelessly for the rest of that week on turning them into a short story, which, after completing a first draft on Saturday morning, was about 10,000 words. Feeling proud and accomplished, I gave myself the rest of the weekend off and vowed to revisit the piece for a round of editing on Monday morning.

With only a week left on my lease, I sipped a cold Japanese beer and ate a light salad for lunch, while I searched Craigslist for available housing in different areas of Los Angeles. The idea of living in Santa Monica, Marina del Rey, or Venice Beach initially appealed to me, but, since beach towns were all I'd ever known, I searched for places away from the water, such as Silver Lake and Downtown, and then—remembering my first conversation with Samy, the bartender—narrowed my search to West Hollywood.

I finally found a house, described as "the famous Sunset House: a mansion in West Hollywood overlooking Sunset Boulevard," that especially roused my interest because it seemed, from the pictures, to be the antithesis of my current living arrangement, and it had one room available "as soon as possible." After reading a strange note on the advertisement—"Just show up at the house for a tour when you're ready to start living here. When you arrive at the gate, call the posted number. No calls beforehand please"—I wrote down the address in my notebook with the intention of seeing the place the following week, if the room was still available.

Next, I checked my email, and my eyes were immediately drawn to a message from Andrew with the boldfaced subject: "Bad News ..."

From: <u>Andrew Martin</u>
To: <u>Jake Reed</u>
Subject: Bad News ...

It's about Steve ... The construction guys found him dead this
morning--just lying facedown in the middle of one of his dirt lots. They
think it was a heart attack. I tried calling you. Left you a message.
Crazy. Everyone around here is in complete shock. Apparently, he has
no family to inherit his land. I wonder if the Coastal Commission will
get the land back? Just unfortunate. Thought you should know. When
are you coming home? What should I tell the neighbors about you?

Dead? Goddammit. I read the email again and felt tears well up in my
eyes until they were sagging with a heavy, tragic weight, on the verge
of spilling over with thick, salty streams down my face. And—as if I
blamed my own eyes for Steve's death or my grandmother's death or
death in general—I angrily wiped both of them with clenched fists to
prevent the spillover of my emotions. *I hate that I care. But this just
doesn't make any sense. Do you see now, Andrew? Was any of it worth it for
Steve, waiting his whole damn life to cash in on those lots?* As images of
my dead grandmother in the open casket flooded my brain, I winced
and shook my head in an attempt to dispel them. I got up and paced
around my living room and then, thinking that doing something with
my hands might distract my mind, filled a kettle with water and set it to
boil over the stove for tea; but when it took too long to heat up, I turned
the flame off, grabbed a towel and a book of short stories, and walked
down to the beach.

Sprawled sideways on the sand, I tried to get through the first sentence of a short story in my book, but each time my eyes reached the
end of it, I'd already forgotten what I'd just read and was forced to start
from the beginning again. I was reading the words, just not processing
them, a realization that frustrated me. Usually, when I concentrated on
reading the words, they traveled from the page into my brain, so, given
my newfound incompetence, I wondered where the words went after I
read them if they never made it into my brain. I doubted the existence
of a word limbo, a special place to harbor all the lost words, but I also
knew that they had to go somewhere. I imagined the words coming off
the page and floating toward my brain, but then, inexplicably, falling
from midair into the sand where they'd be lost forever. *Limbo, I see now*

why you're appealing. You're a safety net. You're there just in case. But if you don't exist, there is nothing, nowhere to go but down into the ground. I feared the guilt I'd inherit when I looked back to the page of my book and saw, in place of the words I'd just read, a blank space. I'd have to be careful not to read any more words in that state of mind, because then I'd be the one responsible for losing them—the infamous monster hated for destroying all the beautiful words in all the great books of literature.

I put the book down and watched a group of bikini-clad girls wander toward the ocean and, as though they were beautiful deer exploring a new meadow for the first time, shoot precautionary glances down the beach in both directions, scanning the land for looks of judgment or looks of desire (I never knew which). I watched a wave form far out in the sea, gain height and momentum as it approached the shore, and then—after extending itself as high as it could—curl over, crash into thick, white foam, and rush toward the shallows, where a young boy, aided by an instructor, was learning how to surf on a longboard. I redirected my gaze to a volleyball game—watched a player dive for the ball—and then to the boardwalk bustling with people, and finally, to a sand-dwelling bug within my reach, charging, with vigor, the vast expanse of tiny desert hills that stood between him and his destination.

But not any of it made sense to me that day; rather, all of it confused me, and I could only find comfort in knowing that I'd felt that way before. The feeling I had after reading Andrew's email regarding Steve Duggins's death was the same feeling I'd had when I heard about my grandmother's death, and later, when I stared inside the open casket at her dead body. The Feeling, nearly indescribable other than to say, for me, it caused a mind-and-body-numbing paralysis, first came into my life when I was ten years old. I was in my father's library, running my fingers along the spines of his meticulously shelved books, when I discovered a very little book, but, because my father wouldn't have anything else, still an adult book. I pulled it from the shelf, read the title— *Of Mice and Men*—flipped through the pages, and then started reading it from the beginning. Several words on the first page were beyond my comprehension, but I loved the imagery created by this John Steinbeck guy, especially from his descriptions of water and mountains and trees and animals; as I read on, I was even more enamored of the idea that two men of such opposites—one man short and clever, the other large and dopey—would ever be walking together through the countryside.

Because the first few pages were fascinating to me and the length of the book wasn't intimidating, I attempted to read the whole thing. Over the next several hours—lying on my stomach, propped up by my elbows, with the book in front of my face and my feet swinging back and forth behind me—I read, with a dictionary close, the entire story of George Milton and Lennie Small. When I finished reading the final sentence of the book, I closed it, set it down, and stared breathlessly in the direction of the floor, but, really, at nothing. I didn't speak to anyone— my parents, my teachers, the other kids at school—for a whole week. When I came home from school, I went immediately to my room and lay in my bed. My mother, frantic in her motherly way, cried, screamed, yelled, and shook me—everything she could think of to fix me. Even my father, a man of very few words, came into my room one night and said, "Listen, cut it out, goddammit. You're driving your mother crazy."

At the end of the week, my mother drove me to the elegant Newport Beach office of one of her cocktail-party friends—a successful psychiatrist—and left me alone with him inside a room with some of the shiniest things I'd ever seen: a fastidiously cleaned and sparkly wood floor, a freshly polished brown leather couch, and a gleaming set of framed awards and degrees hanging on the wall. And in the background, behind a large, spotless window and under a bright sun, a shimmering blue sea sent intermittent flashes of light into the room, which then bounced around, like a pinball, from one shiny thing to another. A red, plastic model Ferrari sat on the table in front of the couch, and I played with it in silence, while the psychiatrist asked me several questions, starting with the bland, prosaic ones ("How was your day?" or "How are you feeling?"), and then shifting to much more personal and intrusive ones ("Have you ever been sexually abused by a priest or a gym teacher?"). Perhaps frustrated by his inability to break through to me, he finally slammed his hand down on the desk, making a smudge on the spotless surface, and said angrily, "What's *wrong* with you?"

"I can't believe George killed Lennie," I said to him.

"Who are George and Lennie? Friends of your parents?"

"No. In *Of Mice and Men* ... George kills Lennie. It's just terrible. I don't know what to do about it. It won't leave my head."

After our session was over, the psychiatrist, with me still in the room, told my mother that he believed I showed signs of depression. "Not sure which kind, but I think it could be manic-depressive disorder. However, I'll have to spend more time with him to properly diagnose him."

"What is manic-depressive disorder?" my mother asked incredulously.

"It's just another term for bipolar disorder."

"But he's so smart," my mother said defensively. "He writes little poems all the time, and he gets straight As in school."

"Many manic-depressives are like that."

My mother never took me back to see that psychiatrist, and I think she cut friendship ties with him, as well; I'm quite sure, given her obsession with public perception, that she was worried about my having a reputation as a crazy person who needed pills to exist in society.

I left the beach and walked back up the hill to my house. I spent the rest of the weekend lounging around, drinking wine, reading, and watching Woody Allen films in my bed; and then, on Monday, as planned, I sat down at the table to polish my short story. After reading it twice over and realizing it wasn't as good as I'd imagined, I felt that I needed to ignore everything else and spend the next week revising the piece—cutting sections out, rewriting sections, writing new sections—until I was reasonably satisfied with it. I knew I'd never truly be content with my work—perhaps, I thought, a sentence could be improved for all eternity—so, at the end of that week (on my last official day in Manhattan Beach), after condensing my short story from 10,000 words to 7,000, I chose to send it out. *Why not?* I went to *The New Yorker*'s website, found the section that accepted written submissions from the general public, pasted my short story in the field box, and checked "Fiction." At the bottom of the page was a large, intimidating button labeled "Submit," which—after thinking, *Fuck it. What could I lose?*—I clicked, prompting an immediate automated response from *The New Yorker:*

> **From**: Fiction, TNY
> **To**: Jake Reed
> **Subject**: Your fiction submission
>
> Your submission to *The New Yorker* has been received by our fiction department. The editors will read your story and reply to you within ninety days.

And then, after overcoming the apprehension of doing it once, I submitted my short story to any literary website with a submit button, hoping that within the next three months I'd receive some good news. Lastly, I erased all the old stuff on my blog, and then divided up my short story into ten parts and posted them sequentially under the title: "The Tales of a Desert Wanderer: A Short Story."

Later in the day, just before sunset, I received a text from Jayson ("Roll through to my house tonight. Having people over. Start filming new season next week. Last night of freedom"), and one from Liz ("Sorry, been so busy lately. Let's hang out again soon!"). I decided, since it was my last night in Manhattan Beach, to stop by Jayson's, so I texted him that I'd see him later; unsure how to handle the text from Liz, I didn't respond and moved on.

The setting sun, flashing a luminous orange through my window, moved me to the balcony, but, after feeling a tremor in my hands and then holding them out in front of my face to verify that they were indeed shaking, I went into the kitchen, found a small bottle of whiskey, and poured myself a drink; I returned to the balcony and sipped the whiskey, as the sun pushed its way down into the blue and my hands steadied.

Over the next hour, I packed my things into the four trash bags I'd originally started with and loaded my car with all of my belongings, except for a toothbrush, a bar of soap, and a change of clothes. After showering and getting ready for the night, I stopped by my favorite bar, ordered a whiskey, and briefly chatted with Samy about my move.

"I think I'm going to do it ... try West Hollywood," I said.

"I think you're doing the right thing. It'll be the time of your life. You won't be able to do it forever, but you'll see some new things."

"Take care, Samy."

"Hope to see you again, Jake. You know where I'll be ..."

I walked along the boardwalk, with the sand and the sea to my left, until I reached Jayson's house and went inside. A large inflatable pool filled with water, three feet deep, was in the middle of the living room; Jayson, in black boxer briefs, and several girls, in bras and panties, were swimming around, splashing and giggling like kids in a pool on a summer day. Not another male guest was present. Some girls, hair and bodies still damp from the pool, danced in the kitchen to music, but the majority of the girls not in the pool massed around a glass table in the back of the living room, taking turns snorting something from the table's surface with a rolled-up bill. I assumed it was cocaine (I'd never seen it in real life). One of the girls, waiting her turn, stepped forward in the line, allowing me a glimpse of the middle of the table, and I saw a white-powdered mound, big enough to mold into a good-sized snowball, resting out in the open, as if someone had casually dumped it there. *Wow. There it is. Cocaine … It is real. People really do it.* I took a second to let the feeling I had settle, a mix of excitement and nervousness—the same feeling I always got when I was a part of or witnessed, for the first time, some sort of deviant behavior. I remembered the time, during the summer before my first year in high school, when one of the neighborhood kids, after his parents had gone to bed, stuffed his pockets with cans of beer from the refrigerator, and a group of us drank them (me for the first time) down on the beach, or the time I went to a high-school party and saw someone pull out a bag of marijuana and roll a joint.

Shaking myself from my trance and approaching the inflatable edge of Jayson's pool, I pretended to be indifferent to the activity in the back of the room. As I got closer to Jayson, I realized his face was badly scraped and bloodied and that he had a black eye, swollen shut and discolored with streaks of dark purple and blue-tinged yellow.

"What's up, my brother?" he said, noticing me for the first time, squinting his eyes and pointing at me the way people do when they've momentarily forgotten a person's name.

"Jake," I said, feeling embarrassed.

"Jake! What's up, my man? Sorry, just a little fucked up … You know the drill."

"Yeah … What happened to you?"

"What—do I look … different?" he slurred, laughing drunkenly at his own joke.

The calm, cool demeanor he'd maintained the night I met him had been replaced by a slightly unhinged, twitchy one; his long hair, wild and wet, was pasted in strands down his face, and his good eye was opened so widely, between two strands of hair, that he looked a bit psychotic.

"Yeah, man, some fuckheads—like five of 'em—jumped me at a bar."

"*What*—really? That's ridiculous."

"Yeah, man, violence is never the answer."

"Why would they do that? I mean—did they have a reason?"

"A reason? Of course there's a goddamn reason: I'm fucking famous. That's why I'm not mad about any of it. They just want what I have. I feel sorry for them. Jealousy is a powerful thing, my man. Turns men into animals," he said, not looking at me but through me, through the room even, perhaps into some other realm where his epiphanic words were being born.

"Yeah, I'm sorry, man. At least you're OK, I guess."

"OK? Look around you, man. I'm *more* than OK. Look at this pool, dude. I had a team of Mexicans bring it in and fill it up today. I do whatever the fuck I want. I fuck whoever the fuck I want."

"Woooo, yeah you do!" some girl shouted from the glass-table area.

"I'm on TV, motherfucker, who the fuck are you?" he yelled, as more girls cheered. One girl swam over to him and whispered something in his ear, and during his moment of distraction, I was able to slip away to search for a beer in the kitchen.

I maneuvered around the dancing girls, who remained unaware of me; whatever world they were in, I wasn't. But as I pulled a beer from the refrigerator, one of the girls tapped me on my shoulder and said, "Valedictorian?" I turned around and immediately recognized her from high school: she was a popular beauty who'd also, at some point during our senior year, gotten involved in reality TV. I'd never spoken to her in person, but we were Facebook friends.

"What the hell are you doing here?" she asked, noticeably confused.

We talked for a minute, but after I declined her request to join her in the pool, she snapped a photograph of the two of us together with her phone and skipped away. I took a sip of beer, and, feeling out of place, walked to the edge of the inflatable pool to say good-bye to Jayson.

"You leaving? Feel free to partake if you'd like," he said, nodding in the direction of the glass table.

"Yeah, I'm good. Moving out tomorrow—have a few things to do."

"Where you going?"

"West Hollywood."

"Jesus, man. I told you I used to live there. I hope you like heroin."

I smiled and said, "Take care, Jayson. Good luck."

At that point, he sank beneath the water, and when he came up for air, he was on the other side of the pool with the girls.

I left his house and sat on one of the stone benches along the boardwalk to drink my beer and listen to the ocean. I awoke, shivering on the cold stone, as the sun was rising and early morning joggers were bustling past; with a bewildered, sleepy squint, I checked the time on my phone and saw forty-three missed calls and eleven texts from Liz. *What the hell?*

I staggered, not fully awake, up the hill to my house. After a quick breakfast, I cleaned the dishes, took out the trash, and started to tidy up the place. When I went into my room, I found Liz, still seemingly wearing her clothes from the night before, asleep in my bed. Seeing her for the first time since our weekend together immediately flooded me, in a matter of seconds, with a cascade of mixed emotions, one after the other: first, utter surprise; next, a rush of excitement; then, confusion; and, finally, suspicion. *Wait ... why is she here?* Trying not to wake her, I walked into the bathroom, closed the door, undressed, and, with my head turned over my shoulder toward the mirror, stared at the scars forming on my back from the first night I'd spent with Liz. With the hope of calming my nerves, I took a long, hot shower, and, after finishing, wrapped myself in a towel, opened the door, and walked back into my bedroom.

"Hey," Liz said, softly.

"Hey, Liz. What are you doing here?"

"You don't want me here?"

"It's not that. I'm just surprised to see you."

"Where were you last night? Tell me everything," Liz said.

"I fell asleep on one of the benches along the boardwalk."

"Did you meet a girl last night?"

"Um—no. Why?"

"Who was that girl in the picture?"

"Huh?"

"I saw you tagged in a photo with a girl on Facebook. Are you dating someone else?"

"Oh, no. I knew that girl from high school. I ran into her when I stopped by Jayson's last night."

"Did you fuck her, Jake? Don't lie to me."

"*No*, I didn't. What's this all about, Liz?"

"Are you over me?"

"You don't respond to any of my calls or messages, and then you show up at my house two weeks later ... in my bed ... asking me these questions. How did you get in here, anyway?"

"I thought we had a good thing going. I don't just have sex with anyone, Jake."

"Liz, sorry, I'm just a little confused here ... I tried calling you, texting you ... You said—I thought—"

"You said you were going to write me something. Why haven't you written me anything?"

"What? Oh—I just didn't take you seriously when you said that ...

What's really bothering you? Did something happen?"

"I texted you last night—you didn't respond."

I shrugged, perplexed that she'd even use that argument since she hadn't responded to me in weeks.

"Why is all your stuff gone?"

"My lease is up, remember? I'm leaving ..."

"When?"

"Today."

"You weren't going to tell me? We had such a fun time together," she said, starting to cry. "Will you stay? You don't have to leave just yet. Stay another couple weeks. *Please* stay. Will you? It'll be fun. Will you?"

"Liz, I didn't think this mattered so much to you. I don't know if I can ... I mean—I don't even know if my place is still available."

She started to cry harder, as tears poured down her face, and then she buried her head into my pillow.

"I still don't understand why you're so upset, Liz. Where have you been all this time?" I said.

"Why would you just leave when we could see where this goes?" she said as she got up from my bed, now sobbing almost hysterically. "You can leave just like that?" And just before she ran out of my house, she said, "Am I not worth staying around for, Jake?"

I paced about, completely bewildered, and tried to make sense of the situation. *Crying? Why was she crying? How did I make her cry? I tried to get ahold of her. I made an effort to see her again. She was the one who ignored me! Maybe the idea of my leaving made her realize that she'd miss me? Maybe she really cares to see where this could go? Maybe it's worth it to see where it goes? To have more fun ...* On a whim, I called my landlord, and, after learning he hadn't secured another renter, worked out a deal with him to stay on a pro-rata basis with the condition that I'd leave if he found someone else to rent the place. After I hung up, I felt fine about my decision because I remembered one of the goals I'd made for my travels—to connect with other people on a basic human level—and Liz was offering me just that. I thought I should embrace the opportunity.

I called Liz, and, surprisingly, she picked up on the first ring.

"Hello?" she said, solemnly.

"Hi, Liz."

"Hey."

"I'm going to stay for a little while."

"You are! Tell me everything!"

"Well, I called my landlord, and my place is still available. Perks of a recession, I guess."

"This is just great. We're going to have so much fun."

"Do you want get dinner tonight?"

"Yes!"

"Good."

"You pick the place."

That night I took Liz to dinner at a Mediterranean restaurant down by the pier. I ordered a bottle of wine from the wine list, and she asked the waiter for some feta bruschetta for us to share before our meals; for dinner I ordered a lamb dish, and Liz chose the ahi tuna. Our waiter brought the wine, uncorked the bottle, and poured a small amount into my glass for me to taste.

"It's OK, man. You can just pour it."

"No! You have to try it first," Liz said. "You don't know if it was a bad year or not."

I laughed. "Right," I said and then sipped the wine, as Liz snapped a photograph of me.

"It's fine," I told the waiter after swallowing a taste, but I really didn't have any idea what was fine or not fine when it came to wine. It wasn't that I hadn't consumed quite a bit of it in the past, just that the bottles I was used to drinking were usually priced in the five-dollar range.

I listened to Liz's stories about her friends, most of whom, according to her, had gone crazy or were about to go crazy or had done crazy things; she paused in her stories during the moments when the waiter brought the plate of feta bruschetta, and, later, our entrees to the table, so she could take photographs (of the food or of me eating the food) with her phone, as if she was chronicling our dining experience.

After dinner, while I sipped my coffee, I asked Liz if she wanted to have a drink at my favorite bar in town.

"I grew up here. I know all the bars in town," she said, and then after I told her which one it was, "Ha ha, *that's* your favorite? I don't think I've ever been in that bar longer than a minute or two."

"You can try something new. We'll make it fun."

"Let's do it."

Later that night—after Liz and I were back at my place, lying in my bed, drunk—I told her that I felt good about staying in Manhattan Beach, that I felt lucky because girls like her weren't usually interested in guys like me.

"I'm glad you stayed, too," she said.

NINE

Liz, this time, was very responsive, almost surprisingly so, often calling and texting me repeatedly when we weren't together, which was a rarity. I still tried to devote part of every day to my writing, but Liz was intent on being with me all the time; on the days I told her I needed to be alone to work, she'd understand initially, but then, usually within the hour, knock on my door with a bottle of wine in her hands and an impish, flame-blue glint in her eyes.

"I know! Sorry ..." she would say. "I just had to see you ..."

I could never resist her, and she knew it. So I put my work aside, and, for the next few weeks—during the dry heat of midsummer, that illusory time of year when the subtle hint of a feeling is enough to seduce one into trusting in it wholeheartedly—I lost myself in my infatuation with Liz. And because she also seemed desirous of my attention, we naturally spent most of our time chasing the thrill of a fresh sexual relationship, initially retreating into the familiarity of my bed, but soon, as evidence of our growing comfortableness, graduating to the shower or a chair on the balcony or the living-room table. And then Liz, her eyes ablaze with adventure, began suggesting that we fuck in public places: "We already did it on the beach that one day. Remember? Think how much fun other places would be!" Soon we'd visited the pier, a tennis court, the park, the boardwalk, and even a restaurant bathroom.

During the day, we stumbled around town in a joyous daze, and, every night, we had dinner at a different restaurant; but when Liz suggested once that we dine at the fancy Mexican restaurant on Highland, I told her to pick another place.

"Why?" she asked.

"I promised my friend, Hector, I'd never eat there," I said.

"Who is Hector? Tell me everything."

"Long story."

"Fine—you pick the place tonight."

After dinner each night, she insisted that we do something fun: do karaoke at a bar, watch the grunion swarm the beaches to mate, get high in the park, skinny-dip in the ocean, or, one time, hit golf balls at the town's night range.

One early Sunday morning late in August, the third week into my extended stay, Liz left my house but then returned before noon with a huge smile on her face, wearing a bright yellow dress, and carrying a bottle of champagne.

"Let's drink this ... and then will you come somewhere with me?"

"OK, sure—where are we going?"

"You can't ask questions. You just have to come. And you have to dress up a little," she said, pouring two glasses of champagne and adding a dash of orange juice to each.

After we finished the bottle, I put on the nicest shirt I had—an un-wrinkled, blue T-shirt—and followed Liz out to her shiny, white Range Rover. She drove south, blasting music with the windows down, for a mile or so, and then east for another couple of miles, until she slowed her car to turn into an enormous parking lot already filled with cars—a vast sea of glistening metal. A massive stone, with a crucifix and the name of the church carved into it, greeted our entrance as she pulled into the lot.

"We're going to church?" I asked, but Liz didn't respond.

After she parked, we walked over a bridge, and I paused to take in the scene over the railing. Directly under me was an immeasurably grand field with impeccably cut grass playing host to a variety of activities: some children played with beach balls, soccer balls, or Frisbees; some played duck, duck, goose and tag; others jumped on a giant trampoline. A stream snaked through the field and poured into a good-sized lake at the far end, in the middle of which was a lavish fountain shooting water high into the air. Beyond the lake were several buildings that looked like classrooms, but one, in particular, might have been a store, because people walked out carrying shopping bags or books or stuffed animals. And on my immediate left stood the church—the most grandiose building of them all, truly a breathtaking tribute to architecture—with pillars jutting into the sky, angling toward each other, and meeting in the middle as the foundation for a giant crucifix, the tip of which knifed through the high clouds. My entire view—the church, the buildings, the field, the lake, the fountain—gave me the impression of a booming city.

"Jake, are you coming?" Liz said. "We've missed most of the service. We'll have to sneak in."

"Holy shit—this is a megachurch, isn't it?"

"Um … I guess. Just follow me."

I followed her around the building, through a back door into the church, and stood in astonishment at the sight of thousands of people filling rows of seats lining the auditorium from one end to the other; looking up, I saw that the church had multiple, tiered levels, each of them spilling over with people. We found two seats in the very back, seemingly the last two available, and quietly sat down. The stage—one large enough to fit several big, yellow school buses—had, on one side, a Tyrannosaurus rex–sized Jesus built into the floor, extending a single hand to all in the crowd, and, on the other side, a rock band and a choir. At a podium in the center stood a white-haired, white-bearded pastor with his hands raised in the air. We seemed to have arrived during the concluding act of the service.

Just then, all the lights turned off, and high-pitched shrills, like those produced by women at a rock concert, echoed throughout the auditorium. Light suddenly flooded the ceiling of the church, where several people—dressed as angels, wearing white-winged gowns and fastened to ropes—dangled from the rafters high above, moving their arms and legs as if they were swimming the breaststroke through the air. The crowd cheered in the dark. And then one young man, illuminated by a spotlight, rose from his seat in the middle of the auditorium and shouted for all to hear, "I used to be addicted to pornography … but now I'm addicted to Jesus Christ!" Just as he finished, he was hoisted by the ropes attached to his body toward the ceiling, where all the angels were fluttering around. The crowd cheered louder, and the pastor called out, "Do you feel that!" A middle-aged woman, also spotlighted, stood up at the far end of the auditorium and shouted, "I used to have promiscuous sex … but now I have a relationship with only two men: my loving husband and Jesus Christ!" And then, as the crowd roared, she, too, was lifted high in the air to join the others. "Salvation!" the pastor shouted. "Salvation! Salvation! Salvation!" *What the hell is going on here?*

One after another, people in the crowd, wearing body harnesses attached to ropes, shared how they'd overcome their sinful ways, and, as a reward, ascended to "heaven," until there were twenty or so "saved" people flying around above us, like Peter Pans of Christ. When the lights finally turned back on, hundreds of people in the crowd were swaying with their eyes closed, reaching toward the heavens in exaltation. The band started playing, and the pastor yelled, "Thank you all! See you next week." The mighty Jesus started moving his arm from side to side, as if he was blessing the crowd, and behind him, on a large projection screen, appeared the words, "Friend Jesus on Facebook," with the appropriate URL underneath.

Liz grabbed me by the hand, pulled me through a smiling crowd toward the front of the church, and then led me into a private room on the side of the stage, where the pastor was mingling with a group of people. A young woman, who looked to be around thirty and was carrying a toddler, approached Liz; they embraced and then exchanged a few words, while I stood awkwardly to one side.

"This is Jake," Liz told her at some point.

"Hello, Jake. We appreciate your coming here today," she said.

Ha! Well, shit, I had no idea I was coming here. "Oh, really—it's no problem," I said.

"So what did you think?"

"Very entertaining show," I said.

"Do you know Jesus?" she asked.

"Do I know Jesus?" I repeated, feeling slightly pressured by her tone.

"Yes, that's right."

"I'm not sure what you—"

"Have you accepted him into your heart?"

"Well, I'm not really … committed one way or the—"

"We really want you to *know* Jesus. Will you try to know Jesus?" she said.

I paused and studied her as she looked directly into my eyes and held her gaze. *You see, passionately aggressive woman, there was a time when I knew Jesus very well. Maybe too well. Our relationship, however, may have already run its course. But there's no use in explaining that to you now, is there?* The toddler, who'd been previously peering over his mother's shoulder in another direction, whipped his head around and stared into my eyes, as well. I looked at him and thought about the time in my early years when, the moment his mother looked away, I would have put my protective, evil-repelling shield around him. *But you already have the shield around you, don't you? Now I'd rather release you from it. But I don't know how to do that. I can't do it, anyway. Your mother won't look away.*

She's still staring at me. I looked back at the mother.

"Yes, I can try to know Jesus," I said.

"That's a wonderful decision. It will change your life," she said.

The pastor, with an attractive middle-aged woman by his side, walked over to Liz, picked her up, and swung her joyously in a circle, as if she were still a little girl.

"Daddy!" Liz said, laughing.

Daddy? Wait—what?

"Hey, Lizzy—so glad you made it," he said, setting her down.

"Thanks for coming, Lizzy. It's so great when you do," the woman by his side said.

"Guys, this is Jake," she said. "Jake, these are my parents."

"Nice to meet you, Jake," the pastor—Liz's dad—said.

"Hello," I said, shaking his hand.

"Did you go to school with Lizzy?" her mother said, squinting at me curiously.

"No, Jake went to Berkeley, Mom."

"Oh no! Ha ha," she said, turning to the pastor and then back to me. "Does that make you a liberal, hippie communist?"

Both her parents laughed, and I tried to.

"I guess it might," I said, smiling politely, making them laugh again.

The woman carrying the toddler said, "Picture time," and the whole group shuffled into three rows; I stood in the back with people of similar height, mostly guys who seemed to be around my age. "How's it going?" I said to the guy next to me, but he didn't acknowledge me. After someone took a few pictures of our group, all of us abandoned our smiley poses simultaneously.

Back in Liz's car, on the way home, I said, "Um ... you really caught me off guard there. What was that all about?"

"Oh, yeah, sorry—my parents just love it when I go. I haven't been in a while, and I hate going alone. So I figured you could come with me, you know?"

"I had no idea your father was a pastor or, for that matter, that you were even religious."

"Well, I'm just a Christian."

"What does that mean?"

"It just means that you have to say, 'I accept Jesus.'"

"And that makes you a Christian?"

"Yep."

"You just have to say, 'I accept Jesus,' and you're a Christian?"

"Yes, Jake."

"Wow—I never knew it was that simple."

"You aren't religious?"

"I don't think so. Not anymore. But … if I had to pick something, I think I'd go with Judaism—that community just seems to have so much genuine camaraderie."

"I don't get it. Why would you *want* to be Jewish?"

"That's not the point," I said. And then, attempting to explain myself, I continued, "So, my freshman year in college, I had a black roommate, and he told me one night that since there was such a small population of black people on campus, they sort of felt … I guess … compelled to reach out to one another—and the way they did this was through a simple nod of the head whenever they passed by each other. Just a little nod, like this," I said, showing her. "I didn't understand it at the time, but I was completely fascinated by the idea of that. So I started reading all these books relating to black American history and literature—you know, stuff by W. E. B. Du Bois, Alice Walker, Toni Morrison—because I think I was trying to understand that nod, searching for any clues about what that nod meant, you know? But in the end, I think I really just wanted to be able to give that nod around campus, too. I think my thing for Judaism is sort of like that," I said, feeling relieved by the thought that I might have clearly communicated something true about myself to Liz, perhaps something I never fully understood until explaining it to her. But when I looked over at Liz, hoping to see on her face a look of admiration, she had, to my disappointment, a noticeably absent expression—the way people stare distractedly at nothing, with wide-open eyes, when they're deep in thought about some matter elsewhere.

"Um …" she finally said, as if my silence had alerted her that it was her turn to say something, and then, as she scrolled through her phone at a red light, "You … are so weird."

We rode in silence back into town until Liz, as she pulled up to my house, asked if I wanted to hang out for the rest of the day, and I told her that I needed to focus on some writing.

"Come over tonight, then," she said. "You've never been to my house."

I spent the rest of the day flipping through my favorite novels and old issues of *The New Yorker,* pausing to write down words that inspired me, and then watching certain parts of films I loved, freezing the frame to investigate, when there was a book, or, even better, a bookcase in the background of the scene—all in a hopeful attempt to tap into the internal well of my own words. *Time to write.* As evening fell, I uncapped a new black pen from my shoulder bag and brought the tip to the smooth, yellowish surface of a fresh page in my Moleskine notebook. But twenty minutes passed, and the page was still unblemished, except for the thickening freckle of ink from the bleeding tip of my motionless pen. I picked up my notebook, brought it close to my face, and rapidly flipped through it, fanning myself with its sweet-smelling paper. I paced around the living room, went out to the balcony to stare at the sea and then back into the kitchen, where I filled a kettle with water for some tea and set it over the blue flame.

I sat back down at the living-room table. *OK—now it's really time to write.* I scribbled a few notes about my church experience earlier in the day. But I had nothing else. *Where are my words?* The kettle hummed on the stove. *Why can't I think of one damn thing to write?* The kettle started whistling softly. *Just write something. Write about Liz. Write about* ... The kettle shook angrily, blaring like a train horn, and I frustratedly slammed my notebook shut. I took the kettle off the flame, put two bags of green tea into a large mug, poured the boiling water into it, and let it steep. My phone vibrated in my pocket; Liz had tagged me in a photograph on Facebook.

During our time together, I became quite accustomed to Liz's frequent pauses to capture our adventures with her phone; but that afternoon, during my rare time alone, I discovered, after catching up on Facebook, that I was in many of her recent photographs, and, as I browsed through them, that she'd created a photographic timeline of our relationship: the first night we met at the lounge, our bike ride along the boardwalk, our nightly dinners and adventures (even one of us kissing in bed), our days of debauchery around town or at the park or on the beach, and, most recently, the shot of us at church with her family. And then, with one simple click, the photographs of Liz and me segued into the ones of Liz and her ex-boyfriend; and it seemed as though my relationship with Liz, in the online world of events, had replaced the one she'd had with her ex-boyfriend—simply made it a thing of the past.

Later that night, after a light dinner, I texted Liz that I was coming over and then took a pleasant fifteen-minute stroll to her place—a large, white, weather-beaten house with stairs that led to a front porch. Her roommate answered the door.

"Hello ... Jake ... right?"

She was a very thin, slow-moving, slow-talking person, as if she were under the influence or medicated, and I was struck by the way she smiled at me; it was a sluggish smile that crept across her face one tiny muscle at a time, stayed in place for a few seconds, and then, like the waves retreating back into the sea, the corners of her mouth retreated back into two pouty lips.

"Yeah, I'm Jake."

"She's taking ... a shower. She told me ... to let you in."

"Thanks."

I walked into a large living room, which, already very white and summery, was also decorated with the feminine touch of beach lovers: seashells on countertops; flowers in vases; a large wicker basket holding thick, bright towels, a volleyball, and sandals with clumps of sand still clinging to them; and, hanging on the wall, framed black-and-white photographs of lovers rolling around in the sand and others, in color, of soft orange sunsets.

"Help yourself ... to a drink from the fridge ... if you want," her roommate said, before sauntering away, like a sloth, down the hall and out of sight.

I found a single bottle of Corona Light in the back of the refrigerator and sipped it until Liz came out and brought me into her bedroom, the walls of which were decorated with collages of photographs of laughing, drunken people. Her bedspread was purple, and she had a nightstand by the side of the bed, with several framed pictures on top; I recognized some of the people in the pictures from church earlier. A sliding-glass door, draped with purple curtains, was at the back of her room, and when I peeled the drapes back to peek out, I got a moonlit glimpse of her backyard and a Ping-Pong table. I walked over to Liz, grabbed her at the waist, and pulled her in for a kiss, but she pushed me away.

"What's wrong?" I asked.

"I don't know ... I just think we can hold off on that stuff for a while. We already know we're *amazing* at it."

"OK ..." I said, confused by her unfamiliar reaction. "So then ... why would we stop?"

"I don't know—can't we just watch a movie or something?" she said, apathetically.

"Yeah ..." I said, unemotionally, trying to veil my frustration. "OK, that's fine."

"Nothing with subtitles—it's way too intense, you know? It's like if you look away for one second, you miss everything."

"You choose the movie."

When I awoke, the movie was still playing on Liz's laptop, but she was absent from the bedroom. I lay still, trying to gather myself, and wondered how long I'd been asleep; but then my ears detected a slightly muffled but audible conversation happening in the next room, presumably Liz's roommate's room.

"Should I ... call him?"

"No. Maybe text him ... Have you guys had sex?" Liz said.

"Yes."

"OK, when did he stop calling or texting?"

"Maybe, like, a couple days ago, after our last date."

"I wouldn't worry. It gives guys confidence to know they have some control, and, in the beginning, all they really have is, like, whether they call you or not. But ... I mean, that won't really change ever, even when he's your boyfriend. He'll still want to feel like he has control. That's just how guys are, you know?"

"Yeah ... totally."

"But, oh my God, it's so easy: when you know he's getting annoyed or, like, boiling up because he feels like he's losing control, just ask him something, like something you know he has the answer to, something you know he's passionate about. But you can't just ask in, like, a normal way. Ask him in a way that says you really need him, like you're dependent on his answer or something. It can even be a question you know the answer to, but, obviously, don't let him know that."

"Obviously."

"It gets him involved, and then he can go on his little rant, and you can smile and pretend you care. But you still need to lock this guy down, right?"

"I mean ... yeah. He still hasn't called or texted me back or anything."

"You *need* to go out with some other guys. Show him that you're strong and doing your own thing. It'll be good for you. He'll call again—trust me. You just have to be prepared when he does, but not act like you're prepared, you know?"

"What do you mean?"

"Like, you have to be witty on the spot. Be on your game. Don't be a dud when you talk to him, but don't overdo it either."

"Now I'm worried—how would I overdo it?"

"Well, he'll probably tell you some jokes. That's what guys do: they try to say something funny to make you laugh—because girls want to be with a guy who makes them laugh, right? So you have to laugh, but you can't laugh too much, because then he'll just think you're, like, patronizing him or something. So you have to make sure that your laughs seem real enough to him, and then you have to have a witty response ready. Then, hopefully, he'll laugh and say something back, you know? That would be the ideal conversation."

"Perfect."

"The most important thing to know is that guys want to *have fun.* You can't give him the slightest impression that you're serious in the beginning because that'll just scare him off."

"Yeah, you're right. I just really want a boyfriend … I mean, I think it's time again."

"You just have to be clever and careful, and then everything will work out. Girls just have it harder with certain things, and this is definitely one of them. Guys don't know what they want until they want it. So it's the girl's job to get him there, you know?"

"Yeah, you're *so* right."

"So it's natural that we have to be, like, super protective of ourselves and always have other options."

"Liz, thanks so much for talking to me. I needed that. Seriously. Thank you *so* much."

"Oh my God, it's nothing. OK, I'm going back to bed."

"See you tomorrow!"

Her bedroom door cracked open, and, in no mood to talk, I feigned sleep, while Liz walked quietly over to the bed and climbed in. As she got settled and drifted to sleep, I realized that on the nights we'd spent together, Liz tended to fall asleep quickly, while I usually lay awake for hours worrying about snoring or drooling or how I looked while I was positioned next to her; it wasn't the type of romantic unease I'd expected to feel while in a healthy relationship. I wondered if my unease was rooted in my fear that Liz and I weren't compatible at all. *Do I just want to believe that we're a good match? Or that a girl like her would be interested in me?* The more I became aware of certain red flags about the nature of our relationship, or that, perhaps, I didn't even enjoy her much as a person, the more I longed to be in her presence. *That makes no sense ... Maybe I just want to convince Liz that we're right together. Is that the issue? My inability to sell myself to her?* I'd allowed her to have some type of control over me. *Why?* I tried to understand what was binding me to her—what about her had captivated me since the first time I saw her, what had made me want to spend so much time with her—and I couldn't come up with anything other than her dark blue eyes and the curves of her body, really just my overall physical attraction to her. *What do you do for me, Liz?* We never had much to say to each other apart from our telling of stories to pass the time—stories that entertained us in the present but faded from our memories the second we moved on to another adventure.

Well, all of this is something new for me. Something different. Maybe it's just that simple. But look at her. She's sleeping soundly ... And I'm awake worrying about all these things. I'm losing myself in her. I'd also started do-ing and saying things I normally wouldn't to ingratiate myself with her: laughing loyally at all of her stories, watching and pretending to enjoy her favorite TV shows, forming opinions on matters I cared nothing about. *Compromise or obsession? Maybe it's because I think she's normal. Normal? Yes, a girl who's in normal relationships with normal guys, a girl's girl, the girl I'd always heard about growing up. Normal as in not weird ... like me. Maybe I'm trying to convince myself that I can participate in all of this—that I, too, can be ... normal.*

But who are you, Liz? You're a shiny doll. What else are you? What am I to you? Maybe she doesn't have any meaningful reason for wanting to be with me, either. Maybe, as she suggested in the beginning, I really am some-one she can simply enjoy her time with. But why me? Maybe I'm thinking about it too much ... But maybe loneliness is like drunkenness, and we're both settling for or justifying things when we normally wouldn't. But even after all the feelings of doubt and uncertainty I had that night, I couldn't imagine leaving the bed with her still in it.

After I spent the next few days away from Liz and in a limbo of irresolu-tion, she texted me on Thursday evening: "Drinks at my house then out to the bars tonight! You have to come!"

A simple, exclamatory text message (along with several mood-themed Emoji characters) from her seemed to put me in better spirits. I made a stop at the town market to buy some beer and have a chat with Ki and

Kwan.

"Hi, Jake," Ki said, thumbing through bills at the cash register.

Kwan, mopping the aisles, looked up at me and nodded hello.

"Hey, guys, how's business?" I said.

"Same, same," Ki said. "Where your girlfriend?"

"I'm picking up some beer before I go see her," I said.

"Yeah, she very, very pretty," Ki said.

I laughed politely and said, "Thank you."

"You a lucky boy," Ki said.

I went to the beer section, decided on a few packs of different micro-brews, all ones I hadn't yet tried, and paid at the counter.

"Bye, guys," I said.

"Good night, Jake," Ki said, while Kwan gave me a wave.

I walked to Liz's house, carrying the bag of beer, and before I ascended the short flight of stairs that led to her front door, I stepped aside for a staggering Brittany—the girl with Liz the night I met her—who, given the unlit cigarette hanging from her lips, was presumably coming outside for a smoke.

"You!" she said.

"Me."

"I thought you ... you were supposed to be gone by now," she slurred.

"I decided to stay a little longer."

"Why?"

"I don't know ... Been hanging out with Liz."

"You should've gone, silly!" she said, giving me a presentiment of an unenjoyable conversation to come.

"Thanks," I said, sarcastically.

"Well, I guess ... we can't blame her for doing what she has to do ... to get what she wants."

"What are you talking about?"

"Let me ask you something, Jake," she said, lighting her cigarette while nearly losing her footing. "What kind of person takes lithium pills and can never ... be ... *alone?*"

"I have no idea, Brittany," I said, growing tired of her.

"Liz! Ding, ding, ding."

"You're wasted."

"Yep and ... just ... fucking bored, man."

"Bye, Brittany," I said, turning to walk up the stairs, but she grabbed my arm.

"What's in the bag?"

"Beer."

"Let's have a drink together."

"The bottles aren't twist-off," I said, looking for any excuse to escape her.

"I can take care of that," she said, as she grabbed two beers from my bag and popped their caps off by angling the bottles along the edge of the stair railing and hammering down with a closed fist. She handed me a beer and said, "She's been using you to make her ex-boyfriend jealous. And I think he finally got the message."

"Liz and I are in a casual relationship ... Just having some fun."

"Ha ha ha, right, Mr. Naive. Look at you—you're not having fun at all. And Liz? A fun girl? You should guess how many happy pills it takes to put a smile on her face. That girl only cares about two things: marrying her ex-boyfriend and having a fuck-load of babies with him. You're in the wrong crowd, Jakey boy."

"I appreciate the concern," I said, starting for the stairs, but she grabbed my arm again.

"Let me tell you a story. When Liz found out her ex was seeing another girl, she went fucking crazy over it. But then! That night at the lounge, she met you ... a good old-fashioned distraction ... for that weekend—a one-time thing, really. But starting that Monday, when all the depression and loneliness set in, she tried getting her ex back for the next couple of weeks, but he just wasn't having it. So she cried to me all day, while she stared at his new girl's Facebook photos. She practically studied the bitch's life and then kept asking me, 'Do you think she's prettier than me?' It was driving me fucking insane, so I helped her with a plan."

"And what was that, Brittany?" I said, exasperatedly.

"To make him jealous. Shit, she even got you to go to church and hang with her family. Hellllloooo! Look at all your online pictures together. Those were taken for his eyes only."

"I don't think it's that simple."

"Of course it is. It's always that simple. What world do you live in? Everything else is always the bullshit we use to hide the fucking simplicity."

"Why are you telling me all of this? Aren't you *her* friend?"

"Uh, yeah, she's my best friend. We've grown up together in this shitty little town. I love her more than anything. But that doesn't mean she isn't bat-shit insane … just … like … me. And, of course, we have our own secrets from each other … like the time I fucked her high-school boyfriend in the bathroom while she was passed out in bed," she said, starting to laugh. "But that was, like, so many years ago. Who cares, right?"

"You know, Brittany, I hardly know you, so it may be wrong of me to form an opinion of you so prematurely but … I think you're full of shit," I said, confidently.

She laughed arrogantly, making me doubt myself.

"Then why would she invite me here tonight?" I said.

"For backup, silly. She always needs someone to give her attention, or she just loses her shit. It's the curse of being a pretty girl and always getting attention, but, like, never really believing you're pretty," she said. And then, stepping closer to me, with a wicked smile, she said, "You want to make her jealous now, don't you?"

"Huh?"

"You don't think I'm hot, Jake?" she said and then grabbed the back of my neck with one of her hands, pulled my face down to hers, and kissed my lips with her smoky, devilish lips, while she grabbed my cock with her other hand.

"You *are* crazy," I said, pulling away.

She laughed, as if she were verily enjoying herself, and, after tossing her cigarette into the street, said, "Your loss. Come on. Let's go party, then. Since her ex is back in the picture now, he'll probably be around tonight. You guys can fight over her. It'll be fun."

"What do you mean by 'back in the picture'?"

"Aw, is Jakey boy sad? They're not officially back together, but they're fucking again." She paused to laugh. "We're all fucked up. We're all crazy. You shouldn't be so serious. There are no rules here, man. What did you expect? To have some fun? To fall in love? Who the fuck *are you* anyway?"

"Fuck off, Brittany." I left her at the base of the stairs and walked up to the front door.

"I read some of your blog the other night!" she called up after me. "I really liked some of your stories, Jakey boy. They were just so lovely to read—" she said, cutting herself off with her own laughter.

I opened Liz's front door and went inside. The TV was set to a pop-music channel. Some people were in the kitchen taking shots of vodka, some were sipping beers while plucking from an assortment of hors d'oeuvres on the counter, and others were playing a drinking game around the kitchen table. I didn't see Liz anywhere in the room. I stood for a while, awkwardly sipping from my beer, on the fringes of huddling groups, unable to break into the conversations—besides a joke or two with someone standing next to me about the benefits of fun-employment—partly because I didn't know anyone and partly because most people were participating in an impressive demonstration of multitasking, dividing their time between intermittent, half-sentence mumbles to those around them and phone browsing. Some guys, in a more active group, were grabbing and hugging each other, sometimes smacking or shoving each other. One guy hit the bottom of his friend's red plastic cup filled with beer, which geysered upward all over his friend's face. Everyone laughed, even the victim, who drunkenly yelled out, "You're gonna fucking get it!"

But generally, the room was filled with individuals who, although probably acquainted with everyone else, seemed far more content to be on their own high-tech phone islands, as if they were plagued by the insatiable need to find out, every passing second, what was happening somewhere else. Forced to entertain myself, I imagined that the neighbors in the house across the street were also having a party, and each of their guests was also texting someone not in attendance or browsing the online lives of others far away. Perhaps, I thought, they were texting the people in Liz's house. I wondered what would happen if the parties combined into one large room: everyone would then start texting someone new or browsing the lives of people elsewhere. I tried to conjure up images of those elusive, ghostly people, who were apparently much more important than the ones already in the room.

When I finally saw Liz, she'd emerged from one of the back rooms with glassy eyes and a drunken stagger; after seeing me, she ran over, kissed me, and said, "I've missed you." But then she disappeared, somewhere down the hall and out of sight, and I didn't see her again until someone, about twenty minutes later, yelled, "Let's go to the bars!" and the herd moved toward the door.

After a series of photo shoots outside, during which everyone moved gracefully in and out of rehearsed poses, we surged toward the nightlife, filling the width of the sidewalk and spilling onto the street, indifferent to the danger of passing cars. An even mixture of guys and girls, we carried along riotously; some of the guys shoved each other, others laughed boisterously; the girls chatted loudly, almost at a shouting level, and slammed their high heels forcibly into the pavement with deep, deer-like strides. And then I realized, at that very moment, I'd placed myself in the middle of The Mob—the one I'd always watched from afar—that gobbled up everything in its path with an unforgiving tenacity. I looked around the group to gauge if anyone had noticed me, the trespasser, but The Mob surged forward—stumbling down the path, making cars slow down, and forcing other pedestrians to step aside and wait for its passing. I wondered how long it would take for some of the members of The Mob to realize I was amongst them. I imagined one of the soberer members detecting an unfamiliar stench, enough to pique his interest, and then, with a flare of his nostrils and a deeper whiff, he'd confirm the certainty of an intruder. I'd watch him scan the group, looking for the source, until, finally, he'd lock eyes with me. With his gaze still fastened on me, he'd lean over and say something to the person next to him; after that, it wouldn't be long before the whole group would come to a halt and stare at me. I anxiously awaited that moment, but it never came.

We crowded around the little entrance to a rowdy bar (or was it a club?) shaking with music, called Twelve and Highland, conveniently on the corner of 12th and Highland, which was packed so tightly inside with drunken, sweaty, fist-pumping people, some of them were nearly falling out of the windows. A long line of similar-looking people waiting to get inside stretched down the sidewalk, and, in the madness, I lost Liz again. I fought through the crowd and looked for her at first, but, un-nerved by the overwhelming mass of partiers and the thought of spend-ing my night finding Liz and then losing her again, I decided to leave.

I detached from the group and walked down the hill until the drunk-en reverberations faded into the sounds of the ocean; then I walked the boardwalk to my street, veered right, and walked up the hill to my house. I texted Liz to come to my house after her night was over and waited for a response until I fell asleep on my living-room floor.

I awoke on Friday morning, and, with the drunken rant of Brittany still fresh in my mind, quickly checked my phone for a response from Liz, finding nothing. Over the weekend, I texted and called her several times, and, after not hearing from her by Sunday evening, decided I'd stop by her house the next morning to talk to her.

After a long, restless night, I had a coffee, early Monday morning, at a café on Highland. Before I left, I ordered another cup of coffee to take with me (in case Liz wanted one) and walked to her house. As I walked up the steps to her door, I was surprised to hear music playing inside at such an early hour. I knocked on the door. No one answered. I called Liz's name a few times and knocked some more. I called her phone a couple of times. Nothing. *Maybe she can't hear me over the music.* I remembered, from the night I spent at her house, that she had a sliding-glass door in the back of her room that opened to the backyard.

I set the two cups of coffee down on the porch and then walked around the side of the house, following the path through an unlocked gate to her backyard. I heard something before I saw anything—the muffled sound of two people laughing—and froze; but then I heard something else:

"Oh my God, tell me everything!" Liz said, giggling.

It was beyond my control then; I inched closer to the sliding-glass door, until one more step would give me a view into her bedroom through the partly opened curtains. I took the step and saw the two of them. They lay naked in the bed together, covered by a single purple sheet; she was resting her head on his chest and caressing his stomach with the tips of her fingers; he had his arm wrapped around her, gently tracing the shape of her lower back with his hand. Her room was cluttered with empty water bottles, a half-eaten box of pizza, stray cans of beer and bottles of wine, and clothes—giving me the impression of a room where two lovers had spent the entire weekend without leaving.

At first I stood watching them, as if I were watching a bad movie at three in the morning when I couldn't sleep—with an empty, lopsided expression—but, like the short delay that occurs after one touches something very hot and then feels agonizing pain, I was rapidly consumed with a much more terrible feeling.

"Tell me everything!" Liz said again.

He laughed and I looked at his face. I recognized him from Liz's photographs of them together.

"I guess ... it is that simple," I mumbled to myself.

I tried to move my feet, but they were held firmly in the ground by invisible roots. I couldn't take my eyes off the scene. Suddenly my vision blurred and faded to black everywhere except the bed, which was illuminated by the floodlight of an ugly, internal rage welling up inside me; I felt it gathering heat—this rage—and then I felt it stirring, as if a monster were coming to life inside me, first learning to crawl, then growing and maturing, and finally, with its ravenous lust for power, trying to take control of me. Now nearly defenseless against it, I stood in the early morning shadows, partly concealed by Liz's purple curtains, and peered through the sliding-glass door at the result of my own naiveté. I'd extended my time in Manhattan Beach so that my oblivion and idiocy could not only be exploited but, far worse, charted in my online world—now a timeline of true mockery. I'd become a pawn in an inane, secret plan devised by Liz, who'd successfully enticed me to chase a feeling and trust a visceral urge. And, ultimately, I'd been misled by a pretense that she wanted to make a real connection with me. *What a fool I am—conjuring up fantasies about the way I believed it could be, and betrayed by my own silly need to seek meaning in everything.*

I felt my blood reach a hellish boil, until, with clenched fists, I fantasized about shattering the glass door with my bare hands, dragging them both out of bed, beating his face while she watched, and then hoisting her by the neck as she gasped for air. Then, suddenly, as if the last remnants of my sanity had regrouped and mounted their own successful counterattack, I felt the monster begin to retreat into the layers of my bowels, like a crab slowly backing into the dark shadows under an ocean rock; and, as my head cooled, I was ashamed of the perverse thoughts that had, only seconds before, nearly governed me. *How could I let myself go to such a dark place so quickly? It was never love. She said at the beginning that she didn't want anything serious with me. What did I think would happen? Get it the fuck together, man.*

I walked, in a cold and numb silence, back around the side of the house, through the gate, and onto the street. A trio of high-school girls walked past, and the sound of their laughter penetrated me like a cold kitchen knife. A couple, holding hands, strolled along the street, and the sight of them together unnerved me. The sound of a car horn startled me, causing me to flinch. And at that moment, worse than my fear of my own thoughts was my fear that the monster inside me had not been dispelled forever, but that he'd only chosen to lie dormant; I worried that he would be part of me from that point on, living within me, ready to surface again with the right opportunity. Perhaps he'd always been there, and I'd only just awakened him.

Back inside my house, I packed my things, tidied up the place, and called my landlord to let him know that it was my last day in Manhattan Beach and that I'd leave the rent check (for the pro-rata total) on the kitchen counter. When everything was in order, I sat on my bed, grabbed my laptop, opened my browser, and, to my surprise, discovered that the "mansion" in West Hollywood I'd bookmarked on Craigslist weeks ago still had a room available to rent.

I closed my laptop and undressed. I ran the shower water until it was warm enough, but just before I stepped in, I caught, in my peripheral vision, an image in the mirror. I backed up to get a closer look at the scars on my back—from the cuts Liz had given me the first night we'd spent together—and, in that moment, likened them to tattoos I regretted getting or birthmarks I wished I'd never had. In the shower, I frantically tried to scrub the scars away with a white bar of soap, but when I got out and checked the mirror, they were still there, reminding me again of the sickening thoughts I'd had at Liz's house.

As I dressed, I thought about the day I first saw Liz, sitting on a blanket with her friends in that grassy park, and then realized that her smiles, her cuteness, her wittiness, her expressions, her stories, her "tell me everything" phrase—even her touches—were never intended for me. I'd just been introduced to all of it in passing, as a random, temporary recipient in a simple, but apparently effective, social media scheme. *It's my fault. A pretty girl sitting on a blanket in a grassy park is everything you want her to be before you know her. She smiles. She laughs. She has fun. She amazes you when she decides to talk to you. She gives you attention. Elation. Excitement. Could this be love? Yes! But you must first make her into something that she isn't. Why? To experience love, of course.*

I drove up the hill, and, before turning toward the freeway, noticed a small, fluorescent sign on a shabby building that read: "Best Psychic in Town." I pulled over and parked. When I walked through the entrance, I saw a disheveled woman sitting behind a desk smoking a cigarette.

"Come in and sit down," she said.

I took a seat in the empty chair in front of her desk.

"Would you like a smoke?" she asked.

"No, thank you."

She smiled. "What can I help you with today?"

"How much is it?"

"I don't know yet. We should talk first. What's your name?"

"Jake."

"Jake, tell me what's on your mind," she said, peering studiously at me.

"What do you want to know?"

"Why don't you tell me what's troubling you?"

"Well," I paused and stared at her cautiously before continuing, "in short, I just spent two months investing in something ... chasing something that wasn't even real ..."

"Go on."

"Um ... I'm not really sure how to describe—I guess I'm constantly looking at the world in a way that precludes me from truly participating in it, and I want to change that. But I don't know if it's possible for me. I think I might have some serious issues."

"Maybe. Let's see," she said, reaching for my hands and then holding them within hers, as her cigarette dangled loosely from her lips. "Please continue."

"I don't do well with people. Rather than enjoy someone's company, I spend my time thinking about why that person chooses to say what he says or do what he does. I never add anything to a relationship because I don't see the point, when I'm so confused about everything—you know, like, if nothing means anything why should I do anything or care about anything or talk to anyone ... ? You see that? I also feel that I've been tricked and duped my entire life. I really just want to know if I'll ever be able to tell the difference between real and fake."

"How do you mean?"

"Well, if someone said, 'I really want to climb this tree,' I'd have no idea if he or she likes the idea of climbing the tree or hates the idea of climbing the tree, and I'd probably sit around for hours and wonder which one it is."

"You're a young boy. Your age?"

"Twenty-three."

She pulled her hands away from mine, removed the cigarette from her lips, flicked away the ash, and then took a final puff before smashing the butt into the ashtray on her desk. "OK ... so let me tell you what I know. I know that you think my business is phony. I know that you just came here to talk with me because you have no one else. Perhaps you've suffered some recent losses and you're incapable of processing your angst. But ... let me tell you what I *also* know. You'll be faced with some decisions in the very near future. The choices you make in these specific cases have the capacity to result in extremely divergent life trajectories, much more so than any choices you've ever made before. I still see an energy in your eyes, feel a warmth in your blood, but it's very important for you to understand that, when faced with these decisions, you should not seek darkness. You're very naive and fragile, because you act as if you don't believe in anything, as if you don't care to believe in anything, but, really, all you want is to believe in *something* with all of your heart. This is a problematic combination. I should tell you that the only way to fit in well with people is to truly love people. And the only way to truly love people is to continue to immerse yourself in social environments where, contrary to what you hope for, you'll find that people are never what you want them to be. It is at this point of acceptance, if you're still willing, that you'll be able to start loving people. And let me enlighten you about something—you must know, for your benefit, that it doesn't really matter in the end if a person says she wants to climb a tree and doesn't mean she wants to climb a tree. That's all I can tell you today."

She lit another cigarette, leaned back in her chair, took a quick puff—smacking her lips as she inhaled—and stared at me. I felt uncomfortable in her presence, then, because the truth was that I *had* come in there to just talk with someone—someone I didn't know, someone indifferent to my issues. But, after our session was over, I felt slightly ashamed of how quickly I was willing to believe everything she told me; I feared what that could mean about me.

"How much do I owe you?" I asked, wanting to get out of there quickly and back on the road.

"Do you write in that notebook you're holding?"

"Sometimes."

"What do you write about?"

"Just ideas that come to my mind for stories."

"Include me in one of your stories, publish it to the Internet, and the session is free."

"How will you know that I wrote the story?"

"Email me the link," she said, handing me her card.

"I can just pay you. No one reads my stuff anyway."

"I'd rather you write the story. Bye now, Jake. Good luck."

I left the smoky dwelling of the psychic, started my car, and drove east on Rosecrans toward the freeway; I glanced at the blue ocean in my rearview mirror, but then, pushing the gas pedal down to accelerate, concentrated on the road ahead of me.

Ten

My wheels spun swiftly away from Manhattan Beach and toward the disharmonious sounds of planes streaking across the sky, buses coughing fumes into the air, car horns blaring, police sirens scolding, and homeless people ranting. The drive to the 405 freeway from the beach was long enough for me to see drastic changes, as well: the houses shrunk and were ramshackle, the sidewalks filled up with hurrying pedestrians, and the streets, which had become much wider to accommodate the traffic, were lined with massive shopping centers.

I drove onto the 405 and inched north in unrelenting traffic, restrained by the brake lights that snaked bright red for miles ahead. After an hour of mostly slow, jerky driving and a few inexplicably short stretches of open freeway—where drivers, tasting freedom, accelerated to sixty miles per hour just before being forced to slam on their brakes for yet another traffic jam—I merged east onto the 10 and battled more traffic for another twenty minutes. When I finally took the La Cienega exit, I was dumbfounded that, according to my GPS, I'd only driven about thirteen freeway miles for the entire trip. I drove north toward the hills in the distance—passing a mélange of fast-food chains, dirty bus stops, liquor stores, massage parlors, strip clubs, and car-repair shops—until I was in West Hollywood, where I was intrigued by the cars on the road: a clashing blend of shiny, new luxury vehicles (Bentleys, Ferraris, Range Rovers) and decade-old, dilapidated hunks of metal, spewing exhaust fumes into the air. I crossed Melrose and Santa Monica, then climbed a steep hill, passing Fountain, before I turned right on Sunset.

I coasted cautiously along a curvy, congested street, straining my neck to look up through my windshield at the advertising that saturated both sides: hand-painted billboards on the faces of tall buildings, freestanding billboards—some old-fashioned, some digital, and some three-dimensional—and all the world's posters and stickers. The sidewalks were peppered with palm trees. I passed a luxury hotel with limos lining the front, valets scrambling around like disturbed ants, and formally dressed guests filing into the lobby. Big trucks, out of which men unloaded various things, were parked along the sides of the street in "No Parking" zones. Car drivers, using their horns to express their frustration, maneuvered around the trucks, and huffing runners wired to MP3 players weaved nimbly through all the activity. The sun shone and the sky was a clear blue, but still, a certain coldness blanketed the city—a sickly, fluorescent chill—as if it could never get warm, even with all the heat in the world.

With the indecisiveness of a tourist, I resorted to stop-and-go driving—provoking an angry honk from behind me—because, according to my GPS, I was supposed to make a left turn within fifty feet, but I couldn't see any street ahead of me to turn on. A line of people, waiting to get into the House of Blues, stretched down the sidewalk and coiled around the corner. A herd of angry picketers, brandishing handwritten signs and chanting in unison, marched in a circle in front of the Andaz West Hollywood hotel across the street. I looked at the time on the clock in my car: 12:30 p.m. *Jesus, look at all this activity.*

Just as I decided to turn around and start over, the house, or mansion rather, appeared in a grandiose fashion on my left, directly behind The Comedy Store. Sitting on the top of a steep ramp, it sprawled four stories high and was nestled against the base of the Hollywood Hills. A magnificent, spiked gate marked the end of the ramp and the start of the private property. After making a sharp left over a double-yellow line to go up the ramp, I was immediately flagged down by a valet. I rolled down my window.

"Pay here," he said, coldly.

"Pay for what?" I asked.

"Pay to park. You can't just park for free."

"Even to see the house? I'm looking to rent one of the rooms."

"*Christ*, man. Why didn't you say you were going to the house? Just pull up and make sure you park inside the gate. I have a party at the hotel and can't have any cars blocking the ramp."

I drove up to the gate and called the phone number that had been posted on Craigslist. On one of the last rings, a guy answered and barked, "What!" as if he'd been woken by my call.

"Yeah, hi, uh—I'm here to see the room for rent," I said. "The guy told me to pull the car into—" He hung up on me.

A few seconds later, the mechanical gate jolted to life and angrily creaked and clattered open along the track. I pulled my car into the driveway, parked, and walked up the steps to the second level—an impressive outdoor expanse that had a full bar along the side, a veranda with comfortable-looking, cushioned chairs at the back, an enormous fire pit encircled by a couch in the front, and, in the middle, enough empty space to throw a baseball back and forth. I leaned against the wrought-iron fence that traced the edge of the deck and enjoyed a glimmering panorama of Los Angeles: Century City's skyline to the west, Downtown's skyline to the southeast, and, to the south, the vast, magnificent horizon embellished with the soft, cloud-shaped contours of the hills rising out of the great Los Angeles Basin in the distance. I pulled out my phone and captured a photograph of the view.

"Incredible," I said.

The only part of the view that slightly unnerved me was the entire side of the neighboring Andaz hotel plastered with Oprah's smiling face; her eyes shone like bright stars over the city in a way that suggested she knew all the answers. I looked into her eyes and then quickly away. I couldn't understand why, in a city of millions, she chose to stare directly at me.

"It's just a house, man," said a deep voice from behind me.

I turned around to a tall, thin, but muscularly shaped, blue-eyed, unshaven guy, walking toward me with both swagger and suavity, holding a folder, his phone, and two cans of beer. He may have been the best-looking, most confident guy I'd ever seen.

"What's that?" I said.

"Once you realize that it's just a house, you're going to do fine in this town. Here, I brought you a beer," he said.

"Thanks," I said, slightly amused by his little canned gift, as I was with everything else happening at half past noon on a Monday in West Hollywood.

We both cracked open our beers and took a drink.

"And I'm sure you noticed that this month we have giant Oprah."

"This month?"

"Every month that advertisement changes, and this month we have Oprah."

"Got it," I said.

"Parker Thomas," he said, reaching out his hand to shake mine.

"Jake Reed," I said, shaking his hand.

"You know, it's funny; I remember taking photos of this view when I first moved in. I looked at it the same way you just did. Everyone who comes through here has the same reaction. Unfortunately, it wears off quickly. But, it's always the same for first-timers, which is why I like to get new people over here all the time—so I can feel it all again by watching their faces. But, again, it's just a house. I figured I could save you the trouble."

I laughed and said, "Thanks. I appreciate it."

Parker seemed uninterested in my response, almost bored by it. "So what's up, man? You're here to see the room or what?"

"That's right."

"OK, let's take the tour."

I followed him along the deck.

"This is the deck level where we hang out a lot—we throw parties here, a DJ plays, people dance. Fantastic shit. On sunny days we just kind of lounge around here and take in the sun. There's one room on this level, the biggest room in the house, currently being rented by a cool, fun couple. Obviously, you'll meet them and see their room if you end up living here. Let's walk up to the next level."

I followed him up the steps to the third level.

"OK, that's the Jacuzzi—gets cleaned twice a month. We try to get in it as much as we can. That path leads around the house to the backyard," he said, pointing behind the Jacuzzi, and then continuing along. "A balcony slash lounge area here with a nice couch … Another great view of the city … Let's go inside now."

He opened a large, wooden door and led me into a clean, capacious living room with a ballroom-like ceiling and a ten-foot-high painting of Jim Morrison's face on the wall. Still, I got the feeling—from the look of the faded walls, the smell of the musty room, and the sounds of the floor under our weight—that the place was urgently in need of repair, as if it was barely able to stand upright after years of abuse. A cleaning crew of about four or five was busy mopping, vacuuming, and scrubbing.

"So," Parker continued, "this is the living room. Good thing the cleaning people are here today, right? They come every Monday to clean the whole house. Anyway, as you can see, that's a pool table in the corner. This is the main couch and TV—we all try to eat together or hang out in this room occasionally. OK, next room," he said, gesturing me to follow. "This is the sitting room, I guess. A few more couches. A couple of desks. Some of us here work from home. A piano. You play piano?"

"Not really. I took lessons as a kid, but probably forgot it all. You?" I said.

"Yeah, I play. OK, next, the kitchen … over here," he said, pushing through a swinging door. "Nice big kitchen. Big commercial fridge. We don't do much cooking, because people are always coming in and out, and it's hard to keep track of everything. You want another beer?"

"Sure."

He took two beers out of the fridge and tossed one to me.

"The door back there opens to the backyard. OK, let's go upstairs."

I followed him up the stairs to the fourth level, which was just a long, narrow hallway with several doors.

"This floor has the rest of the rooms. A total of six rooms up here, and the one in the very back is available to rent. Let's go see it," he said, walking down the hall and opening the door to a room that hadn't been fully emptied—a bag of trash, a box spring, and a mattress had been left behind.

"So it's the smallest room in the house, but it's also the cheapest. You have your own bathroom with a shower, a little walk-in closet, and a great view of the city through the window. The guy before you just sort of picked up and left. So you wouldn't have to buy a new bed if you don't mind using his."

"How much is the rent?"

"Seventeen hundred a month, but that includes utilities. Rin Tin Tin is probably in his room if you want to meet him."

"Rin Tin Tin?"

"Yeah, he's a DJ here in Hollywood, and that's his DJ name. He's out all night and home all day. Now that I think about it, I can't even remember his real name," he said, walking me out of the room for rent and down the hall.

"Tin," Parker said, leaning against the closed door.

"What?" someone yelled from inside the room.

Parker opened the door. Rin Tin Tin, sitting in a chair with his back to us, had two widescreen monitors set up on his desk, both of which displayed his Facebook profile; and although I could only see the back of his real head, I had a clear view of his digital face.

"Tin, this is Jake. He's checking out the room."

"Oh, hey, what's up, man?" he said without turning around.

"Nice to meet you," I said, looking into the eyes of his profile picture. I followed Parker out of the room, and he closed the door.

"OK, let's go downstairs and talk for a second," he said.

"Sure."

Downstairs, we took a seat in the sitting room, and Parker lit a cigarette. "You want one?" he asked.

"No, thanks. I'm good."

He set the folder he'd been carrying on the desk and said, "You want to take a look at some of your competition ... for that room?"

I chuckled and said, "OK."

"Seriously, man, people have been giving me their fucking headshots. Look at this guy ..." he said, opening the folder and pulling out a glossy photograph of a shirtless, blond male posing with the squinty-eyed, smoldering look. "Anyway, the point is that nothing is for sure—but we're looking to lock down a new renter immediately. The room has been vacant for too long ..." He paused, seemingly gathering his thoughts, and I wondered why the room had been vacant for too long if there were so many applicants. "OK, let's talk details so you know ... Everyone who lives here is on a month-to-month contract, simple as that—you pay for a month, and you're good for a month. After that term you're free to leave, as long as you make sure to give me a week's notice to find someone new. It seems crazy, but that's how the owner wants it. Oh, did I tell you who owns this place?"

"I don't think so," I said. And after he told me the owner's name, I said, "I don't think I know him."

"He did all those goofy comedies in the nineties ... Remember? He was pretty famous at one point. Anyway, he'll be around. He likes his house to be rented by young, active people—probably because it reminds him of his glory days. Anyway, month-to-month it is. Cool?"

"That's fine."

"Which also means people come and go quite frequently. Still, a few of the guys have been here for a while ... Rin Tin Tin, the guy you just met, has been here for two years. I've been here the longest—this will be my fifth year—so I sort of manage the place."

"I see," I said.

"How old are you?" he asked.

"Twenty-three."

"I was your age when I moved in here. Crazy shit."

A long pause ensued, and I stared at him. He had a very odd, distant quality about him, as if he was aware of the situation just enough to recite his spiel about the house but nothing more. His eyes had an illusory quality about them: instead of pools filled with a natural, clear-blue water, they were more like drained pools with the floors painted a gluey blue. Often, throughout our conversation, he'd pause and stare vacuously, and then, when he spoke again, he'd carry on as if he'd never stopped speaking.

"So I should be honest with you, man. *This is it* ..." he said, making eye contact with me for the first time in a while. "The heart of it all. The thick of it. This is the only house actually hanging over Sunset Boulevard in all of West Hollywood. You're in it, man—in the heart of a soulless city. It doesn't get closer to all the shit than this."

"Meaning ... ?" I said.

"Meaning: you don't really make decisions anymore when you move into a place like this. Things sort of just happen to you, and then you move on. Some people have moved out pretty quickly in the past, so I decided it's better to be upfront with potential renters from the start."

"Well, I think I like the idea of living here."

"Why do you want to live in a place like this?" he asked.

"I don't know. I guess I want to try something new ... experience a new way of living."

"Good answer. You're employed? Can you make the rent?"

"Not currently employed—but I can make the rent."

"You saved some money or something?"

"Yeah, I never really spent the money I made while I was working, and my grandmother left me something. It'll be fine."

"OK ..." he said, leaning back on the couch, crossing his legs, and getting more serious. "You seem like a go-with-the-flow type of guy, which it's very important to be in a place like this. Do you like music?"

"Yeah, sure."

"Do you have a problem with partying?"

"No, I don't mind it."

"Do you believe in love and all that shit?"

I laughed, thinking he was joking, but he stared earnestly at me.

"I'm trying to understand which phase of life you're in," he said.

"Oh, OK—well, I mean, I don't know ..."

"Well, do you have a girlfriend?"

"No," I said.

"Very good to hear," he said. "And you said the main reason you want to live in a place like this is for the new experiences … right?"

"That's right."

"So you're willing to embrace trying new things?"

"Sure."

Then after a long pause, he said, "The room is yours if you want it."

"Really?"

"Yep, but you have to tell me your answer right now."

"OK … well, all right, let's do it. I'm in."

"Sweet, man. Write me a check today for two months' rent, which will include a security deposit of one month's rent."

"You know, I was surprised this place was even still available. I saw the advertisement weeks ago."

"It's very important to me that I choose the right person."

"I see."

"Welcome to the Sunset House."

Because hauling a new bed up four stories seemed far too laborious for a potential short-term stay in the house, I decided to use the bed left behind by the previous renter. I applied the same logic to buying anything else for the room, except for some brand-new sheets for my bed, which I went to pick up at a store down the road. I hung my clothes—a few T-shirts, a couple pairs of pants, and one thick, black pea coat—in the closet, and organized my books in a horizontal line on the floor along the back wall. I looked around my new room—at the small bed in the corner, the row of books along the wall, the bare, yellowish walls, the rug-less, old, wood floor, the little four-paned window—and got an empty but strangely satisfied feeling.

I checked my email and found, much to my surprise, twenty or thirty messages notifying me about comments made on my blog by those who'd discovered the short story I'd posted, and had, apparently, enjoyed it. After reading several encouraging comments, I wondered why so many people at once were interested in my writing, a short-lived curiosity resolved by the next email I read.

From: Stone Fox
To: Jake Reed

Where have you been all my life, Jake Reed? After reading your short story, I shared it with my followers. See, I've been posting (just my thoughts) on my blog for a long time and have, along the way, aggregated quite a following, which is not nearly as impressive as it sounds, because I also follow my followers. At this point, it is beyond me who followed whom first. So, in reality, it's just a vast sea of followers following followers. Nevertheless, I felt it more than appropriate to introduce your writing to my followers. I hope you don't mind.

Best,
Stone Fox

I decided to respond.

From: Jake Reed
To: Stone Fox

Dear Stone Fox,

Very cool name. And, no, I don't mind that you shared my short story. Perhaps it would have been wiser for me to have opened an account under a pseudonym, as you've done. Nonetheless, it was exciting to receive such complimentary comments from your followers, who, it seems, have now become my followers. I now look forward to reading your thoughts. Talk soon.

--Jake

Parker charged into my room. "You know, this was my room when I first moved into the house. Have some great memories in here."

"Ha, I bet."

"I'm in the room next to yours now. Come take a look," he said.

I followed him into his much larger room, the ambience of which, in stark contrast to mine, seemed to be the outcome of Parker's attentiveness to the latest trends. I looked around, in awe of the elaborate decor: several pieces of abstract art; a large bed in a dark, wooden frame adorned with black sheets, fluffy pillows, and a thick comforter; an electric and an acoustic guitar propped up next to each other; a full musical keyboard; a white-lacquered wooden desk with two flat-screen monitors on top; an exhaustive DVD collection; a flat-screen TV; a closet neatly organized with fashionable clothes; windows draped with shiny, silky curtains; a complete sound system; chic rugs; and a bookshelf filled with best-selling business books. I wondered if he'd hired an interior decorator, or, at the very least, modeled his room exactly after a photograph in a voguish home-furnishings catalogue.

"I've had a long time to put this room together ... over the years," he said.

"Very impressive."

"You know, you're moving in at a great time—we're having a party this weekend."

"Oh yeah?"

"Our parties are infamous. Everyone tries to get in, so we have to make guest lists and hire bouncers—shit like that," he said, as my mind drifted to a Friday night during my freshman year in college when my roommate and I, on a mission to meet some girls, strolled down frat row and stopped in front of a house party. When we tried to walk in, a large bouncer, flanked by a few rookie frat boys with proprietary smirks on their faces, blocked our entry and said that the party was limited to members of the fraternity and their guests.

"You'll get the experience soon enough," Parker continued, breaking me from my trance. "More important to the time being, you should get settled, then I'll take you out to celebrate your first night in the house. You'll meet the others in the house later, also," he said.

"Sounds good, Parker. I appreciate it."

Back in my new room, I listened to music from my laptop, as I lay on the wood floor with my hands joined behind my head and thought about how Parker had hinted at the lifestyle of a resident at the Sunset House. I wondered if I knew what I was doing or what type of lifestyle I was willingly signing up for, but finally took comfort in the idea that experiencing something completely unfamiliar to me, something previously off my radar, was part of my plan—reminding me of the day, when I was a young boy, that I'd gone around my house setting my family's dog on high tables or benches or the hoods of my parents' cars, so that he could see the world from a new perspective.

I read the headlines on CNN.com, had a brief online chat with an old high-school acquaintance, and then wrote short thank-you messages to some of the people who'd commented on my short story. After accepting a friend request from Rin Tin Tin, I briefly browsed his pictures, the majority of which were shots of him playing music in front of a sweaty, hands-in-the-air, tongues-sticking-out crowd. He seemed to be quite a prolific sharer, sometimes several posts a day, of self-aggrandizing photographs and his personal—some snarky, some incendiary—thoughts. I closed my laptop and plucked *The Complete Stories* by Flannery O'Connor from my row of books along the wall and read for a while, until I fell asleep. Hours later, when the little window in my room showed black outside, I awoke to Parker's voice.

"Why did you go buy those new sheets if you're just going to sleep on the floor?"

"I don't sleep very well in a bed," I said.

"You sleep pretty damn good on a floor though," he said.

"I didn't get much sleep last night."

"Vodka or whiskey?" he asked, holding a bottle of each.

"Whiskey."

"OK, we'll start with whiskey. We can share the bottle as we get ready. By the way, I hung some clothes on your door … for tonight. Your clothes won't really work for this place."

"Thanks," I said, amused by the thought that people never seemed to want me to wear my own clothes. *My fashion sense must be terrible …*

He went back into his room, turned on the music—which blasted from his speakers with a thunderous roar, causing the floor to vibrate and the walls to shake—and came back into my room pumping his right arm to the bass.

"Dubstep is the music of choice in this house. You ever listen to Rusko or Zomboy or guys like that?" he shouted over the music. I shook my head. "What about Skrillex? I bet you've heard of him. He's more brostep but whatever."

"No, I don't think so," I shouted back.

"You can feel this shit in your fucking core. Wait … here it comes—it's going to really drop hard."

He raised his hand slowly, matching the rise of the music, and then, on the right key, dropped his hand and jerked his head to a repetitive, distorted grind that sounded almost like a chain saw and ripped at my insides like one, too. My initial impulse was to plug my ears, but watching Parker dance—his eyes tightly closed, his arm pumping, and his head bouncing—gave me a momentary understanding of the sound's appeal, as I began to subtly bob my own head: I thought it was music that could invigorate anyone with life no matter how dead he was inside.

I sipped from the bottle of whiskey, and, not sure what to do while Parker danced, watched him until the song ended. He opened his eyes and said, "Rin Tin Tin is spinning tonight at this club. We always get in free wherever he spins. Also, Brad is working the door—another one of your roommates."

"Nice. Do you have work tomorrow?"

"Yeah, but I work from home."

"I'll shower and be ready in a few minutes."

I handed him the bottle, but, after he took a large swig, he handed it back to me and said, "Keep it. It's good to have during a shower."

I showered and dressed in Parker's clothes and found him sitting naked at his desk, smoking a cigarette and sifting through a girl's Facebook photographs; when he noticed me, he said, "Fuck, she's gorgeous, isn't she? She might be there tonight. If not, who cares—she's right here whenever I want her," he said, tugging at his flaccid cock and smiling at me. "Ready to go?"

I laughed and said, "I'm ready."

After he dressed in clothes that were nearly indistinguishable from the ones he'd given me, we walked downstairs and Parker said, "Let's pound a beer before we go and then take one for the road."

We took four beers from the refrigerator and opened two; tilting my head back, I let the cold beer stream down my throat and pour over the warm whiskey already in my belly. *I feel damn good.* We walked out the front door, each sipping from our other can of beer, and, as Parker carried on obliviously, I paused to take in the view of a majestic city burning with fluorescence. The billboards, the palm trees along the sidewalk, the tiny, lighted windows of rooms in distant buildings and hotels, the fronts and backs of passing cars and taxis, the eyes and teeth of giant Oprah—all of it, under the fluorescent lighting, bled together and emanated blotchy blazes of vivid color, as if the scene was too much for the eyes to absorb all at once. And although the sky directly above me was flawlessly black, the horizon was still tinged with a streak of glowing orange. It was all part of my new view from my new balcony at my new house. *I live in West Hollywood!*

"Let's go, man," Parker said. "We need to get there and get ourselves some of the bottle before it gets too crazy."

We descended the levels of the property and then went through the gate and down the ramp; after finishing our beers and throwing the empty cans into a bin at the base of the ramp, Parker hailed a cab and told the driver, "Take us to Hollywood and Cahuenga. I'll tell you where to go from there."

"No problem," the driver said.

"Can I smoke in here?" Parker asked, already lighting his cigarette.

"Roll down the window," the driver said.

"The most important thing about LA," Parker said to me, pausing to thumb his phone and then flick his cigarette ash out the window, "is eye contact. No one does it anymore; everyone is too distracted. So, by doing it you set yourself apart from the rest of them, and then, you'll notice, getting into places, making connections, getting pussy, all of it becomes much easier. If you want something, just make eye contact, and it'll be yours. If you want pussy, just look her in the eyes until she looks you in the eyes, and then hold your gaze steady until she looks away. When she looks back, you've got her. It's that simple, man. That's Los Angeles." He pulled out a flask from his back pocket, took a drink, and handed it to me. "Just remember that it's all bullshit, man. Don't be nervous around the girls. Men in lab coats create the scent of women's perfume. Women smell the way us guys think they should smell. Knowing *that* will help you. It's just shit, man—complete fucking bullshit."

Within ten minutes, we arrived in front of a club, and Parker paid the driver. We joined a herd surging toward the entrance, as if we were barn animals charging the fresh trough that had just been filled with the evening meal. At least a hundred people—smoking, texting, posting, shouting, pacing, arguing—were waiting in line, and several large bouncers, blocking the entrance to the club, waddled around like angry walruses in black suits wearing headsets. When Parker walked in front of the massive line to talk with a bouncer, I felt intimidated by the hundreds of furious eyes on me.

"Jake, up here, dude," Parker said, noticing that I remained several feet behind him.

I put my head down and walked over to him.

"Wait here," the bouncer said before speaking into his headset.

Parker gave me the look a dissatisfied mentor gives his pupil in the early stages of training. "See this?" he said, pointing to the line and then to the bouncers crowding the entrance. "It doesn't mean anything. It's all bullshit, man."

"Parker Thomas!" someone yelled from behind the entrance.

I saw the guy squirm his way through the bouncers, who tolerated his passing, but, in their body language, showed their contempt for him.

"How's it, brother?" he said to Parker.

"Meet Jake. He just moved in today. I'm taking him out for his first night," Parker said.

"No shit? You're fucked," he said to me, laughing. "Welcome to the house."

"Brad lives at the house with us and promotes this club," Parker said.

"Good to meet you," I said to Brad.

"So what's up? Are we good?" Parker said to Brad.

"Yeah, come in. No worries," he said, as he unhooked the rope and let us through. "These two are with me," he said to the bouncers. He gave Parker and me bright green wristbands. "Put these on."

He led us through a door and down a short hallway that opened up to a dark, glowing room packed with sweaty, moving bodies.

"I have to handle some shit. I'll stop by the table in a bit," Brad said before darting off.

On the right side of the room, thirsty nightclubbers clustered around a long bar, as overworked bartenders scurried around taking their drink orders. On the left, tables lined the wall, and further down, in some sort of hierarchal fashion, the tables became booths, and then the booths became larger booths; those inhabiting the tables and booths helped themselves to bottles of liquor from fancy buckets filled with ice in the center of the table. A few waitresses, dressed in black lingerie and carrying sparklers that rained blue and yellow sparks over the crowd, delivered two bottles of champagne to one booth. A group of girls in the back, using thick Crayola markers, drew shapes all over each other's faces.

The music, the same type Parker had danced to in my room, boomed and reverberated throughout the club, rattling my rib cage. A sea of electrically charged people in trancelike states—on a sweeping dance floor in the center of the room—moved to the beat in synchrony, as if all of them were wind-up toys programmed to a certain repetitive movement. The girls, with their legs hip-width apart, jerked their lower torsos back and forth to the beat while flipping their heads from side to side; the guys stood tall and narrow and threw one arm forward repeatedly, as if they were attacking invisible enemies with tomahawks; some danced while hoisting their phones high above their heads to capture the scene. And everyone was focused on the DJ—my new housemate, Rin Tin Tin. The dancers honored him—their musical god, the creator of the sound that set them all free—with a lemming-like praise; the girls worshipped him by shaking their asses toward him, the guys chopped their hands in his direction, and they all cheered for him.

Rin Tin Tin stood hunched over his equipment—his right shoulder holding headphones up to his right ear, his hands turning dials and readjusting switches, his body bouncing along with the crowd. He was a master at teasing his followers, tickling them with the touch of a button or the flick of his wrist, slowly introducing new sounds and letting them rise up in intensity until no one could take it anymore. When the escalation of the music could reach no greater height, like the car on a roller coaster hitting the highest point before the great plunge, a wave of anticipation rolled through the crowd, little yelps of pleasure erupted like tiny volcanoes all over the floor, and the dancers held their hands high in the air. Then, Rin Tin Tin, indulging his followers, dropped the synthesized beat, and the room went wild with screams and cheers and lights and lasers. *My God, this is something.*

"Jake!" Parker yelled through the noise before appearing at my side. "There you are, man. We have a table over here. Come on."

I followed him through the crowd and toward one of the nicer booths.

"I'll get you a drink," Parker said, shoving his way through the crowd at the booth.

Two Persian girls—tall, thin, with caramel skin and huge breasts—walked up to me. "And who are you?" one of them yelled over the music.

"Jake," I shouted back and, sensing they weren't satisfied with my answer, "I just moved into the Sunset House with Parker."

They both laughed. "You'll be seeing plenty of us, then," the same girl said. "I'm Yaas and this is Lily."

"Nice to meet you two ... too," I said, awkwardly.

"Ha ha, he looks so innocent, doesn't he?" Lily said, giving her friend a look. "Is this your first time living in Hollywood?"

"Yes."

They both laughed again. "Are you ready for this shit, Jake?" Yaas asked, smiling, raising her eyebrows and playfully nudging me.

"I'm not sure," I said.

"Lily," Yaas said, "what do you say we show Jake a good time tonight?"

"Jake, have you ever had a threesome with two girls who have fake tits?" Lily said, moving closer to me.

"Nope. Never," I said, as they giggled, seemingly enjoying my timidity.

Parker came back with a bottle of vodka and two glasses filled with ice.

"Here, Jake, take some from the bottle real quick, and then I'll pour us a drink," Parker said to me.

I grabbed the bottle from him and took a mouthful; he did the same and then poured vodka into the two glasses with ice and handed one to me. I nodded my thanks.

Parker looked at the two girls and said indifferently, "Hey, Yaas. Hey, Lily."

"Who's the new guy, Parker? Your new best friend?" Yaas said.

"Suck a dick, Yaas," he said, which made the girls giggle again.

"Hey, follow me," Parker said to me.

We maneuvered through the crowd and went into the bathroom. Parker signaled me to come into his stall, and, when we were both inside and the door was locked, he pulled from his back pocket plastic wrap twisted tightly several times around a pure white, chalky rock. With enough sense to understand what was happening, I suddenly felt trapped in the stall and consumed with apprehension: my hands trembled and my heart palpitated.

"Let me mash it up a little bit," Parker said, breaking the rock into little pieces with his fingers and then rubbing the pieces together until they turned to a fine powder; then, with a key, he scooped out a fresh, powdery mound and put it under my nostril.

"Wait ... how much is too much? Can I overdose from that much?" I said, quivering.

He laughed. "First time?"

"Yes."

"Ha, dude, you're fine. It's barely anything. Just breathe it in normally—you don't have to snort it all crazy like they do in the movies."

I looked down at the key under my nose and thought about running out of the stall. But I didn't. I stayed. *Fuck it.* I breathed it in, as he'd instructed, and promptly felt a concentrated rush of wonderful energy to my brain—the top of my scalp tingled, my facial hair tickled my skin, my eyes surged open—and the apprehension I'd experienced just seconds before was ousted by a happy-to-be-alive confidence. The stall that used to confine me became the enclosed territory I presided over as a crowned king.

"Wow, that's intense," I said to Parker who, being fair to both of his nostrils, was busy helping himself to far more than he'd given me.

"Told you. Here, have another," he said, scooping out more for me; after taking it in, I felt, to my surprise, even better than before. "OK, let's go," he said. "I'll have it ready when you want some more."

Still wearing my crown, I walked out of the stall, unconcerned with the impatience of those who'd been waiting and indifferent to the obviousness of what I'd just been doing. Parker playfully slapped the bathroom attendant on the shoulder with a smooth nonchalance as we sauntered out of the bathroom, bringing the joy from the stall with us.

"Wait here," he said in the hallway before walking out toward the bar.

I happily looked around at all the people near me and even nodded, with a smile on my face, at a few strangers. My upper gums felt numb, and, with my tongue, I rubbed back and forth on them; the numbness then expanded to the front part of my upper jaw and my teeth, reminding me of the feeling I'd had once after Novocain injections from the dentist—at the point when the feeling started to return but some of the numbness was still there.

Parker came back holding two beers. "Here ..." he said, giving one to me. "Nothing better than a cold beer after some blow. Let's go outside."

We walked out the back door to a patio, where everyone was smoking, and Parker, removing a pack of cigarettes from his back pocket, put one in his mouth and handed one to me. "It'll intensify the feeling."

What else does this guy have in his back pocket? He lit mine before lighting his, and then we both took a deep drag. He was right. I felt the smoke rush into my lungs and cling to the blood my heart was pumping to my brain. I felt light and wonderful, as if the smoke had unlocked the safe in my brain that stored all my endorphins, and let them loose inside me like hundreds of colorful balloons. I felt the urge to be chatty: I wanted to tell Parker about Liz and ask him about his life in Los Angeles and what his greatest memories were, or tell him how much fun we'd have together and everything else. But he started a conversation first.

"I read some of your story, man," he said.

"What?"

"I was researching you earlier and came across your blog. I don't normally read shit like that, but I was into it from the beginning."

"I appreciate it, man."

"So that's what you want to do? Be a writer?"

"I think so."

"Cool, man. I'd say stick with it. I like having talented friends who do cool shit."

"Yeah, we'll see. I'm glad I live in the house now—I'm excited for a change."

"You have no idea," Parker said. "Here, take a quick one," he said, pulling out the bag, swooping stealthily into it with his key, digging up another snowy mound, and shoving it under my nose.

I breathed it in and felt some of it drip down my throat; I swallowed a few times and felt it numb my esophagus on the way down. I felt so high and alive. I guessed that Parker was feeling that way, too, because over the next several minutes we went off on a series of chatty tangents: he told a story, I interrupted him, I told a story, he interrupted me, I said something, he passionately agreed, he said something, I passionately agreed, and then we complimented each other's points of view.

"Remember one thing tonight ..." he said, starting to walk back inside.

"What's that?"

"Make sure you find a girl before one thirty."

Back at the table, he made us each another drink, and I sipped mine cautiously. Parker, however, guzzled his whole drink in one swig, and his eyes glassed themselves with a blue emptiness. I said something to him, but, not hearing me or perhaps not processing it, he turned around and walked off toward the dance floor. I had a glimpse of him a few minutes later dancing with a girl.

The two girls I'd met earlier, Yaas and Lily, were in front of the booth taking pictures of themselves, studying the results, laughing, and then taking more pictures. One girl, sitting in the booth, lowered her face to the table and snorted cocaine from a key—something I would have normally overlooked if I hadn't just been introduced to that world.

Yaas and Lily, noticing me, impishly walked over and positioned themselves on both sides of my body; I held up my drink as they bounced against me to the music. When Lily detached herself from me to thumb her phone, Yaas kissed me on the cheek, said, "Let's go get freaky-deaky," and pulled me to the edge of the dance floor. I was too high to keep a rhythm with even the simplest repetitive bassline, but I danced with her anyway.

A lanky, bearded, squinty-eyed photographer, wearing skinny jeans and a leather jacket with a hood pulled over his head, came along, and, with a digital SLR, snapped several photographs of us dancing; Yaas, seemingly ready for him, naturally assumed her pose, while I stood awkwardly looking into the camera. The photographer was flanked by an attractive, hippyish, wild-eyed girl with thick curly hair, who used her phone to take photographs of the photographer taking photographs.

"Brilliant," the photographer said, looking down at and admiring the images he'd just captured.

"Let me see them before you post," Yaas demanded.

"Fine. Fine," he said, showing her the images.

"Erase the first one. Don't post the first one," she said, almost scolding him.

"Whatever you say, Yaas. Whatever you say," he said.

"Let me see you erase it," Yaas said.

While he let Yaas watch him delete it, his wild-eyed partner snapped a photo of them and studied the image. "That's fucking beautiful—she's protecting her memories." And then both photographers vanished into the crowd.

Yaas and I continued dancing, and, when she pulled my face close to hers, I kissed her lips but she pulled away. "I want to but … I can't. I'm sorry," she said, walking away.

I looked around the club, and, in that instant, realized how inebriated I was; the repetitive boom of the music, the sea of sweaty dancers, the bright, flashing lights, the glaring lasers, and the smoke Rin Tin Tin released into the crowd blended into a blurry mass that came toward me in a halting rhythm, as if it were a giant, blobby puppet guided by jerky strings. *I need to go home.*

I hailed a cab outside and told the driver, "Get on Sunset and go west until I say something," and when we reached the base of the steep ramp in front of the Sunset House, I told him, "This is fine," gave him a twenty, wobbled up the four levels to my bedroom, and fell, like a giant redwood tree, onto my bed.

I was awakened (a few hours later?) by a booming bass, pounding the inside of my head, rattling the four little panes of my window, and shaking my bed on the wood floor. Groggy, heavy-eyed, and already hungover, I plugged my ears with my fingers, and, after that didn't stifle the loudness, tried putting in earphones with different music and burying my head under several pillows. Still, the music coming from downstairs was far too overpowering, so I gave up trying to find peace and left my room.

The bass was blasting from the sound system under the TV in the living room. I didn't recognize any of the twenty or thirty people dancing, because, in the darkness, they all looked the same, with their darkly shadowed bodies and their vacant, pallid, laser-lit faces—the only hint of their aliveness coming from their bright eyes bouncing around like fireflies on a dark, country road.

"You must be the new roommate," someone said from behind me.

I turned around to a short, plump Asian guy with spiked black hair and sharp, greenish brown eyes, wearing a red leather jacket and a V-necked T-shirt that revealed most of his chest and a gold chain. And, next to him, clutching his hand with both of hers, was a fair-skinned girl—sucking on a lollipop and wearing hardly anything at all—with short brown hair done in two pigtails.

"Yeah," I said. "I'm Jake."

"I'm Jackson, one of your roommates, and this is my girlfriend, Jenny," he said, gesturing toward her.

Almost a head taller than her boyfriend, she was smiling with her lips closed over the lollipop, swaying to the music, tossing her head from side to side like a happy little girl, and other than a quick look in my direction from the corner of her eye, she didn't acknowledge our introduction.

"Come with us to our room," he said.

"OK."

We walked outside, down to the deck, and into their "room"—which was more like a small house—with a full kitchen and sitting area, a living room with a large TV, a bedroom, a bathroom with a Jacuzzi-sized bath, and a walk-in closet almost the size of my entire room.

"Jesus, nice room," I said.

"Thanks."

In the light, I could see that his pupils were as large as pancakes. His girlfriend, Jenny, who still hadn't said a word, was swaying and smiling by his side. The three of us sat around the kitchen table, the surface of which was clear glass, and Jackson took out a ziplock bag holding several rocks of cocaine; he dropped one of the rocks on the table, mashed it up with a credit card, minced it to a fine powder, and then separated out six white lines that reminded me of fat, albino slugs inching across the glass.

"We shouldn't do too much since we're coming down off the E," he said and then, after handing me one half of a straw, "You first."

I used the straw to vacuum up a line. The rush returned to my head, and although the intensity was a little less powerful than it was earlier, my headache and hangover instantly disappeared.

"How long have you been living at the house?" I asked him.

"About nine months now," he said, coming up from snorting a line.

"That's cool. Are you working?"

"Not right now. Just kinda hanging, trying to figure it out, you know?"

"Yeah."

His girl, Jenny, picked up the straw, pulled the lollipop out of her mouth and stopped bouncing and swaying just long enough to snort her line; when she came upright, she was smiling wider. We each did another line, and then Jackson, reading my mind or perhaps a victim of a dry mouth himself, walked to the fridge and brought us back a few beers. I cracked mine open and drank much of it down, but my senses were gone, and I couldn't taste it; still, it felt good to wet the inside of my mouth.

"Let's go back up and party," Jackson said.

We walked up a level, and in the Jacuzzi sat two guys and two topless girls, all of them staring vacuously through each other; the girls' breasts floated on the water like flesh-colored balloons.

"You want one?" Jackson said.

"What?" I said, before realizing he was referring to a cigarette from the pack he was fingering through. "Oh, sure."

"Here, take the whole fucking thing. I've smoked a pack already," he said, tossing me the pack.

We smoked and drank on the balcony, until Jenny tugged Jackson's arm, and he said, "Well, we're gonna go dance. Good meeting you, man. See you around."

"Take care," I said.

When I realized I was licking my gums like a crazy person, I took a big mouthful of beer and kept it there for a few seconds before swallowing; then I lit another cigarette and watched, far down below, yellow cabs zoom by and drunken pedestrians wander aimlessly.

"Hey, man, you need anything?" said a guy who'd crept over to me.

"Huh?"

"I have everything: blow, E, molly, Vicodin, percs, acid, everything," he said.

"I'm fine."

"I know I shouldn't be selling shit here because of Jackson, but I'm just trying to make some quick cash—then I'll leave."

"Really, I'm fine, thanks," I said.

"Let me know, man," he said, walking away.

Back in my room, I locked my door and lay on my bed and stared at the ceiling; when my mouth got too dry, I angled my can of beer over my lips and let some pour in. I closed my eyes. My thoughts came to me in little flashes of white light that exploded against the backs of my eyelids. I opened my eyes again, set my beer down on the floor, and clenched my head at the temples with my open palms. *Please slow down.* I lit another cigarette from Jackson's pack and smoked it. Soon after, I heard Parker go into his room with a giggly girl, and, through the apparently thin walls, heard them fucking, until they went silent. The music downstairs carried on for another two hours before it, too, went silent. The sun came up an hour after that, and, a few minutes later, I fell asleep.

I awoke to my own violent coughing, and, realizing I couldn't breathe through my nose and that my mouth was parched like the summer desert, I lurched forward in a bit of a panic. In the bathroom, I put my mouth under the running faucet, at first just rinsing and spitting but then taking short, quick gulps of water.

"Oh my God," I said, coming up for air.

I felt terrible, as if everything inside me had been gnarled and mangled and my internal organs had shriveled down to little black raisins, and, with a single touch, my brittle, hollow bones would collapse into a pile of dust. My head throbbed, and my face was swollen. I tried blowing my nose but, being so congested, nothing happened. When I heard a knock at my door, I limped over and opened it to Parker holding an unopened can of beer in one hand and a bottle of nose spray in the other.

"I heard you struggling in here," he said, and after handing both things to me, "Just get a couple good sprays up in there. Once you can breathe, the headache will go away. The beer will balance you out."

"Thanks," I said, as his bedroom door creaked open, and Yaas slithered out.

"Oh ... hey," she said to me, and I nodded at her.

Parker didn't turn around to acknowledge her. She made a gesture to me to indicate that she was leaving, then she tiptoed down the hallway and turned right down the stairs.

"You went home alone last night, huh?" he said.

"The end of the night was pretty hazy for me."

"Yeah, I blacked out early. I don't remember anything after midnight," he said.

I walked back into the bathroom, jammed the bottle of nose spray up one of my nostrils and pumped it, but the spray flowed back out of my nose, as if it had hit an impenetrable wall, and dripped down my upper lip. I sprayed a few more times in each nostril and sucked in strongly, almost theatrically, but nothing happened, until finally, after one unforgettable pump, my nasal passage opened up and fresh oxygen shot into my brain. I took a big drink of beer. I *did* feel much better.

"Come into my room, and let's find out what happened last night," Parker said. And then when we were in his room, he said, "This guy and his girlfriend take pictures of us when we go out, and then he posts them either later that night or the next morning. It's perfect. It's like"—he paused to pull up the guy's Facebook profile—"watching a slide show of all the shit you don't remember from the night before."

I looked at the guy's main profile photograph and remembered him as the photographer who snapped photos of Yaas and me on the dance floor. "I remember that guy."

"We wouldn't have any good memories without him. He has a popular nightlife website. But he posts everything here, too. Found it," he said, bringing up the album with all the previous night's photographs and rapidly skimming through them until he saw one of himself with a girl. "*God*, she's a babe. Look at her."

"She *is* cute."

"I'm stoked I was dancing with such a babe. I wonder why she didn't come home with me," he said, clicking to the next picture of the two of them. "Jake, look at her. She's so fucking gorgeous—I'd suck a fart out of her ass." And then at the next picture, he said, "*Look* at her, man. Does she look like she was into me?"

"Yeah, she does," I said, obliging him.

"She had to have been into me."

"I bet she was."

"I wonder how I lost her."

"Maybe she didn't want to go home with you ... you know ... the first night she met you."

He laughed and said, "Jake, girls want to fuck, too—remember that. Hey, look at you. Dancing with Yaas, huh?" he said, pointing to a picture of her posing, and me, the stoned fool, staring into the camera.

"I didn't realize you two—"

"You didn't realize what?" he said, cutting me off.

"That you were—"

He laughed again. "We're nothing. I don't even remember being with her last night. When I woke up, she was there, slobbering on my pillow. I can't stand the girl. She's insane—literally fucking crazy."

"Really?" I said.

"And she's a starfish in bed—just lies still with her legs spread out and her arms up like a goddamn starfish. Every time I fuck her I have to do the Jedi mind thing just to make myself come. I focus and tell myself that I have to come. 'I *will* come,' I say in my head. But I never understand why she just lies there like that. It might be different for you though," he said.

"No, it's fine. It's not like that."

"Now, let's see if we can get a closer look at my babe," he said, ignoring me, as he finished browsing the night's photographs and then clicked through to his dancing partner's profile. "You can tell a lot about a girl by the profile pics she chooses to represent herself. See, look at this girl … partying, and another one of her partying," he said, rapidly clicking through her pictures. "Oh, look, she's backstage. She wants to show the world that *she* was cool enough to be backstage at a concert. A picture of her legs by the pool. One of her in a bikini. You really make a statement by making one of your main pictures a bikini shot. Look— she does the same pose again and again and again, see? So we get it: this girl wants to be seen as a cool partier. Not very original. Boring. Cliché. Still a babe, but I'm over it."

I laughed.

"We all have a weakness in trying to impress people with our online identity—sometimes the pattern is very easy to pick up, and that's just fucking embarrassing, you know? The trick is to make it hard to detect," he said.

"Show me an example of a girl who does it right," I said.

"Sure," he said, typing a name into the search field. "Look at this girl. So hot, right?"

"Yeah, sure."

"Look at her pictures—firing a machine gun in Thailand, lying on railroad tracks … Look—she's driving a *fucking semi* on the freeway in this one. Who do you know that drives a semi on the freeway? You can tell she's beautiful, but she doesn't excessively flaunt it. This is a cool babe with cool photos."

"I see," I said.

"And then you, Jake Reed—you have one profile picture to represent yourself. You're in a T-shirt staring at the camera, not even smiling. It looks like you took the picture with your shitty webcam. I love that."

I gave him a half-smile and a shrug.

"You excited about this weekend?" he asked.

"This weekend?"

"Yeah, man, I told you, we're having a huge party—Saturday night."

"That's right, I forgot. Do we have to set up the place?"

"No, given our prime location, we get sponsored by this liquor company. They set up all the shit and provide their booze until it runs out. So keep a stash of something you like to drink in your room. Rin Tin Tin sets up on the main deck outside and plays until the cops come, and then he plays until they come again, and then he moves it inside and plays some more," he said.

"Jesus," I said.

"We have a pretty big guest list. You want to add anyone? If they aren't on the list, they can't come in."

"I don't know anyone around here."

"You will. Oh, by the way, Tin told me some famous blogger is coming to our party. You should talk to her."

"She's famous?" I said.

"Well, Internet famous, you know," he said.

"What does she blog about?"

"No idea. You want another beer?"

"You don't have to work today?" I asked, hoping to get some writing done.

"Already made a few phone calls while you were sleeping. The luxury of working from home," he said.

Rin Tin Tin walked into the room wearing bright green shoes. "Do you guys like these shoes?"

"Yeah, cool shit," Parker said.

Rin Tin Tin glared at me.

"Yep," I said, nodding.

"I'm wearing them for our party. I'm going to post a photo of them in a few minutes. Can you guys give it some love?"

"Sure thing, my man," Parker said.

Rin Tin Tin glared at me again.

"Sure," I said, nodding again.

"Thank you," he said, storming out of the room.

"I'm going to take a shower, then let's order some food," Parker said to me.

"Sounds good."

I left his room and went back into mine. I sat on the floor and picked up a book I'd already read, skimmed a few pages, and, in the process, stumbled upon a section I remembered really enjoying and read until the chapter's end.

"Fuck! Goddammit! Fucker! You fuck!" Rin Tin Tin screamed from his room.

I set my book down, walked down the hall and into his room, where I found him hovering over his keyboard, slamming his finger down repeatedly on the refresh button as he stared at the screen, presumably waiting, or hoping, for something to happen.

"What's wrong?" I asked him.

"Not one of my 4,000 friends 'liked' my latest post."

"Maybe give it a little time, for people to, you know, see it …" I said.

"No, wrong, dude—if people don't start 'liking' it and commenting on it right away, it won't catch. Sometimes it catches once the first person paves the way. Can you make a comment, man? You said you would."

"Yeah, sure, no problem," I said.

I went back into my room, opened my laptop, made a short, complimentary comment on the photograph of his shoes—something I thought he'd like—and walked back into his room.

"Did that help?" I asked.

"Fuck! Still nothing. There's no way it's the photo—look, those shoes have swag. It must be my caption. I'm erasing it," he said, banging the refresh button one last time. "You're a writer, aren't you? Can't you think of a witty caption?" he said in a panicky tone.

"I'm not really—"

"I got it!" he said, erasing the post and starting over. "OK, same photo, new caption—posting now," he said, clicking the post button, then refreshing the screen a few times. "Yes!" he yelled, watching his social network victories pile up. "I'm good."

ELEVEN

It was Saturday afternoon, the day of our party. In the living room, all the residents of the Sunset House—Parker, the house manager; Brad, the club promoter; Rin Tin Tin, the DJ; Jackson and Jenny, the couple; two others I hadn't yet met; and me—were sitting on the couch, drinking beer, and eating cheap Thai food out of Styrofoam containers.

Parker introduced me to the two housemates I didn't know. "This is Levi and that's Drew. Levi makes videos, and Drew is a singer." And then he said to them, "This is Jake—he's a writer."

Eight of us sat comfortably on the enormous L-shaped couch with our laptops open on our laps, the screens casting pale light on our faces as we stared numbly down at them. While reruns of Jayson's reality show played, almost inaudibly, on the TV in the background, we were all displaying a certain behavioral pattern that—after the point in our lives when laptops had become supplements to our bodies—we'd nearly perfected: rapidly type a few words, open a new tab or window, scroll down, scroll up, click back to a previous tab or window, type again, breathe, take two quick bites of food, take a sip of a drink, check phone, glance at the TV, and repeat. We'd become seasoned veterans of human multitasking.

I had several unread emails in my inbox, most of them notifications from more people commenting on or sharing my short story, or following me or friending me. But there were also a few messages from my mother—her latest one being, "Will you at least send me your address? I'd like to mail you something"—one from Andrew, and another from the mysterious Stone Fox.

From: <u>Andrew Martin</u>
To: <u>Jake Reed</u>

Jake,

You doing all right, friend? I haven't heard back from you. People are wondering about you. What should I tell them? When are you coming home?

Also, something has come up ... When I went to the Thai place for dinner (it's strange without you there), Tamarine said she had a little scuffle with her boss, and now she needs a place to stay. Is it OK if she moves into the condo for a little while? I really do understand if it's not OK. But, if it is, maybe she can move into your room ... just until she figures something out? Things aren't looking too good for her. Her visa runs out in six months--she'll probably have to go back to Thailand. Just trying to help her out. On the MBA application to USC there's a section to talk about community service. Well, I think trying to help her would be an impressive act of community service. Don't you?

Cordially,
Andrew

I clicked reply.

From: <u>Jake Reed</u>
To: <u>Andrew Martin</u>

Sorry about the delay. News of Steve's death put me in a funk for a bit ... Anyway, just tell the neighbors I'm traveling for a while. And, sure, Tamarine can stay. I think it's good that you're trying to help her. Take care, friend.

--Jake

"Ha, you idiot," Levi said to Drew, breaking, for the first time in a while, the monotonous pitter-patter of fingers tapping on laptop keys.

"Crazy, right?" Drew said back to Levi; I guessed that they'd been chatting on the Internet and part of their online exchange had carried over into the physical world.

"Attention, everyone in the room," Levi said, as all the screen-lit faces slowly elevated and focused on him. "I've been hired to make a video for a luxury rental car company, and I have artistic freedom to make anything I want, dependent upon approval by them, of course. But here's the thing: I don't get paid unless the video gets one million views, and I get a large bonus if it hits ten million views. Anyone have any bright ideas? Jake, you're a writer, right?"

"The goal is that this company rents more cars, right?" I asked.

"Too much, Jake. Let's think views ... They care about views," he said, as the room unexpectedly came alive with chatter.

"Use animals," Drew said.

"Yeah, get a dog to do something funny on camera," Rin Tin Tin said.

"Yeah, use puppies!" Jenny said in a high-pitched voice, smiling and still slightly swaying to the music in her head. It was the first time I'd heard her speak.

"Babies ... Do you have access to any babies?" Jackson said, creepily.

"Take two really expensive cars and crash them together. You don't have to damage the real cars—you can just cheat it," Brad said.

"All of the above—put a bunch of babies together, a bunch of animals together, and then crash two really nice cars, all in the same video," Parker said.

"Yeah, and keep it under a minute," Jackson said.

"No, make it under thirty seconds," Drew said.

"Ten to fifteen seconds would be best—you have to give the people what they want," Rin Tin Tin said.

Give the people what they want. I wondered who the "people" in question were and then imagined a huge room of faceless humans sitting side by side—in front of their laptops, at rectangular tables stretching for miles—as they scrolled endlessly down the screen, 'liking,' commenting, sharing, but never reaching the bottom, because it didn't exist. The scrolling would go on for eternity, because there was always more scrolling to do. Maybe, I thought, they were paid by the amount of 'likes' and comments and shares they gave back to the world, but, because there was always more scrolling to do, they were never able to use the money; it would just pile up in their bank accounts until they died, and then it would be passed to their offspring, who'd also never be able to use it because they would have already fallen behind on their own scrolling.

When I stopped daydreaming, the room was silent again, except for the familiar sound of people typing, which reminded me of raindrops hitting pavement. I read the email from Stone Fox.

From: <u>Stone Fox</u>
To: <u>Jake Reed</u>

Mr. Reed,

It seems that *someone* hasn't posted any new writing in a while. Jake, you have to keep writing your words as often as you can, because, otherwise, they'll dry up and be gone forever. Writing, for you, will become a distant memory of an old hobby. *Trust me.*

I had a dream of being a writer once, but, unfortunately, it was something I could never pursue. Why? Because I'm deathly afraid of failure--the mere hint of it has the power to keep me bedridden for weeks.

But you ... you might still have a chance if you keep at it.

In my world, where everyone is seemingly the same, I'm constantly reminded of how different and lonely I am. I often feel overwhelmed with confusion--enough to drive me crazy. My solution (to quell my uneasiness) is simply to expect nothing from everyone--this way, I can at least get through the day without hyperventilating. Weird, right?

See, I'm the worst breed of human. Let me explain. Some people are dead inside. They go through life knowing this, and they manage fine enough, because, well, they're dead inside. They aren't bitter because they don't care enough to be. They just try to get by with the things they can control. Others live in the fucking clouds, watch romantic comedies, and dream about everything being perfect one day. These people are always fine because they have an everlasting well of hope inside them, and no matter what happens they'll just romanticize their existence.

But when it comes to me ... I'm someone who's mostly dead inside but still has a little hope for something extraordinary, which, as I said, is

175

the worst breed of human, because it means that I know everything is bullshit, but that I secretly hope for the day when it might not be. The tension makes me wish I were just completely dead inside. It would make things much easier for me. See that?

Anyway, then I met you, or read your writing rather, and now I feel connected to someone for the first time in ... forever. So, please, if you can't write for yourself, write for me.

Best,
Stone Fox

Who the hell puts this much thought and time into writing an email to a stranger on the Internet? I didn't know what to make of this outspoken, persistent, and strangely revealing Stone Fox character. Although I couldn't deny feeling connected to, even intrigued by, some of her thoughts about people, or, more important, the way she'd described herself (it reminded me a little of the way the psychic in Manhattan Beach had described me), I still couldn't deny the signs that she might be crazy. So I went to her blog—the title of it read, "One Simple Thought Every Day"—which appeared to be, as I scrolled down the page, exactly that: one of her thoughts posted every day. I read her latest entry:

BABIES

We have this desire to protect and take care of babies. Babies are cute. We all love babies. But this feeling extends to babies of other species: baby lions, baby dolphins, baby alligators, baby bears, baby anything. So it must be deeper than just our having the urge to take care of our own young. Perhaps it's the realization that babies of all species are existing in their purest state. *Innocence.* They have not been hardened by the world yet. And for us, babies evoke a feeling of nostalgia because we were once babies. And we want to go back to being babies. A baby wolf is the cutest thing in the world because it's not worried about survival. It's only driven by curiosity. The baby wolf changes when its mother, already hardened by survival, teaches it how to kill. And I think we all change when we begin to worry about survival. It hardens us. It makes us nonbelievers in enjoying our time. So, naturally, we long for the days when we were innocent little babies, because we know we can never go back to that. Back to that purity. Back to that curiosity. Life prohibits it. So what do we do? We spend our time thinking babies are the cutest things in the world. And where is the place to do that? YouTube.

I decided that, given her lengthy, seemingly candid email to me, I should respond to Stone Fox, at the very least to acknowledge her effort.

From: Jake Reed
To: Stone Fox

Stone Fox,

I promised myself that I'd write much more than I currently am. Thanks for giving me some new motivation.

Also, I read some of your blog today, your thoughts on babies, right after, coincidentally, my roommates discussed some of the same things. I prefer your eloquence. You have my interest.

Until next time,
Jake

"Time for some business," Jackson said, excitedly. He opened the backpack that had been resting at his feet and poured its contents onto the table: clear plastic bags of differently sized pills, cocaine, weed, and whatever else. "Here are the goodies for tonight, or whenever, for that matter," he said.

"Yes!" the guys said in unison, while Jenny's eyes brightened and her smile widened.

"Who wants what?" Jackson asked. "Of course, y'all know you get the roommate discount."

Jenny pointed to a bag of colorful pills and smiled at Jackson.

He looked at her and said, "Oh, I *know* what you want, don't worry." And then she smiled even wider.

"I'm rolling tonight, for sure," Rin Tin Tin said.

"No shit, when do you *not* roll?" Levi said.

"Fuck off, like you're one to talk," Rin Tin Tin said.

"Do you have any Molly?" Drew asked.

"Yep, sure do," Jackson said.

"I'll take a gram."

"Yeah, give me some of that, too," Brad said. "And what was that grass I smoked last time?"

"Master Kush," Jackson said.

"I'll take an eighth of Master Kush, also," Brad said.

"Me, too," Levi said. "Also, I need an eightball and some Klonopin."

"No problem," Jackson said, and then he looked at Parker.

"First and foremost, give me some fucking blow—I'll take an eight-ball for tonight. Give me four E pills—fuck Molly—and an eighth of Kush, as well," Parker said. "Oh, I'm out of Xanax. I'll need some more of that, too."

"Actually, fuck E and fuck Molly. Give me some GHB," Rin Tin Tin said.

"Oh, shit, how could I forget? I need some 5-HTP," Drew said.

"Me, too!" all the guys said in unison.

All of them had produced cash from their wallets, and I watched them work out their deals with Jackson.

"Anything else?" Jackson said, then looking at me, "Jake, what do you want?"

"Um—" I said.

"Here," he said, gathering all of his new cash and perhaps feeling happy about it, "welcome to the house," and threw me two thumb-sized ziplock bags of cocaine. "OK, since business is done, why don't we celebrate with a line each, huh?" And then, with a credit card, he scraped some coke into lines, and we each did one.

Parker and I stood on the balcony trading pulls of whiskey from the bottle and smoking cigarettes and closely watching the steep ramp for the first signs of party attendees. It was a chilly September night, at least for Los Angeles, and the sky was a cloudless black.

"When do you plan to take down your first girl in the house?" Parker said, while exhaling smoke from his lungs, distorting the sound of his voice.

"No plans," I said.

"You should probably do it soon. If not, it'll become this thing with all this pressure. I'd recommend getting it out of the way, and then everything else will fall into place for you," he said.

I brushed him off casually with a nod and a half-smile, and then watched the team of men on the deck below us organizing bottles of liquor at the bar, and Rin Tin Tin setting up his sound equipment. Parker, however, was staring at something else, much farther in the distance.

"Look at that fucking city ..." he said with a wistful flash of bright blue in his eyes. "There's so much fucking pussy in that city—pussy in those houses, pussy in those hotels, pussy in those taxis, pussy walking down the street, pussy everywhere. It's so wonderful to imagine all the fantastic pussy out there in that city and how good it'd be to have it all. But the fantasy only works when that pussy stays hidden out there in that city below us ... because when the pussy grows legs and arms and a body and a brain and hair—well, sometime during that development it becomes a girl. And that girl with a pussy comes walking up our ramp and into our house, and you get to meet that girl and talk to that girl ... And then you might get a chance to fuck that girl—but, my friend, here's the terrible news: once you fuck that girl, she becomes a real person ... and it's all over."

Just then, a taxi pulled halfway up the ramp, and several girls got out, readjusted themselves, and, with their legs shining under the fluorescent lights, walked up the rest of the ramp to the front of the gate. They were stopped by a giant bouncer, who flipped through some pages on his clipboard, made a few scribbles with his pen, and then let them pass. From the level we were on, we could watch them ascend for another thirty seconds before they would be within a conversational distance. Parker put a key with cocaine on it under my left nostril and I inhaled it; then he shoveled some into each of his own nostrils.

"Here we go," he said, walking away.

I stood alone on the balcony and watched more taxis drive up the ramp, more yellow doors open, and more eager people begin the climb to the desired destination of the evening—the large beacon of a house, the Sunset House, the place with the music, the place with the liquor, the place where everyone would live on forever in photographs. The guests morphed from tiny, faceless figures on the ramp into full-sized individuals on the deck just below me, most of them pausing, in the same spot I'd once chosen, to take pictures of the view. I made a game of trying to predict a characteristic of each tiny figure approaching my house—something that would remain true when he or she became a real person with eyes and a mouth and an expression right in front of me—and realized I was more drawn to the tiny figures in the distance, because they all shared something: a hurried, childlike excitement in their step, as if, unaware of being watched from above, their movements were purer. By the time they'd become real people in front of me, they'd retreated into the comfort of their rehearsed poses, and their faces only showed the expressions they wanted others to see. *I want to live in the tiny-person world.*

Still, the full versions of the people were far too interesting to ignore. I saw guys with thick, pointy beards, long hair, shaved heads, mohawks, earrings, full sleeves of tattoos, neck tattoos, face tattoos, tank tops, big-faced watches, silver-chained necklaces with crosses, big rings, hats with flipped-up bills, hoodies, top hats, beanies, square-rimmed black sun-glasses, skinny jeans, bright blue and green and yellow shoes, skin-tight shirts, multicolored wristbands, thick flannel shirts, shirts with animals printed on them, backpacks, ties over oxford shirts, leather jackets, pea coats, scarves, and, on one guy, a loose-fitting, thin black cloth that hung past his knees like a dress, showing his entire chest covered with a giant tattoo of an angel with its wings spread.

I saw girls with shiny dresses, big fur coats, black-rimmed glasses with clear lenses, sandals that coiled halfway up their legs, black tights and short shorts, denim shorts and high-heeled boots, tight, high-waist-ed jeans, leather pants, flowing white dresses, furry knee-high boots, scarves, leopard leotards, loose shirts with black bras underneath, little white T-shirts, bodysuits with hoodies, flowery dresses, bandanas, big hair, afros, long hair on one side and buzzed on the other, dyed blonde hair and dyed pink hair and dyed purple hair, feathers in their hair, big, shiny purses, black coats with gold trimming, lacy see-through shirts of black netting, and thick, gold necklaces. One of the most beautiful girls I saw all night was covered in tattoos. Some of the girls had suckers in their mouths.

Everyone carried a phone in one hand, and some also held a pack of cigarettes or a little camera or a bigger professional camera in the other hand.

The photographer from the club on my first night in Hollywood ap-peared at my side and snapped a photo of me smoking a cigarette and staring down at the crowd.

"The solo experience from the balcony above," he said in a slow, lulling, almost vacant tone. "Beautiful."

"So you're *the* photographer, huh?" I said.

"No, man, not a photographer, just a person. I capture ... fucking memories," he said, dragging the *s* for a second or two, almost hissing. "It's not about the photo; it's about the memory—two different things, man."

"That's cool," I said, enjoying him.

"Yeah, man, I love getting fucked up and creating art with memories," he said, as his wild-eyed companion appeared—her knees slightly bent to indicate that she was in concentration mode—and, with her phone, took pictures of us talking. "It brings joy to people's lives. And my girl here takes pictures of me in the process, so I have my own memories."

"To really enjoy a party," the girl said in a voice just as slow and lulling as her companion's, "you have to let loose and get really fucked up and not remember anything. So, obviously, people need photographs to remember. Dude, we fucking solve *that* problem," she said with bohemian zest.

"And who takes pictures of you so you can remember?" I said to her.

The photographer laughed and said, "Clever man. My girl's clever, too. She writes the greatest one-liners for our blog."

"You should check out our site," the girl said, handing me a card with a URL on it. "People love it. We have a huge following."

The photographers each snapped one more photograph of me before walking away to create more memories.

I saw Parker talking to a girl on the deck, and then they both looked up at me; soon after, she started walking up the stairs in my direction.

"Your friend, Parker, said I should come talk to you," she said when she was next to me.

"Oh, *did* he?"

"Yeah, he said you're his best friend and roommate and big in the blog world, too."

I laughed. "He's kidding. I'm not much of a blogger," I said, lighting another cigarette.

"Can I have one?" she asked.

I handed a cigarette to her and then lit it for her. "So you're the famous blogger ... What do you write about?"

"I don't write. I post photos of myself naked in small places."

I laughed again, but then realized, from her expression, that she wasn't joking. "Sorry, what?" I said, trying to rebound.

"I used to be a gymnast, so I can get into really small places. I have someone take the photo of me, and then I post it. I started doing it a year ago, and it blew up. I make money on sponsorships and advertising."

"Sponsorships?" I said.

"Yeah, like, this one guy owns a washing machine company, and he paid me to take a photo crammed inside one of his washing machines—stuff like that."

"That's amazing," I said.

"Yeah, that photo actually went viral and got his company a lot of attention, so he was happy about working with me. Anyway, I was thinking I should probably get a photo tonight. You want to take one of me?"

"Um—"

"Is there a really small space I can crawl into somewhere in your house?"

"Well, maybe, I mean—probably," I said.

"Let's go look. Let's try the kitchen first," she said.

"OK."

I followed her into the kitchen, and she said, "This sink is perfect. Let's do the sink."

"Are you sure you can fit in there? That's pretty tight," I said.

"Here, hold this," she said, handing me her camera. "Can you lock the kitchen door?"

"Sure."

She started undressing as I went to lock the kitchen door, and when I turned back around, she was fully naked—her face plain and expressionless, but her body nearly flawless. I tried not to look at her.

"Ready?" she said.

"Yep."

She put her feet in first then, turning her body sideways, dropped her lower body in so that her bent knees touched one end of the sink and the bottoms of her feet rested on the other; she then scrunched her upper body into a ball and wiggled and writhed, until she was bent so far forward her nose was smashed against her knees. I thought she resembled a fetus in a cold, white, hard womb.

"Try to take ... several photos ... from a good angle," she struggled to say between short, seemingly painful breaths.

"Sure thing," I said, climbing on top of the counter and snapping a few shots. "I think we're good."

"Turn the water on ... so people know it's ... a real sink," she said, drooling on her knees.

I turned the water on, and it poured over her ribs and trickled one way down her stomach and one way down her back.

"Oh! Cold!" she said.

"Sorry," I said, adjusting the handle to make the water warmer.

"OK, take a ... few more."

"Got them," I said, after snapping a few more.

"Help me," she said. I pulled her out of the sink, and she put her clothes back on. "I'm going to go home and post it. Your house is considered West Hollywood, right?"

"Yeah, I'm pretty sure," I said.

"OK, good. I've done a few sinks before but never in West Hollywood. I always include the location. So this will say, 'Sink in West Hollywood,' or something like that."

"Cool."

"OK, I'm leaving now."

"Where're you going?"

"I don't want to waste my energy. I have to go home to edit my photo. I post a new one every day. If I don't, my followers get angry."

"So why come to a party?"

"My manager thinks it's a good idea to get out and see people in the real world once in a while." She reached into her purse, pulled out a card, and gave it to me. "This is my site. I should have the photo up in an hour. It'd be cool if you followed me."

"Yeah, sure."

"Thanks. Bye," she said.

"Bye."

I followed her out of the kitchen, and, as I stood on the balcony, watched her morph into the tiny person hailing a cab at the base of the ramp. *What the hell was that about?*

Rin Tin Tin shouted from a loudspeaker below that his show was starting in a few minutes, and the herd began to move toward the middle of the deck. Parker, on his way down, inadvertently bumped into my shoulder, and when I looked at him, the emptiness had already started showing in his eyes; I wasn't sure, at that point, if he knew who I was, until he said, "You take down that blogger?"

"No, she went home, I guess."

"Shitty …" he said, looking through me.

"She might have been … a *little* crazy," I said.

"Find someone else. Here, take this, and let's hit the floor, buddy," he said, handing me a blue pill and walking away.

Rin Tin Tin shot smoke into the eager crowd—happy screams sliced into the night chill, hands reached toward the sky—and then, when everyone's anticipation was peaking, he let his synthesized bass boom for the whole county of Los Angeles. His show had begun.

I took the pill and washed it down with a drink of beer; the feeling, one that crept up on me and rose steadily, started with tiny, warm pulses of pleasure undulating at the top of my head, which then showered down through the rest of my body and tingled at the tips of my fingers and toes.

In the middle of the dance floor, I smiled at those around me, whom I then considered my partners in the pursuit of pleasure, and pumped my arm to the music, as we all moved in synchrony, all played our roles to foster the feeling. The energy of the music streamed out to us, and, after we absorbed it and processed it, we sent a new energy back into the environment, as if we were undergoing our own version of photosyn-thesis—the music as our sun and us as its flowers, with pumping arms as petals (a true symbiotic relationship).

Jenny, my smiley roommate, bounced over to me to the rhythm of the music, her body brushing against mine; the combination of her aro-ma and the feeling of her body against mine made my skin float, and I closed my eyes to enjoy the sensation. When I opened them, I watched her lustfully, as she smiled and swayed to the music; her exposed thighs and kneecaps were, in that moment, the most sensuous things I'd ever seen.

After the cops had come to the house twice to issue warnings, Rin Tin Tin moved the party inside, and, in the darkness, I made many faceless friends, some of whom I led to my room to share some of the cocaine Jackson had given me earlier in the day. After we crammed into my small bathroom, I stood close to the greatest friends I'd ever known and nodded happily at everything they said, laughed with them, and complimented them regardless of their blurry bodies and blurry faces and unmemorable stories—all while we huddled together and helped ourselves to more white magic. And then, back in the living room, in the dark madness, I lost them, but soon discovered new best friends, until I ran out of cocaine, and all my faceless friends were forced to find someone else to try to keep them satiated.

Stumbling out of the living room, I caught the blurry scowl of Yaas, who stood in a dark corner watching Parker lead a girl by the hand up the stairs and then disappear down the hall. Yaas marched over and pulled me outside.

"You know he's only with me when he doesn't find someone else to fuck," she said, while I tried to focus on her face. "He came to LA five years ago after leaving a girl he was going to marry. He was a virgin before her. Imagine *that*—the perfect fucking Midwestern couple! But then he watched a few episodes of a stupid reality show and decided to leave her for Los Angeles, to, like, experience it all, you know? She was devastated—cried for a whole year. Now she's married to someone else. They just had a baby."

"Why are you telling me this?" I asked, squinting and swaying.

"It fucked him up so much when he heard about the baby. Now, his mind is, like, half gone. I'm pretty sure he's gone insane. And *you're* the new guy."

"New guy?"

"Parker brings people into the house who he thinks can save him. Has he called you his best friend yet?"

"Why do you wait around for him, then?" I stammered.

"Because I love him."

Jackson came up to me and whispered in my ear about a secret party in his room, and, in a haze, I left the heartbroken Yaas alone on the balcony. In Jackson's living room, a group of us passed around a bottle of champagne, while we danced in little circles; we took breaks from dancing to do lines of cocaine off the glass table in the kitchen. To us, at that point in the night, the outside world (anything beyond the walls of Jackson's room) existed only in our minds as a frightening thought of vast, dark, cold, and unforgiving terrain, and the idea of leaving his room brought a chill to our bodies; so, for warmth, we bunched up in the corner of the room, until even the small space we occupied became much too big for us. To solve our problem, we all squeezed onto the three-seater couch in the living room, but after the comfort of that haven had worn off and we felt exposed again, we gathered inside Jackson's walk-in closet and sat, with the door closed, cross-legged in the darkness; then, we moved inside the bathtub, where we huddled together closer than ever before without saying anything, only passing around a bag of coke and one of Jackson's steak knives to dig out little mounds.

After some time in the bathtub, the girl next to me touched my leg, and I stared into her large, empty eyes for the first time.

"Do you live here?" she asked.

"Yes," I said.

"Will you show me your room?"

"Yes."

"Let's split this pill first."

"OK."

Back outside, we staggered with trepidation across the deck, using our hands as visors to shield our faces from the harsh light of the rising sun. The music had stopped, and an eerie silence blanketed the Sunset House, as crazy-looking, pale-faced people loitered about on the property, as if they were nocturnal animals forced into the daylight.

On our way to my room, a naked Parker walked down the hall—his eyes empty, his upper lip smeared with cocaine, his big, flaccid cock flapping between his thighs—and passed between us without saying a word. Inside my room, I locked the door and hung a sheet over the window to block out the light, but some still sneaked in through the uncovered corners of the panes. When I turned around, the girl had already undressed and slipped under the covers in my bed; she reached down to her purse, pulled out a little bag of cocaine, dipped the butt end of a Parliament cigarette into it, put the filter tip up to her nostril, and breathed it in.

"You want one?" she asked.

"What the hell," I said and did one.

I undressed, pulled back the covers, climbed into the bed, lowering my body on top of hers, and tried kissing her.

"Fuck, dude, just get it in already," she said, breathing heavily.

At some point, she told me to choke her.

"What?" I said, still fucking her.

"Choke me," she said again.

I put one hand around her neck and squeezed softly.

"Use two hands," she barked.

I used two hands and squeezed softly again.

"Harder," she said.

I squeezed harder and heard the sound of her starting to choke.

"Harder! Don't be a fucking pussy," she yelled and then choked.

Are you kidding me? OK, fine. I squeezed harder. Her face turned bright red, and then she went silent. I quickly pulled my hands away in fear that I'd killed her.

"Don't stop—I'm going to come. Choke me," she said, gasping for air.

I squeezed hard again, and, at first, she made the gurgling sound of someone choking, but then—when little veins surfaced at her temples, and the red of her face bled into the whites of her eyes—she went silent again. As I looked at my hands clenched tightly around her red neck and then at her red, bobbing face, I still couldn't escape the thought that I was killing her. I closed my eyes and shook my head to dispel the image. When her body loosened under me, I opened my eyes in a panic and removed my hands from her neck. *Oh, Christ—I killed her.* She gasped ferociously for air. *She's alive!*

"I ... came. Oh ... my God—I came," she panted.

That was too fucking intense. My heart is going to explode. "I'm glad," I said.

"You've never choked a girl before ... have you?"

I apologize for not having made killing people a priority in my life. "No, I haven't."

"Girls like to be choked. They like to feel something."

"Oh, well, now I know." *I want to be alone. How do I get her out of here?*

I walked to the window, partly pulled back the sheet hanging over it, and looked out over the city. I usually enjoyed the way the land looked under the fresh morning light, but, that morning, I felt very exposed by the light, almost scolded or judged by it—so I quickly moved the sheet back over the window. I picked up a pack of cigarettes that rested on the floor by my feet, plucked one with my teeth, and lit it with a nearby book of restaurant matches. I inhaled deeply, held the smoke in my lungs a bit longer than usual, and then breathed it out slowly—I felt it in my head. I looked down at the books on my floor and then looked away ashamedly. "You want a beer or something?" I said to the girl. "I'm going to get a beer. I'm thirsty."

"I'm gonna get going," she said, dressing. And then, leaving my room, she said, "We should do this again sometime."

When I opened my eyes a few hours later, memories of the night flashed in my head, as if I were watching a slide show of absurd images in no logical order. Some of my memories were so ridiculous I took comfort in the possibility that they hadn't happened, that I'd only dreamt them. I took a shower and watched blood from my nose run down my body, trickle off my toes, and stream red down the white ceramic. "No more of that shit," I said, suddenly feeling moved with an energy to do something, to achieve something, to be productive, to be proud of myself, but first, to feel clean; I lathered myself with an extra layer of soap, and, before I rinsed, twisted the shower handle a little more toward the heat.

Wrapped in a towel, I grabbed one of the books along my wall, flipped through it, and smelled the pages. I picked up another and did the same. I decided that I'd spend the day reading and then, after my head cleared and my fingers stopped shaking, maybe try to write something—a new story, something better than anything I'd ever written.

Parker barged into my room with beads of sweat massing on his forehead.

"God, I feel terrible," he said. "But, man, what a night. I don't remember anything ... Did you take down a babe last night?"

"I think I was with someone."

"Who's the winning girl?"

"I don't know. It happened so fast, and then she left."

"Let's find out," he said, leaving the room, coming back with his laptop, then taking a seat on my bed and finding the photographs from the night before.

"I met her much later in the night," I said, prompting him to skip toward the end of the night's photographs. "That might be her," I said, pointing. "Yeah, I think that's her."

"Fine first choice. I think I was with her once, too, a while ago."

"You were?"

"The photographic evidence points in that direction. OK, let's get out of here and fix this shitty feeling."

"I have to get some work done today. I've been neglecting my writing—something I promised myself I wouldn't do."

"A writer needs experience, man. You'll never live in a place like this again in your life. Embrace it now, write later," he said.

"Not today. I can't even think straight yet."

"You should eat. I know a good Mexican place down the street. It'll make you feel a lot better."

Well, I guess I should probably eat something ...

A few minutes later, after I'd dressed, I met Parker in the hallway, and as we passed Rin Tin Tin's room on the way to the stairs, we heard him cussing at his computer screen. Downstairs, the scene was disastrous: hundreds of cans of beer, some of them only half empty, and several bottles of liquor, some of them shattered, were scattered all over the floor and furniture; outside, the most cigarette butts I'd ever seen in one place paved the entire balcony in a cancerous yellow. As we tiptoed around shards of glass and unidentified pools of spilled liquid, Parker said, "Don't worry about the mess. The Monday Mexicans make it all go away."

Down on the deck, several people were spread across the couch in a deep slumber. Parker, hovering above them, clapped his hands loudly twice with a proprietary confidence, making me shut my eyes and turn my head and forcing some of the sleepers to stir and groan.

"Get the *fuck* out!" Parker yelled, as one sleeper's eyelids cracked open slowly, as if his sockets were giving birth to his eyeballs. "Get … the … *fuck* out!" he yelled louder.

After the sleepers were jolted into consciousness, they scrambled off the deck, down the stairs, and down the ramp, and I considered the possibility that some of them had been my best friends at some point during the night—a thought that mystified me. *Best friends during the night, but trespassers during the day?*

When I got into the passenger seat of Parker's shiny, black BMW convertible, he handed me a pair of sunglasses, and, as he drove down the ramp, said, "This is the best Mexican food you'll ever have." He turned the music up and headed east on Sunset, weaving around the Sunday traffic. Except for a layer of haze I'd realized would always be there, it was a clear, cool day, and the sun and the breeze felt good on my face. I put my hand outside the frame of the car to let the wind hit it, while we zoomed past liquor stores, strip clubs, restaurants, hotels, and paparazzi bubbling at the side entrance to the Chateau Marmont.

Parker made a hard right turn into the dirty parking lot of El Compadre, a shabby Mexican restaurant with an ambience that seemed to be at odds with the new, glimmering blue Ferrari parked in the lot.

"A down payment on a Ferrari is a down payment on road head," Parker said, not seeming to care if I heard him or not.

As we walked toward the entrance to the restaurant, a family of three—a young couple and a little toddler just learning to walk—passed by on the sidewalk; I was struck by how attentive the parents were to their child, as if their own existence and relevance were fully dependent on that little heart and those little lungs.

Parker, following my gaze, said, "Having kids is a very selfish thing to do, man. I mean, I can't really think of a more selfish thing to do. You didn't ask to be brought into this world. Your parents just did it so they could stare at little versions of themselves all day. And then they wonder why we do the things we do, like we shouldn't have a choice or something. But they had a choice. They chose to bring us into this fucking world. And why? Because they hit a point in their own lives when everything became boring and meaningless, and they needed something to make it all more interesting. It's a fucked-up way of validating their own lives. It's all bullshit, man."

"This conversation is way too heavy for my hangover, Parker," I said.

Inside the restaurant, the decaying walls were wet with the heat from the kitchen, and the floors were caked in grime, but the wonderful aroma of fresh Mexican food hovered in the air, kick-starting my salivary glands. A Mariachi band—each man dressed in a black suit lined with silver studs and wearing a wide-brimmed hat that reminded me of a giant coffee-cup saucer—played a lively Mexican tune in the back; some of the waiters, carrying trays of sizzling food, sang along as they walked by.

We took a booth in a quiet corner. Parker nodded toward another booth, where a middle-aged man with long, shaggy gray hair wearing tattered, trendy jeans and a "styled-to-look-cheap" T-shirt cuddled a tanned, blonde-haired girl of twenty or so.

"See that?" Parker said. "I guarantee the Ferrari in the lot is that guy's. Look at his girl … Man, she's just sucking the coin out of his old cock."

I was still too hungover to laugh or even acknowledge him. The waiter came over to take our drink orders; Parker asked for a Tecate, and I asked for a Bohemia.

"We're all just animals, man," he said, continuing his tutorial. "Any attempt at monogamy is a crock of shit. And it takes seeing people in their rawest state to know the truth. People who live in a small town in the Midwest don't know any better, because they don't have any choices. But when you put people into the madness, right in the center of it all, with all the choices in the world, they become who they really are—just a bunch of animals trying to get some pussy or dick and make some fucking money."

The waiter brought the beers, and Parker told him to bring us two more.

"Sure," the waiter said. "Ready to order?"

"Give me the steak fajitas," Parker said.

"The *albóndigas* soup," I said, after skimming the menu briefly for the first time.

"People are fucked up," Parker said after the waiter left with our orders. "I've never met a person who isn't crazy. So you have a shit-ton of fucking crazy people running around town and fucking each other. At some point, they get scared that they're getting too old and ugly to fuck who they want, so they get married and sit around all day dreaming about the days when they ran around town with the freedom to fuck anyone they wanted. After a few years of marriage, the dude hides in the bathroom to masturbate after work because his wife doesn't want to fuck him anymore … Or maybe he can't even get it up when he sees her naked. Who knows. So what comes next? They decide to have a kid to distract themselves from how pathetic their lives are. Then they raise this kid and tell it what to do, like they have some sort of fucking clue. And then they are furious when the kid grows up and starts disobeying them. Because the kid isn't allowed to live life differently than how they want it to live, right? And all the kid can think about when he gets older is when he'll be able to start fucking someone, and the pattern repeats itself."

"Shit, that's depressing, Parker," I said.

"I'm not depressed. I'm happy as a clam and horny as a billy goat. It's just better to know how it really is, don't you think?"

"I guess so."

"Do you know how many married babes I've been with in Los Angeles in five years? One time, I fucked this girl, a friend of mine, and then, a few weeks later, went to her wedding and listened to her father give a heartwarming speech about how his baby girl had found the man of her dreams. She winked at me during the speech."

I laughed and said, "She winked at you during her own wedding? That's pretty shameless."

"It's not about shame."

"What's it about?"

"It's about people needing those speeches. Or needing a religion. Or a gym membership. Or a vacation. Or a new job. Or a new husband. Or a new kid. Why? Because people need to feel like they can start over—you know, feel alive and fresh again. It's like those teachers back in the day who started you off with a perfect A in class. Everyone was so happy. Everyone felt smart. Anything was possible. But what happened? We kept fucking up every day, and our grades kept dropping until they ended up as the grades we were always going to get, maybe even worse. But then, a new semester or quarter or whatever begins, and everyone has a perfect grade again, and everyone is happy and alive and so smart. People need that feeling to get by, you know?"

Half an hour later, after we'd filled our bellies with chips and salsa and our entire meals and a few beers, it seemed that Parker had been rejuvenated, but I was still queasy and shaky, as if my body still wasn't sure how to handle the influx of new drugs. The waiter brought the bill, and I paid it.

Parker screeched out of the parking lot and snaked west on Sunset with an indifference to living or dying, as if he were playing a car-racing video game that would allow him, if we crashed or died, to just start over from the parking lot of the restaurant with another life. A girl, staring down at her phone, was slowly crossing the street when the light changed to green, and Parker, who'd hit the gas pedal right when the light changed, slammed on the brakes and yelled out the window, "What the *fuck* are you doing?" The girl's head shot up, and she froze, seemingly surprised by her whereabouts, as if someone had blindfolded her, placed her in the middle of the street, and removed the blindfold. Her eyes focused on the row of cars inching angrily toward her, and then she finally sprinted to safety on the other side of the street. Parker drove on.

"We might as well keep it going. No point in starting to feel shitty again this early," Parker said.

"I really should—"

"Just a drink or two. I can tell you need something. You look like shit," he said, as he pulled into the parking lot of a Midwestern-themed bar, a few blocks from our house, with cowboy figures bursting through the walls on their horses and harlot figures waving good-bye from the windows above. Inside, a mechanical bull was positioned in the very center of a large room. Any guy who mounted the bull and tried to impress the crowd with his heroic endurance was quickly and dramatically tossed to the mats below, much to the delight of the drunken spectators. However, any attractive girl who mounted the bull lasted, conveniently, long enough to ignite testosterone-laden cheers and grunts from fist-pumping frat-boy armies in the crowd, before she, too, was tossed, legs flailing, onto the mats below with the rest of the defeated.

We sat at an outside table and started off with a round of Bloody Marys because Parker said that they would be "a good base" for the rest of the day. Before my drink came, with my eyes hidden behind a pair of sunglasses and my legs quietly trembling under the table, I hoped that the terrible feeling within me would soon go away. The commotion inside the bar and out on the street annoyed me, especially the afternoon joggers zooming by on the sidewalk with healthy sweat on their brows and motivating music in their ears. One of my eyelids drooped lower than the other. My head was pounding. My throat had dried up, and every time I swallowed I thought I might gag or do something potentially far more embarrassing—something I couldn't quite comprehend, like have a seizure or burst into flames or faint or bite off my tongue; my mind, seemingly unhinged and poisoned, was roaming free of my control and conjuring up hellish images. But then the drink came—a tall Bloody Mary with celery and olives inside—and after guzzling it down, my shaking subsided, and I felt much better.

"What's it going to take to get your mind out of the shit?" Parker asked.

"What do you mean?"

"You're always staring at things like they're supposed to tell you something. Once you realize that this is just a table and that's just a tree and those are just people, everything starts to make sense, and then you don't have to give a shit anymore. Then you can start having fun. It's that simple. So how can I help? What do you want?"

"What do I want?"

"Like what are you striving for?"

"I don't know ... To be good, I guess, or to be good at something. To find some sort of peace of mind—you know, find something in the world that means something to me, that I'll never get tired of doing or thinking about or being part of for the rest of my life ... or that, at least, won't confuse the shit out of me. Because, at this point in my life, I haven't done anything that makes sense to me other than sit around and read fiction and drink all day—which is just ridiculous, you know?"

"What about the writing?"

"Sure, but I think I'd have to make something of myself before I could ever find peace with it, you know? I'd probably have to get something published ... or at the very least get some respect from other writers. I don't know. Writing for me, right now, is sort of like therapy—I just write stories as a way to better understand myself and the people I meet ..."

"You know, I think I have a good idea for you—for your blog. You should write something about the illusion of fake tits."

I laughed and said, "Come on, Parker."

"What do you think of fake tits?"

"I don't know. I've never been with a girl who has them."

"Yeah, but what do you think of them?"

"They're OK to look at, I guess."

"I just can't stand fake tits anymore," he said. "You fantasize about them. You think about them all those years. You think about them and you think about them and you think about them. And then you finally have them, and it's fine because it's something different and exciting— and you can play with them and bounce them around. But then everyone in this fucking town has them, and you start to really know fake tits. Soon you figure out that they're just these two manufactured mounds of flesh on a girl's chest. A doctor goes in there and does some shit and makes the tits look pretty, and then the girl has these fresh new mounds on her chest. Round bulges of skin. I could go to that doctor and say, 'Hey, Doc, can I have one of those fake tits installed on my kneecap?' You know? Right here on my kneecap, I could have a fake tit that, if you zoom in on it, looks like everything we fantasized about before we knew the truth. There's something deep in that, man. Think about it."

"Already taking mental notes ..."

After our second Bloody Mary, Parker told our waitress to "switch us to mimosas." When the champagne was in me, I was recharged and felt balanced and fresh; but I knew it wasn't *real*, just as the pleasant feeling a gravely wounded soldier presumably gets after a morphine injection isn't *real*. We were drunk, again, and Parker suggested that we "take it easy tonight with a couple bottles of white."

"White?"

"White wine. It's nice in the evening on the deck."

"OK," I said, too drunk to care anymore about getting any work done.

Parker pulled the car into the tiny parking lot of a place called Liquor Locker, and I followed him inside. Parker paid the middle-aged, straight-faced Mexican guy at the cash register for a carton of cigarettes, three bottles of white wine, and—"Just in case," Parker said—a bottle of whiskey, a bottle of vodka, and a few mixers.

Back on our deck, with the white wine in a bucket of ice, we reclined on the couch and sipped from our glasses and smoked cigarettes; I stared at the city below me and then squinted in the direction of the sun, which had begun its descent into the world's other half. Parker browsed the web on his laptop.

"I like the pussy to be tucked in a little bit. Not too far out in front, but up and under a little bit and tight like this," he said, holding his index finger and middle finger together.

"I have no idea what you're talking about," I said.

"Here, look at this," he said, turning his laptop screen toward me so I could look at a picture of a tall, skinny girl in a bikini standing on a beach. "You can't really see anything, but I've been with her, so I know. See how the legs come up, and the thighs curve in a little so they don't touch. The pussy is right up under there. It's the perfect spot. You see? And she doesn't have any of that big-hip bullshit. She's skinny, skinny, skinny all the way through, with a nice, round butt in back. She's perfect."

"Maybe you should ... spend the rest of your life with her, then," I said, deliriously.

"Some guys like to come home to a challenge—a smart girl who can talk and argue and exchange ideas. Some guys want to come home to a pretty smile and a blow job and a good meal. You can't have both. I take you as a guy who wants to be with a girl who talks to you, right?"

"Yeah, I imagine talking would be nice," I said.

"You fucker, you're going to go off and get married and leave me behind with all this pussy."

"I don't think so, man. I've never even had a real relationship before."

"Well, what's wrong with you?" he said, his attention divided between me, his laptop, and some other insatiable craving buried deep behind his blue eyes.

I took a drag on my cigarette and said, "I have no idea."

"Wrong. Nothing is wrong with you. Relationships aren't real. They're only a temporary antidote for loneliness ..."

In the early evening, when the orange of the horizon had faded to purple, we doused a few logs in the fire pit with lighter fluid and got a small fire going. Parker played "Champagne Supernova" by Oasis on his guitar and sang the lyrics, while I watched razor-tipped, red-yellow flames dance around each other to the song's soothing rhythm.

"I told you, dude," Parker said, when he'd finished the song. "I told you we'd take it easy today."

But we still ended up at The Den, a lounge down the street, and stayed until closing time.

"I just want to say," he said to me, as the bartender announced last call, "that I've never connected with someone so quickly in my life. I think we're going to be friends for a very long time."

I awoke, cracking one heavy eyelid open before the other, late Monday night, after sleeping through the entire day, to the most dismal room I'd ever known—the walls looked bare and lonely and cold, and they were beginning to yellow, as if they'd been poisoned by the air I breathed out while I slept. My window showed four panes of a hauntingly silent and infinite darkness.

As I looked exhaustedly around my bleak room, I was surprised at my own irritability. I kicked repeatedly at the sheets annoyingly tangled around my legs, until, finally, I was free of them. My books were distastefully scattered all over the floor. My pillow, wet with my cold sweat, disgusted me, and I frustratedly flipped it over to its purer side. Just noticing a little crack in the wall next to me caused my heart to palpitate and my lungs to tighten up. But more overwhelming than anything else was the profound loneliness that was smothering me. I was quite familiar with loneliness, but this feeling was ... more intense. I felt empty, as if all the goodness inside of me had been vacuumed up and dumped into space.

I walked down the stairs, making the only sounds in the starkly quiet house, and into the kitchen. I found a loaf of wheat bread, removed a slice, nibbled at it slowly, fearing that food would be an unwelcome visitor in my stomach, and drank several glasses of water, the whole time standing alongside the kitchen counter. It was then that I realized how clean the kitchen was; all the appliances, the counters, and the floor shimmered in the moonlight. I walked into the sitting room with the piano, and it had also been thoroughly cleaned. I walked into the living room and then out onto the balcony. *Everything* had been cleaned. There was no trace of all the beer cans and the cigarette butts and the broken bits of glass. The trash had been taken out. All the spills had been mopped up; all the furniture had been straightened. All the evidence of the past week's debauchery had simply vanished. All the sins had been forgiven. Everything was pure and clean, ready to be dirtied again.

"The Monday Mexicans make it all go away," Parker had said earlier. Perhaps a team of them had arrived early in the morning with the focused mission to clean the house as Catholic priests clean the guilty minds of sinners. They must have worked quietly and stoically, while the nocturnal animals slept. And they had succeeded. They had transformed a menagerie into a normal-looking house, and, in doing so, they had given us the opportunity to feign wholesomeness, at least for a day or two.

I assumed that inside their dark rooms, my housemates were clinging tightly to their pillows, trying to sleep off their pain. I sat down on the balcony couch and took a deep breath. The cleaning crew had forgotten one thing, perhaps purposefully, since it still had some value: a half-consumed bottle of Jameson whiskey resting on the stand next to me—my sole companion on that dismal Monday night, when everything else was dead. I unscrewed the cap and took a sip. I grimaced at first, but then it felt warm going down. I welcomed the new feeling. I reached into my back pocket and pulled out a crushed pack of cigarettes—two left. I lit a bent one and leaned back against the cushions.

As I stared out over the fluorescent city, I thought about how I'd been oblivious to drug culture my entire life. The world of drugs had always been, for me, an intangible one, an isolated place far removed from my reality—much in the same way an American, uninterested in traveling, might think of Europe: he knows that it exists somewhere out there, and, during dinner conversations, he might even offer, based on stories he's heard, his opinion about it, but, really, he never cares to spend too much time worrying about a place that'll never influence his own daily routine.

In my early years, drugs had been defined by all the atrocious labels given to them by my teachers or the media; and I grew up believing that a person who did cocaine one time was a cokehead, and that a person who smoked pot one time was a pothead. And, as far as I understood, there wasn't a difference between the terms "cokehead" and "crackhead"; they were synonyms, simply referring to terrible people who did terrible things.

I remembered something a teacher had told my class in middle school long ago. She stood in front of the classroom, glaring at us with her pious eyes, and, trying to instill fear in us, said that alcohol and tobacco were gateways to the evil world of drugs. Sitting at my little student desk attached to a blue, plastic chair, I imagined walking down a road fringed by trees with low-hanging, red-colored needles for leaves—brimming with horrific, unspeakable drugs—that, as I walked past, tried to lure me away from a moral life. The red apples, I thought. Stay on the path.

Stay away from the forbidden fruit. Keep walking.

I stopped daydreaming about my past and took a sip of whiskey and lit another cigarette.

Back in my room, I got into my bed and lay still in the silence for a few minutes, wishing the sun would rise and flood the land with light; the darkness and my loneliness were, especially that night, a destructive combination. But then I heard something I hadn't heard in a long while. It was the sound of crying. Someone was crying. And the sound came from Parker's room.

I opened his door quietly and walked into the blackness, guiding myself toward his bedside with the light from my phone. Parker, with his head turned away from me, lay on the far end of his bed. I shone the light over him and saw that his pillow was stained with a head-sized pool of fresh, red blood coming from his nose.

"Parker, are you OK?" I said, softly.

"I'm—in it, man … So in it," he said, turning to face me, between guttural gasps for air.

"What's wrong?"

"She … was smart. Pretty hair—kind eyes—a good … person … to the core. Perfect for … me. We were … engaged," Parker said, struggling, with thick streams of tears gushing down his face and onto the pillow, mixing with the blood and brightening the red. He paused, took a deep breath, and then seemed to get control of himself before continuing. "My mom cried for three months when I left my girl. Everyone loved her. It was serious shit, dude. We lost our virginity to each other. We used to make love face to face three fucking times a day."

"What happened?" I asked.

"I couldn't sit still anymore. There was nothing ever to do in that little town. No one ever left. I saw what it did to my parents. They hated their lives. So I left and she stayed. After the first month, I regretted leaving her. She was going to come to LA, and we were going to start over."

"She didn't come?" I said.

"No." His wet eyes twitched, as if my question had stirred an ugly memory. "I fucked it all up."

"How?"

"I got chlamydia from some girl at a club around the time she was going to come see me. She had her flight booked. Everything was set. But I didn't want to give her anything, you know? And I didn't have the heart to tell her I fucked another girl. She would've never understood.

So I told her that I didn't want her to come—that I needed more time. She was heartbroken, man. I crushed her. And then, somehow, more time turned into never. She's married now ... to some guy. They have a kid. I know she's a wonderful mother ..." he said, his voice trailing away.

I need to help him. I need to say something or do something. I rested my hand on his shoulder and tried to comfort him, but I was too late, for he had already fallen asleep.

TWELVE

The midday sunlight streamed through my window, warming my forehead, and when I opened my eyes and heard Parker on a work call in the next room, I knew the house was alive again. I decided I'd take a walk, have a bite to eat on the street, explore my new city, and, most important, get some writing done. After a shower, as I toweled off, I heard a knock at my door.

"Come in," I said.

My roommate, Levi, came in. "Hey, Jake."

"Hey, Levi. What's up?"

"So this actress I've done some work with is looking for a writer. She's, like, trying to make a big comeback or something. Anyway, I told her I live with a writer, and she wants to meet you. Would you be interested in meeting her? She might give you some work."

"Levi, have you ever read anything I've written?" I asked.

"No, but it's a good way to get you out there."

"I'm not exactly an established writer. Why would she want to work with me?"

"It can't hurt," he said.

"OK, who is she?"

"She starred on a hit TV show a while ago. You might recognize her," he said.

When he told me the name of her show, I remembered seeing an episode or two at some point several years before, but I hadn't heard anything about her since.

"When does she want to meet?" I said.

"Today."

"Today?"

"Yeah, she's sort of ... spontaneous."

"What time?"

"In fifteen minutes."

"Jesus, Levi," I said.

"I told her you'd be there. It's not far. You can walk. It's at a place called Palihouse down the street," he said.

"I don't know if I'm right for this."

"Just have some lunch and talk to her. Maybe it'll be a good fit," he said.

"OK, fine."

"One thing ..."

"What's that?"

"She's sort of fucking crazy, so just ride it out."

"What does that mean, Levi?"

"Just, you know, let it settle."

I shook my head and smiled incredulously, as he turned and walked out of my room. On my way out, a few minutes later, Parker whipped open his door and greeted me jovially, as if our interaction the previous night had never happened. "Goddamn—how nice is a clean house? *Whew*—I feel great. A new week. Where're you going, my man?"

"To take a meeting Levi set up," I said.

"Good kid. I'll be here when you get back."

On my walk to the Palihouse, I paused to observe a crowd, near the corner of Holloway, that massed in front of a cement wall covered in stenciled graffiti art; the piece showed a dog urinating a bright yellow stream, one that defied gravity, up the entire face of the wall. Some of the spectators were pointing and gawking, others were taking photographs, and two guys within earshot of me were passionately arguing.

"How the hell is this not a Banksy?" one of them said, throwing up his hands.

"Banksy would never reduce himself to this. This dog-pissing thing has already been done. Banksy would never do something unoriginal. It's that simple."

"How the hell do you know? You Banksy fanboys are forgetting one thing: he might not even be a real person. No one even knows who the hell he is. It could be anyone or no one or a whole shitload of people!"

"You're a goddamn idiot!"

I continued half a block east on Holloway until I arrived at the entrance of a small, fashionable lodge; I paused in front, realizing I was grossly underdressed, then unassertively walked inside and told the hostess whom I was meeting.

"She hasn't arrived yet. Would you like me to seat you, anyway?" she asked, contemptuously.

"Yes, thank you."

She sat me at a small table around a few decorative plants and scattered groups of trendily dressed people helping themselves to small-portioned appetizers and drinking colorful drinks in fancy glasses. The waiter came to the table and asked me if I wanted bottled water or "normal" water. I found it a bit odd—perhaps it was the tone of his voice—that he referred to water in that way; and, although it made me feel unremarkable to do so, I told him "normal" water was fine. I waited twenty minutes and then decided to wait, at most, ten more, before leaving. My back was to the restaurant entrance, so I didn't see her come in. She took a seat in front of me, along with a middle-aged man in a suit with gelled, slicked-back hair and black thick-rimmed eyeglasses. I stood up to greet them.

"I'm Jake," I said. "Good to meet you guys."

The man shook my hand without telling me his name, while she fidgeted with her purse. "Thanks for meeting us," he said.

"No problem."

"Before we discuss anything, we'll need you to sign this nondisclosure agreement," he said, handing me a pen and a document filled with legal jargon. "Basically, with your signature, you're legally agreeing that anything we discuss during lunch is private."

"OK, no problem," I said, signing the document.

The waiter came to our table with a pitcher of water; as he picked up the actress's glass and began pouring, she instinctively swung her arm to block him, knocking the glass from his hand and spilling the water all over the table.

"No!" she yelled. "I brought my own."

"I'm very sorry, ma'am. The gentlemen here," he said, pointing to me, "said this water would be fine."

"I brought my *own*," she said again, refusing to look at him.

"I do apologize, again. Sir," he said, looking at me with a dignified disdain, "would you still care for this water?"

"Yes, that's fine. Sorry about that."

He filled my glass and then left us in an awkward silence; I nervously readjusted myself and took a sip of my "normal" water. The suited man, who sat by her side, stared directly into my eyes, and I stared back into his. He looked away, and I looked at the actress, while she scrolled through her phone, pausing to look at me for just a second before looking down again—but long enough for me to meet the glossed-red whites of her eyes and the droopy, tired flesh that hung underneath them. She must have been in her middle to late thirties, and she looked stoned and lifeless; I remembered her being much prettier on television. No one said a word. So I decided to break the silence.

"So … you guys are looking for a writer?" I asked.

After an insufferably long pause, the suited man said, "Well … maybe. We can't really talk about that. We just want to casually chat with you at this point."

"Sure. What would you like to talk about?" And then, not getting a response from either of them, I decided to try something else. "I really enjoyed watching your show," I said to the actress, immediately disappointed in myself for resorting to a line like that.

She looked up at me, and a slow, stony smile crept across her face. But, again, our table returned to silence.

"Is there something I can do for you guys? My roommate said—"

"We don't know yet," the suited man said, cutting me short.

When the waiter returned to the table to take our food orders, the actress, ignoring him, held the menu up to her companion and pointed to a few items.

"She'll have the plate of olives and the soup," the suited man said. "And I'll have the chicken salad."

"I'll take the chicken salad, as well," I said when the waiter scowled at me.

"Should be out shortly," the waiter said.

The actress reached into her purse, pulled out a metal container that looked, to me, like a giant bullet, unscrewed the cap, and poured *her* water into a glass; after sipping it with an air of smugness, she resumed browsing her phone.

"Well, what are you guys working on?" I asked, attempting one more time to create some meaning out of the seemingly pointless, and, at that point, most bizarre meeting I'd ever experienced. *Wow—this experience is making my social media meetings at my old company seem almost pleasurable by comparison.*

"Nothing we can really talk about. We have some interesting projects on the table, but we can't really discuss those," he said.

"OK," I said, slipping into a slight smile that was intended to reveal my unwillingness to put forth any more effort. It didn't work.

As we sat together, like a mismatched trio of mutes, both of them took several breaks from whatever they were fidgeting with to stare awkwardly at me. The waiter brought our food to the table and left. With a fork, the actress rearranged the olives on her plate without ever eating one of them; the suited man, like a little rabbit, nibbled gently on the lettuce in his salad; and, with nothing else to do, I finished my salad rather quickly.

"Can we get all of this to go?" the suited man said to the waiter, referring to half of his salad and all of her untouched food.

After the waiter brought back their meals wrapped in gold, swan-shaped foil, the suited man looked at me and said, "It was really nice meeting you. Do you have a number where you can be reached?"

I gave him my number and watched them leave the table. *What the fuck was that about?* The waiter brought the bill and laid it in front of me. *One hundred dollars!* I paid the bill and left the restaurant, intending to voice my anger to Levi when I got back home; but, as I turned toward La Cienega, a black town car with tinted windows crept up slowly from behind me and, when it was even with me, came to a halt. The back window rolled down, and the suited man stuck his head out.

"She really likes you. Are you available to talk some more about the job?" he said.

"What job?"

"Can you hop in the car with us back to her house? We can talk more about it there."

The driver, a stocky man with naturally brown skin, exited the vehicle, walked around to my side, and opened the door. I stepped in.

"Where are we going?" I asked, not expecting a response.

"Just a few minutes up the hill," he said. "Don't drive yet," he told the driver and then said to me, "Before we go anywhere, you'll need to sign this nondisclosure agreement."

"Haven't I already signed one?"

"That one only covered what we discussed at lunch. This is a different one. If you decide to sign it, you're legally agreeing that anything you learn about my client or her work is strictly confidential. Let me stress that signing this document prohibits you from discussing *anything* with *anyone*." He handed me a pen and the document, filled to the bottom of the page with more legal jargon, and waited for me to sign it.

I stared at the document for a few seconds, looked at the actress (she was still absently scrolling through her phone), and then looked back at him. *Who are these people?*

"We don't have all day, you know?" he said.

I signed the document and handed it back to him.

"Drive," he told the driver.

The driver weaved professionally through traffic, turned left on Laurel Canyon, and cut back and forth through a maze of little streets, all of which climbed the Hollywood Hills, until we were as high as the clouds, and driving by fancy homes overlooking the vast San Fernando Valley on one side and the bustling city of Los Angeles overrun with normal-water drinkers on the other side.

I followed them through an enormous, password-protected metal door, and then through a veranda with a pond full of big, colorful koi mindlessly swimming in circles. We took cement stepping-stones over the pond to a large glass door that required another access code. The house, constructed in a modern-minimalist style, was a series of connecting rectangular-shaped, ground-level rooms with large-paned windows.

We went inside. The living room was spotlessly clean, flooded with natural light, and angelically white wherever there wasn't a window—white ceiling, white floor, white couch, white table. The room was decorated with strange art: gold statues of animals lounging on the floor, grotesque paintings on the walls, and a life-size portrait of the actress, naked, riding a white tiger above the fireplace. One of the paintings near me, done with watercolors, showed a nude woman with a huge penis and the inscription: "A very small, little, tiny woman with a very big, large, enormous cock." The floor-to-ceiling, back window in the living room showed a view of the sprawling hills dipping into the valley and a panorama of the hazy horizon. The backyard had an elegant fire pit and an infinity pool filled with crystal, sky-blue water that stretched across the length of her property; and, in the far corner, there was a tiny house with a door and a window, which I imagined to be a guesthouse.

She took a seat on her white couch, and, motioning with her hand, told me to do the same.

"I'll let you two be," the suited man said and left the house.

"You have a really beautiful home," I said to her.

"I've heard that before. You know, I just moved back to LA from New York. I like my place in New York—it's on the Hudson—much more than this dump. But LA is coming back again. No one cares about New York anymore. Years ago it was all about LA, then everyone moved to NYC, then it was about London for a little bit, now it's LA again. So here I am. Do you smoke cigarettes?"

"Sure."

She dug into her enormous, shiny purse and pulled out a pack of Capri cigarettes; after plucking from the pack two of the thinnest cigarettes I'd ever seen, she handed one to me, lit hers, and tossed me a pink, penis-shaped lighter.

"I think your writing is brilliant," she said, leaning back on the couch as she exhaled.

"You've read some of it?" I said, awkwardly lighting my cigarette with the flame that shot out of the penis.

"That's just what we say."

"OK ..."

"If someone says it's brilliant, then it's brilliant," she said. "Would you rather it not be brilliant?"

"Um—well ... I don't know," I said. "I'd probably rather it be what it is."

"I have a gift, you know. I know when someone is special or talented, without even knowing them or seeing their work. I know right away. I feel it in my soul. I'm like a fucking psychic or clairvoyant or whatever. My sixth sense has never failed me. And I think your writing is brilliant."

"Thank you," I said, accepting her meaningless compliment with my meaningless expression of thanks, hoping, at that point, she would move on.

"Something to drink?" she said.

"Yeah, what do you have?"

"I only drink my water or absinthe. You want a glass of absinthe?"

"That's fine."

She rose from the couch and sauntered regally into her kitchen. I heard the clinking of glasses, while I sucked at my thin cigarette, waiting for something to happen. She brought back two glasses of absinthe and gave one to me.

"I need to stay current," she said.

"Sure," I said, sipping the drink and letting a new kind of burn travel down into my stomach.

"I need an online voice. Frankly, I hate that shit, but my manager says I need to interact with my online fans. Something *big* has to happen for me *now*."

I nodded.

"I don't have the time for it, you know?" she said, pretentiously.

"Yeah, I understand."

"All this social media bullshit. I mean, I have to read scripts ... I can't just sit around and waste my time trying to be clever," she said, pausing to take a drag on her cigarette and to thumb her phone for an amount of time that would easily be considered rude when in company. "I want you to do it," she said, finally looking up at me.

"Do what?" I said.

"Be my Internet voice."

"You mean post for you in third person?"

"No, I want you to post as me, in my voice, for my fans," she said.

"But I don't know your voice."

"Be clever. Be witty. Say some cool shit. It's up to you. Just make it cool."

"I think your fans will probably want your real voice," I said.

"Yes, and *you* will be my real voice."

"Right, but how do I know your inner thoughts, the things that make you ... you?"

"You wouldn't be sitting here on my couch next to me in my home if you weren't able to do this. Let's try it now," she said, grabbing a nearby laptop and flipping it open to one of her social networks. "Post something now—the best thing that comes to your mind."

I laughed. She didn't.

"OK, I'll try something," I said.

Trying to channel a TV celebrity I knew nothing about, I wrote down a few phrases.

"I wouldn't write that," she said, reaching over me and pressing the delete button to erase my words.

"That's what I mean—"

"Try it again."

I wrote something else.

"Ha, I would never write that."

"Right, what I'm saying is that I don't—"

"Try it again."

"I'll try one more time. You may need someone else," I said, and then wrote something outlandish, even gratuitous, having nothing to do with her.

"That's much better. I might write that. Let's keep it," she said, posting it for her hundreds of thousands of followers to read. "Congratulations. The job is yours."

"Sorry, what job is it again?"

"You are now my voice."

"Well—"

"The pay will be good. Someone will email you a contract. Congratulations, again," she said, forcefully, with no intention of really congratulating me, as a way to end the conversation in her favor. She looked away and said, "OK, business is done. That's all we have to talk about."

I stared at her, thought about declining her offer, but, already too aware of her incorrigible nature, decided to figure out a resolution later. "Thanks for your time," I said, and then finished the last of my absinthe and put my cigarette out in her ashtray.

"Can you find your way home?" she asked.

"I guess I should be able to."

I stood up from the couch, shook her hand, and walked toward the glass door; but as I opened it and took one step out, she said, "Jim ..."

"Jake," I said, stepping back inside.

"Jake," she said, patting the cushion next to her to tell me to sit back down.

I walked back over to the couch and took a seat. "What's up?"

"You don't find me attractive?" she said, inching closer to me.

"Huh?" I said,

"Do *you* find me attractive?" she said, as if she were upset with an employee.

"Well—I mean ... sure I do."

"Then do you want to kiss me for a little bit?" she said, putting her hand on my knee.

"I wasn't looking at it like that. We're working together. Wouldn't that—"

"What's wrong with a kiss?" she said.

"Nothing, I guess."

"Then kiss me."

"But—"

When she kissed me, the feeling of her cold lips and cold tongue made me slightly recoil, but, getting more aggressive, she pulled me on top of her as she lay back on the couch. "You aren't going to sue me, are you?" she said, grabbing my cock through my pants.

"I'm not sure."

"Are you scared of sex?"

"Scared of it?"

"Oh, shit," she said as her phone vibrated underneath us. After reading the text message, she said, "He'll be here in a minute."

"Who?"

"I'm going to rinse off in the shower. Can you buzz him into the house? Just tell him the usual and then, after he leaves, meet me in the bedroom ... *Hello?* OK?"

"OK."

The actress disappeared around the corner, and, within a few seconds, a male voice on the intercom said, "Delivery," and I buzzed him in. He appeared at the glass door holding a black suitcase, and I let him inside.

"How's it going? Is she here?" he said.

"Yeah, she's in the shower. She said just the usual."

"Sure. No big thing. Let's go over to the table," he said.

I followed him to the table, where he opened his black briefcase, and inside were organized rows divided into little compartments holding clear ziplock bags of weed and pills. He gathered a few bags of weed and a sack of pills.

"So what do you do, man?"

"I'm a writer," I said, deciding to go with it.

"No shit, man? Me, too."

"Really?"

"Absolutely. I'm a ghostwriter."

"That's really cool."

"You'd be surprised how many people don't even write their own shit," he said.

"Oh yeah?"

"Yeah, man, I'm talking powerful politicians, actors—I mean, I can't drop names, cuz it's against my contract, but believe me when I say that I write for some very famous people. It's crazy, man. The words they claim are rarely their own."

"Damn," I said. "That's disappointing."

"Nah, man, not for me. Just the other day, I heard my speech on fucking TV. No one will ever know it was mine, but I was like, fuck yeah, that's my speech! Good shit, man," he said, handing me her order. "She's paid through the month. Good talking, man. You're a cool dude.

Take care."

"Take care," I said.

I heard the shower water running, and, in that instant, decided, as a matter of self-preservation, to disregard etiquette. On the counter I found a pen and a piece of paper and wrote, "Thank you for the opportunity, but it's not for me. I think you'll find someone much better for the job," and then signed it "Jim."

The sound of an opening door startled me, and, initially, I feared that I was too late to sneak out, but then I realized that the sound had come from the guesthouse in the backyard. When I glanced outside, I saw a very small man, dressed like a Tibetan monk, emerge from the guesthouse and walk toward me. *What the fuck is this place?* As he walked by me, I said, "Hey," but he ignored me, continued into the kitchen, filled a glass with the special water, and then went back outside and into the guesthouse. I stared incredulously into the backyard for a few seconds before realizing that I needed to leave.

I left her drug order by the note and walked quietly out of the house, over the pond of fish, and through the metal door onto the street, where, once my feet were planted on the asphalt, I had the sudden urge to run. Without any sense of direction other than to go downhill, I sprinted—not with the rhythm of an afternoon jogger, but wildly, as if I were a feral animal darting between cars, hopping back and forth from the sidewalk to the street—until my muscles ached and sweat, streaming down from the pores in my forehead, stung my eyes. Whenever I heard a car approaching, I ducked behind a parked car, and, hidden behind the shiny side of a Porsche or Mercedes, waited to see if her black town car was tracking me.

Finally, after forty minutes of downhill running, I made it to the base of the steep ramp below my house on Sunset, and, as I panted my way up, Jackson greeted me at the gate.

"Do you need anything?" he asked.

"Need anything?" I said, sweating and resting my hands on my hips.

"You know—for the weekend. It'll be here soon enough."

"Oh," I said, realizing what he meant. "No, I'm good."

"Are you sure? Everybody always thinks they're good, but then the weekend comes, and everybody's knocking on my door after they've had a few drinks. I get almost 200 texts on weekend nights—it gets crazy. It would just be easier if you bought what you needed now."

"I'll let you know."

"Thanks," he said.

"Jackson, do you ever worry about … you know … the cops?"

"No, man," he said, laughing uproariously. "I have a good lawyer. And besides, I keep everything locked in cases. Only I have the key. They need a fucking warrant to open that shit. Dealers have rights, too, man. Don't worry."

Through the window, on my way into the house, I saw Levi on the living-room couch with the pale light of a laptop screen on his face, and, when I opened the front door, he quickly looked up, momentarily startled.

"Oh, so, how'd it go, man?"

"Jesus, Levi, you told me she was crazy. But you didn't tell me she was fucking insane. I had no idea what I was walking into."

"Did you fuck her?"

"If she'd had it her way."

"I fucked her the first time we worked together. That's what she does—she pays younger guys good money to do very little work, but then she holds them captive. I must have stayed there for a week— swimming, eating, fucking, massaging her, all that—"

"Why would you knowingly throw me into a situation like that?"

"Hey, I thought I was doing you a favor. Everyone needs work. Did you meet the little Tibetan guy?"

"Yeah, he didn't say a word."

"He only spoke to me once while I was there."

"What did he say?"

"'Move.'"

"Move?"

"I guess I was in his way."

I laughed and said, "All right, Levi, I appreciate your thinking of me, but in the future, skip me if it's for work like that."

"No problem," he said, without interest, looking back down at his screen, and then, in the quick flash of remembering something, he looked back up at me, said, "By the way, you got a package in the mail today," and pointed to the base of the stairs.

I peeled off the envelope taped to the front of a thin, square cardboard package, and, after detecting a whiff of spilled white wine, opened it. The handwritten note read:

Jake,

Let this remind you of all the hard work you've done. Let it remind you of the great opportunities you've been given. Most important, let it remind you of the great responsibility you must bear.

Love,
Your Mother

I ripped open the cardboard package to find my glistening, framed college diploma, along with the necessary pieces to hang it on a wall.
"My God, Mom," I said.

THIRTEEN

I don't know why I stayed in the Sunset House as long as I did. I stopped writing altogether; I didn't even scribble thoughts in the notebooks my grandmother had given me. Parker Thomas loved the idea of telling others that I was a writer, but he hated the idea of my spending time to actually write. "Get experience now, write later," he liked to say. It wasn't his fault. I let myself become seduced by the lifestyle.

The weekends always created the urge to do more, to go beyond present limits, to experience crazier things, to chase new feelings. After a month or so, my weekends were starting much earlier in the week—Thursday at first, then Wednesday, and so on, until, except for Depression Mondays, my time at the Sunset House had become one long weekend. The mornings were the toughest, but, after the lesson from Parker that a beer when I woke would settle me down, they became much more manageable. I kept a supply of beer under my bed and came to enjoy the ten minutes I spent each morning sipping from the can. I made a ritual of it: a few sips while still in bed, another sip after I sat up to play music from my laptop, a few sips in the shower, and the few remaining sips while I toweled dry. But then I needed two beers to bring me the same balance I used to get from one, and then three to get me where two used to. I added a cigarette to my morning routine, but then the short length of a single cigarette left me craving more. Soon I was smoking half a pack before noon. And eventually the moment came when beer and cigarettes alone weren't enough to keep me at peace, at which point I justified having a touch of whiskey or vodka in the morning, kick-starting my far-too-powerful-to-ignore craving for cocaine or some other drug much earlier in the day.

Jackson was right. I began spending hundreds of dollars on multiple trips per week to his room for my own supply. My usual order included cocaine and Molly, but sometimes, when I was feeling like a change, I bought something different that Jackson was pushing me to try ("*This shit will get you there, man,*" he often said). When the drugs became part of my daily diet, I stopped eating food regularly; one week, I ate nothing but a bag of baby carrots dipped in hummus. I began to get panic attacks. I always found it odd how easily or randomly they could be triggered—having an unpleasant thought, hearing an unfamiliar sound, seeing a piece of furniture out of its place, stumbling upon the carcass of a dead bird in the backyard ... Sometimes the attacks never came, but the fear of them happening was just as terrible of a feeling as actually having them.

Perhaps it was my dramatic leap into a hedonistic lifestyle, but my re-membrance of my time at the house at some point was just as hazy as the Los Angeles horizon; the only real proof of my experiences was charted by a timeline of photographs on the Internet, while all of my other memories remained unverified, floating around in a fluorescent limbo.

MEMORY

Somehow Parker and I are at the house of a rapper named Famous. He lives with two hookers. It's their night off, and they're wearing pajamas. The four of us snort a mysterious blue powder through a straw. Parker plays "Champagne Supernova" on the guitar, and we sing along. Then Famous raps freestyle for us while the girls cheer.

Memory

It's four in the morning at the Sunset House. Rin Tin Tin is playing music for a crowd in the living room. He falls and cuts his head on the corner of his DJ table. No one notices but me. The music keeps playing. The people keep dancing. I go to check on him. His forehead is bloody. I grab a towel to wipe the blood from his head.

"What are you doing?" he says.

"You have blood on your head," I say.

"At least get a picture of it before you wipe it off," he says.

I pull out my phone and snap a photo of him lying on the floor with a bloody forehead.

"I'll send it to you," I say.

"You post it. It would be too weird if I posted it."

"Yeah, fine," I say.

He grabs the towel from my hand and wipes his forehead. He gets up and continues playing music for the crowd.

MEMORY

It's early morning at the house, a few hours before sunrise. One guy tells me he's an artist. I say, "OK." He asks me if I have anything for him to paint. I bring him a chair from the living room. He lights a joint and takes a paintbrush to the chair. Soon, others with paintbrushes join him. Some of them bend over the top of the chair. Others lie underneath it. All of them stroke the chair with their colorful paintbrushes. The painters pass around the joint. The room fills with a thick smoke.

"It's beautiful," one girl standing next to me says. "Paint me," she says to them and takes off her clothes.

The painters turn their heads toward her in synchrony, as if they're a pack of wolves hearing the same unfamiliar sound. They move slowly toward her. They surround her and start painting her nude body. The tips of their paintbrushes—looking like sharp, colorful teeth—are nipping her all over. When they finish, the chair and the girl are covered in chaotic, squiggly lines.

MEMORY

It's early evening. The sun is setting. Parker and I are sitting on the deck. We hear the pitter-patter of the girls' high heels as they walk up the stairs. The girls come into our view, standing tall and thin on their high heels and wearing pretty dresses. One of the girls notices that we aren't dressed in the right clothes and says, "What the fuck, Parker? We're not going anywhere?"

"What's out there in that city that you don't have right here?" Parker says.

The girl says to her friend, "Don't you hate it when a cute dress goes un-photographed?"

"It's a completely wasted outfit," her friend says.

"Whatever, we'll stay here tonight, but can we at least take some pictures?" the first girl says.

I take photographs of the girls posing together. Then one of the girls says Parker and I should get in the picture. We ask Jackson, who is passing by, to take a picture of all of us. After the photos, Parker buys four E pills from Jackson. We all take one.

When we get the feeling of euphoria, we smile and breathe in and acknowledge how happy we are. Parker asks me to describe my feeling. I say that I feel as if I'm flying through the sky and hovering above the trees, rubbing my bare feet against the soft leaves. Everyone laughs. Parker tells me to keep going. I say that I feel as if I'm drinking the cold blue water from the pools on hotel rooftops and then doing the backstroke from cloud to cloud, resting on one sometimes to take a nap. Everyone laughs again. One of the girls moves closer to me.

The four of us are naked in the Jacuzzi, passing around a bottle of vodka, smoking cigarettes, and using Parker's car keys to dig out little mounds of cocaine from a baggie. We are very careful not to get the coke in the hot water. Parker starts fucking one of the girls. The other girl sits on my lap. I begin to fuck her. The Jacuzzi water splashes over the sides.

It is morning. We go to breakfast at a place on Sunset. Parker's girl tells us about a Chinese man in town who goes by a single name: Pink. Pink is worth $1 billion, she says. Pink asked her out at a club, she says.

"I told him I'm not sleeping with him. I'm not that easy," she says. "Still, he invites me to Vegas and tells me he'll get me my own private suite, and that I could invite my girlfriends. So, I mean, my girlfriends and I obviously decide to go. When we get there, he lets us go shopping with his credit card. So we bought new clothes, facials, massages, purses, everything! Then we joined him and his friends for dinner ... Our dinner bill was, like—can you believe this?—$30,000! It was all the wine, appetizers, entrees, desserts, and champagne. The next week, I ignored his phone calls. I mean, I can't be bought."

"At least he treated you right," my girl says. "I just dumped a guy because he was a thirty-five-year-old *writer* still renting a place. *Ew!* He couldn't afford to buy me anything."

MEMORY

A famous actor from a popular TV show comes to the Sunset House at three in the morning. He is drunk. He has a bottle of whiskey in his hand. He screams Jackson's name and falls over. He gets up. He screams Jackson's name again. Jackson finds him and brings him into his room. The actor was in the news recently for getting his second DUI and announcing that he's very serious about fixing the problem and going to rehab to get clean. The actor leaves the Sunset House. I ask Jackson what he wanted. Jackson says he is a client. Jackson says that he has many clients like him.

Memory

Parker, Yaas, her friend, Lily, and I are lounging around the rooftop pool of the Andaz hotel, drinking sangria on a sunny autumn afternoon. A group of three married gay couples occupy the space next to us. They are dancing and laughing loudly. Parker starts a conversation with them. They tell us they're in LA on vacation from Utah. Parker asks if they party. They tell us that they're high on GHB, and then they share some with us. Parker asks them about their sex lives. They say that they have more sex than straight people. "Guys are just so much hornier!" one of them shouts. Everyone laughs. Parkers asks for more details. They tell us that some gay men are "bottoms" and some are "tops" and some like "to take turns." Parker says, "Who would be the bottom and the top with Jake and me?" Parker points to me. One of the guys studies us both and says, "You would be the bottom, and he would be the top." Parker gets offended and says, "That's bullshit. He's quiet. I'm the aggressive one. I would be the top." The guy says, "No, honey, that just makes you a bossy bottom." Everyone laughs.

MEMORY

Parker, Levi, and I go to a party at a warehouse in Silver Lake. The streets are quiet. We wonder where the party is. Parker knocks on a garage door. Parker keeps knocking. We wait a few minutes. The garage door slides up. The music booms into the street. The bouncer asks for the password. Parker tells him. The bouncer lets us in and shuts the garage door.

Inside, it's packed with people. The film *Chinatown* is being projected onto the huge back wall. People are dancing. I see their silhouettes over Jack Nicholson's face. There's a performance art show in one corner of the warehouse. A guy is cutting his hair on a stool and repeating, "I don't know what to do. I don't know what to do," while a woman is riding a unicycle in circles around him.

I'm tired from not sleeping the night before. I go to the bathroom and do some blow to wake up. Inside the bathroom, a fifty-year-old man in a suit is crying. I ask him what's wrong. He says he's crying because his girlfriend just dumped him. I ask him why she dumped him. He tells me she was getting in trouble for cutting so much class. He tells me she's still in high school.

I ask him if he wants some blow. He says he does. I give him some. He tells me that he feels better. I ask him what he does for a living. He says he produces movies.

MEMORY

Parker and I make friends with some crazy Australians at a bar down the street. One of the Australians says to me, "Have you ever been snorkeled, mate?" I say, "What is snorkeled?" He says, "It's when you shovel cocaine up a sleeping person's nostril right before he inhales."

We bring them back to the Sunset House. I fall asleep sometime around sunrise but violently lurch forward in bed soon after. Parker and the crazy Australians are hovering above me, laughing.

"You've just been snorkeled, mate," one of them says.

MEMORY

I'm smoking a cigarette on the balcony after eating mushrooms. The glowing red embers at the end of my cigarette catch my attention. I think I see something moving around in there. Sure enough, there they are—hundreds of little men working with shovels and axes and wheelbarrows and brooms. They seem to be working together to build up a village or something. I watch them labor harmoniously, as beads of sweat flow down their faces. They are efficient and determined. But I decide to take a drag on my cigarette. When I suck in, it brightens the glow of the embers and catches all the men and the entire village on fire. A sickly smile spreads across my face when I hear them screaming in the flames.

MEMORY

"We're going to hang out with some fags tonight," Parker says to me, while we drink beer at an outdoor café.

"What?" I say.

"My gay buddy has a table at Voyeur tonight for his birthday. He wants us to come," he says.

"OK."

We sit around the table at the club. I look up at naked girls crawling around like spiders in nets that hang from the ceiling. Parker has sex with a girl in a bathroom stall. We bring our gay friends back to our house. One is named Nicky, and the other is named Pat. Parker suggests that we play a game of pool.

"Fags versus straight boys," Nicky says.

"Losers have to do a booty bump," Pat says.

"What's a booty bump?" I ask.

"You know, take it on the ledge," Nicky says.

I'm confused.

"Ecstasy pill up the asshole, babe," he says to me.

"Deal," Parker says.

"We better fucking win," I say to Parker.

After we win, Parker says, "Ah, fuck it. We'll all do it."

All of our assholes start to burn. Parker shoves several ice cubes up his asshole. He says it doesn't work. We try to numb the pain by taking shots of whiskey. Then Parker brings out a bag of cocaine. We go into my room, and Parker searches for a good surface to snort cocaine from. He sees my college diploma on the ground and picks it up. I watch Parker divide a mound of cocaine on the glassy surface of my framed diploma. I imagine that he's editing my diploma using white lines to cross out the words he feels are unnecessary. He uses one white line to cross out "UC Berkeley." Another white line to cross out "With a major in English literature." Another to cross out the governor's name. And one more to cross out the year I graduated. For the first time in a while I think about my mother.

When I stumble into the bathroom, Nicky stumbles in after me.

"Nicky, I like you fine enough, but I'm not into it like this," I say.

"Just take a piss," he says.

"Whatever," I say, pulling out my cock and pissing, while he watches.

"Why do I always fall for straight men?" he says after I finish.

I wake up in the morning on the floor next to him.

MEMORY

Parker and I are driving along Sunset with two girls. One of them is in the passenger seat next to Parker, and the other is in the backseat with me. We pass around a bottle of whiskey. Each of us takes a couple of swigs before passing it on. Also in the rotation is a bag of coke. The girl with me in the backseat offers to let me use her keys to dig it out.

"Put it all away," Parker says, urgently.

I look up as the traffic slows. I notice the flash of red and blue lights ahead.

"It's a checkpoint," Parker says.

My girl has the bottle of whiskey in her hand. I have the bag of coke. I grab the bottle from her and hide it under the seat. I put the bag in my shoe. Parker's girl in the front seat turns down the music. My girl straightens her posture.

"Turn the fucking music back up," Parker says. "Everyone act normal. Don't act guilty."

She turns the music up. We bob our heads and fake laughter. I realize I've done too much cocaine. I begin repeatedly swallowing to prevent myself from gagging. Parker's car inches forward in a long line of cars. I fear that I'll ruin it all by gagging and vomiting in front of an officer. Four cars are in front of us. Then three. My throat closes around the back of my tongue. I start to gag. Two cars are in front of us. I reach down under the seat. I unscrew the bottle of whiskey and take a gulp. I hold some in my mouth, so I can wet my throat again if I need to. One car is in front of us. I put the bottle down under the seat as we pull up to an officer.

"How we doing tonight?" the officer says.

"Just fine, Officer," Parker says.

"Where we coming from?"

"Dinner with these beautiful girls," Parker says.

"Anything to drink tonight?" the officer asks.

"Some wine with dinner," Parker says.

Another officer approaches my back window with a flashlight. I swallow the rest of the whiskey in my mouth. He points his flashlight into my eyes, forcing me to squint. Then he moves the light down to my feet. My eyes nervously trace the path of his light. When I look up, the officer is looking directly at me. I hold my gaze on him, until he turns around and walks toward another car.

"Carry on," the officer at Parker's window says.

At a safe distance away, Parker cheers and leans over to kiss his girl. Both of us in the backseat laugh at Parker, who begins to lick his girl's face in exaltation.

"Jake Reed, hand me that fucking bottle of whiskey," he says.

"Coming right up," I say.

MEMORY

"Nothing excites me anymore," Parker says to me one night.

"What do you mean?" I say.

"I'm scared out of my fucking mind. I can't feel anything," he says, and then he walks out the front door.

"Where are you going?" I say out the window.

I hear the gate open below and his car screech down the ramp. He comes back an hour later.

"Let's do this," he says.

"Do what?" I say. I follow him into his room.

"Only take one hit," he says.

"One hit of what?" I say.

"Acid, my good friend," he says, and then he puts something in his mouth.

"How much did you do?"

"Just do one."

"Yeah, but how much did *you* do," I say.

"More than one," he says with a smile.

"What do I do?"

"Just let the tab dissolve on your tongue and wait," he says.

"Fuck it," I say and put the tab on my tongue.

"Another journey," Parker says.

"What now?" I say, feeling anxious.

"We wait."

The minutes pass very slowly. I remember being in school as a young boy, sitting at my desk in the classroom, waiting for the last bell of the day to ring. The minute hand on the large, round clock on the wall always seemed to move more slowly during the last fifteen minutes of the day.

"Is anything going to happen?" I say to Parker.

"It takes an hour or so," he says. "Let's listen to some music."

Parker feels something first. "Oh God, here it comes."

My hands tremble in anticipation. I start to feel something. I look at Parker. He is glowing. I watch his body pulsate with every breath he takes, with every pump of his heart. His movements appear blurry, with a trailing effect. I don't know anymore where his movements start or finish.

"Holy shit," I say.

"Feel that?" he says.

I feel as if I'm dreaming. All of my senses are distorted. Parker's skin changes colors and textures. Soon, my brain registers the music, but I don't hear it. I can only see it. I can see the sounds emit from Parker's speakers and hear the colors pulsating from Parker's body.

"What the fuck," I say.

"Right?" Parker says.

The hours pass, and the feeling intensifies. Rin Tin Tin brings the party back to the house and plays music in the living room. Parker and I follow the blurry trail down toward the action. We walk through the crowd and up to the front next to Rin Tin Tin's equipment. We are stupefied by every sound we see and every color we hear. Parker puts another tab on his tongue.

"Fuck, man. Another one?" I say, but my words are drowned out by everything else in the room.

Parker stares at me as if he's seeing me for the first time. Hours later, I feel myself gradually come down. But Parker goes in the opposite direction.

"You're my best friend," he says.

"Huh?" I say.

"You're my best friend."

"Let's go back to the room." I pull him upstairs.

"You're my best friend," he says.

"I know." I take him into the bathroom and put his head into the sink and splash his face with water.

"You're my best friend," he says, again.

I try to hold myself together, as I put him in his bed and pull the covers over him.

"You're my best friend," he says.

He keeps repeating the phrase—over and over again.

I lie with him for half an hour, but he doesn't stop repeating himself. I bring him a glass of water, but he bats my hand away. The glass falls to the floor and shatters.

"Parker, you have to get it the fuck together," I say.

"You're my best friend," he responds, with empty eyes.

I turn out the lights in his room and close the door behind me. I lie on my bed. Parker won't stop. He starts screaming the phrase repeatedly, until the words begin to haunt me. Sometime in the morning, Parker's room finally becomes silent.

MEMORY

I buy a woman a drink at a club. She's wearing a ring on her left hand.

"You're married?" I say.

"Not tonight," she says.

The next morning, after she leaves my room, she finds me on Facebook. I browse pictures of her and her husband smiling on different vacations.

MEMORY

Everyone goes home for a few days during a holiday. I stay at the Sunset House. It's early in the morning. I'm standing on the deck and staring down at the city. Los Angeles is deserted. It's eerie, like a ghost town. I see no one for a long time. Then I finally see someone. I see Jesus Christ walking down Sunset Boulevard. He's wearing a white robe and brown sandals and has a thick, brown beard. I call to him from the deck railing. He walks up the ramp, through the gate, and up to the deck.

"Hey, Jesus," I say.

"Hello, my son," he says.

"How's it working out for you ... being Jesus?" I say, lighting a joint.

"You don't know who I am do you?"

"You're Jesus."

"I'm Hollywood Jesus."

"Well—in that case, you want a hit?"

"Sure," he says.

I watch Hollywood Jesus bring the joint up to his lips and take a big puff. It makes me laugh to see Jesus smoke weed. After we're both stoned, Hollywood Jesus tells me how hard it is to be him.

"Being a celebrity, I'm expected to act a certain way. People always want me to do Jesus stuff for them."

"Why don't you put on normal clothes and move somewhere else?"

"Because I'm Hollywood Jesus. I have a huge following. This is my life."

Memory

I wake up facedown on the sidewalk in front of a bus stop on Sunset. I'm wearing my black pea coat. It's raining. I'm soaked in rainwater. I look up. A Mexican woman is staring at me, while she waits for the bus.

During one of my rare lucid moments on one cold morning, as I shivered under thin, cold sheets, I thought about how, for me, the world of drugs was no longer an intangible one. I'd become quite masterful at identifying people in clubs or at bars carrying drugs, almost as if I could sniff them out, and after a silent nod and a quick smile in their direction, they would become my friends for the night, my teammates fighting for the same trophy. It was us against all those who didn't do drugs. Nonusers were the enemy, because the curse of their naiveté would never allow them to understand us; until they became users, they would always be ignorant and judgmental of our ways.

And the girls—college students, aspiring actresses, aspiring models, bartenders, club girls, Santa Monica girls having a Hollywood night, tourists visiting Los Angeles for the first time, married girls—were always one drink and one adventurous urge away from coming back to the Sunset House; by that time, they'd become for us warm, scented shapes of tits and asses with blurry faces who possessed, between their thighs, the key to the highest of highs.

I never remembered much of the intimate moments I shared with girls—a realization that often caused me much torment during sober moments. I futilely searched the layers of my brain for sensual memories of how they kissed, how they moved, or how their skin felt against mine; I rarely remembered even the way we were with each other, how their bodies were positioned relative to mine, how it began, how it ended. Often the kissing part was skipped over, and the rest of it became quite transactional: my cock, if it could still get hard after a night of certain drugs (Parker always kept a bottle of Viagra handy), might as well have been a phallic-shaped piece of wood, still attached to me but dead of feeling, functioning on its own behalf, while I watched myself in action, as if I were a third person in the room watching two other people mindlessly fuck. But the aspect of my intimacy with these girls that proved to be the most frustrating was my inability to recall the sounds they made, if they made any at all, the cadence of their voices, the sounds of their breathing. It was all lost on me, as if none of it had ever really happened. The silence that came to represent my sexual experiences haunted me.

During my relationship with Parker Thomas, I came to know that he had a profile on every relevant Internet dating site, even a Jewish one (he changed his last name for that one). He posted the same information on all of his profiles: blue eyes, tall, sales account manager, speaks multiple languages, cooks, plays the guitar, plays the piano, lives in West

Hollywood. His descriptions of himself weren't entirely fabricated: he'd taught himself several conversational phrases in Italian, Spanish, and French; he could cook one dish very well using an original Italian recipe for spaghetti Bolognese he'd found on the Internet; he knew how to play one song on the guitar perfectly, and he'd mastered another song on the piano. On the days when people weren't over, usually early in the week when the house was still recovering from the craziness of the weekend, he had girls over from the dating sites, and on the days when those girls weren't able to come over, he called upon Yaas, who always seemed willing to oblige him.

When it came to seducing girls, the most elaborate attempt I'd witnessed, before meeting Parker, was when one of my roommates in college, before the arrival of a girl to our apartment, scattered the floor of our living room with vinyl records and books (ones he thought would impress her) and then, on the table, set up a chessboard with the pieces strategically arranged to suggest a battle so hard fought that it was still ongoing. The girl ended up canceling the date. Parker Thomas, however, was a master at a much more advanced level of subterfuge. Throughout my stay in the Sunset House, I rarely knew a night when he slept alone.

But the madness, after a week in which each day it steadily crescendoed, tapered off by Sunday and dissolved into depression by Monday, when the house was hauntingly quiet and dark throughout the day, the bedroom doors locked, the curtains drawn shut. No one stirred. No one ate. No one lived. And, as we Xanax-dazed zombies slept off the pain and battled the loneliness, the stoic Mexican warriors worked ceaselessly to erase our sins and give us a shiny, clean house ready for the spoiled, self-indulgent madness of a new week.

Every Depression Monday, late at night, Parker brought his crying into my room, huddled close to me on my bed, and told me stories, mostly about the love of his old life—a ritual that enlightened me to the understanding that even those whom you've initially come to believe are nearly empty inside have something, usually someone, that's a source of pain responsible for shaping the current versions of themselves. Parker would, between short sucks of air and with a blue-grey tinge of nostalgia in his wet eyes, reminisce about long-ago summers with his ex-girlfriend—camping around fires or staying in log cabins or taking road trips out in the country—but, after he was through pining for her, he'd make the conversation about us.

"We have to get the fuck out of Los Angeles, man. It's too much. It's killing us," he said on one Monday.

"Let's travel. See the world. How about Thailand? Maybe Spain? I heard they eat dinner at midnight in Barcelona. Let's buy some flights right now. We need to get the hell out of here," he said on another Monday.

And, usually, right before he fell asleep in my bed, at the tail end of his emotional release, he would speak hopefully about the future of his romantic life.

"Jake, she might be the one," he would say. "I'm really into her. This is it."

"Who?"

"The girl I had this weekend."

"Really? That's great, Parker. You should do something about it."

"Yeah, man, this girl's different. She just does it for me. I feel something when I'm with her. I love a new feeling."

But on Tuesday morning he was back to his desensitized ways—his mentality hardening, his sentimentality drying up—acting as if Monday had never happened. When I asked him about his new girl, the one whom he was "really into" just the night before, I could always rely on the same response—"Who? What are you talking about, Jake?"—and then by Wednesday we were focused on new prospects.

"Would you fuck her?" Parker, pointing to a random girl on the street, would say as we stumbled home on Sunset from wherever.

"Yeah, I'd fuck her," I'd say.

"Look at *her*. I'd fuck her."

"I'd fuck her, too."

"What about that one?"

"Maybe I'd fuck her. Yeah, I'd fuck her."

"Me, too."

I started to understand that Parker's angst on Depression Mondays would never be resolved by my comforting him or our leaving Los Angeles or his having a new love interest. And as for the girl he'd left behind, the one he seemingly still loved, I was convinced that she only lived in his mind as the girl from a simpler time, a time that, in hindsight, made sense to him. She was, I presumed, just a memory he'd have when he was sad; he was sad on Mondays because he was coming down from all the drugs he'd done throughout the week. It was never about anything else for Parker Thomas other than just getting through Monday. So I slipped into the routine of just letting him talk until he fell asleep.

Fourteen

I only had one connection to my past life—the emails Andrew sent me—and, admittedly, every morning, when I was still somewhat sober, I checked my new messages, hoping that one from him would be waiting for me. Because I never responded to his emails, I knew that the day he'd stop sending them was imminent; and, since I hadn't received one from him in quite some time, I thought that day had finally come. But one morning I heard from him again.

From: Andrew Martin
To: Jake Reed
Subject: Alive???

Jake? Are you still alive? Where've you been? It's been way too long ... I thought you might have a good opinion on something ... My bosses at work called me into a meeting and asked me why I didn't have a girlfriend. Usually I'm prepared to answer their questions, but I wasn't prepared to answer that one. They said it looks good when the employees are in committed relationships. They said it shows that we are good people with good heads on our shoulders. I'm sure they're right. I trust them. They both have their MBAs and earn a shitload of money. They definitely bring a lot of value to society. Well, I guess I better find myself a girl, right? What do you think? Anyway, must go back to work. I've already gone 1 minute over the time I set aside to write this email. Oh, yeah, Tamarine says hi.

Cordially,
Andrew

I was still chuckling from reading his email when an instant message popped up on my screen.

Stone Fox: hi
Me: there she is ...
Stone Fox: i'm about to walk to starbucks. need to get out of the office. can you talk on the phone? i want to ask you something.
Me: yeah, call me
Stone Fox: ok, 2 Min

Stone Fox is no longer available to chat.

My relationship with Stone Fox had developed gradually throughout my time at the Sunset House, usually during my solitary moments when I was resting (or recuperating) in bed: first it was emailing, next instant-messaging (because she had a full-time job, she was always available to chat during the day), then texting, and, finally, talking on the phone. Each new layer of our connectedness, something we sort of graduated to each time, was, to me, a testament of our mutual interest to learn more about each other. I was, of course, skeptical of her at first, given the slightly suspicious nature of our email introductions to each other, but she slowly convinced me of her sincerity each new time she reached out to me. It also helped that she seemed interested in many of the same things that interested me.

She still, however, maintained a seemingly impenetrable layer of privacy between us: her identity to me had always been "Stone Fox," and she refused to tell me her real name or connect with me on Facebook so I could learn about her that way. I had no idea what she looked like, so I was a bit relieved that, when we started our phone relationship, she didn't have the voice of a dirty old man but, rather, a very sweet, confident voice, ripe with femininity. Over time, I became more intrigued by her, or, rather, her voice, or maybe even the girl I imagined behind her voice. And, of course, as I'd always been accustomed to doing, I started to piece together her image, one that appealed to my fantasies, from little clues in the messages she sent me or the sound of her voice or the way she laughed or told stories.

I learned through our conversations (we communicated briefly in some medium every day) that Stone Fox, five years older than me, had studied English literature in college.

"You went to Cal, right?" she asked once.

"Yeah. You, too?"

"No. Stanford."

"No shit? Now we're required to hate each other."

She laughed and said, "Forbidden love."

She went on to tell me that her relationship with literature had started with her love for Shakespeare and how, with a dream to act on Broadway one day, she'd memorized some of the great Shakespearean speeches. She mentioned her Jane Austen, Virginia Woolf, and Brontë sisters phases, and, later, much to her surprise, her fascination with dirty realists Charles Bukowski and John Fante.

"I know, I know. That doesn't make sense," she said.

"I think it's cool. It doesn't have to make sense," I said, enjoying a topic I had, during my time at the Sunset House, drifted away from. "Is your job in the arts?"

"Nope. I'm a content manager at Viacom."

"Wow—that sounds important."

"I'm older than you. I hit a point when my imagination kind of lost stamina—just couldn't focus on one creative thing long enough to … you know, really accomplish anything. Then there were bills, student loans—all that," she said.

After I told her where I was living, during a later conversation, Stone Fox loved to ask me about the goings-on at the Sunset House—a conversation that, because I wanted to keep her separate from that part of my life, I always tried to avoid. So I usually found something else partly related to talk about instead.

"I think one of my roommates might have a serious social media addiction," I said to her once.

"Don't we all?"

"Probably. And, really, I'm not one to talk—I used to work for a company as the social media guy. I mean, I used to do that stuff all day. But I think my roommate has achieved his own honorary status."

"How so?"

"Well, he's this DJ guy—actually pretty popular in Hollywood—but he spends nearly all of his free time, I'm talking about all day, posting stuff on Facebook and hitting the refresh button to gauge the immediate reaction. He gets depressed—well, more like incredibly angry—if his posts don't do well."

"Do well?"

"Yeah, you know, get a bunch of 'likes' or comments from his 'friends.' Some of his posts are actually very clever. And when one of his posts does well, it's the best day of his life. It's like all of his emotions stem from his online world—like he hates it, but he's also dependent on it or something."

"You know, I just read an article about a study that, I guess, sort of tries to prove that people get, like, this euphoric rush of endorphins from every comment or 'like' or mention or heart or favorite or whatever else happens on social networks. Then the author compared that feeling to the one people get from taking certain drugs, like Ecstasy, I guess." She laughed. "Now that I'm talking about it, I feel like it's a bit out there, but it still made me think."

"No, no, I believe it," I said, feeling a bit culpable.

"Anyway, the article goes on to say that, basically, we're all going to lose that special human element of making a connection in the real world with real people. Scary stuff, huh?"

"I can see that … I'm sort of convinced no one knows one true goddamn thing about anyone else."

"Yeah, it's just where we're at. But, of course, critics accused the author of being a disgruntled old-timer who doesn't get the Internet. 'We are actually more connected now than we've ever been,' was the general sentiment of the critics. I'm not sure what I think yet."

I began to feel comfortable with Stone Fox, to trust her. Perhaps it was her willingness to share her thoughts and ideas with me, or maybe it was that I felt connected to her, or that I could relate to her, or that we seemed to have similar mentalities about our existence. During our conversations, even if they lasted for just a few minutes each day, I began to allow her access to a very private side of me. Our exchanges, on the Internet or on the phone, carried on smoothly as we shared stories or talked about our doubts and loneliness. She had become my outlet, and I had become hers.

"Jake, did you write about your own life … you know, in the short story you wrote? I mean, is it autobiographical?" she asked me once on the phone, during her lunch break.

"I guess—well, some of the time. Sometimes I made stuff up."

"Do you really feel that out of place, that lonely? Because I feel that lonely, too. Sometimes I feel like I'm just watching my daily life play out on a giant projection screen, while I'm living my real life in my head, or something. I don't know. If I was in a room with a thousand people, I'd still feel alone."

"I know exactly what you mean."

My phone rang. I answered it.

"Sorry, got caught in the elevator. We must've stopped on every floor on the way down," Stone Fox said.

I laughed and said, "I don't miss those elevators."

"I've decided I want to meet you. Do you want to meet me?"

"Of course."

"We have to do it within the week, because after that I'll be out of touch for a while."

"I'm free whenever."

"I took the day off tomorrow. How about then?"

"Let's do it."

"Cool. I'll come to you."

The following afternoon, I was in my room sipping a beer and listening to an Andrew Bird album when Stone Fox called and told me to meet her in the lobby of the Andaz. I walked quietly down the hall, to avert attention from Parker or Rin Tin Tin, and out the front door. From the balcony, I had a clear view of the adjacent Andaz—the hotel that, when I first moved in, had an advertisement of Oprah's face on the side of the building. Oprah had been replaced, two rotations before, first by an advertisement for an upcoming 3D film and next by a giant Jesus Christ with outstretched arms and words above his head that read: "The end of the world is coming. Only Jesus Christ can save you for all eternity."

I left my house, sidestepped a few scurrying valets on the way down, and made a left at the base of the ramp toward the entrance to the hotel. Inside the lobby, I tried nonchalantly scanning the area for the girl I imagined to be Stone Fox.

"Jake," said someone behind me in a voice I recognized.

I turned around. She was short, built with wide hips, yet still shapely; she wore unfashionable jeans and a sweatshirt, reminding me of the way girls at my college used to dress for class. She had straight brown hair up in a loose ponytail and a plain yet attractively kind face with a pleasant, inviting smile. But *her eyes* … She had big, intelligent, emotional, sober, reddish-brown eyes that were full of life—the kind of eyes that have their own set of features, as if they could smile on their own or share their own bits of wisdom with anyone gazing into them. Although she looked very different from the girl I'd imagined her to be, Stone Fox looked like a real person, and I was happy that she was such a change from the girls I'd shared time with at the Sunset House.

"Stone Fox," I said, smiling.

"Rachel," she said.

I laughed and said, "She has a real name ..."

"Would you like to get a drink in the hotel bar?" she said, nervously.

"Definitely," I said.

We took a seat next to each other on the leather-padded stools along the bar. I shifted my stool toward her as she shifted hers toward me, the simultaneous timing of which drew a smile and then a soft laugh from each of us, as we both tried to figure out what to do next.

"Here we are—in real life," I said.

"Yep," she said, still smiling. "This is weird, huh?"

"We're just not used to it."

The bartender—in a white dress shirt with a bow tie and a black vest buttoned down the front—approached us, polishing a wide-mouthed wineglass with a hand towel, and asked, "What are we drinking this afternoon?"

I gestured to Rachel that she should order first, and she glanced down at the drink menu on the table, held her finger on the drink of her choice, and read it to the bartender. "Um ... I'll have a glass of this ... Chateau St. Didier Parnac, Malbec."

"Certainly," the bartender said. "Good choice."

"Can you just bring the bottle and two glasses," I said.

"Coming right up."

As he walked away, leaving me alone with her, I felt the slight, wet heat of anxiety surge through my body. Stone Fox was someone I'd gotten to know quite well and engaged with rather effortlessly over the last couple of months—but only from behind a high-tech wall. I considered the thought that I might be more comfortable with her if we could set up our laptops along the bar and chat with each other that way; but after the waiter brought our bottle of wine and poured us each a glass, our first few sips seemed to resolve the issue.

"When I knew I was going to see you, I decided to read 'The Tales of a Desert Wanderer' again," she said, bringing me to marvel at the thought that our relationship—the calls, texts, emails, and now the drinks in person—was a result of my deciding to start a blog and post a short story. *Incredible, really.*

"Oh, great—it got worse the second time around, didn't it?"

"No, but I think you're a bit of a romantic deep down."

"Shit—your man Bukowski would kill me," I said.

"I think he was a romantic, too."

"Well, there *was* a 'bluebird' in his heart …"

She laughed and said, "*Right?* So"—pausing to sip her wine—"has Hollywood gotten hold of you yet?"

"How so?" I said, trying to fight back the guilty look on my face.

"Hey, I lived here once, a while back. It's not a place for world-weary thinkers, you know."

"I'm still alive," I said, playfully.

Then, after a quick exchange of smiles, she said, "I feel very drawn to you … like we've known each other for a very long time."

"I feel that way, too. I'm happy we decided to meet," I said, feeling that warm, mellow buzz that comes after finishing a glass of smooth red wine.

"Have you ever looked into supernovas?" she asked.

"You know what—my roommate, Parker, has played that supernova song by Oasis on his guitar so many damn times, I should be a professor of supernovas. But, sadly, I'm not sure I can even say what they are."

"So a star explodes and creates this light—so brilliant, so powerful, so bright that it shines more spectacularly than every other star in the sky combined, but just briefly—then it's gone. A black hole. Nothing can escape. No light. But during that brief amount of time it might be the single most powerful thing in the entire universe—nothing shines brighter."

"I like that," I said.

"I read about supernovas the other day and, for some reason, I thought … I thought about you and me—I mean, well … I thought about us."

I smiled and then she smiled. The waiter came to check on us, and when I was about to order a second bottle of wine, she told him we were fine and he walked away.

"Cutting us off, huh?" I said.

"Let's go do something."

"Sure, anything."

We got into one of the cabs lined up outside the Andaz, and Rachel told the driver to take us to the West Hollywood Library.

"The library is brand-new. They just built it. It's supposed to be beautiful," she said.

With its natural lighting and airiness and rooms filled with elegantly polished wood and floor-to-ceiling windows showing views of palm trees, the hills, and the curvy San Vicente Boulevard below, the library was indeed a beautiful structure. We spent our time browsing books in the paper-scented aisles and reclining on soft, leather chairs to talk quietly.

"So ... have you worked on any more short stories?" she asked me.

"I've been a bit distracted lately. But I need to get back into it."

"You need to get out of that house. How do you expect to get any work done there? I mean, I guess I don't know you *that* well, but I don't think of you as the type to be living there. Am I right? Come live near me in Santa Monica. You can get a place in my neighborhood, and we can read books all day, while we lie in hammocks and drink ice tea."

"You know me better than you think you do."

After we'd had our fill of library books, we hailed a cab and made our way down to the Los Angeles County Museum of Art—a short two miles away—where we browsed the art for a while, including an exhibition of Larry Fink's black-and-white photographs of celebrity life in Hollywood, and then hopped in another cab up Fairfax to get Chick-fil-A sandwiches for dinner. The cab driver looped around to the drive-through window, where a smiley, maroon-shirted employee handed us our food, and then took us west on Sunset Boulevard toward the glowing orange of the setting sun, while we ate in the backseat.

"Well, I don't mean to come off like this," Rachel said, after we'd been dropped off at the entrance of the Andaz, "but I have a room here. Do you want to come up?"

"Are you sure?"

"Yes," she said, a shy smile stretching across her face.

"Lead the way."

The room was immaculate and brisk—the type of air-conditioned quality only found in decadent hotel rooms—and the pure-white sheets were pulled tight, without a single wrinkle, and tucked into a queen-size bed with six large pillows resting on top of it. There was a flat-screen TV resting on a desk along the wall in front of the bed, a leather chaise longue next to a small, round table in the open space next to the bed, and, at the far end of the room, a sliding-glass door that opened to a balcony and a view of the hills. I opened the sliding door and looked down at the Sunset House. I thought it looked very different from my view, almost peaceful in a way.

"We have such a great view of my house from here," I said.

"The house of hedonism," Rachel said, coming up behind me.

I turned around and she kissed me, and we continued for several seconds. I slightly opened one eye, noticing both of her eyes were shut passionately tight, then shut my eye and kissed her some more until she pulled away, as if to slow herself from taking things too quickly.

"Do you do this with all the girls?"

"I'll tell you this: I don't remember the last real conversation I had with another girl. Besides, I've never spent time with a girl quite like you," I said.

When my body was on top of hers under the cool, white sheets, and it was happening, she looked at me through her big brown eyes, as if all her love over the span of her lifetime was meant only for me.

"Tell me you love me," she said.

"What?" I said, her words catching me unprepared.

"Tell me you love me."

I moved into her—her neck arched back and she wrapped her legs tightly around me—and, seduced by the moment, said, "I love you."

After it was over, I lay on my back, my forehead beaded with sweat, and she lay next to me, tracing my chest with her index finger.

"Have you heard of the 'irresistible force paradox'?" she asked me.

"I'm starting to feel uneducated around you," I said, lightheartedly. "What is it? Please tell me."

"So there's an unstoppable force, and then there is an immovable object, both things said to exist. The paradox arises when an unstoppable force meets an immovable object. So let's say I was an immovable object, and you were an unstoppable force ... What would happen when you ran into me? Sometimes thinking about stuff like that drives me crazy all day. I feel like my head is going to explode."

I laughed and said, "I like the way you think."

"I want to ask you something ..."

"OK ..."

"What is it that drives you to write? Where is that coming from?"

"Um ... well—I'm not really sure."

"You have to know *something*," she said.

"OK ... Let me see," I said, pausing to gather my thoughts, and she kissed me on the cheek. "Some of the best memories I have of college were from the nights before one of my papers was due. You remember—the teacher gave us a list of prompts relating to the novels we had to read during the semester?"

"Oh, I remember," she said.

"Well, the writing was never the hardest part for me. The hardest part for me came before—like, during the time I spent trying to understand the characters and themes in one of the novels. But when I was finally ready to write something—and it was always super last minute, really late at night—all my confusion was gone, and for the next several hours I was able to write continuously with this ... lucidity ... or rhythm, I guess. I was sort of strange about it, too—like, I used to bob my head and sway my body as I banged away at my laptop keys—you know, like some concert pianist playing in front of a large crowd or something. I drank several cups of coffee, talked to myself, paced around my room, and worked into the early hours of the morning. And when I finished, usually right before I rushed off to make it to class, I printed out this crisp, clean ten-page paper, and it felt perfect in my hands, almost like ... biblical or something. One time, a professor read my paper aloud to the class, and later, some of the students asked me about my ideas or just made small talk with me. I don't know ... I felt like ... I had a voice ... I guess I spent most of my college years confused, really, and the more I got involved with people, the worse it was. But writing always made things simple for me. It made me believe I could contribute something. I guess I'm still sort of chasing that feeling." I paused and looked at her for the first time during my monologue, and it seemed as though she'd soaked up with her eyes every one of my words. "But then, right when I walked out of that classroom with no paper to go home and write, everything was confusing again."

"I think I'm falling for you," she said. "Can you handle that?"

"Which version of me?" I joked.

"Just ... you."

We were with each other again, and when it was over she said, "Maybe we should order another bottle of wine and drink it on the balcony."

"Perfect," I said.

We dialed the concierge, and they said someone would be up in fifteen minutes with our bottle of red wine. When we heard the knock, I got out of bed, walked down the hall, slipped into one of the two robes hanging in the closet, and opened the door.

"Wine delivery," he said.

I recognized his accent. "*Sei Italiano?*" I said.

"*Si.* You speak Italian?" he said.

"A little bit. I studied abroad there."

"*Dove?*" he asked.

"Siena."

"Ah, very beautiful city."

"*Di dove sei?*" I said, inquiring where he was from.

"*Roma,*" he said.

"How do you like living in the States?" I asked, signing the bill on my knee.

"Well, I came to Los Angeles for a new life and to live a dream. But all I think about now is the money. I never think about the money in Italy. You don't need so much over there. It is so different here. I don't much like the stress."

I smiled and said, "I think I know what you mean."

"*Ciao, bello.* Enjoy the *vino. Piacere.*"

"*Piacere,*" I said, closing the door.

We sat in robes on the balcony, with two glasses brimming with dark red wine, while we stared down at people already proliferating on the Sunset House deck.

"I think I like my house better from up here," I said, lighting a cigarette. "Up here with you."

She smiled and touched my hand and then looked at me curiously. "How did you get those scars on your back? I noticed them earlier."

"War wounds from another life," I said.

When I awoke early the next morning, Rachel, with her hands crossed over my chest and her chin resting on her hands, was staring at me.

"Good morning," she said.

"Morning," I said. "Jesus, I passed out, huh?"

"You looked so peaceful."

"Did you sleep well?"

"I didn't sleep," she said.

"Didn't sleep at all?"

"I wanted to soak in all my time with you. I enjoyed watching you sleep."

"I haven't slept that well in—God, forever," I said.

"But, unfortunately, I have to go to work now," she said.

"When can I see you again?"

"I hope soon."

She kissed me good-bye and pulled away against the volition of her sullen eyes, but I pulled her back for one more kiss and then watched her walk out of the room. I had a cigarette on the balcony and spotted a few deep sleepers scattered across the deck of my house.

I left the hotel and made the short journey up the ramp to my house with an excitement in my step. My time with Rachel, the girl I'd met on the Internet, had enlivened me with the sweet feeling of connecting soberly to a real person, an event made even more thrilling by her being an attractive and intelligent person. She had also reminded me of my passion for literature and reinvigorated my desire to accomplish something remarkable, and ideas were already ripe in my head for more stories I wanted to write.

But my elation was short-lived. My phone vibrated, alerting me to a new email, and, standing in front of the gate at the top of the ramp, I read it, then read it again three times, each subsequent reading worsening the feeling in my stomach. It was an email from the editors of *The New Yorker*. Although I'd hoped something good would come from my submitting a short story, I always knew that expecting anything to happen in my favor would be impractical, maybe even pretentious; still, something about receiving a rejection letter made it gruesomely real. I read it again just to be sure.

From: <u>Fiction, TNY</u>

To: <u>Jake Reed</u>

Subject: Your fiction submission

Dear Mr. Reed,

We appreciate your desire to be published in *The New Yorker*. Regretfully, we will not be publishing your short story. We advise against your submitting another piece for at least six months.

Sincerely,

The Editors

Goddamn it. And then, to make matters worse, throughout the rest of the week several more rejection letters from the other literary publications I'd submitted to appeared in my inbox, seeming to hurl themselves at me like deadly daggers. The most positive response I received was from an independent publisher: "It seems a literary career is ahead of you. Unfortunately, your content is not for us. Best of luck, Jake. Keep writing." I read them all multiple times, as if by doing so I could replace the words with the ones I wanted to read, the ones I needed to read. And, in some sort of cosmic succession of misfortune, Rachel sent me an unforgettable email one afternoon, after I hadn't heard from her for more than a week.

From: Stone Fox
To: Jake Reed

Jake,

I'm sorry that I've been avoiding our daily chats and haven't responded to your recent emails or texts. It's important that I tell you something. First, I want you to know how unbearably difficult it was for me to walk out of the hotel room that morning. I feel that I left my soul in that room, somewhere between those white sheets. Before meeting you, I'd nearly given up on making a real connection in the world-- something I believe, as silly as it sounds, I've done with you. There's a depth in you I've been searching for in others my whole life. I felt drawn to you after reading a single sentence of yours. And then after our time together, I knew that I'd made the right decision in meeting you.

(As you continue to read this letter, I can only ask that you try to trust me ...)

But I also knew that if our connection was what I believed it could be, I'd be writing this email with a broken heart.

See, most things are never as good as they seem. It's the curse of a species that relies heavily on an imagination. But what we had, at least for me, was real, not something conjured up by the imaginations of two lost souls hoping for something better in their lives. Although I've thought myself to be dead for a long time, being with you made me realize I'm not impervious to feeling something wonderful in my core. It also, however, made me realize that I am not impervious to pain.

It's only fitting that someone like you came into my life in such a grandiose flash of brilliance. It reminds me that I am so small, so powerless against anything real. You did it. You managed to penetrate every layer of me. You know me better than any person I've ever been with. I'll always fantasize about where all of this could have gone ...

But now I must face reality.

I told you that I would be out of touch for a while. Well, that's true, but it's a bit more complicated than that. The truth is ... I'm getting married this weekend.

I know it sounds absurd. It feels absurd to write it. I'm already dead from reading it. I'm sorry for being dishonest. I'm sorry for everything, really. I only ask that, once your anger for me fades into apathy, you try to understand why I wanted to be with you, even for just one night. It was just something I couldn't pass up, even at the expense of your feelings or mine.

But out of respect to the next phase of my life, I need to cut ties with you. Again, I'm sorry.

I know that the world confuses you. I fear that you have a tendency to float through life without showing anyone who you truly are, but I also know that deep inside of you is a desire to make a real connection with someone. Why else would you agree to meet me?

I think you're capable of something great, Jake. I hope that you find the courage to believe in yourself more than you do. I know that I'll always regret not being the one to experience your journey with you. Goodbye.

With love,
Rachel

"What the *fuck?*" I yelled, slamming my laptop shut in confusion and anger.

Parker opened my door and, with sleep still imprinted upon his face, stood there scratching his head while drinking from a can of beer. I caught a glimpse of Yaas peering sheepishly at me from behind his shoulder.

"You good, man?" he said.

I didn't respond.

"Let's go get some coffee," he said.

"Yeah, let's get the hell out of here," I said.

I flipped open my laptop and quickly wrote a short email to Rachel.

From: Jake Reed
To: Stone Fox

It is what it is. Supernova ... I get it now.

--J

Parker and I walked along Sunset in the warmth of a Los Angeles sun slightly chilled by a subtle fall breeze. Perhaps on any other day it might have been a lovely scene to me. But not that day. The sun shone irritatingly in my eyes, the sky looked artificially blue, and the breeze blasted the stink of the city into my nostrils. The horns blared at an octave far too piercing for comfort, and red tour buses roared too noisily down the street.

Parker told stories from the night before, or that's what I imagined him to be doing, as I heard only the sound of his voice, not his words. Rather, I was distracted by anyone who came into my line of vision. I observed a family of American tourists—with their swiveling heads and pointing fingers—gape with excitement at the unfamiliar sights of Sunset Boulevard; the father and his two teenage sons wore cowboy boots and cowboy hats, and the mother was plain-looking and overweight. I stared at a baby (only the second child I'd seen my entire time in West Hollywood)—strapped to his father's chest with his arms and legs dangling impotently—whose view of the new world was blocked by the phone his daddy typed into. I looked at two homeless men, with dirty faces and dirty hands and tattered clothes, against the chain link fence that ran along the sidewalk, one of them sleeping, the other vacuously sipping from a bottle of cheap liquor. I noticed a Mexican guy in an apron taking a smoke break in a parking lot, and then a pigeon on the ground in front of me stupidly walking in circles, looking for something to eat.

"Let's get coffee here," Parker said, turning toward a coffee shop that had a large outdoor patio with several tables.

"Large Americano for me," Parker told the barista and then pointed to me.

I held up two fingers, and Parker paid her for both drinks.

We sat at a round table at the back of the patio. When the barista called Parker's name, he left the table to retrieve our coffees, and I lit a cigarette. The headline of an abandoned newspaper on our table caught my attention: "Well-known Pastor Accused of Statutory Rape With High-School Student." The familiar face in the photograph accompanying the headline compelled me to read more.

"No fucking way," I said, after confirming that the photo was indeed of Liz's father, the pastor. "Unfuckingbelievable."

Parker came back, set the two cups of coffee down on the table, and lit a cigarette. "Yaas was giving me all sorts of shit this morning," he said. "I guess I fell asleep while we were fucking. She was on top. I don't remember any of it, so I told her ..."

I stopped listening when I noticed two guys around my age sitting at a nearby table, who seemed particularly interested in Parker's story. They sat in silence with the concentrated, furtive expressions people often have when they resort to eavesdropping. As Parker continued his story, I watched the two eavesdroppers intermittently glance at each other—the same type of glance two people in agreement share while hearing the dissenting opinion of a third person.

"You know?" Parker said.

"Definitely," I said, losing momentary interest in the eavesdroppers and focusing on Parker.

"Like when I'm watching porn—I have to see everything. I always have to see initial penetration in every stage. If I skip to a new scene, and they're fucking in a new position, I have to go back and watch the part when they first started fucking in that new position, or I just can't get off. But, anyway, she just gets mad at the stupidest shit, like, this morning, after she calmed down, I was trying to teach her how to give me good head. And then she gets mad at me when I tell her to stop sucking my dick after I busted. Our dicks are just way too *sensitivo* for that shit, you know?"

"Yeah …"

"And that's about the time we heard you yelling in your room," Parker said. "So what's up with you, dude?"

"I think," I said, pausing to take a drag on my cigarette and a sip of my hot coffee, "I'm just sort of … disillusioned with a few things."

The eavesdroppers abruptly rose from their table, walked over to ours, and hovered silently above us. I felt uncomfortable in their presence.

"What is it?" Parker said to them.

"We think it'll benefit you two to read this. Please keep it. I have plenty more. Remember, there's always time," the guy closer to me said, handing me a folded leaflet.

Distracted by the self-righteous tone of the speaker's voice, the crossed arms of his right-hand man, both of their tight-lipped, expressionless faces, and the overall condescending manner in which they carried themselves, I accepted the leaflet without inquiry. The two guys returned to their table.

"What the fuck?" Parker said, confused. "What is it?"

The folded cover of the leaflet showed a picture of Jesus Christ with his hand raised and a golden halo above his head, and page one had a series of common Christian phrases—"Have you found peace with God?" and "Jesus loves you" and "Prayer will save you in the final hour"—in bright, big letters alongside pictures of people smiling. I flipped one more page, and, before closing the leaflet, noticed a long list of vices, some of them being, "Drugs, Drinking, Smoking, Premarital sex, Cussing …"

I stood up, feeling the wrath of the monster within me, and marched over to the eavesdroppers' table. "I don't think I'll be needing this. You can have it back," I said, forcibly slamming the leaflet on the table.

"Are you sure? I think it'll be good for you," the one who spoke earlier said in a calm tone, which seemed to unsettle me even more.

"Let's chat for a second," I said, pulling a chair over to their table and sitting down.

"Sure," he said.

"I had this dream once that I visited every motel in America and replaced the Bible in the drawer with *The Great Gatsby*. What do you think that means?" I said, angrily.

"Well, I'm quite certain it means that you—"

"It means that I had a goddamn good dream. Do me a favor and keep your bullshit to yourself, you priggish fuck."

"What's your name?" he asked, condescendingly.

"Hazel *Fucking* Motes," I said, fuming.

"Jesus loves you, Hazel Motes," he said. "I hope that, for your benefit, you learn to love Him."

"Fuck off," I said, leaving their table and walking back to mine.

Parker was laughing. "What's gotten into you, dude?" he said. "Leave the poor Jesus freaks alone."

"Let's go get fucked up," I said.

"Sounds good to me."

Later that evening, one of my housemates was having people over, and, at some point, I found myself in the bathroom doing cocaine with a girl.

"Don't tell me you're out of blow?" she said, hungry for more.

"I sure hope I'm not," I said.

"Are you OK? You don't look so good. You're really sweating."

"I'm fine," I said, leaning in to kiss her. She kissed me back, and then, as she pulled up her skirt, I sat on the lid, and she climbed on top of me. I couldn't feel anything.

"What the fuck are you doing?" she screamed, as I tried to choke her. She pushed me away and fell to the floor.

"I thought that's what—"

"You're a fucking *psycho*, dude," she said, back on her feet, fixing her skirt and then charging out of the bathroom.

"Wait, don't leave!" I said, pulling up my pants and chasing after her. "I have some more blow in my room. I'm sure. I just have to find it," I yelled, as people huddling in the hallway lifelessly stared at me. "I'll come find you, then. I'll be right back." I then staggered into my room.

Convinced a bag of cocaine was somewhere, either hidden purposely or misplaced accidentally, I rummaged through my entire room on my knees; I searched under the bed, tore through everything in my closet, upturned all my books and searched between their pages, scoured the cracks in the floor, checked the drains in the shower and the sink. As if I were a rabid, heaving, feral animal pausing to rest after a long bout of madness, I stood up and looked at the mess I'd created in my room, and then a subtle movement caught my eye. *Someone's in the room with me.* I jerked my head to the right and saw him standing there, looking at me, with sullen, sunken eyes, hollow cheeks, taut flesh, and a pale face.

"Who are you?" I said to no answer. "Oh shit," I said. "*You* … are me."

I reached out, touched the bathroom mirror, and incredulously traced the contours of my face's reflection, one I hardly recognized. My right knee wobbled as I braced myself with both hands on the sink, and I watched the face in the mirror sway erratically. The eyes looked dark and dead.

"I'm going down," I said to him.

I fell sideways through the bathroom doorway and hit my bedroom floor without bracing myself. When I awoke, it was still night; I'd fallen on top of my books, and one of my hardcovers was painfully digging into my cheek. I raised my face off the book and looked directly into the eyes of Ernest Hemingway on the back cover of *The Short Stories*. He had a mustache, his hair was loosely parted, his right eyebrow was raised curiously, and his right eye was squinting at me disapprovingly.

"You want to be a writer?" Hemingway said.

"I think so," I said.

"That's a problem. You must *know* so," he said.

"I know so."

"Then forget what you think are your problems and write. You think you're flawed? You *are not* flawed. Get yourself together and focus. I wrote at least 500 words a day, every day, and I never drank while working. This is what it takes," he said.

I pulled two other books out from under me that had been jabbing my stomach, *Sputnik Sweetheart* and *The Bell Jar,* and another that was lodged in my thigh, *Franny and Zoey.*

"I'm up every morning at four to write," Murakami said. "Then I go for six hours straight. I go to bed at nine and wake up and do it all over again."

"I was up at four, too," Plath said.

"I wrote fifteen hours a day," Salinger said.

I peeled *The New Yorker* off my lower leg. "You aren't showing that you have the discipline to be a writer," Joyce Carol Oates said.

"A minimum of ten pages a day, even on holidays," Stephen King said from a dark corner.

Balzac laughed at me and said, "Get a pot of coffee going and work, young man."

James Joyce didn't even acknowledge me.

"Writers are in the business of creating sentences. Where are your sentences?" DeLillo asked.

"You're turning into a cliché," Langston Hughes said.

Henry Miller chimed in, "I wrote while I was poor, hungry, and in a bed full of scrambling cockroaches. You have money."

"Yeah, I lived in *Bunker Hill* ... You live in a *Hollywood mansion!*" John Fante said.

"I partied all the time—did a hell of a lot more drugs than you—but I still managed to write some fantastic shit," Hunter Thompson said.

"Get a grip on reality, man. Stop worrying about who you aren't, and start being who you are," Joan Didion said.

"I would get up, enjoy a light meal, take a walk, and then spend the rest of the day in search of the perfect word," Flaubert said.

"I left the throne to them," Foster Wallace said, flashing a look across the room. "Do you really think you can compete?"

I followed his eyes and saw Eugenides, Franzen, and Zadie quietly observing me from a distance.

"I get it," I said to them all.

FIFTEEN

The romantic thought of myself as a promising writer had, unjustified as it may have been, given me a reason to be OK with the way things were going in my life. It was OK to be dwindling away within the menagerie of West Hollywood, because I had my writing. It was OK to be jobless and spending my dead grandmother's money, because I had my writing. It was OK to get dressed in the morning or laugh at a friend's joke or go to a bar down the street when I woke up every day believing I was, regardless of whether I wrote anything or not, a writer waiting to bloom.

The rejection emails I'd received from the little publications on the West Coast or in the Midwest had indeed stung me, but they'd only given me surface wounds; the pain, although bothersome, was manageable. The rejection email from *The New Yorker*, however, had delivered a much deeper stab wound. Somehow, over the years, I'd been convinced that intellectualism flourished in the East, that the esteemed literary critics, the good writers, and all the other smart people, far superior to me, lived in the East. And these intellectuals of the East probably had, I presumed, a contemptuous perspective on Los Angeles or, for that matter, any of the aspiring writers in Los Angeles. New York, therefore, had always intimidated me.

But as long as I didn't know I wasn't worthy of *The New Yorker*, I could keep the fantasy alive in my mind that I was. Once I'd been disillusioned, however, I began to see my life through a much darker lens, and, consequently, began to pay more attention to things I'd previously been oblivious to, like the dark purple blood in the toilet after I stood up or how much I coughed throughout the day or the frequency of my headaches or the incessant shaking of my hands.

I'd known early on that something had died within Parker Thomas, but, for the first time during my relationship with him, I think I understood him better than I ever had, giving me a glimpse of the world the way he saw it. It was not pleasure that Parker so desperately sought; rather, his life had become defined by his relentless search for something that would simply ease his pain. He'd been doing everything out of necessity, out of a need to stay afloat. He was barely alive. He never remembered the stories he told shortly after telling them, and, with empty blue eyes, he'd often stare right through anyone else telling him a story, as the limits of his consciousness were always confined to the unending hunt for something that would make him more numb so that he could feel less. He was constantly moving around—scratching his head, tapping his foot, playing with his hands—and when he was in one place, he craved being in another. You could be near Parker, in the same room with him, even touching him, but you were still as distant from him as two people living on different continents.

"I hate the taste of alcohol—beer, wine, whiskey, all of it," he said to me once, a statement that confused me initially because he was always drinking. But there came a time when I understood that, for Parker, it was never about the actual act of consumption or sex or, for that matter, his obsession with the thrill of experiencing a new feeling; rather, it was about doing what he could to keep himself desensitized, because his pain couldn't thrive within his numbness; it could, however, prosper within his aliveness, latch on to his hope and ambition, flourish with his love and passion. But, as Parker had discovered, his pain withered with his apathy and detachment.

Unlike Parker, who used people, mostly girls and me, as a means to forget himself, I started avoiding people altogether. I stopped going out to bars and clubs. In truth, I rarely left the Sunset House, and, as a result, it became my territory—I knew every nook, every concave area in the bushes, every pathway, every sitting spot on the roof. During the time in the night when all the after-hours people showed up at the Sunset House, I was ready for them; my objective was to become camouflaged by the house, to be unrecognizable, to be within the madness but to remain unseen. I hid out in my dark room with the door locked until a lost soul—wandering up and down the stairs looking for something to keep his high going—pounded on my door and yelled, "Open up! It's me," and then I would climb out my window and guide myself down the thick pipe that ran all the way to the ground. One of those times, as I landed on my feet and turned to walk down the path leading to the back of the house, something stirred in the tall bushes next to me, and then a middle-aged man popped his head out. I thought he might be lost, or perhaps drunkenly relieving himself, but then I noticed a young girl, around my age, partly shrouded by the dark greenery.

"You spying on us, bro?"

"No, just passing through," I said.

I looked at him as he stepped forward into the moonlight; his face was emaciated, and his shark-like black eyes, with loose bags of discolored skin hanging underneath them, protruded unhealthily from his skull. If it weren't for his trendy clothes, the magnificent, big-faced watch on his left hand, the pretty girl in his clutches, and the confident air with which he carried himself, I would have taken him to be a homeless man who'd wandered drunkenly onto the property.

"Did you take a photo of us, bro?"

"No. I live here," I said.

"I see ... Well, I own this house. Enjoy the best time of your life," he said before redirecting his attention to his tryst in the bushes.

"Take care," I said.

But I usually made it around the dark path to the back of the house, unnoticed and unmolested, where I'd scale another pipe to a ledge from which I could jump and grab an overhanging part of the roof and pull myself up onto it. Once I was on the roof I never had to worry about being noticed—even when I stared down, in clear view of the people below me, because, after adventurous experimentation, I discovered that no one ever looked up.

I started spending the later parts of the night in the backseat of my car, where my mind tiptoed on the cusp of unconsciousness, making it difficult for me to gauge the validity of approaching footsteps, or, on one particular night, the sound of crying and the eventual sounds of tapping on my car window.

"Help," she said.

When I opened my eyes, I saw my housemate, Jenny, hovering outside my car window with the frightened look of a girl who'd been separated from her parents at an amusement park. I unlocked the door and opened it.

"What's wrong, Jenny?"

Tears poured down her face while she gasped for air, the way that frightened little girl hyperventilates when she's crying and can't speak.

"He—" she muttered before her own gasp cut her off.

"What is it, Jenny?" I said.

"He—He—" she said again in the same fashion.

I gave her a minute to find her words.

"He—"

"He what? He who?" I said, noticing she was holding her left wrist, which was bruised, the skin rubbed raw as if it had been forcibly yanked.

"He did too much," she said finally. "Did too many."

"Who?" I said.

Her head whipped over her shoulder in a panic, while her wild eyes scanned the darkness—her apparent fear enough to awaken my own trepidation over whatever or whoever had driven her to her current state.

"He's ... going to ... find me," she said, as her hyperventilating resumed and more tears overflowed from her eyes.

"It's OK. You want to stay in here for a little while?" I said.

She nodded, climbed into the backseat, and, as she laid her head on my chest, I felt the dampness of her face soak through my shirt and the pounding of her heart on my stomach.

"Nothing bad is going to happen," I said, resting my hand on her head. "It's OK, Jenny."

I knew she'd fallen asleep when her breathing had slowed to a regular pace and her body had quit trembling, and, for a while, I stayed alert—the sounds of the party above still lively—but no one came for her. I fell asleep.

When I awoke, Jenny was gone, and I lay shivering in the morning crispness, which was exacerbated by the cold metal of an unheated car. I decided to walk to Jackson and Jenny's room to see if Jenny was OK. I knocked on their door and she answered.

"Hey, Jake," she said, smiling widely in her underwear and a T-shirt and showing no signs of the fear that had paralyzed her the night before. "You want breakfast? Jackson is making some breakfast."

I followed her inside and saw Jackson cooking eggs and bacon over the stove. "Hey, man," he said. "A mimosa?"

I nodded at him and then, glancing at Jenny's left wrist, noticed it had been adorned with several shiny bracelets; she smiled wider and played with them when she saw me looking, as if she thought I was admiring their beauty rather than searching for what was underneath.

"Jackson bought them for me," she said, holding her wrist out for me to see.

Jackson handed me a mimosa, and the three of us clinked our glasses together.

"Cheers!" Jenny chirped.

We sat at their kitchen table, them facing me, and drank mimosas and ate scrambled eggs and bacon. Jackson and Jenny told me about the craziness of their night, but also that they couldn't remember much of it.

"There were five people passed out in my bathtub when I woke up today. I had no idea who they were. I kicked them out," Jackson said. "I don't think they knew who I was, either."

Jenny hopped happily over to the counter and poured herself another mimosa. I looked Jackson in the eyes, and he looked away. I decided to let it go.

"Thanks for the breakfast, guys. I need to get some stuff done. See you soon," I said.

"Bye, Jake," a smiley Jenny said as she waved her hand, making the bracelets on her wrist jingle a merry tune.

Later that evening, a rare occasion when the house was empty on a Friday, Parker pounded on my locked door.

"Jake! Open up, dude," Parker said, as I was halfway out my window. "I really need to talk to you," he then said with an urgency that made me reconsider my escape.

I walked over to the door, unlocked it, and let him in.

"Jake, where the hell have you been lately? I need you to come with me somewhere. It's a little out of the way, but I really need you to come with me."

"Where?"

"Just come. You haven't been around for me lately. I need my best friend tonight."

"You can't tell me where we're going?"

"Please?"

We rode along Santa Monica for a while. I sipped from the flask in Parker's car and passed it to him when we were stopped at lights so he could have a drink. Parker merged onto the 101 south, took it to the 110 south, and then took Ninth Street to South Hill Street.

"What are we doing downtown?" I asked to no response.

He parked the car along the curb in front of a dark establishment with a large bouncer guarding the entrance.

"Is this a strip club?"

"Just wait here," he said, getting out of the car.

He walked up to the bouncer, and they engaged in a lengthy conversation before Parker was allowed inside. When he came back out, twenty minutes later, he wasn't alone, but rather, flanked by two Asian girls dressed to entertain, and, as they neared the curb, he gestured to them to stay put.

"Parker, what the fuck is this?" I said, as he got back inside the car.

"I'm in the mood for something a little different," he said.

"Fuck, Parker, they're hookers?"

"Girls, strippers, hookers, escorts, people, whatever. Who cares?"

"Why did you bring two?"

"One for you."

"I don't want one."

"Who gives a shit?"

"*Jesus Christ*, Parker. It's just not for me."

"Oh, come on. Don't take the fucking moral high ground here. *Really?*"

"Fuck off."

"It's something new and exciting. It'll be fun."

"Not doing this, man, sorry. Not this."

"It'll be a fun memory. Do it for me—your best friend."

"Why do you care if I do this? Do what you want with your own time."

"Come on, Jake. Please. I've already paid for them. They don't even speak English. It'll be fine," he said, starting the car.

"Where are you going?" I asked.

"Just around the back. They have rooms there. It won't be a big deal," he said, leaning out of the window and signaling the girls to get inside the car.

"I'm not doing this. You've gone too far."

"Please, man. For me. Please?"

"Not a chance. Sorry."

"Fine. You can just wait in the car with your girl."

"No, man. Fuck that. Take me home."

I quickly glanced at the two sheepish, young-looking girls as they noiselessly got into the backseat and stared blankly down at the floor. Parker pulled behind the establishment and drove a hundred feet down an alley to rows of little rooms next to each other.

"We're good here," he said and then, handing me a gold, greasy key,

"Just in case ..."

"You're an asshole."

He took one of the girls into a room and closed the door, while I sat in the car with the other girl. Because I didn't want to draw attention to myself in the car with a girl Parker had paid for, I got out, told her to follow me, opened the room door, and closed it behind us. The room—with a dirty, pale yellow carpet, no windows or bathroom, and only a cheap, filthy bed in the middle of shit-stained walls—was a very dismal sight. The girl began removing her clothes.

"No," I said. "Don't do that."

She glanced up at me, and then, quickly averting her eyes, stared at the wall behind me with a confused expression.

"Do you speak English?"

"Little," she said.

"Where are you from?"

"Vietnam."

"How old are you?"

"Sixteen."

"Is that your friend in the other room? Your friend?" I said, pointing toward the wall we shared with the other room.

"Yes."

"Is she Vietnamese, too?"

"Yes."

"Does she speak English?"

"No."

I removed a pack of cigarettes from my back pocket and showed it to her; she plucked one with shaky fingers, and I lit it for her, then lit one for myself, and we smoked in silence for a few minutes.

"Are there more girls like you in that place?" I asked. "More like you," I repeated slowly.

"Many, many."

"Are all the girls from Vietnam?"

"All over world."

"How old are the girls?"

"Sometime ... fourteen, sometime ... eighteen."

"*Christ*. How old is your friend?" I said, pointing to the wall again.

"Fifteen."

"Why are you here?" I said, not explaining myself properly. "How did you end up—" I heard a loud scream from within Parker's room, so

I hurried out of my room and pounded on his door.

"Parker! What the fuck is going on?" I said.

"Everything is fine. Just a misunderstanding."

"Parker!"

"Really, Jake, everything is cool. Give me a few minutes."

I opened the door to my room and beckoned the girl to follow. "Your friend—ask her if she's OK. Do you understand? Ask your friend in Vietnamese if she's OK."

She nodded and then said something to her friend through Parker's closed door, and, after a pause, her friend responded.

"She OK," the girl said to me.

Parker and I didn't speak to each other on the way home; he blared the music, and we both chain-smoked cigarettes until our packs were empty.

During the final week of autumn—in some form of seasonal trickery— angry, dry winds, full of summer heat, blew through Los Angeles, and the streets, boiling under the sun, breathed thick, wavy lines into the sky; then, as the winter season began, rain poured over the city for two consecutive weeks.

"It's so bizarre. I've lived here for fifty years and never seen anything like it," said the cashier at the liquor store, ringing up my carton of cigarettes.

The stormy weather of early winter possessed a stored rage, as if it were lashing out after a long period of mild-mannered behavior, which the complacent denizens of LA had come to expect, or, given how angry everyone in the city seemed during the rainy streak, even demand. Frigid gusts of wind, erratically shifting in every direction, whipped and knifed the faces of all those who ventured outside. The streets flooded. Parts of the freeways were shut down. Brown rivers surged and flowed. The Sunset House, however, evolved to accommodate the weather. Parker had the guys clear out all the furniture in the main rooms and stack it in one of the rooms we hardly used—that way, there was more space for people to be inside, and the parties and the after-parties could carry on, unaffected by the weather.

During one of our after-parties that raged into the early morning, I stood on the balcony, shielded from the rain by an overhang, and smoked a cigarette. I could feel the sound from Rin Tin Tin's bass inside the house more than I could hear it; it was the kind of sound contained behind thick walls, shut windows, and closed doors, muffled yet powerful, that would blast anyone opening a door or window from the outside with an unpleasant, amplified noise—something that happened to me every time a person went inside.

But it was a much different sound responsible for shaping that rainy night for me. When I heard it I thought of my skull fracturing or every one of my ribs snapping at once, but then, immediately after, I realized the sound was much too powerful and resonant to occur within me. It was the sound of metal smashing into metal, a sound that travels in through the ears, shoots down the spine, slices into every internal organ, momentarily stops the heart from beating, and burns the stomach in its own acid—an ungodly, unworldly sound that poisons the air with a sickly uneasiness and registers fearfully foreign in the ears of all human beings. I whipped my head toward the street and saw that two cars had collided on Sunset in front of the ramp below my house. The cars, horrendously misshapen on the wet street, looked like two heaving, steaming metallic beasts after a gruesome caged battle that had claimed all their energy and possibly their lives.

"*Oh my God,*" I said.

I quickly descended the levels of my house, and, while sprinting down the wet ramp, slipped and fell forward, bracing myself with my outstretched arms. The thick pea coat I was wearing protected my arms during the ten-foot slide down the ramp, but my hands got severely scraped and bloodied. I picked myself up, not registering the pain as adrenaline pumped through my veins, and hurried, a bit more cautiously, toward the crash. I was the first person on the scene. One of the cars had flipped over on its roof after the collision; the other, just as badly damaged, had ricocheted across the street and onto the sidewalk. The rain came down harder as I approached the car closer to me, the one that had flipped over, and then, shielding my eyes with a bloody hand, I crouched down to look inside. A guy, maybe twenty years old, was in the driver's seat, and a girl of similar age was in the passenger seat, both dangling upside down, held in place by their seat belts. Because the car had flipped over sideways, I was on the side of the girl in the passenger seat. Other cars began to pile up, and one driver got out of his car and said something to me.

"Call the goddamn ambulance!" I yelled and then tapped on the passenger window. "Are you OK? Can you hear me?"

The girl didn't move. I crawled around to the driver's side, but didn't bother tapping on the window when I saw his open eyes, drained of life, staring ahead at nothing, and the thick, fresh blood dripping out of his ear, and, since he was upside down, onto the inside roof of the car.

"Goddamn it," I said, as a few people hurried over to me. "Did someone call for help?" I frantically said to them.

"Yeah, they're on their way," one of them said.

"Check on the driver in the other car," I said, rushing around the car back to the girl on the passenger side. "Can you hear me?" I yelled, back down on my hands and knees, tapping on the window.

Her nose looked broken—hot, pulpy, bright red blood trickled out of it and ran down to her forehead—but the skin on her face looked as soft and pure as a newborn baby's, and, in a flash, I thought about the girl's father at home tucked comfortably in his bed, sleeping, unaware of his daughter's accident.

"Are you alive?" I shouted, knocking on the window harder, and this time her eyes cracked open. "Thank God! Help is coming. Don't worry. We're going to get you out of there," I yelled to her.

She slowly turned her head toward me and looked into my eyes, and, in doing so, shattered my entire understanding of anything I'd ever known. She pressed her open hand against the glass and mouthed the words, "Help me."

"Help is coming. We're going to get you out of there."

She mouthed the same words again, but this time tears poured out of her eyes, mixing with the blood on her forehead.

"Goddamn it," I said when she closed her eyes, and then turning to the people gathering around me, "Where the *fuck* is the goddamn help!"

"I don't know. We've all called. They said they're on their way," one of them said.

"There isn't enough time," I said.

I positioned myself for leverage near the backseat window, and, lying on the ground with my feet facing the car, tried shattering it with a kick, but the way in which the car had been smashed prevented me from making strong contact. I kicked again as hard as I could with everything I had. Nothing.

"Come on, break!" I begged.

I flipped around and, lying on my side, pounded the glass with the bottom of my clenched fist. Nothing. I swung harder. Still nothing.

"Fucker!" I screamed.

Summoning all my strength, I swung vigorously at the window several more times until I felt my hand go numb; when I pulled it away, my own blood was smeared across the unbroken glass. I checked on the girl again and, after seeing that her eyes were still closed, put my hand up to the window, near where her head dangled, and said, "I'm so sorry." I felt my hot tears being washed away by the cold rain.

"Move out of the way," a paramedic said, pulling me back to make room for his team to investigate the scene.

I stood up and noticed two large fire trucks and about ten police cars surrounding the area. I hadn't even heard the sirens. Flashes of red light lit up the night sky. The paramedics, after assessing the situation, convened in the middle of the street; the police began roping off a large perimeter with yellow tape.

"The girl on the passenger side … she's dying in there," I said desperately to the officer who passed in front of me while unraveling yellow tape. "Aren't you going to help her?"

"Stay back. We'll handle it," he said, perfunctorily.

Some paramedics treated the driver in the other car, who, although bleeding and bruised, seemed relatively fine, while other paramedics, after deliberating for what seemed like forever, finally decided to bring out the Jaws of Life to use on the car that had been flipped over. I stood up against the yellow tape, while they began to operate the hydraulic tools. Two cops, one of them holding an umbrella over the other, stood a few feet away from me.

"I did Bill a favor tonight and took his shift. The wife's pissed. She hates it when she has to sleep alone," one of them said, making the other laugh.

I glanced at the people within the growing crowd: many were capturing pictures and video of the scene, some were talking on the phone, and others were texting or posting. I could feel the resounding, synthesized boom of Rin Tin Tin's music from above.

They were able to remove the body of the male driver from the car first, but, after they had him on the stretcher, they quickly covered his corpse with a sheet. *Goddamn it.* I watched anxiously as they focused on getting the girl out, angry that they hadn't tried for her first but hopeful that she was still alive. As they pulled her out, I held my breath, fearing the appearance of the sheet, but, when they rushed her over to a nearby ambulance to treat her, I exhaled in relief. *Thank you. Thank you. Thank you.* I watched a few paramedics attend to her inside the ambulance until one of them shut the back doors; I expected the ambulance to drive off in the direction of the hospital, but it never did, and when they reopened the doors, I saw that a sheet had been pulled over the girl's body and face.

"No, no, no, no! *Please*, no ..." I said, the tears welling up in my eyes again.

When an officer with a clipboard approached me and asked me to give a statement, I wiped my eyes and told him in a shaky voice what I knew.

"Well, that's what happens when you kids act like you own the road," he said, indifferently.

"*Fuck you*," I said, heating up with anger. "How about showing some respect? She's dead. What the hell took you guys so long?"

"Young man," he said, stepping closer to me. "I suggest you seriously consider the consequences of whatever you say or do next."

"She was still alive ... You could've saved her," I said, turning and walking away from him.

I numbly climbed the ramp and then the stairs up to my house, where nothing had changed inside; the dark living room, intermittently lighted by flashing laser beams, was still brimming with dancing shadows cheering in ecstasy and fist-pumping to the music. As I stood on the balcony, the dead girl's face, mouthing her final words, flashed in my head.

Help me.
Help me.
Help me.
Help me.
Help me.
Help me.

I ran over to the bushes by the Jacuzzi and vomited until her words were out of my head. Back on the balcony, I smoked cigarettes—not moving except for the motion of my arm to my mouth and the slight rise and fall of my chest as I inhaled the smoke and breathed it out—while watching them clear the mess off the street below.

"Hey, what's up, man?" someone on a smoke break said to me. "We've met before, right? You need anything?"

I ignored him.

"You need anything, man?" he said again.

I turned toward him, and, in a rage, pushed him with my good hand against the front of the house and said, "No, goddamn it. I don't *need* anything. Do you understand?"

"All right, man. Chill out. What's your problem? I was trying to help you out."

I let go of him, turned back around toward the view of the city, and stared at the horizon until the sun began to rise. Minutes after the mess on the street had been cleared away, the music finally stopped. Everything was back to normal, as if the terrible crash had never happened.

"What up, Jake?" said a sweaty Rin Tin Tin as he came out for a cigarette.

"Is that tree pretty?" I mumbled.

"What?"

"That tree," I said, nodding in its direction on the side of the house. "Is it pretty?"

"What the fuck are you talking about, man?"

"I think it's pretty just the way it is, you know? Look at the way it sways naturally, just the way it is, in the breeze, you know?"

"How fucked up are you, Jake?"

"I think ... very."

"Dude, your hand is dripping blood on the ground."

"Oh, *really?*" I said, leaving him and walking up to my room. When I opened the door, a couple was kissing on my bed. "Get out," I said.

"Be cool and close the door, man," the guy said.

"Get the *fuck* out," I snapped.

When they left, I immediately lay facedown, fully clothed, under the covers in my bed, holding my injured hand up against my chest. When I awoke a couple of hours later, I tried to lift up my body, but fell back onto the bed when a cutting pain shot through my hand and up my entire arm. After I struggled out of my wet clothes, I spent ten minutes rolling a joint with mostly one hand and then lay in bed smoking it until I was high. I felt fine for a while, until I glanced at my injured hand, which was bruised a dark purple, covered mostly in blood, and swollen, as if it had been filled with air. As I stared at it, my body began to shake uncontrollably, lightly at first, a soft tremble; but soon after, it began to violently convulse. My bed shook against the wall. My heart palpitated, and I couldn't breathe. Parker staggered into my room—staring at me vacantly while swaying back and forth, barely able to hold himself up—kneeled alongside my bed, bowed his head, and began to pray for me. After twenty minutes, the shaking had subsided, Parker had quit praying, and I passed out.

"Oh, shit, look at all that blood on your arm," Parker said, smiling above me as I awoke in the late morning. "What happened?"

"I may have broken my hand."

"Shitty, man. It'll heal. Don't worry about it. Here, numb the pain," he said, handing me his flask.

"Hey, I had a panic attack earlier this morning, and when you came into my room and saw me, you started praying. Do you remember that?" I said and then sipped the whiskey in the flask.

"I don't even know any prayers. Maybe you imagined it."

"Maybe."

"Let's get you to the hospital."

Parker drove me to Cedars-Sinai and pulled up in front of the emergency room to let me out.

"They'll fix it. Just call me when you're done, and I'll pick you up. We'll go out for some good Mexican food at El Compadre," Parker said.

I got out of the car, closed the door, and walked inside the hospital toward the woman behind the counter.

"I need a doctor," I said.

"What's wrong with you?" she responded without looking up.

I paused, startled by the question, but then realized what she meant and said, "I think I broke my hand."

"Fill this out and take a seat. We'll call you when we're ready."

Two hours later, an old nurse led me into a small room to check my blood pressure, heart rate, and weight, and then moved me into an examination room. "The doctor will be with you shortly," she said, closing the door.

I stared nervously at a set of metal tools resting on top of a moveable table near me. I held out my uninjured hand, and the tips of my fingers trembled erratically. The cold, white sterility of the room made me feel uncomfortable, as if its cleanliness was a facade masking the dirtiness brought in by all the previous patients with terrible illnesses. I heard two soft knocks on the door before a young female doctor entered the room.

"Hello, Jake?"

"Yes."

"I'm Doctor Chow," she said.

"Hi," I said, softly.

"Let's take a look at your hand," she said, and then, after her examination, "OK, we'll need to do an X-ray, but I'm guessing that you've broken this metacarpal," she said, pointing to it. "Assuming that it's just a fracture and not a displaced fracture, you'll probably need to be in a hard cast for six weeks or so. If you don't have any questions, we can get you started right away on the X-ray."

"Well …" I said, pausing to gather my thoughts. "Lately, I've been experiencing these panic attacks, or, I guess, anxiety about having a panic attack. But the fear of it possibly happening is just as bad. Usually I feel like … like something is boiling inside me … or my internal organs are just going to spontaneously implode … or I won't be able to breathe and my heart will stop beating. Earlier today, I had a panic attack, and my whole body shook violently. I thought I was dying."

"Whenever we experience a new terrible feeling, it scares the hell out of us, and our first thought is to wonder if we are dying. It's human nature," she said, loosening her professionalism in response to my candor. "Do you mind my asking if you use drugs recreationally?"

"No, I don't mind. The answer is yes," I said.

"Which ones?"

"Probably most of them."

"How many times a month would you say that you use drugs?"

"I have no idea."

"Well, when was the last time you used them?"

"Late last night … or, I guess, early this morning."

"And what about drinking—when was the last time you had a drink?"

"Maybe just a couple hours ago."

"Have any of your friends told you that you have a problem with your alcohol or drug use?"

"I don't think they would."

"Why's that?

"Because they do the same things I do."

"Look, Jake, you seem like a nice boy. You're young enough to get healthy. Perhaps you should get your priorities together and embrace the time you've been given. We only get one chance, you know. I can prescribe you something for the anxiety. Would you like me to?"

"OK, yes, thank you."

"Sure. One last thing: have you ever been diagnosed with depression or any other mental illness?"

"Not really …"

"Not really?"

"Well, when I was younger, a psychiatrist thought I showed some signs of depression, but my parents never followed through with it."

She handed me a card with some information on it. "Call this number and set up an appointment. Take care of yourself. Bye, Jake."

After part of my hand and lower arm had been placed in a cast and I was free to go, I hurried across the street in the rain to the nearest pharmacy to fill my prescription. Inside, I threw away the card the doctor had given me, and, fifteen minutes later, walked back outside—with the bottle of pills in my front pocket—to hail a cab. On the ride home, I caught myself, more than once, gripping the bottle of pills through my pants; I hadn't taken a single pill yet, nor did I really want to, but the idea of having them made me feel at ease.

Parker was asleep on his bed with the door open. Because of the quietness of the house, I assumed that the rest of my housemates were also sleeping behind their closed doors. I glanced at the stack of the notebooks my grandmother had given me and then stared ashamedly at the cast on my hand. *I broke my goddamn writing hand.* I decided to leave nearly everything in my room—my clothes, my shoes, my diploma, my hidden bottles of liquor, my drug stashes—except for my books, notebooks, and laptop, which I quietly packed in two large trash bags. I clumsily wrote a check (with my unbroken hand) for one month's rent, grabbed the trash bags, closed my door softly on the way out, and set the rent check on the floor at the entrance of Parker's room; I walked stealthily out of the house, and, when I reached the deck, turned around for one last glimpse of the Sunset House. The rain fell hard on my face, while my eyes drifted to the spot along the railing where I'd first met Parker Thomas.

City of Angels. City of Dreams. City of Lost Memories. City of Neon. That was it—the neon lights: manufactured color pouring down over the city, like acid rain, slowly eroding the souls of the city-dwelling youths, while poisoning their minds with an insatiable craving for manufactured highs. It was the lights. It had always been the lights.

I never saw Parker in person again; he never called or messaged me. I guessed that he'd discovered the rent check when he awoke and knew that I was gone, that my time—everyone had a time—had come. He probably posted an advertisement for my room the same day I left the house. That way, he could start the process of finding his new best friend, as he'd done after the departure of my predecessor, when he'd found me.

I imagined the new guy walking up the steps, amazed at the grandiosity of the house, and then staring in awe at the view of the city; he would hardly be able to contain his excitement for the new life that awaited him. And just as he snapped a photo of the view with his phone, Parker Thomas would appear majestically behind him.

"It's just a house, man," he would say.

BOOK 3: REVELATION

SIXTEEN

I drove east on Sunset, away from the house, in the pouring rain. My mind was wildly ablaze with thoughts, each one sparking up, quickly flashing bright, and then fizzling immediately into the next one, as if they were hundreds of firecrackers attached to the same long fuse.

A sea of lost souls—chasing illusory feelings, smiling in ecstasy, crying in sobriety. Needing something more, something enhanced: drugs, choking, doctored sunsets, doctored conversations, doctored lives. Hello, Doctor.

I'm looking through you. You're looking through me. We're never looking at each other. Always searching for something else behind the glossy screen of a phone—something to make us feel better, feel ... anything. Chasing the feeling all day and night. Hunting for it.

Wait! We're more connected than we've ever been! But ... no one is talking to the person right in front of him. Well ... we're still communicating with our friends, more than ever!

Happy Birthday!

Happy Birthday!

Happy Birthday!

And we're sharing more than we ever have! But ... we're missing the real moment, are we not?

Lying. Fucking. Crying. Cheating. Stealing. Snorting. Swallowing.

So many friends everywhere. Enough friends for a lifetime of lonely nights. But who are these friends? And which versions are we talking about? The Internet versions of people are accomplished. They went to universities. They studied abroad. They speak multiple languages. They've visited South America and India. They like art, films, music, books. They're interested in cooking and traveling and reading and playing sports and hiking and photography. They make things. They have fancy job titles. They're happy! You want proof? Don't you notice the photo-timeline of smiles and laughs and sunsets and beaches?

And who are you? I must ask. I recognize your face, but I don't know your name. Oh, so you're the flesh version of your online identity? The storyteller? The one forced to defend an image? The one cornered into the predicament of pandering? The one imprisoned by a lifetime of indentured servitude to the online self? Yes, you must go out in the world and do the things you've already claimed to have done and then capture proof to show everyone else. Proof makes us believe. And what better proof than enhanced proof? Doctored proof? Real is boring. Real is never good enough. So what do we do about it? We become the documentarians of our own lives. How? We become artists and photographers and painters and writers to tell the story we want told. We must be professional curators of our own identity—so that we always seem shiny and pretty. We must contribute to the abyss of doctored and filtered photos. Bright eyes. Fake smiles. A pretty girl in a nice dress means nothing. But a pretty girl in a nice dress captured in the right photograph is immortalized. But why do we laugh in our photos and cry in real life? Real or fake? Real or fake? Real or fake?

Click.
Like.
Click.
Like.
Click.
Like.
Click.
Like.
Click.
Like.
Click.
Like.

But we don't really want to do any of it. We just want to feel better. To distract ourselves. To feel the warmth. But we're slaves to the public images we've created. Now we always have more work to do. The flesh versions of ourselves are too tired from all the work—we have nothing to say to each other in person. We just numbly stare at each other and wonder how to better please our master, who lives behind the computer screen. And now we've become masters of our own, haven't we? Masters of affectation. Affectations. Affectations. Affectations all around! We are … professionals—professionals who'll never achieve satiety.

Oh! Look at the people walking around, getting soaked in the rain. I see you, young, suited man, hiding under your umbrella, with your 401(k) and delayed life plans. I see you, parents, rushing your children across the street, trying to protect them from the inevitable. I see you, young couple, fighting over your jealousies under the overhang of a restaurant. I see you, middle-aged, bored, silent couple, in the car next to me, still sitting side by side after all these years, because you both think you're too old to find someone else. I see you, sad woman in a yellow raincoat, walking that dog you bought to cure your loneliness. Your plan didn't work, huh? I see you, pedestrians, huddled under umbrellas, waiting for the light to change, making small talk with each other, as if it matters. And I see you, shivering old man with a cane, waiting for death. Death ...

Death.

Death.

Death.

Death.

Death.

"Help me," she said. But I didn't help her. No. Instead, I let her die.

I veered sharply to the right side of the road, threw open my car door, and, to the ugly, angry tune of several car horns, heaved into the gutter, already gushing with filth, until her image had, at least temporarily, faded from my mind again.

"How can I help you today, sir?" she said, setting her Kindle aside.

"I'd like a room," I said, setting down the two large trash bags, soaked in rainwater and filled with my books.

"Sure, do you have any preferences?"

"I'd like a room with a kitchen."

"Sure, we do have a few of those available ... How long will your stay be?"

"I don't know—can we start with a month?" I said quickly, starting to feel queasy and shaky, hoping to get into a room immediately.

She suspiciously lowered her eyes to the two large trash bags resting near my feet, quickly studied them, looked back up at me, paused in thought, and then said, "Sure, sir, we have a long-term rate. Let's get you set up."

I set the two trash bags down in front of my hotel-room door, unlocked it, propped it open with my foot, and reached for the bags; as I hoisted both of them over my shoulder with my unbroken hand, one ripped, and my books spilled out into the hallway. I continued into the room anyway—indifferent, in that moment, to everything else in the world but the bed in front of me—and plopped facedown on top of the comforter. *Alive and well ... then dead ... forever. Grandma, dead in the open casket. Steve Duggins, dead among his lots. "Help me," she said. That sheet ... over her face. God, not the sheet.*

I couldn't move; I lay still in bed and stared at the wall. *We just die ... Why move? Why eat? Why talk to other people? To enjoy life? To make the best of our time here? Bullshit. We die ... and never remember anything. We don't even get to keep the knowledge we acquired during our lifetime. It's ours—and we still can't keep it. Eyes closed. Black. Nothing. Forever. Dead. Christ. I'm in it. I can't get out of it.*

I curled up into a ball, not moving, barely breathing. My teeth felt grimy against my tongue, but I didn't see the point in getting up to brush them. *Why shouldn't I just kill myself now? What would it matter? But I'm too scared to do it. I'm too scared to close my eyes and not know anything. But I'd be dead, right? So not knowing anything would be fine—I wouldn't know that I knew nothing ... But the idea of that still scares me. It doesn't make any sense. We're all ants, just bigger versions, scurrying about until one day ... Smash! Dead! Killed in a car accident or struck down by a heart attack ... for no reason. Life and then death. Alive and then dead.*

But, wait ... We're worse than the ants. We love to accumulate things. We accumulate things like cameras and cars and swimming pools and necklaces and coats and shoes and watches and 'likes' and vacation time. It'd be easier if we were just like the ants, scurrying about for food. Their queen is far more forgiving than our master. But we must have all these things so that when we die ... we die with things. Then our things are passed to another person, who eventually dies with more things. My head's going to explode. My heart's going to stop beating. I have cancer of the brain and the eyes and the ears and the mouth. I want to kill myself ... now. I reached for my pocket and gripped the bottle of prescription pills, feeling a momentary wave of calm wash over me. *Is suicide really the answer? Maybe ... But I shouldn't kill myself today, because I don't know what I'll discover tomorrow. Maybe, tomorrow, I'll find the answer.* I had an itch on my leg but ignored it, and then felt it working harder to get my attention, until it got bored and disappeared back under my skin. *Try harder next time, little itch.* I stared at the wall, wishing I wasn't who I was, wishing I were a dog instead, because a dog, when he's tired, simply goes to sleep. *Wouldn't that be wonderful—to be tired and just fall asleep ...*

The late afternoon faded to dusk, then to blackness, and the dark hours of the night were long and cold, as the wind whipped the heavy drops of rain against my window. And then, in the early hours of the morning, I began drifting to sleep, waking each time within a few minutes, gasping for air. My sleep was taunting me; its intentions were never to rest me, but only to make me feel more tired. It was a short-lasting sleep that drained me, aged my face, and paled my skin. Then, seduced by an act of trickery, I fell into a deep sleep; but, with my eyes sealed shut, I was still conscious to the dismal world of darkness around me. As I drifted in the black nothingness like a rock in space, I felt my heart stop beating and wondered if I was dead. It was then—the moment in which I thought myself to be dead, left to float aimlessly for all eternity in the nothingness—that I wished for life again. I lay in the bed—writhing in the agony of my inability to wake up, drowning in the darkness of the world behind my eyelids—gathered my strength, and tried to will open my eyes. But I seemed to be powerless against whatever sinister force kept them tightly shut. I felt the monster laughing inside me.

With the fight still in me, I finally discovered how to beat the monster with my own trickery: I feigned apathy. It was quite astounding the level of control I was able to regain when I'd convinced the monster that I didn't care whether I lived or died in that moment. And, with an air of petulance, he finally acknowledged his defeat, released his hold on me, and vanished; my eyes shot open and soaked in the angelic sight of natural light and clean, white sheets. On the bed I found a note on a ripped-out page of my notebook, scribbled in my shaky handwriting, that I didn't remember writing. In large letters across the page, it read: "Help me."

I walked to the sink in the bathroom and turned on the faucet just enough to release a few drops onto my tongue. *Fuck you, water, for extending my life and prolonging my pain.*

I stayed in bed for three days, eating nothing, drinking only a few sips of water from the bathroom faucet. The trembling started on day two; I thought it had to be, at least in part, related to the symptoms of drug and alcohol withdrawal. Regardless, it was truly a terrible experience, one that seemed to worsen with every passing second. I clung to my bottle of prescription pills, fighting the urge several times to twist off the cap and pour pills into my mouth. *I want to fight this the real way, not by fixing the feeling with more drugs.* Still, I felt a bit better knowing I had the option.

By the early afternoon of my fourth day in the hotel, my trembling had calmed to a slight quivering, and when, after a shower and a large glass of tap water, it had ceased altogether, I silently hoisted the un-opened bottle of pills in the air as a self-congratulatory nod to my small victory.

I heard a knock at the door and decided to answer it that time (I'd ignored all the previous knocks from the housekeeper, and had, at some point, hung the "Do Not Disturb" sign on the outside door handle). I wrapped myself in the soft, white robe provided by the hotel and opened the door to no person, just neatly organized stacks of my books, a large plastic container of tomato soup, and a note that read: "I'd prefer not to interfere, but you should take comfort in knowing that the thoughts that haunt you, the ones you feel you're battling alone, are usually the same thoughts that haunt us all. You are much less alone than you think. At the very least, perhaps you would allow these precious books back inside to keep you company? Also, I imagine you must be hungry. Enjoy some hot tomato soup—fresh from the deli."

After carrying my books inside, I found a spoon in one of the kitchen drawers, removed the lid on the container of tomato soup, and hungrily shoveled mouthfuls of the thick, red paste into my mouth—burning my tongue, but not caring. The heat of the soup travelled down my esophagus, warming my chest, and rested at the base of my stomach like red-hot coals in a fire pit, and my stomach roared alive, like an animal on an operating table the second after the effects of a tranquilizer had waned. My strength of mind and body slowly returned.

Reading the note a second time inspired me to read the words of my favorite writers, to search the pages of my books until I found some sort of solidarity. I picked up one book, touched the spine, rubbed the cover, and then flipped through it, holding my nose close to take in the smell of the pages. I read all through the remaining hours of the day and then through the night until the morning, going from book to book, reading select passages, and sometimes, with the shorter novels, reading them in their entirety. Two paragraphs of writing from separate novels affected me the most profoundly: one, from Henry Miller's *Tropic of Cancer*, about being truly alone in the world, about passing the time with only one's thoughts and agony and longing; and another, from Albert Camus's *The Stranger*, about how to deal with what little difference it makes to the world if a man dies young or old. I took out my notebook, and—laboring awkwardly with my broken writing hand—wrote the passages down, each one on its own page, ripped out the pages, and stuck them to the wall, one next to the other. I read over the passages one more time, enlivened by the connection I felt with the dead writers.

Now to write.

I set up my laptop on the table, opened a new page, and took a deep breath. *Write about West Hollywood. Write about the Sunset House. Write about Parker Thomas.* But the white blankness of the page intimidated me, and I couldn't conjure up one word worthy of any true human emotion. So I tried writing about my room instead—the bed, the window, the kitchen—but the mediocrity of my sentences depressed me; I'd forgotten how to use the semicolon and the em dash and the comma, or even how to spell simple words. At one point, I spent twenty minutes writing one short sentence about the window in my room, and another twenty futilely trying to make it worthy of human eyes. I read it over. *Fucking terrible.*

I checked my email, partly because I hadn't checked it in a while, but mostly because I thought I could ease into writing by simply replying to an email—any email would do. *Perfect. A new email from Andrew.*

From: Andrew Martin
To: Jake Reed

Jake,

How have you been? When are you coming home? What do I tell everyone? Anyway, I have a couple updates for you. Here goes ... I'm applying for this incredible life insurance package. It's term life insurance. Lasts for thirty years. So if I die before I turn fifty-five my family will get $2 million. And get this ... If two years go by after I sign the deal, I could commit suicide and my family would still get the money. Obviously, I'd never do that but what an incredible perk, right? It's just too good of a deal to pass up. But to get approved, they need to send a doctor out to examine me and ask me a bunch of questions like, 'Do you smoke?' (NO!) or 'How much do you drink?" (only a little), etc. I'll let you know how the test goes and if I get approved.

And secondly, Tamarine has been living here at the condo for a while
now. Everything's going great! And get this ... I asked her to dinner
and she said yes. I'm taking her out tonight! Too bad I can't take her to
the Thai place--they are having a special tonight.

Cordially,
Andrew

I hit reply and typed, "Dear Andrew," erased it, then typed, "Hey,
Andrew," but, still, couldn't find it in me to type another word; in my
frustration, I closed my laptop and decided to leave my room for some
fresh air.

The hotel I'd chosen for my stay, or rather, randomly stumbled into,
called Farmer's Daughter Hotel, was adjoined to a restaurant called Tart,
which had an inside-seating area (with a few cushioned booths and a
bar) and an outside courtyard with more tables, nestled between the
hotel rooms. At the far end of the courtyard was a gate that opened to
a small, old-fashioned pool—really just the size of a large Jacuzzi—with
a few wooden chaise longues around it. The unpeopled pool was very
clean-looking and glassy blue, and it rested with the flatness of a lake in
the early morning just before sunrise.

The courtyard was quiet except for the unrelenting hum of traffic on
Fairfax and Third, the muffled chatter of the only other people sitting
outside (two women in their thirties at a table at the opposite end of
the pool), and the soft acoustic tunes playing from the outdoor hotel
speakers. The courtyard curved around the restaurant and opened up to
a grassy area with trees and a small garden with flowers; I took a table
in that section.

The rain had finally gone, and only a few clouds—fluffy and rung
dry and inching across the sky like puffs of white smoke—had stuck
around to bear witness to the sun's takeover of the land: to me, a welcome transfer of power from the storm that had ruthlessly governed the
sky for weeks. Just above me, strings of soft, blue lights stretched across
the courtyard, and, jutting into the sky, behind the rooms of the hotel
from the street, the tops of palm trees swayed gently, as if they, too, were
relieved by the storm's passing. The air smelled fresh and pure in the late
morning, and I felt better.

A tired-looking but attractive waitress in her early twenties approached my table, fighting a yawn, and asked if she could get me any-

thing.

"Two eggs, sunny-side up, and a coffee, black," I said.

As I waited for my coffee and eggs, the sounds of approaching emergency sirens disrupted the serene ambience of the courtyard; they grew louder, peaking just outside the hotel at a nearly intolerable volume, then faded away down Fairfax. I closed my eyes—*the sound of trouble, the hateable sound*—and felt the bottle of pills in my back pocket, hoping to tame a slight wave of anxiety. *I'm glad you faded away, sirens. I'm glad that today you have nothing to do with me.*

"Here's your coffee and eggs," the waitress said, setting my order on the table, as I opened my eyes.

As the song "Laurel Canyon" by Jackie DeShannon started playing in the courtyard, I ate my breakfast, and, to distract myself, browsed the restaurant menu, noticing one of their featured deals, called the "American Recession Suggestion," which was a shot of Jack Daniel's and a can of Pabst Blue Ribbon beer for five dollars. Normally, such a deal would interest me, perhaps even excite me, but at that moment, the idea of a drink special—one that entailed spending money at an elegant restaurant in Los Angeles during a real recession—seemed ludicrous, as if the whole thing were a mockery of the rest of the country's misery. Or maybe I felt that way simply because I was running out of money.

After finishing my meal and paying the waitress, I decided to get groceries for my room. I walked through the courtyard and out of the hotel. As I strolled toward Melrose, the air felt different as I breathed it in, and the pavement under my feet felt as if it had been borrowed from a foreign country. People hurried along the street to wherever it was they intended to be, and I fantasized that I could see them but they couldn't see me, that I could observe them as much as I pleased without the fear of being noticed. But I realized, then, I wasn't alone in making observations; certain people—the cripples, the homeless, the disabled—who'd held dominion over the streets for some time, had become, in the process, the keenest of observers. I felt the cast on my arm. *Perhaps I'm one of them. Perhaps these are my people. Maybe they've always been my people.*

I was particularly drawn toward one man, in tattered clothes, slumped against a building wall on a street corner. He sat in silence, observing the passersby and the cars and the lights, as they changed from green to yellow to red. A few times, I watched him raise his hand to his mouth and sip something shrouded by a brown paper bag. *The Dolphus Raymond of Los Angeles! I found you!*

287

I walked toward Dolphus and greeted him: "Hey, friend, can I sit here with you?" He looked up at me without saying a word, and I handed him a five-dollar bill, then sat next to him against the wall, smelling the hot stench of liquor on his breath. Together we sat for nearly an hour, watching and studying the street activity; sometimes a passerby would toss Dolphus some change or a dollar bill, but he didn't seem to care.

I noticed two parents leading a toddler down the sidewalk; the mother guided the toddler from behind, and the father, facing them both, walked backwards while pointing a camera toward the little one.

"Do you think she'll do something funny today?" the father said.

"I don't know. Kayla, say something to Daddy. Look at Daddy. Kayla, say something to Daddy," the mother said.

The three of them, now directly in front of Dolphus and me, inched along slowly. The father grew frustrated. "Kayla, where are we? What are you doing? Kayla, what do you see?"

"Just keep the camera on her," the mother said.

As Kayla passed me, she looked into my eyes, and I nodded at her.

Kayla, don't listen to them. They're trying to get you hooked on something. It's not for your benefit; it's for theirs. Just keep doing what you're doing. Enjoy yourself. Don't let them turn you into a whore, Kayla. Be yourself. I'd save you if I could, Kayla. You have to believe me. I couldn't save her, I know, but I'd try my hardest to save you.

I watched them continue along and then turn right, out of my view, on the next street.

"Thank you for the company," I said to Dolphus. "I'll see you again. Maybe, next time, I'll bring us a couple bottles."

Dolphus looked up at me.

"Take care," I said.

At the grocery store, I bought meats, broth, vegetables, eggs, fruits, juices, coffee, and a few bottles of red wine, and then walked back to the hotel. As I set the groceries down in front of my door to retrieve the room key from my front pocket, the door directly across the hall opened.

"Hello, there," he said.

He was a very old man, but he looked quite healthy for his age; he was freshly shaven, very clean—as if he'd just showered—and impeccably dressed in a gray wool suit, a vest, a matching gray wool tie, a pressed white dress shirt, and shiny, black wing-tip boots. He wore thinly rimmed, round eyeglasses, and, on his head, sported a wool flat cap with white hair showing at his temples. He had warm, sky-gray eyes, and his face was craggy in an artistically aesthetic fashion, as if his wrinkles were carved by a sculptor and his blotches and slight discolorations done by a painter. I thought he was the most elegant-looking old man I'd ever seen. He stared at me with eager eyes, smiling in the doorway, emitting gentle wafts of aftershave into the hall.

"I wonder if I have you to thank for the soup and the salvaging of my books?" I said.

"Henry Shapiro," he said, still smiling.

"Jake Reed."

"Lovely to meet you, Jake," Henry said. "Do come in for a minute. What happened to your hand?"

"I broke it—it'll be fine in a few weeks."

I left the groceries outside my door and followed Henry into his room, which was similar to mine in layout but much more of a home. The bed was neatly made, and its base was lined with several pairs of polished dress shoes; pieces of art hung on the wall; a sitting area—a table flanked by two small couches—was positioned near his window; a vintage typewriter rested on the dining-room table; several beautiful suits hung in his open closet, and several flat caps, similar to the one he was wearing, were stacked above on a shelf. But most impressive was the one wall stacked to the ceiling with vinyl records, and every other wall in the room stacked to the ceiling with elegantly timeworn hardcover books.

"My God, look at all these books," I said in admiration.

"The forty-year collection of a retired professor, I suppose," Henry said.

"That's really something. Where did you teach?"

"UCLA."

Also alongside the wall was a neatly stacked pile of newspapers—*The New York Times*—all of them still fairly crisp-looking, but just tattered enough to show that he'd gone through the different sections and then fastidiously put them back together.

When he caught my gaze, he said, "I get the paper delivered every morning, because it reminds me of a simpler time, a time without electronic readers, when people could smell the pages of the books they read."

"Ha, nice," I said, immediately infatuated with him. "It seems you've been living here for some time."

"For the last two years. I've been the only long-term guest at the hotel for a while."

"You and me, then."

"I heard," he said, enlightening me to the possibility that he'd spoken with the concierge about me. "How long are you staying?"

"Not sure—at least a month."

"Great," he said, walking into his kitchen and coming back out with a platter of fruit. "Try the melon, it's wonderful."

"Thanks," I said, grabbing a piece.

"And grab a few of those berries—fresh today."

"I appreciate it. Are you going out somewhere?"

"Oh," he said, catching my drift, "I always dress like this—it gets me excited for each new day. Would you like something to drink?"

"I'm OK. I'd better get back. Have some work to do. But, listen, I'm grateful for the tomato soup—it put me in a much better place," I said.

"Well—" he said, his own cough cutting him off. I waited as he tried to control his coughing, taking in giant sucks of air, as his eyes started to water.

"Are you OK?" I said, walking over and standing above him, while he was hunched over, holding his chest. "Can I get you some water?"

A few seconds later, his coughing bout had ceased, and, after standing upright, wiping his eyes, and taking a deep breath, he said, "No, I'm fine. That seems to happen from time to time. Anyway, what I planned to say is why don't you come back for dinner tomorrow night, seven thirty? I'll cook."

"I can do that. Should I bring us something to drink?"

"I don't drink alcohol unless, of course, it's a nice bottle of wine, red or white, a good microbrew, or a single malt whiskey," he said, smiling and extending his hand toward mine.

I laughed. "Fine by me. Good to meet you, Henry," I said, shaking his hand.

Back in my room, I had a cigarette, breathing it in deeply to let it lighten the weight in my head, and then read over the passages I'd posted on the wall. I sat down in front of my laptop and tried to write something. *Nothing. Goddamn it.* I had another cigarette and noticed a spider spinning a web in the corner.

"I see you," I said, reaching for my shoe.

I stood on top of a chair, putting myself at a height within striking distance, and slowly cocked my good arm back, but, in doing so, alerted the spider to the imminent danger, at which point he sprinted along the wall away from me. I dismounted the chair and positioned it a few feet to the right, under the spider's new resting place, but when I rose up, the spider evaded me again, moving further along the wall.

"You elusive little fucker," I said.

After two failed attempts to kill him with the hurling of my shoe, I decided to let him live.

"I'm sorry for trying to kill you," I said to him. "I'll make you a deal. I'll let you spin your webs if you let me write my words. We can coexist peacefully if we learn to respect each other. Eat all the flies and bugs you want. But don't eat me. We're both trying to survive. All we have now is each other."

I sat back down in front of my blank laptop screen and looked at it hopelessly until evening fell. I lit another cigarette and, halfway through smoking it, felt a burning sensation inside my lungs. I looked at the pack resting on the table and then at the burning cigarette between my fingers. *You fucking cancer inside me. I can feel you sizzling in my lungs.* I walked over to the window, opened it, and tossed the pack out, along with the rest of the cigarette I'd been smoking. My room looked directly into the hotel garden, and I saw that my pack had landed at the base of a tree that grew high over my window, its branches blocking my view of the sky.

I resumed my position in front of my screen, but still couldn't produce a single word.

"Fuck, spider. I have no words. I'm no writer."

I crawled out the window, scooped up my pack of cigarettes, and smoked one while sitting on the grass and trying to find the stars in the night sky through the branches. I gave up searching and crawled back inside.

After drifting to sleep in front of my laptop, I awoke in the late morning with a trail of bites down my good arm, and, in a fit of anger, rose from my chair and tried to find him; he was in his corner, lounging in webbed comfort, unmoving, with his belly full of my blood.

"What about our deal?"

I moved the chair so it was positioned under him, stood up on it, and, with one unrepentant hurl of my shoe, undid the hours he'd put into his webbed artistry and sent him flying to the floor, where he erratically limped about. While hovering maniacally over him, I turned the missile of a shoe into a hammer of a shoe, and brought it down swiftly upon him; he twitched twice and then fell eternally still.

"No. *Goddamn it.* I'm sorry."

My shoulders sunk and fell forward in remorse, and my eyes pumped tears down my face in thick, salty streams, which rained down around the spider's corpse; the deadness of his smashed body haunted me.

"What have I done?"

I fell down next to him and cried. I cried for him. I cried for her. *Help me.* I cried until I was drained of tears.

"I'm sorry. I'm so sorry. Please forgive me."

SEVENTEEN

Before my dinner with Henry, I decided to visit Dolphus and found him in the same spot I'd discovered him.

"Hey, friend, I brought us something to drink," I said, handing him one of the two brown-bagged bottles of whiskey I'd brought with me and then sitting along the wall next to him. He accepted the drink with a nod, and we sat in silence while observing the street's activity and sipping the whiskey. I lit myself a smoke and offered one to Dolphus; he accepted it with another nod.

"Dolphus, I want you to have something," I said, after we'd sat together for some time. "Maybe you can sell it. I don't know. Do whatever you want with it." I handed him my phone. "It's in good condition. Good-bye for now. I'll visit you again."

I'd been wearing the same dirty clothes (the only ones I'd brought with me) since I checked into the hotel, so I found a thrift store on Fairfax and bought two large bags of white T-shirts and a few pairs of pants. Next, I went to a wine store on the other side of the street and bought two bottles of red wine and a bottle of white. I knocked on Henry's door at seven thirty that evening.

"Come in, Jake. Come in," Henry said, after opening the door, holding a fillet knife and wearing a neatly pressed white dress shirt, made of oxford cloth, under a chef's apron. He was bald on top, but elegantly so, and the white hair at his temples was smartly combed back.

"Thank you."

"Full menu tonight—egg-lemon soup, green salad, fresh halibut with russet potatoes and asparagus, and, finally, some fruit and a scoop of ice cream for dessert."

"Sounds wonderful. You really didn't have to go through this much trouble," I said.

"But then it wouldn't be worth it, would it? Why don't we open a bottle of your red now, and then, maybe we can work our way to the white in time for dessert?"

"Perfect."

"Take a seat," Henry said, directing me to the sitting area with a table and two couches.

Often, in the company of an old man, I would try to find the young man within him, imagine the youthful version of him behind his now tired, wrinkled eyes, and when I was able to, he became, in a way, very vulnerable to me, as if he were a sad man tormented by the passing of time. But I wasn't able to do that with Henry; he was simply a beautiful and confident old man. He went into his kitchen, returning with two wineglasses and a platter filled with crackers and different cheeses and some olives; he also handed me a corkscrew.

"Open the bottle and give us a pour," he said.

"Sure."

"Try the cheese on the left. I think it might be the best thing I've ever tasted," he said, taking a seat on the couch across from me.

"So what did you teach?" I asked with a mouthful of cracker and cheese. "Oh, that *is* good."

"Professor of English literature—poetry, history of the language, creative writing, all the beautiful stuff worth learning and teaching."

"Really? I studied English in college," I said, filling his glass with red wine and then filling mine.

"Oh yeah? Where?"

"Cal."

"Were you a student of Carolyn Carver?"

"I was! Wow—yeah, small world, huh? My senior year, I took her class on early twentieth-century fiction—probably my favorite class in college."

"Any particular reason for it being your favorite?"

"Hmm ... Probably because I made friends with two other guys in the class, and all we did was sit around and drink whiskey and study and pretend we were writers living in Paris."

"Fine reason, if I do say so myself," Henry said, laughing. "Carolyn's a wonderful woman and a wonderful teacher. I've grown quite fond of her over the years. She just published a beautiful book on Faulkner's contribution to American literature. I helped her through the editing stage."

"I'll have to buy a copy."

"I'll dig one up for you."

"That'd be great."

"Do tell me, Jake. What is it that brought you to this place and made you my neighbor?"

"Well—I just sort of ended up here, really. I'm originally from Laguna Beach, in Orange County. After I quit my job, I spent some time in Manhattan Beach, then moved to a house in West Hollywood not far from here. And now ... I live here."

"Yet another journey," Henry said, momentarily pausing, with a look in his eyes that suggested he was interested in knowing more.

"What about you? You've lived here a couple years ... do you have family in the area?" I said, eager to redirect control of the conversation back to him, partly because I enjoyed his candor, and partly because I wasn't ready to go into any details about my previous adventures.

"Not anymore."

"What happened?"

"Well, sadly, my wife battled cancer for years and died from it ten years ago. My only daughter died young, also of cancer—pancreatic cancer. She was married, but they didn't have any children."

"Jesus, I'm sorry. My grandmother died of pancreatic cancer, too."

"It's the worst kind."

"That's what I hear."

"Well, I'm hoping I get dealt a heart attack—the organ that holds, locked within it, a lifetime of love and pain just simply explodes. A brilliant way to go, wouldn't you say?"

"I've never looked at it that way."

"Well, Jake, there's always more than one way to look at something," he said, giving me a playful wink.

"You seem to have a good handle on all of it."

"On what?"

"You know ... the idea of, um, dying."

"How old are you?"

"Twenty-three."

"Ah yes, right in the throes of it. You're much too old and far too young to be immune from the paralyzing thoughts of death. I was in

World War II around your age—well, a little younger—and death was all around me. I remember trying, every day, to accept the likelihood of death finding me. The strangest moments for me came after hearing the news of someone's death—someone I shared a drink or card game or conversation with the night before. But there was nothing quite as horrifying as witnessing it for the first time. I thought if God existed, He or She must be a goddamn son-of-a-bitch," he said.

I nodded with a tight-lipped, solemn expression.

"But, far too grim a subject for a first dinner. Let's eat, shall we?" he said, gesturing me over to the dinner table.

I sat in the chair meant for me and guided my hand along the soft, red tablecloth, admiring the exquisiteness of Henry's place settings: the pristinely white dinner and salad plates and soup bowls, the variety of thick, shiny cutlery, the crystal wineglasses, the porcelain coffee cups on saucers, and the neatly folded cloth napkins. And in the middle of the table, to complement the decor, were two lit candles, their flames slow dancing to the rhythm of the light breeze allowed in through Henry's open window.

"How about some music?" he said.

"I'd love that."

"Because … 'It appeared that nobody ever said a thing they meant, or ever talked of a feeling they felt, but that was what music was for. Reality dwelling in what one saw and felt, but did not talk about …'"

"Who wrote that?"

"Virginia Woolf, *The Voyage Out*."

He walked over to his collection of vinyl records, reached for a stack, thumbed through them, and found one he liked. "How about some jazz?" He slid the black record out from the cover and set it on the player, his placement of the needle scratching the sounds of jazz to life.

"So you're alone now?" I asked.

"Alone? You mean excluding all my friends stacked along the walls?" he said, pointing to his collection of work from dead musicians and writers.

"Right," I said, my smile igniting into a light chuckle.

"But, really, I'm quite busy. I still do a guest lecture here and there. I've also started a discussion group that meets weekly here at the hotel. Each week we choose a specific topic to discuss, but generally we limit our discussions to films, music, and literature. And once a year, I travel with a company called Elderhostel, which, as the name suggests, organizes trips for old geezers like me to places like Europe and South America. My latest journey, if you're interested, was to the Italian Lakes, specifically Lake Como and Lake Maggiore. Jake ... Perhaps the most beautiful places I've ever seen. Have you been?"

"Not those places, but I stayed in other parts of Italy when I studied abroad."

"Oh, Jake, you must go. The Alps seem to rise right from the lake shores, and, of course, all the old, wonderful villas are tucked along the shoreside ... well—quite spectacular, really. I also learned how to make," he paused as if to prepare himself for proper pronunciation, "*panettone*—Italian sweet bread—while I was there. A few weeks ago, I baked a loaf. If you were here, I would've sliced you a piece and let you enjoy it with some cream. So anyway, I suppose I'm much busier now than I've ever been, and, of course, I'm doing the things I want to be doing with my time."

As he ladled egg-lemon soup into my bowl and tonged green salad onto my plate, he told me about his love of jazz, "especially early Armstrong, early Basie, and early Ellington." I served myself another helping of both appetizers, while he regaled me with stories of his early childhood, a time he described as being about "friendships and explorations and mischief and boredom" during the "unbearably hot, asphalt-jungle summers" that were typical of his neighborhood in Brooklyn.

When he served the halibut and potatoes, and while I opened another bottle of wine, he told me about the effect the Depression had on his mother's cooking: "I've never quite gotten over the cheap, horrible blandness of the dinners that tormented my taste buds night after night." But he also said that good had come from it: "So I then vowed to make food and its preparation a lifelong passion of mine."

Finally, while we enjoyed another glass of wine (white this time) and tastes of vanilla ice cream topped with fresh berries for dessert, Henry spoke, with nostalgia in his eyes, about his love of women. "They're so beautiful, aren't they? I was in love with my daughter from the day she was born. I loved my wife very much. And there's not a woman I've stumbled upon yet in my life who is devoid of an entirely lovable characteristic. They all have something, Jake. They are women. They are magical."

I gave him a warm smile, much more inclined to hear his words than contribute my own.

"Many men of my age tend to shun romantic involvement, but I don't see the point of doing such a thing. A little love is always the answer, wouldn't you agree? I believe that life can be just gorgeous if you're willing to give yourself to someone, and that you'd be a fool to hold yourself back from experiencing something like that."

"So I'm guessing that you're still dating now?"

"Oh yes!"

I laughed and said, "That's great, Henry. That's really great."

"How about some coffee to settle the meal?" Henry said, rising from the table and walking into his kitchen.

I noticed on his counter the lineup of a coffee bean grinder, a shiny, semiautomatic espresso machine, and a cylindrical French press. I watched him move with an acute attention to detail as he loaded the beans into the grinder, ground them, packed the portafilter with freshly ground beans, and then secured it tightly to the machine.

"Coffee is always one mistake away from being terrible. Jake, come take a look," he said, prompting me to walk over to him. As the coffee began to stream out of the machine—after about twenty seconds—and into two demitasses placed underneath, Henry said, "Look at that beautiful shade of red. See that? Coffee is so much about color. See that *crema*, Jake? This will be a good drink. Would you like me to steam you some milk?"

"No, it's OK. I'll just have it straight."

"Bravo, Jake. Two *caffè espresso* coming right up. I should mention that I get a shipment of these special beans delivered from a coffeehouse in New York—my parents' favorite—every two weeks. They produce such a nice aroma and flavor."

And when he began to explain the coffee-roasting process—"The beans, before they were roasted, of course, were at one time green" (a fact I hadn't known before meeting Henry)—I picked up on his tendency to go into long-winded descriptions of even the most insignificant details. But I found his use of language so alluring, his imagery so lush, it would have been disingenuous for me to deny my growing fascination with Henry Shapiro and anything he talked about.

But, inevitably—as we paused our conversation for a tabletop glimpse of nearly-scraped-clean plates and bowls; empty, green-tinted wine bottles; and steam-less ceramic demitasses—the natural moment to part ways revealed itself, and I rose from the table.

"Let me help you with all this," I said, bringing some of the dishes from the table to the sink in the kitchen.

"No, no, please," he said.

"Are you sure?"

"Please, it's OK, really. Doing the dishes is therapeutic for me. Instead, you can have me over to dinner sometime."

"Sure. I'd love to. I haven't had a conversation and a meal like this in a long time. Thanks again, Henry."

He walked me to the door, shook my hand, and closed the door behind me. But while I was still in the hall, digging in my pocket for my room key, Henry opened his door again.

"Jake, do you still have aspirations to write?" he said. "I thought I'd ask, since you mentioned your fantasizing about being a writer living in Paris."

"Well—"

"I'll read anything you give me, Jake. Good night," he said, closing the door.

After considering Henry's offer for a few minutes, I left the hotel and found a store on Third Street that offered printing services. Using one of the computers, I printed a copy of my short story, "The Tales of a Desert Wanderer," and paid the man at the front for the twenty pages. On my way back, I paused to stare at a line forming outside a bar across the street, felt the bottle of pills in my back pocket, and continued on. Inside the hotel, I quietly slid the pages under Henry's door and then darted across the hall, into my room.

It was just after noon the next day. I was sitting on a chair in front of my window, staring at the tree branches, some of them scratching the windowpane with nudges from the wind, when I heard a knock at my door.

"Your narrator's voice is, at times, believable," Henry said, after I opened the door. "The piece, however, needs significant work, and there's much to improve in your style."

"I appreciate the honesty."

"No time for bullshit, Jake. Only one life to get it right. I've gone through the piece and given you notes," he said, handing me pages tattooed almost entirely in intimidating red ink. "We can discuss it at length later."

"I'd like that."

"Now ... how about some lunch at the hotel restaurant?"

"Sure."

In the courtyard, Henry picked a table under the shade of a tree in the corner furthest from the other diners.

"Henry, what can I get you this afternoon?" the waiter asked.

"How about a spritzer? Jake, would you drink a spritzer?" Henry said.

"Never had one but sure—let's do it."

"Bring us a bucket of ice with the bottle of white wine and the soda water. We can pour it," Henry said to the waiter. "And I'll take the club sandwich. Jake, I think you should try the paella—it's quite wonderful here, nearly as good as it is in Spain."

"I'll take the paella, then," I said to the waiter.

"Sure, no problem, guys," the waiter said.

"Also, Timmy, can you bring the chessboard after lunch?" Henry said.

"Yes, sir."

A family of four was having lunch at the far end of the courtyard; the two children played under the table in a shielded little world of make-believe, while their parents seemed concerned with much more solemn matters up above.

"You know," I said to Henry, "every time I see a child playing, I have the same feeling—this warm, nostalgic sensation for the days when summers were magical and time itself seemed infinite. You remember that? I mean, as kids we could unlock a world of imagination simply by climbing a tree. We could fantasize about everything, imagine ourselves growing up and doing anything, because the possibilities were endless, you know? We were still young enough not to be laden with thoughts of doubt and meaninglessness. It just made more sense."

"You speak fondly of childhood. I've also noticed it in your writing," Henry said. "I hope you don't let it tarnish your experiences in the present. Surely you remember the miserable times of childhood: the braces, the bullies, the heartbreak, the insecurities, the fear of darkness—"

"'It is an illusion that youth is happy,'" I interrupted, "'an illusion of those who have lost it; but the young know they are wretched, for they are full of the truthless ideals which have been instilled into them, and each time they come in contact with the real they are bruised and wounded. It looks as if they were victims of a conspiracy; for the books they read, ideal by the necessity of selection, and the conversation of their elders, who look back upon the past through a rosy haze of forgetfulness, prepare them for an unreal life.'" I paused, proud of myself, but then, noticing Henry's widening smile, felt defeated. "You know it, don't you?"

"'They must discover for themselves,'" he said, continuing where I'd paused, "'that all they have read and all they have been told are lies, lies, lies; and each discovery is another nail driven into the body on the cross of life.' Somerset Maugham," he said, still smiling. "*Of Human Bondage.* Courageous effort, though, Jake."

"Damn you! It took me a week to memorize that passage. I think I read it a thousand times," I said, playfully shaking my head. "Thought I had you on that one."

The waiter brought the bucket and two wineglasses over to our table. Henry pulled out the bottle of white wine and nearly filled two glasses with it; then he grabbed the bottle of soda water, unscrewed it, topped off each of the glasses with a pour, and handed one to me.

"Cheers," he said, as we clinked glasses.

The soda water added a refreshing crispness to the white wine, and I very much enjoyed drinking it at the table, next to Henry, who, at that moment, seemed to be studying me.

"Are you mad at something, Jake?" Henry asked.

"Right now?"

"In the general sense."

"I'm not sure."

"Well, if you had to choose one thing to be mad at, what would it be?"

"Well ... I guess at the way everything is supposed to be," I said.

He took a sip of his spritzer and then looked into my eyes. "I almost married another woman once. I started dating her during high school before I left for the war. And, my God, was I in love with her. The kind of love that makes even the most mundane things seem magical. 'That's not just a table over there; it's the most beautiful table in the world. Look at this fork. Isn't it so shiny and lovely? And this cold weather isn't so bad, it could be worse!'—that kind of love."

"Right," I said, smiling and nodding.

"Anyway, I wrote to her as much as I could, at least a couple of letters each week. The hope, every day, of getting a letter back from her was exhilarating. That feeling, the anticipation, the whole letter-writing process, really, distracted me from all the suffering around me. When I finally came home, we got back together, and, at first, it was lovely and passionate and wonderful, but we soon realized we knew nothing about each other, and that, after all the time that had passed, we were really quite different. After we parted ways, I found out she'd been having an affair with another man throughout my letter-writing war days. But she, the idea of us, got me through the war, Jake. It was the same for many of the other soldiers, too. We buried ourselves in our letter writing, much like the subjects in your short story bury themselves in their phones. For us, it was not only a means of distraction but also a way to fantasize about a far-off world, a better life, a more peaceful life, about waking up in a warm bed next to someone we loved, you see?"

I was staring at the table, but when he paused, I looked at him. "And you're fine with that? With none of it being real?" I said.

"'Lift not the painted veil which those who live / Call life: though unreal shapes be pictured there, / And it but mimic all we would believe … I knew one who had lifted it—he sought, / For his lost heart was tender, things to love, / But found them not, alas!'"

"Who?"

"Shelley," he said with a wink.

"I just don't know, Henry. I think I'm becoming a misanthrope or, maybe, a Luddite or something like that. But I never wanted to be any of those things. I never wanted to be someone who hated anything or anyone. I'm convinced something is very wrong with me, like my mind won't ever just let me be OK with the way things are."

"I should warn you that being a Luddite is very risky business. You'll be accused of being small-minded or holding on to the illusion of an ideal past. Be prepared to defend yourself. Also, the women tend to hate Luddites," he said, chuckling.

"Well … no Internet connection or cell phone, stacks of newspapers, and piles of books and vinyl records in your room," I said, smiling. "I'm guessing you qualify."

"Hey! Am I really to be implicated when music simply sounds better on vinyl?" he said, smiling back. "Or for loving a time when—it's possible that you'll remember—one could answer a phone and be truly surprised by the voice at the other end? I'm just more fond of my generation, that's all."

"Well, when you put it like that …" I said.

"And I do just fine with the women," he said, making me laugh.

The waiter brought Henry's sandwich and my paella, and we took a short break from conversation to taste our dishes and sip the spritzer.

"Jake, I love to teach," Henry said after the pause. "But, at times,

I tend to be—and it's a blatant, personal flaw, if I do say so myself—
overly passionate about my own discoveries and truths. I'm still working
on it, even after all these years, if you can believe that. So I encourage
you to always listen to what I say with a filter—it's important that you
seek your own truths."

"I think it's fine, Henry. I've always dreamt of having my very own
sage."

He cracked another smile and then let it fade before starting up
again. "Now, reverting to our earlier discussion, I feel that there's always someone disillusioned by his generation's preoccupation with
something or detachment from another thing. Gutenberg—that damn
bastard, right?—with his printing press, destroying every man's need
to rely on his memory. And in my time, all the math guys ran around
screaming about the calculator ruining all of our math skills. It all makes
for something wonderful to write about, but to write it well and write
the time well, you must learn to love your subjects to their core, even
if you hate them, because, as a writer in the present, they're your only
beautiful muses in this world. I'm quite convinced that very few, if any,
can do it alone. Jake, you must understand something ... you must
understand that momentary rage is good, but that abiding hate is ruin-
ous. Don't hide from people in hate when you can rage silently in their
presence. Rage means you're alive. Rage brings you closer to the truth.
Misanthropes have nothing to write about, because they're already dead,
and writing is for the living."

After noticing that we'd finished the bottle of wine and our meals,
Timmy, the waiter, brought a chessboard to our table and asked us if we
needed anything else.

"Put the bill on my room, Timmy. How about some tea? Jake, do
you drink tea in the afternoon?"

After I agreed to have tea and Timmy went off to get it, Henry said,
"'Stands the Church clock at ten to three? / And is there honey still for
tea?'"

"Who wrote that one?"

"Rupert Brooke," he said, with a wistful smile, as if he were remembering a time when he and Rupert Brooke had shared a pot of tea and
discussed poetry.

Henry's profound love for quoting the works of others often spilled
into the opportune moments of his own stories, and rather than identifying him as a pretentious literatus trying to impress those in his com-

pany, I got the impression of a man who truly believed that the beauty in life was hiding in all the great words of men and women throughout the ages, waiting to be shared. Henry Shapiro simply loved literature so much it was seeping out of him.

"One thing, Henry ..."

"Go ahead."

"Did the girls ever write back ... I mean, did they ever respond during the war with letters of their own?"

"Much less frequently than we would send our letters to them. But they did. I believe it was, for us, much more about the writing and the sending and the hoping. Their responses were always much prettier in our imaginations. Now, how about a game of chess?"

"It's been a while," I said, still ruminating over Henry's words.

"You'll be fine."

Over the next couple of weeks, I spent much of my time in Henry's room, partly because his room was far more interesting than mine, with all of his books and records and paintings and pastries and fresh fruit and newspapers and coffee steam rising from within porcelain cups resting on top of porcelain saucers, but mostly because I loved his company and the stories he was always willing to share with me.

One afternoon—as we sipped red wine and nibbled on hors d'oeuvres while relaxing on his couch—I learned that Henry Shapiro, then in his late eighties, was raised by impoverished, devout Jewish parents in a tenement house in Brooklyn.

"My ongoing battle with my parents, until they died, was over religion, starting at a young age, when I decided that I felt more comfortable not knowing what was going to happen to us all, not subscribing to any sort of truth—agnostic, in short," he said, pausing to drink wine from his glass and then top a cracker with cheese. "But, until high school, I still went to temple, because my friends went to temple, and the pretty girls went to temple. I had a fear that I was missing out on something special. It was much later that I had the confidence to graduate myself to atheism. It can be very difficult to be an atheist as a young man—it's a strong statement—a religion of its own, you could say."

"Did your parents ever let up?" I asked.

"No ... never. But I was always sure, at least during my more mature years, to remain respectful of their beliefs. Still, it always pained me to know that I was breaking my mother's heart, perhaps even more so when I could no longer argue with her—after she'd passed."

"And now you live in a Jewish neighborhood," I said, knowing, after reading online about the Fairfax District of Los Angeles, that we were very much in the middle of a Jewish community.

"You're right. Maybe as a tribute to them. Maybe because I miss them."

One night, when he came to my room for dinner (I roasted a chicken), Henry told me more about the girl he'd met early in his high-school years and how he'd fallen in love with her—"She was poor, too, just like me. We were so in love. All we ever worried about was being next to each other, feeling the warmth of each other's bodies. That was always more than enough"—and that they'd decided to stay together after he was drafted to fight in World War II, because "at the time neither of us could imagine it any other way."

"So this is the same girl you wrote the letters to during the war, right?" I asked.

"That's right."

"Were you upset that she was seeing another man while you were away fighting and writing her?"

"Well, I wasn't made aware of that until much later, after she'd married him. Of course, at first, I felt betrayed and hurt, but, over time, I realized she was right to seek her own happiness. See, when I finally came home from the war, I'd changed so much. She'd changed so much. We could no longer fight for our relationship because the ideals that bound us together in our young lives didn't seem to make sense anymore. But, as I told you before, my love for her, and hers for me, got me through the war—and I'll always love her for that."

And during one warm winter afternoon under a powder-blue sky, as Henry and I reclined in the chaise longues around the pool in our hotel robes (the first time I'd ever seen him out of a suit), sipping beer from the bottle, I learned that he'd been drafted into the US Army, and, after being trained in the United States, had been sent to England for more training, then to fight in France and later in Germany; then, after drawing it out of him, I discovered that for his exemplary leadership, Henry had been made a second lieutenant, overseeing a platoon of sixteen soldiers, and, eighteen months later, had been promoted to first lieutenant.

"War, for me, was about *waiting*—waiting to take orders, waiting to give orders, waiting to go home, waiting to die, but mostly it was about helping the guys under my command deal with the anguish of all the waiting. The downtime was tortuous. Apart from the letter writing, some guys distracted themselves with drinking and prostitutes. Some played cards. Some turned to books."

"The army supplied you with books?" I said.

"Oh, sure ... along with pens and paper so we could write our letters—they supplied us with anything we needed, really, except a ticket home."

Henry, one of the men who'd turned to books, had grown to love literature while waiting to die in the war.

"I was never much into reading before the war," he said. "I never saw the point of it. But when faced with my own mortality, the idea of losing myself in the imaginary world of fiction was quite appealing. I read everything I could find, everything the army provided us. Then, at some point, literature, for me, became much more than escapism—it became my life."

And when Henry made it out of the war alive, he decided that he wanted to pursue an education in the humanities, preferably literature; so he applied to several colleges and was both surprised and delighted when he, the poor boy from Brooklyn, was accepted to Princeton University to study English.

"And, in New Jersey, it wasn't far from my parents, so I could still be around to help them, as they seemed, perhaps psychologically, at that point, to still be dealing with the ramifications of the Great Depression."

"I spent some time in New Jersey several months ago. It was so beautiful," I told him.

"Oh yes, isn't it?" he said, his eyes flashing blue, then fading to a glimmering gray.

And then, over a game of morning chess in the courtyard, Henry told me that he'd met his future wife in one of his college classes.

"Which class?" I asked him, capturing one of his pawns with an L-shaped attack from my knight.

"It was—ha ha!—as cliché as it may seem, a class on Shakespeare, and we were in the middle of reading *The Winter's Tale* when I first fell in love with her," he said, pausing to make his move, capturing my knight with his queen. "But she fell in love with me, as she used to tell it, much later in the course. I believe we were studying *A Midsummer Night's Dream* by then."

"How did you get her to fall in love with you?"

"I simply told her I loved her every day, until, finally, one day, she said it back to me. That was a wonderful day."

Sometimes, in the late afternoon, as angled shafts of sunlight filtered glittery yellow through the trees, we relaxed in the hotel garden and drank white wine, while Henry read me poetry from Keats, his favorite poet.

"Isn't that just wonderful?" he said once, after he'd finished reading one of Keats's poems aloud. "If heaven existed the way I wanted it to, I'd be allowed to have conversations with Keats all day."

"Sort of like how I get to have conversations with you all day?" I said.

And, of course, Henry loved his music, and he was always excited to expose me to his favorites: "How about some Billie Holiday today, or perhaps some Josephine Baker?"

I joined Henry's weekly discussion group two weeks in a row, during which his gray-haired posse gathered in his room and chatted about the arts; I remained voluntarily quiet until someone within the group—it happened both times—called for my opinion: "Let the boy talk. This issue is related much more to his generation than ours."

My first experience with Henry coming undone happened when, for the first time in our relationship, we got a bit too drunk inside the hotel restaurant as we sat along the bar, chatting up a young waitress Henry knew well. She left us momentarily to tend to an equally drunken group of guys playfully demanding the TV be turned on so they could watch "the game," and when she obliged them, Henry went into a spontaneous rage.

"Damn philistines," he said, slamming his fist on the counter, catching me by surprise. "The art of distraction is indeed a requisite for an enjoyable human life ... but what an awfully unfulfilling way to distract yourself, watching football all day—such mindless, gladiatorial entertainment. Cheering for your teams. Seeking your happiness through the successes of other people. It's a goddamn *waste*—I must say."

"They're watching a basketball game, Henry."

"What's the difference? They'll never be part of the real *conversazione*. You want to mingle with the damn *hoi polloi*? Be my guest. I'd love to join you," he said as he struggled off the bar stool, "but I'm going to bed." He staggered outside, across the courtyard, toward his room.

As I finished my drink, I tried to think, with a bias in favor of Henry's opinion, of justifications for his outburst, but, no matter how much I found myself agreeing with him, his rationale seemed flawed, in that, if "the art of distraction is indeed a requisite for an enjoyable human life," why should it matter the way different people chose to distract themselves? But, going against logic as I swallowed the last of my drink, I decided that Henry had to be right because he was Henry—a decision that inexplicably pleased me as I stumbled back to my room.

The next day I found Henry in the courtyard sitting at a table with the same group of game-watching men from the night before, entertaining them with a story.

"What a terribly uninteresting, happy bunch," he said, describing them to me later. "I quite enjoyed them."

And then, a few days later, I got another glimpse of Henry's temperamental side, when he invited me to join him for lunch with someone—a retired English professor from USC—whom he described as his best friend, "because our relationship has stood the test of time and is still ongoing."

The man, named Jim, perhaps five or ten years younger than Henry, looked disheveled, at least compared to Henry, with his thin, scattered strands of white hair sticking straight up in an Einsteinian fashion, and his wearing of a plain, seemingly unwashed, sweatshirt (which made me aware of how third-rate I must have looked sitting next to Henry every day). Their conversation—a pleasant discussion of the best films adapted from novels (Jim said 1946's *The Best Years of Our Lives*, Henry said 1946's *Great Expectations*, but then they both agreed on 1939's *Goodbye, Mr. Chips*)—carried on smoothly until Jim shifted to a new topic.

"Unfortunately, the novel, inherently prone to novelization, has become much too limiting as a form of creative writing. I'd prefer to eliminate it altogether. Let's kill the novel, if it's not already dead, in favor of the essay, a medium that enjoys few limitations," Jim said.

The comment launched a debate that, over the next twenty minutes, escalated, until Henry lunged over the table, knocking over glasses, to, apparently, shake some sense into his friend. As I pulled Henry back, I was surprised by his old-man strength. Red in the face with anger, coughing violently, and hands trembling, he still broke free of my grip, and, between coughs, said, "Jim, I wish ... you would try ... using your ... goddamn brain." He walked away from the table, leaving Jim and me to awkwardly stare at each other.

"Oh, that's just Henry being Henry," Jim said, breaking our silence.

"He'll call me tomorrow, as if nothing happened, and ask me what I think about this or that, and then we'll get into it again over something else."

Eighteen

After we'd spent two weeks learning about each other, discussing life and literature, and enjoying good meals, Henry, as if he'd used that time to appraise my seriousness, insisted that we focus more on my writing. So after lunch that day, I brought my short story into Henry's room.

As we sat side by side at his dining-room table, Henry began by saying, "The single most important thing about writing fiction is finding your authorial voice. I cannot do that for you. And apart from 'work hard every day,' I won't give you any specific advice on finding your voice. I can only *try* to help you discover it. The rest will be up to you." And then, when Henry was ready, he reached for my short story resting on the table, stacked the pages neatly together with a few tabletop taps, and laid the pile flat in front of us; then, after smoothing out the title page with the back of his timeworn, brown-spotted hand, Henry flipped to the first page of prose, and, together, we started going through the piece line by line.

He told me about the current habits in writing that irked him, several of which I was guilty of in my short story. He'd crossed out several of my weak sentences in red ink and rewritten them in pencil in the space just above. "I'm not going to tell you what to write," he said. "But, do you see how a simple revision here adds a bit of rhythm to the sentence?" And then, pausing on a page branded with a giant red *X*, he stressed to me the importance of compression in narrative writing. "It's an art. You must learn to identify the parts of your story that would benefit from some cutting, as in this section here," he said, tapping on the page with his finger. "But you must also, in the same fashion, pay attention to," he said, flipping a few pages ahead in the short story, "sections like this one that could use some more exposition."

Our first official day of working together seemed to be carrying along smoothly; that is, until Henry paused to take a closer look at the notes he'd made in the margin of a page around the middle of my short story, and then—his expression darkening, his eyes hardening into cold gray stones—erupted in anger over my grammar. "Have you any respect for the language in which you write your stories? Look here," he said, pointing to a section on the page, "and here and here and here. Please, borrow my copy, and study the rules." He left the table, returned with a one-thousand-page hardcover copy of *The Chicago Manual of Style*, and handed it to me. "You *are not* Shakespeare!"

"How do you mean?"

"'Come what come may / Time and the hour runs through the roughest day.' Shakespeare wrote that. Did you notice he used the singular verb form, 'runs,' with a plural subject, 'time and the hour'? Grammatically incorrect, you see—but he's *Shakespeare*."

"Henry, I forgot a few commas. I'm more interested in content. I can always go back and fix grammar later."

"No, *goddammit*, writing begins with grammar. Why is your generation so insistent on butchering the English language? Only *after* you've learned the rules are you allowed to break them. A writer shouldn't break the rules out of ignorance—only when he knows them so well that he craves something more and wants to run free, so he *needs* to write his own rules to grow. But he must *earn* that opportunity."

"Look, I didn't mean to—"

"You kids, these days, are so goddamn self-entitled and disillusioned. You want fame and recognition and affirmation without doing any of the work. And, even worse, it's not that you just *want* it, it's that you *expect* it, and, if you don't get what you want, you complain and whine without ever *doing anything* to change it. It's the end of the world should you ever be denied. Sometime early in your lives, you all started to believe—perhaps because your parents showered you with compliments and told you that you were capable of anything—in your specialness, and from then on you embarked on the mission of trying to sell your specialness to the rest of the world. Why? Because you all want to feel as if you matter. But you must *do something* about it, not sit around and seek empty compliments."

"Henry, I get it—"

"If you care about literature, you must *live* it, *feel* it, *bleed* it, and *respect* it by reading the great works of others."

"Jesus, Henry, aren't you generalizing just a little bit?" I said, fed up with Henry's tirade. "And, for fuck's sake, look at you! You preach about all this shit. You scoff at the idea of someone not loving literature. But, of course, you won't associate yourself with any literature or music that's been created in the last fifty years! Why? Because all the contemporary crap is beneath you, right? That makes you an *elitist*, doesn't it?"

"Perhaps *purist* is the word you meant to use, Jake. I'm not sure. Nonetheless, I feel that we are done with our discussions today."

"I think you're right," I said, angrily leaving his room.

Back in my room, after a cigarette and several paces back and forth, I opened *The Chicago Manual of Style* and began angrily flipping through it. But then, as I started to calm down, I stumbled upon a passage that aroused my interest. I spent the entire rest of the day and the whole night, in my bed, absorbed in the manual, studying it, going over many of the rules, taking notes, committing as much as I could to memory— the whole time, amazed, embarrassingly, at how much I didn't know or had forgotten.

At six the next morning, I was awakened by the loud ringing of my room phone on the dresser next to my bed.

"Hello," I answered, groggily.

"Jake, let's get the day started. How about a fresh cup of coffee from the French press?" said a familiar voice, with—just as his friend Jim had described it—no discernible tone suggesting Henry's remembrance of our previous night's argument.

"Henry, it's a little early, don't you think?"

"We have work to do. If we don't start early today, tomorrow becomes more appealing."

"OK ... Fine. I'll be over in a few minutes." Then, after a short pause, I said, "Look, Henry, I didn't mean—"

"Why don't you bring over some of your favorite contemporary fiction for me to read? That's all," he said, hanging up.

I hung up the phone, smiling and shaking my head, still unable to open my eyes. After a few minutes, I pulled myself out of bed, dressed, gathered an armload of what I thought to be the best contemporary fiction I had, and walked over to his room. His door was cracked open, and when I entered I saw him, already dressed in a suit, in the kitchen, bent over his French press, holding his tie close to his chest with one hand, and delicately plunging the fresh, black coffee with the other hand. I set my books down on his table. He poured two cups of coffee and handed one to me.

"Let's enjoy the coffee down in the courtyard, before we get to work," he said, reaching for his just-delivered *New York Times* on the counter.

After we were seated at our table in the courtyard, I watched Henry take a sip of his coffee, glide his hand across the smooth surface of the newspaper, and delicately unfold it; but then he paused, looked up, readjusted his eyeglasses, and focused on me.

"Jake, I want you to imagine a world where writing is a very uncool talent. Imagine that there's very little money in it. Imagine that your parents will hate you for embracing it, that your friends will make fun of you, that no girl will be impressed by it. Imagine that you'll never truly be fulfilled by anything that you write. Imagine a life stacked with frustrating days and lonely nights. Imagine a life of unrelenting criticism. And then imagine that after you finish writing something you're proud of, no one will read it, and that if someone does happen to read it, he will hate it. Now … if you learned that all those conditions were part of the world you were currently living in, would you still believe that you were capable of rising from bed in the morning with the desire to write?"

As he stared at me earnestly, I dutifully imagined living in the world he'd described, looked at him in the eyes, and then answered him truthfully, "Yes."

"All right. We'll continue, then," he said, his smile brightening my own face.

And so most mornings following our argument that started over grammar, Henry woke me up early with a phone call, and we'd meet to enjoy a cup of coffee from his French press at our table in the courtyard, the table that had become so unambiguously defined by our strange coupledom: the wise old man and the lost young boy. And in the brisk wintry air of early morning, with the whole day ahead of us, Henry, thriving in his old-fashionedness, wearing a crisply pressed suit and holding a pristine copy of *The New York Times*, would share with me the most interesting bits of news.

I began to eagerly anticipate that morning call from Henry, because each time I was awakened by that obnoxious ring, I knew that I still had Henry's attention—that he still cared enough to work with me. And for half an hour or so, I was able to sit across from him in the intimacy of a quiet courtyard—as we were circled by a couple of yawning waiters or waitresses with tired, hungover eyes (a look I recognized in myself from the Sunset House chapter of my life)—and secretly revel in the thought that I'd made a true connection with a person I admired. Then, after our coffee had been drunk and the news had been shared, the work would begin back in Henry's room.

"When you take a pretty girl to dinner," Henry said once, never one to shy away from making analogies to writing with pretty-girl narratives, "should you tell her everything about yourself right away, or should you let her come to her own conclusions? Maybe even allow her to fantasize about who you are, or, better, who you might be? Keep her guessing! Keep her interested! Right? Similarly, when you take her dancing later, do you want to drag and jerk her all around the dance floor, or do you want to let her find her own rhythm under your guidance? Do you see my point?"

"I think so—well, I'm not completely sure, Henry," I said.

"You must practice *obliqueness* in your writing. Got that? Get it in your head. *Obliqueness!*"

After we finished going through his notes on each page of my short story, he began sending me to his typewriter, and, after giving me a random topic, telling me to write about it.

"You have until dinnertime. Write me one sentence, write me ten pages—it doesn't matter as long as *every* word that you write has a true feeling behind it. You like music, right? Think of yourself as a pianist. You're striving for euphony in your work, and that's achieved first with a feeling. Look around you—at the books along the wall, look at the records, look at that vintage typewriter in front of you. All the inspiration you need is in this room. Get up. Walk around. Touch the books. Smell the pages. Breathe in the words of all the great writers who lived before you. And then write me something, Jake. I'll be right here if you wish to discuss anything. Maybe it'll take you ten minutes; maybe it'll take you several hours. But you must get in the habit of disciplining yourself to write every day. And please don't ruin my paper by smearing it with platitudes. *Ever.*"

Once, it took me a few hours to write one sentence. Another time, I wrote several pages in twenty minutes. But I always handed Henry some words before dinnertime, and he always read them aloud.

"You must *feel* your words more," he often said after reading my work. "Close your eyes and feel every word you write—even the conjunctions."

Only on one occasion, about a month into our routine, did Henry Shapiro, not one to give compliments, read the words I wrote using his typewriter (two paragraphs in ten minutes, that time), pause, look at me, and, fighting back a smile, say, "Not entirely bad."

Henry always had something new for me to read. I guessed that he had his reasons for wanting me to read certain works, but I could never detect a pattern to his assignments: first, he gave me ancient copies of John Webster's *The Duchess of Malfi* and John Dryden's *Mac Flecknoe*; later he sent me back to my room with Thomas Mann's *The Magic Mountain*, Henry James's *Daisy Miller*, Herman Melville's *Moby-Dick*, Willa Cather's *The Professor's House*, even a translation of Miguel Delibes' *La sombra del ciprés es alargada*, and, one time, with a proud smile on his face, he handed me a collection of short stories by T.C. Boyle, with whom he said he'd developed a great friendship over the years. I read everything he gave me.

When Henry wanted to take a break from teaching me, he would pour us a cup of tea and bring out a plate of fruit, and then usually try to make the conversation about me. Once, during one of our breaks, Henry said, "Jake, what did you discover with your time in Los Angeles before you met me?"

"Hmm ... Let's see ... *Fucking*. People fucking people. People fucking people over. Oh, and everyone is crazy," I said.

"Ah, but of course you must remember that 'the crazy old lady in the elevator every day turns out to be, when you finally speak to her, perfectly lucid,'" Henry said.

"You read *The Virgin Suicides*!" I said, surprised and excited that he'd actually touched some of the contemporary fiction I'd lent him a while back.

"Quite a lovely book, I must say. I also enjoyed reading *Bel Canto* and *The Sea*."

"I'm glad, Henry."

"I'm a fan of all literature, Jake—not just the much richer and far superior works of my generation and previous centuries," he said, shooting me a smile.

"Right," I said, chuckling. "What about you, Henry—what is Los Angeles to you?"

He looked away in thought for a few seconds and then said, "Well ... Los Angeles, to me, is quite a lovely city in all of its ugliness, just as a beautiful patch of blooming flowers is still lovely, even if it's surrounded by weeds and muck and filth and barren land. There's no place I'd rather be than Los Angeles. I love this town."

"Who said that?" I asked with a quick, playful nod.

"Well, that one is Henry Shapiro, of course," he said, smiling. Then, after glancing down at my arm, he said, "How long have you had that cast on, Jake?"

"Probably long enough. I have to make an appointment."

"Let's go see Javier."

"Who is Javier? A doctor friend of yours?"

"Just follow me," he said, walking toward the door.

I followed him out of his room, down the hall, and out into the courtyard.

"Javier!" he called out to the groundskeeper, who was busy trimming bushes.

Javier turned toward Henry and said, "*Hola,* Henry."

"Javier, my friend, Jake, here, needs a little help with his cast," he said, pointing to my arm. "Let's put those garden shears to good use and help the boy. What do you say, Javier?"

"No problem, *compadre,*" Javier said before sliding one of the sharp blades under my cast, and, in three or four snips, cutting it off.

It was also then, during our breaks, that I finally opened up to Henry about my time in Manhattan Beach (I told him about Liz and Jayson, the reality TV star) and at the Sunset House (I spoke to him at length about my lifestyle and my time with Parker Thomas). I also decided one day to talk to him about the macabre thoughts that had haunted me for years.

"I'm not sure what triggers them, but I get these images and thoughts that won't leave my head. They just stay there and hover. I can't get out of bed until they're gone. I just lie there, paralyzed. When it gets really bad, I think about killing myself, because, I don't know, sometimes I feel like there's no point in anything, anyway—that we're all just sitting around waiting for cancer," I said to him.

"No, Jake, we're enjoying our time before getting cancer. We have our passions and our relationships and our work and our pastimes—and then we move on. It's that simple, really. So just try to enjoy your time. That's all you can do," Henry said, always one to bring light to my darkness.

After that, I only tried to explain my malaise to Henry once more, and he immediately interrupted me.

"Jake, I once looked into the eyes of someone who'd truly given up—it was a terribly depressing sight. I'll never forget my experience with that man—or boy, I suppose—during the war. Some of the guys wanted me to talk to him. They said he was acting strange. So I pulled him aside—oh, that damn look in his eyes still haunts me—and asked him if he was OK. He then said in a very detached, nearly lifeless voice, 'It's winter now, soon it'll be spring, then summer, then fall, and then it'll be winter again. That's how it'll be, and it just scares the hell out of me. I feel trapped—almost claustrophobic—just thinking about it …' He said it just like that, and, regrettably, I couldn't find the right words to help him. He shot himself the next day. I often wish for another opportunity to speak with him, but truthfully, I still don't know what I'd say to him. But I don't worry about you in that way, Jake. You don't have that look in your eyes."

I stopped reaching to feel the bottle of pills in my pocket when I was with Henry, and soon after, I left the bottle in a drawer by my bed, forgetting about it altogether.

But the conversations I most enjoyed having with Henry during our breaks were ones about women. He told me about the woman he was casually seeing, and, more important, about the one woman he really wanted to be seeing. "She's a little young for me at seventy," he said, "but, damn, she's a looker."

"Why don't you ask her out?"

"Soon, Jake. Soon. Waiting for the right moment."

One night soon after, when I heard the sound of approaching footsteps in the hall, I watched a woman, through my peephole, pause nervously before knocking on Henry's door. He opened the door, holding a glass of wine in his hand, and gave her a kiss on the cheek; I caught the sweet aroma of his cooking and knew that he'd finally asked her out.

Sometimes, during our breaks, Henry would tell me, with a rare showing of despondency in his eyes, about life without his wife. "I think what I miss the most is the warmth—that warm feeling of someone next to me. 'The grand necessity, then, for our bodies, is to keep warm, to keep the vital heat in us.' That's Thoreau in *Walden*, by the way. Anyway, it gets cold, sometimes, when I sleep alone," he said to me the first time he spoke about it.

And, invariably, he would, in some way, urge me to pursue a romantic interest of my own. "Let's get you a girl, huh, Jake? I probably have a few student connections I can work for you," Henry said to me once.

"Come on," I said, laughing.

"You need to get out of your damn head, Jake. When you have a girl, it's the little things that seem like the most important things in the world: opening a car door, worrying about if she wants to hold your hand at a certain moment, deciding what topping you want on your pizza delivery. It's a hell of a lot more fun."

"I had the warmth once, too, Henry, but mine was fake heat," I said.

"Oh, Jake, it's a wonderful feeling to fall in love with someone, again," he said.

"Would you get married again?" I asked.

"Sure, if I met the right girl," he said, bringing me to a smile.

"You know, I seek solitude, but then I think I fall in love with every girl who gives me the slightest bit of attention," I said.

He laughed and said, "About the girls, I can't say that I blame you, Jake. But regarding solitude—it may feel right to you at this point in your life. But I wonder if it's because, right now, you know you have the option to change it. You're a young, smart, handsome boy—and having that option makes your solitude seeking seem romantic. It won't feel that way as you get older—your looks fade, your intelligence is doubted, your propensity to make friends weakens. It's a terrible thing, then, to be alone."

"I know that you're right, Henry ... It's just that—"

"Sure I'm right, Jake. So let's find you a girl, and then perhaps you can take her to Canter's Deli, just down the way on Fairfax, and buy her a fried honey ham and cheese sandwich with tomato—the best in town—or, for breakfast, a nice, big, golden-brown Belgian waffle. Both quite delicious, I assure you."

But Henry was old, and sometimes his terrible coughing bouts or shortness of breath or nausea or trembling would cut short our time together. One afternoon, two months into my relationship with Henry, he started wildly sucking in air to combat his coughing, refused the glass of water I brought him, and then waved me out of his room. Outside in the hallway, I stood listening, until he was finally able to regulate his breathing, and when I heard him moving around normally again, I retreated into my room.

When I awoke the next morning, two hours later than usual, without having received a call from Henry, I jumped out of bed in a panic and dialed his room number to no answer. When I rushed out of my room to check on him, I noticed a handwritten note taped to my door.

Jake,

I think you're ready to rewrite your short story. I've thrown away the original with my notes. Start over with a blank page. No copying from the old piece. I'll be gone for a little while, but when I return, I expect to see a new draft.

—HS

While Henry was gone, I tried to keep a routine. Each morning, I had a coffee in the courtyard and worked on my short story for a few hours. At noon, I took a break for lunch, ordered a sandwich and a beer, and read or chatted briefly with one of the servers, who always inquired about Henry's absence. After lunch, I took my laptop and sat around the pool and worked for another couple of hours. I made dinner in my room, took an hour-long walk around the neighborhood, and went to bed early. After nearly a week had passed, I'd finished a new draft of the short story; and after reading through it, I was surprised at how much my writing style had changed. I didn't know if the new draft was any good, but I was sure then that the previous draft, the one I'd originally given to Henry, was truly terrible. With the new knowledge I'd acquired from Henry's teachings, I felt embarrassed that he'd read the earlier draft and ashamed that it had represented me as an aspiring writer. But then I remembered Henry telling me once that all writers, if they were work-ing persistently to improve their writing, have to deal with the constant feeling of dissatisfaction toward their previous work.

That night, as I slid my short story under Henry's door, I suddenly felt very alarmed by the darkness in the crack under his door, as if my preoccupation with my routine had distracted me from the thought of Henry's absence, and I was, for the first time, confronting it. Without Henry at the hotel, I realized how alone I was. But the next evening, on my way back to my room from a trip to the market for groceries, I bumped into Henry, in the hallway, dressed in his usual.

"Henry! Where the hell have you been?" I said, excitedly.

"Hello there, Jake. Ah, I just had to see to some things. Everything's fine. How about some dinner at the restaurant? I'm buying," he said.

"I read your short story," Henry said after we'd ordered our meals at the restaurant. "You fixed it up nicely, Jake. It's getting to a good place. I did, however, make some new notes. I slid the pages back under your door," he said, smiling, in a way that suggested I still had much more to learn.

"Thank you," I said. "I look forward to going through it again. So ... you really aren't going to tell me where you've been all this time?"

"Oh, I needed some tests done at the hospital. Quite ordinary procedures for someone my age. Nothing to worry about," he said with such a recognizable fragility in his eyes, that I wasn't persuaded by his attempt to reassure me.

"They kept you for a whole week?"

"No, I stayed with an old friend for a few days. I hadn't seen him in quite a while. We went to school together."

"And what does he do?" I said, probing him.

"Well, he's retired now, but he was a lawyer—a great lawyer in his day, I must say."

"*Your* lawyer?"

"Well, I suppose the few times in my life when I needed one, yes, he was my lawyer."

"Henry, are you sure you're OK? What were the test results?"

"Everything's fine," he said, as the server brought our meals to the table. "Why don't you bring us the chessboard in a bit?" Henry said to the server. "Jake here thinks he's going to get lucky tonight and beat me."

"Sure thing," the server said. "Oh, and welcome back, Henry. We've all missed you around here."

"Thank you. It's good to be back."

But the way Henry had casually brushed me off made me more worried than relieved; so, during my after-dinner walk the following night, the sight of red flashing lights from a fire truck parked in front of the hotel drew me to a full sprint down the street.

"*Fuck*," I shouted as I ran, knowing somehow what I didn't want to know. When I arrived at the scene, I grabbed a paramedic. "Henry?" I said, gasping for air. "Is it an elderly man from the hotel? Henry Shapiro?"

"I'm sorry," he said, as I let go of him and stepped back, assuming the worst, and perhaps because the paramedic realized this, he said, "He's not dead."

"He's not! Oh, thank you, thank you. Where is he?"

"They've rushed him to the hospital in the ambulance."

"What happened to him?"

"He had a heart attack."

"Which hospital?"

"Cedars-Sinai on Beverly—just down the way."

I'd been waiting in the emergency room lobby for a few hours, when the hospital admitting clerk, who seemed to take me less seriously after I told her I wasn't part of Henry's family, finally called me up to the desk.

"I've been told that Mr. Shapiro is asleep for the night. I recommend that you return tomorrow during normal visiting hours. This is the room he'll be in," she said, writing his room number down on a piece of paper and handing it to me.

"How is he?"

"I've been told that he's stable."

Back in my hotel room, I remembered a time Henry and I were having lunch in the courtyard, and I asked him about music. "I already know you love jazz. What else do you like?"

"My love for music is quite comprehensive," he said, raising his eyebrows and giving me a look.

"Well, tell me about it."

"Sure ... Let's start with the wonderful composer of the Renaissance, William Byrd, and then jump ahead three hundred years to the lovely twentieth-century composer, George Gershwin. Let's go in a different direction here. Perhaps American folk? Seeger, Odetta, and Dylan, early Dylan, of course. In Bluegrass, the Carter Family and Doc Watson. How about some Blues? Ma Rainey, Bessie Smith, and Robert Johnson. Oh! Can't forget Leadbelly. Pop singers Jo Stafford and Dinah Shore, and—ah yes! How could I be so slow to recall?—the lovely Ella Fitzgerald. Country, Patsy Cline, of course. How about the chanteurs and chanteuses, Charles Trenet and Josephine Baker. Oh, let's see ... Oh yes, the tango singer, Carlos Gardel. I must include the Mexican Ranchero music performers, Pedro Infante and … Lucha Reyes and … Mariachi Vargas. And I mustn't forget to mention the Portuguese fado singer, Amalia Rodriguez. Would you like me to continue?"

"My God," I said.

"Hey, you asked."

As I thought back to that conversation, I downloaded onto my laptop several songs from some of his favorite musicians, and then one of his favorite films, *Sunset Boulevard* ("A classic Los Angeles film," he called it, during another one of our talks), so that I could lend him my laptop when I visited him in the hospital.

I awoke early the next morning, took my laptop down to the courtyard, and had a coffee, while I read my latest email from Andrew:

From: Andrew Martin
To: Jake Reed

Dear Jake,

Are you coming back soon? I have some good news and bad news. Actually, more good news than bad news. So I qualified for my life insurance plan! Now, if anything happens to me, at least there will be a lot of money for my family. That's a relief. Also, Tamarine and I have been on several dates now! It seems to be going really well. I want to introduce her to the guys at work soon. I'm sure they'll like her. But we'll see. The bad news is she doesn't have much longer here in the US before her visa runs out. She'll have to go back to Thailand. She's really upset over it. I am, too. Anyway, take care, good friend.

Cordially,
Andrew

I paid the bill and then walked the mile or so to Cedars-Sinai. Inside the hospital, I walked, seemingly in circles, through a maze of white, brightly lit corridors, until I was convinced I'd never find Henry's room; but when I finally found it, I paused in front of the closed door, nervous about opening it, and then saw a doctor walking toward me with his gaze fastened on the clipboard he was holding.

"Excuse me," I said.

"What is it?" the doctor said, looking up at me.

"Is Henry Shapiro your patient?"

"Yes."

"How is he?"

"And who are you?" he asked, looking back down at his clipboard.

"I'm Jake Reed, his—"

"The kid from the hotel, yes. He was insistent that you weren't to be given any trouble when visiting him. Your friend, Henry, had a heart attack, which, in this case, was a momentary blockage to the heart muscle, a brief episode, and then he passed out. We were able to stabilize him and make sure all the vessels are clear. He's going to be fine. We'll keep him here until tomorrow."

"That's such great news. Thank you. I really appreciate it," I said, delightedly, as the doctor hurried off in another direction.

I knocked on the door before walking into the room to see Henry in bed, hooked up to IV lines and the EKG device, reading a medical pamphlet. He was uncharacteristically disheveled—his hair uncombed, his suit replaced by a hospital gown, and his unshaven face invaded by sprouting patches of white stubble. And he seemed, to me, noticeably out of place without all the things that made Henry Shapiro who he was: the early morning smell of fresh coffee made from beans flown in from New York, a crisp copy of *The New York Times*, the old hardcover books, the stacks of vinyl records, all of which—paired with his detailed storytelling, his fits of temper, his aged elegance, his debonair manner—complemented his character and made him perfect to me. I didn't like seeing him lying in the hospital bed, deprived of his Henry-ness. I felt deeply saddened by the sight, almost heartbroken, as if I were bearing witness to the exact moment a worshipped hero had fallen from glory and become ... ordinary.

"Jake!" he said, looking up.

"Hey, Henry. What're you reading?"

"The only thing I could find. Goddamn doctors won't let me out of this white, shiny hell of a place. I was quite sure that, as they rolled me in here, a sign on the door read, *'Lasciate ogni speranza voi ch'entrate!'* Did you notice that, too, Jake?"

"No, Henry," I said, not sure what he was referring to, but chuckling with relief in knowing that his spirit was still intact.

"They could, at the very least, put a piece of literature in this uninspired room. Don't you think? Who would have thought that after all those years of education, doctors would embrace anti-intellectualism?

Christ."

"Well," I said, "I brought you some music to listen to and a film to watch."

"Brilliant. I thought I could rely on you."

"I'll leave the laptop with you, but that means you may have to lower your standards and use modern technology."

"Hey!" he said with a smile.

His bed was positioned alongside a wall with a window facing the hills. I stared at a few of the mansions in the distance, and then looked several stories down at the little cars driving along the road, before sitting on the short couch positioned on one side of Henry's bed. The linoleum tiles of the floor were that type of immaculately clean I believed to be, in hospitals at least, a shiny veil concealing filth and tragedy.

"I think I'm falling apart here, Jake," he said, a pall of gray sadness clouding his eyes.

"Nope. The doctor said you'll be fine. I just talked to him. You can come home tomorrow. We'll celebrate with lunch in the courtyard. I'm buying."

He didn't seem to hear me, as he set the pamphlet down and stared out the window. "Jake, what is it that you want to do?"

"What do you mean?"

"Well, you don't plan to live in that hotel and be my neighbor forever, do you?"

"I haven't given it much thought. I'm happy with the way things are now."

"Jake, I think you're a passionate boy. We've worked together for some time now, and I think you have something worth pursuing. But I want you to understand a few things ..."

"What is it, Henry?"

"After the war was over, all of us guys came home, confused as hell. The confusion is always there ... in every generation. You should look up Wilfred Owen's *Anthem for Doomed Youth*. Anyway, after being around all that death for so long, it was a pleasant surprise knowing that, when I returned, I still had the power to love. See, at some point during the war I became numb to all the deadness around me. I got used to it, I guess, which was a much scarier thought than fearing it. I thought I, too, was dead inside. What I'm hoping to convey here is that it's okay to strive for something different, but if you continue rejecting people in the process, I fear that you'll lose something ... lose your ability to ever really connect with anyone—and that, my friend, is the point of all this. OK?"

"OK, Henry."

"Another thing I want to talk to you about is specific to your writing … Whenever I guest lecture, many of the young students, the aspiring writers, often approach me with the same question, essentially, 'How do I write my generation well?' They simply want me to tell them how to capture their generation's zeitgeist. This is not the reason to write, Jake. Write to write. Write because you *need* to write. Write to settle the rage within you. Write with an internal purpose. Write about *something* or *someone* that means so much to you, that you don't care what others think. Your readers will appreciate you more for it. And once you realize that you don't need validation to find happiness, there is a wonderful world waiting for you—the world that lives in your imagination. Treasure your imagination. Happiness is in there, and so is good literature. You don't need to reminisce about childhood to find it. Unhappiness is not a requisite for good writing. You need to understand that you can be happy being happy—just allow yourself the chance, Jake."

I nodded, taking in his words.

"And the last thing I want to say is this: the greatest tragedy in life is *ennui*. Do you know what *ennui* is, Jake?"

"No."

"It's the pretty French word for boredom. Life is too goddamn short to spend one minute of it bored. OK, that's it. I'm done."

"Henry, I always appreciate everything you have to say, and I appreciate what you just told me now. I really do. You're the greatest mentor and friend I've ever had," I said with utmost sincerity. "But—" I paused, loosening up and smiling, "don't you think that you could've spread out this speech of yours over … like the next ten lunches or something? Come on!" I said, and Henry broke into a half-smile. "The doctor said you're fine. I'm sure you won't be feeling this sentimental when I beat you in chess tomorrow."

"OK, OK, you're right."

After my visiting period had been extended a few times by an understanding nurse (Henry and I were deep into a conversation that bounced around from films and books and music and women), I finally decided that it was time to leave and told Henry that I'd pick him up in my car the following day.

"Wow, it'll be the first time you've driven that thing in a long while," he said, smiling.

"The royal treatment."

The next morning, I drove my car to the hospital and parked in a near-by lot; I went to Henry's room and knocked on the door, but when I walked in, another man was in the bed. I guessed that they'd moved Henry to another room, or that perhaps he was signing some papers before he was free to go. In the hallway, I noticed the same doctor I'd spoken with before.

"Excuse me, Doctor. Sorry to bother you again," I said to him. "But the man who used to be in that room, Henry Shapiro—where is he now? Have they transferred him out already?"

"Your number was not listed. I believe one of the nurses looked for a way to get in touch with you."

"What's the problem?"

"Unfortunately ... your friend, Henry, suffered a free-wall rupture late last night. The result was fatal. I'm very sorry."

"A free-wall wha—I'm sorry—I'm a little confu—what the hell are you talking about? You told me he was recovering fine!"

"He *was* doing fine. A free-wall rupture sometimes occurs three to five days after a heart attack. It's when the muscles that control the valves are damaged structurally, and the heart just sort of explodes. Death, in this case, is always instantaneous. There was nothing we could do. Again, I'm truly sorry for your loss."

A week had passed when I received a knock on my door. I was sitting by my window, smoking a cigarette, replaying in my mind one of the last conversations I'd had with Henry; we were in my room, and I'd just finished trying to articulate, without much success, the reasons why people caused me such confusion.

"Jake, you're waiting for people to be extraordinary—in fact, you're expecting them to be extraordinary. And when they aren't, you feel betrayed and disappointed. You can't wait for people to make mistakes. If you want people to become extraordinary, you have to help them get there. If you're just looking for bullshit, that's all you'll ever see. Don't seek meaning in the empyrean; learn to seek meaning in the earthly," he said.

I answered the door to an old man in a suit. He almost reminded me of Henry.

"Mr. Reed?"

"Yes."

"My name is Al Connors."

"You're Henry's lawyer, aren't you?"

"Yes, that's right."

"He told me about his visiting you."

"Well, he met with me about you, actually."

"Is that right? He didn't mention that part."

"According to a final adjustment in Henry's will, he's stipulated that you should receive all of his books, his typewriters, and his unpublished memoirs. I have the boxes here. He was also very adamant that I give you this card," he said, handing it to me.

After all the boxes had been carried into my room and Henry's lawyer had left, I opened the card.

Jake,

I'm quite pleased I stayed around long enough for you to come into my life. We had a damned good time, didn't we? Oh yes, I should mention that I spoke to an old student of mine, who's now a literary agent in New York, New York. I may have mentioned to him that I'd made friends with a young, promising writer. Anyway, I must've said a few good things about you, because he seemed very interested in speaking with you. Should you ever write something you're truly proud of, perhaps you'll give him a call. I've written his number down here. Remember to always feel your words more. I believe in you and your writing.

With love,
Henry

TATIANA

After Henry's death, I relapsed into a paralytic, unhealthy state of mind, as nightmarish images of both my grandmother in the open casket, and, more profoundly, the girl in the car crash—the girl I couldn't save; the girl I let disappear under the sheet … forever—flashed unsympatheti-cally in my head. Soon after, my haunting visions were being triggered by the faces of every woman I saw in the hotel, or on the street, or in the grocery store, and then by the faces of all people, both women and men; so, naturally, I stopped looking up when anyone was around me.

I ate in the seclusion of my room. Just a casual glance toward our favorite table in the courtyard, in the shade along the back by the gar-den, now empty of the energy and devoid of the conversation that once flourished above it, was far too emotionally draining for me. I became stricken with a loneliness that, over the next few weeks, distorted my ap-pearance; I caught a glimpse in the mirror one morning of a gaunt face, a rat-nest beard, unkempt hair, and sad, sunken eyes—a vision of myself I'd grown accustomed to seeing during the depressive phases of my life.

At night, I often sat upright in my bed, searching for a sound within the walls, floating through space, alone in the universe, only the faint purr of a far-off motorcycle in the night reminding me of where I was. I turned to a side of the Internet I'd never known. I lived in chat rooms and conversed, behind the veil of a pseudonym, with complete strang-ers, long into the night. We talked about where we were from; I told them about my hometown, and, in exchange, I learned about places like Detroit or Kansas City or Vancouver; sometimes we chatted about places we'd always wanted to visit, and our good-byes were always cou-pled with some sort of fanciful, feel-good comment like, "Let's meet in Montana!" or "See you in Thailand one day," or "You should come visit here. I'll show you around."

But my craving for something more than the exchange of typewritten words on a screen led me to the discovery of a video-chat site that paired me up face to face with a random person in the world, and, with a simple click, I could leave the chat with that person and be paired up with another. After long, grotesque stretches of clicking through camera-ready penises, I occasionally stumbled upon the face of a person with expectant eyes and furrowed brows. Sometimes I waved and said hello, and he or she said hello back; sometimes we'd make small talk for a few minutes; one time I had a two-hour conversation with a guy who lived in a small, hilly town in Austria. But most times, we just stared at each other for a few seconds—our lonely faces like mirrored images—before we moved on to another person, always in search of someone better.

One night, I even attended an online funeral that I'd learned about in a chat room. Apparently, the spouse of the deceased couldn't afford a proper funeral, so instead she had decided to host the funeral on her husband's Facebook page, with instructions that people who visited his page post their condolences. I'd never met the person who had died, but, nevertheless, I visited his page, and, after watching the comments pile up from his friends and family, wrote and posted: "I wish I had the chance to get to know you. But I know that you'll be missed."

One afternoon, I searched the web for nearby churches, and, in doing so, discovered a little synagogue on Beverly Boulevard that appealed to me. I took the ten-minute walk, but once I'd made it to the entrance, couldn't summon the courage to go inside.

Every freshly lit cigarette—with the flow of smoke into my lungs and the rush of feeling to my brain—was a new beginning, an injection of warm energy into my quiet, stagnant world; but the cigarette always dwindled to a smokeless butt, and the next one created less of a feeling, until cigarette butts piled up around my room like little, bent-paper corpses. I watched porn and masturbated until I was sore, or it wouldn't work anymore, or my wastebasket overflowed with moist tissues.

On one sleepless night that carried over into the early morning, I opened the drawer by my bed, removed the bottle of prescription pills, unscrewed the cap, and stared lifelessly at the pills, as if they were the only remedy for my problems. But I quickly threw the bottle back into the drawer and shut it. I knew I had to pull myself out of my funk naturally, mostly out of respect for everything Henry had tried to teach me; so, starting the next day, I forced myself to get up early every morn-

ing, made breakfast, cleaned my room, read books from my newly acquired library, and lunched—at a different table than the one at which
I'd sat with Henry—in the courtyard. After lunch, I tried, unsuccessfully, to write about my relationship with Henry and then took walks
around town before coming back to my room for an early dinner. I
often checked my email, with the hope of finding another message from
Andrew, and, finally, one came.

> **From**: Andrew Martin
> **To**: Jake Reed
>
> Jake! Man, we miss you around here. Tamarine and I are doing
> great. She's officially my girlfriend now! Exciting, huh? We're still
> trying to figure out the whole getting-deported-to-Thailand thing. I've
> been researching options like hell. Also, a bit of bad news. I was
> hospitalized for two days. Can you believe that? I fainted at work. The
> ambulance came and everything. Embarrassing! The doctor said my
> blood pressure is through the roof and that I need less stress in my
> life. Ha ha, doctors! Life *is* stressful when we have our futures to worry
> about! What do they want me to do? Stop working? It's a good thing I
> have that life insurance plan now, right?! Anyway, I hope to hear from
> you soon.
>
> Cordially,
> Andrew

Still, my loneliness, determined to survive, affected the way in which I
observed people: each time I ventured out onto the streets of Los Angeles, I became preoccupied by thoughts of my social deprivation: every
young man who passed me on the street was my lost best friend, every
older man was my mentor or my father, every group of people was my
posse still waiting for me to pull up in a taxi and join the fun, and every
older woman was my mother looking to comfort me and cook me a hot
meal.

And, my God, the girls ... Every girl I saw walking down the street
became the only girl in the world for me; I found in each one, regardless of her appearance, a terrifyingly beautiful quality—a smile, a scent,
a curve, a gait, a face, a hand, an ear, a neck. I fell in love with all of

them. I dreamt of our marriages. I lusted after our first kiss, our first fuck. I wanted to meet their families, firmly shake the hands of their fathers, make their mothers laugh, persuade their sisters to love me, and win the approval of their brothers. I wanted to kiss their collarbones and watch them sleep peacefully. I wanted to feel their hot breath on my face. I wanted caress the curves of their bodies and kiss their open mouths. I wanted to spread their legs and see what was between them, that goddamn untouchable, hidden paradise that eluded me and drove me rabid—the paradise that was within all of them, waiting to be discovered, lush, ripe, tucked away like a secret garden, a forbidden path for gawkers like me. I could only imagine my own map: start at the toes, run up the calves, circle around to the kneecaps, and coast along the thighs, but then what?

I stood still on street corners and stared at passersby like an idiot, but no one ever paid me any attention, just walked by, unaware of my importunate stares, or, perhaps, pretending to be. The more everyone ignored me, the more disconnected I felt, and the more I desired to be wanted. Nothing made me feel more alone in the world than being blatantly dismissed by my own species.

On one occasion, a curious toddler, unbiased and trusting, had wandered over to me during one of my midday walks; the mother, who had indulged in just a few seconds of window-shopping, quickly came to her senses and yanked her child by the collar, away from me and back toward safety—an action that awakened me to the crazy-person vibes I was exuding out on the street. I only took night walks after that.

One warm spring night, while walking north on Fairfax, I realized I'd been thinking about *the place* for some time. I didn't want to think about it, but the idea of going back there hovered in my mind with such persistence, I was forced to consider its inevitability.

"You're in the wrong place, man," said someone in line for a bar called The Dime.

I anxiously hurried on, veered right into an empty parking lot, and skulked about until an available cab rounded the corner in my direction. I knew then that the moment had arrived. I flagged down the cab, hopped inside, and told the driver to take me downtown to the corner of Ninth Street and South Hill Street. I slouched in the backseat, unsure of what to do once I arrived at my destination. Several times I caught the driver's eyes studying me through the rearview mirror, but he didn't say a word to me until our time together was ending.

"You know, my life used to be shit until I realized how much worse it continued to get. Then I knew the current moment I was living in was the best moment of my life. *Then* I started to enjoy myself," he said.

"Good to know. Drop me here. Keep the change," I said, handing him cash.

It looked the same as I remembered it from the night months before when I'd come with Parker Thomas. As I walked toward the entrance, guarded by the same giant bouncer, I could almost taste the awful stench emanating from within the establishment's walls.

"What do you want?" the bouncer said, holding me back with his thick arm.

"Take your hand off me. You know what I want," I said.

"Why have I never seen you here before?" he asked, skeptically.

"I'm not here to cause any trouble."

He looked at me suspiciously, then studiously. "Do you have cash?"

"Yes, plenty."

"Go on."

I walked down a long, dark hallway, toward the entrance, opened the door, and walked inside. The room was dimly lit, and cigarette smoke clouded the air. Several girls danced on a large stage in the front of the room, some danced around the small tables that filled the center of the room, and, presumably, more of them danced within the little curtained-off areas along the back wall, as I could see the tips of men's scuffed shoes peeking out from underneath. I looked around the club and recognized, on the faces of all the occupants, the same loneliness that had contorted my own face; I stared into the desperate eyes of broken men driven to the only place in the world that would have them, the only place that would offer them companionship.

"Do you want to meet a friend?"

I looked down at a repulsive little woman with a mouth full of rotten teeth. "No, just a table."

"This way," she said, and then led me to a little table in the back of the room, facing the stage. "Drink?" she asked.

"Bourbon, neat," I said.

She brought my drink, and I sipped it slowly and smoked a cigarette and became part of the place. I knew what had driven the men there, for it had driven me there, also. *These are my people now.* But when I saw *her* face, my attitude instantly changed. *She doesn't belong here.* She was cowering in the corner of the room, in the dark shadow of a much older man towering domineeringly over her, while his hands rested possessively on her shoulders and rubbed them in a way that sickened me to my core. He moved closer to her and touched her face, while she stared through him, but, even in the darkness of the room and the man's shadow, I thought I detected a soft flicker of light in her eyes, like two beacons in the distance on a foggy night. But then the man grabbed her by the hand and pulled her along a path between the tables—*Where are you taking her?*—nearer to me, and I grimaced at the sight of his yellow teeth and red eyes. As they passed my table, I looked into her green eyes, but her gaze was fixed on the floor a few inches in front of her feet. *"Help me."*

I stood up from the table and trailed them, as they zigzagged between the tables of vile men. *He's taking her to one of those rooms!* I quickened my pace, nearly bumping into them, but then dropped back and waited for the right opportunity. When he turned the corner toward the mouth of a dark hallway, I made my move. I charged toward him, grabbed his arm, and forced him back against the wall.

"I'm taking her. If you get in my way, I'll fucking *kill* you. You hear me?" I said, looking directly into his wicked eyes and tightening my grip.

He angrily mumbled something, and I felt him tense his arm muscles, but I squeezed him harder and kept my eyes fastened on his, until, finally, his body loosened, and he let go of the girl's hand.

"Now leave us," I said, releasing him. "Find someone else. Don't make any trouble."

He left us. The girl, still staring at the ground, was alarmingly motionless, except for her fingers, which were trembling. I didn't have a plan. I thought, or hoped, rather, that one of the hallways would lead us to a back door that might open onto the street. *And then we can escape.*

"Hey," I whispered to her. "I'm going to get you out of here. I'm going to help you."

She didn't move or look up. I reached for her, but she flinched.

"It's OK. Just trust me. Can you do that? We'll be out of here soon."

I took her by the hand and led her down the dark hallway, but froze when I heard voices in a nearby room. I knew we wouldn't be able to escape unless the people believed I'd paid for the girl. I took a deep breath, gathered myself, and then pulled her down the hallway, feigning confidence; we walked past the group of people in the room, and they ignored us. I found a door, and—as the suspense shortened my breath and sped up my heartbeat—quietly turned the handle and gave it a nudge; to my great relief, the door cracked slightly open, and, with the thrill of escape rushing through my body, I looked at the girl and gestured to her to be quiet, but she still stared blankly at the floor, seemingly unaware of her imminent freedom. She did, however, come alive in protest as I pulled her hurriedly down the street and away from the club.

"No! No! No! No!" she screamed, trying to resist me.

I stopped running and whisked her around the side of a building, at a safe distance from the club. "I'm here to help you. Not hurt you. Do you speak English?" I said.

She stared down at the dirty cement, her eyes fixed on a point and barely blinking.

"My name is Jake. I want to help you. What's your name?" I said.

Her hair fell down over her sad, green eyes as she started to raise her head to look at me, but, as though she were stopping herself from doing something terribly wrong, she quickly lowered it again.

"I'm Jake," I said, tapping my chest with my finger. "Your name?" I said, pointing to her.

She didn't respond. I repeated myself a few times until she, noticeably exhausted and drained of her fight, finally answered me.

"Tatiana," she said very softly in a foreign accent.

"Tatiana ..." I repeated. "OK, that's good. Let's get out of here, Tatiana."

I took her by the hand again, led her toward the main street, hailed a cab, and told the driver to take us to Fairfax and Melrose, and that I'd tell him where to go from there.

"What the hell is going on here?" he said, swinging his head over his shoulder to look at Tatiana.

"It's not what you think."

"Get out of my cab."

"Look, man, I'm only helping this girl. If you drive us away from this place, you'll be helping her, too. Trust me. I'll pay you whatever you want. Just fucking drive, man."

He looked at me, shook his head, and then started driving. Tatiana curled up in the backseat, resting her head against the window, as she hugged herself in a defensive pose and stared blankly at the floorboard.

We got onto the freeway and, coasting along at a smooth pace, drove away from Downtown, away from that place, away from harm. As I calmed down, I mulled over, for the first time, my predicament. *What have I done? I'm really in some shit now. I'm getting involved with the wrong people. This can't even be legal. But I had to save her. But how am I going to help her? Take her back to my hotel and then what? Call the police?* About twenty minutes later, after we crossed Melrose, I told the driver to take us a few more blocks down Fairfax.

"This is fine here," I said, and then, after he'd pulled over to the curb in front of my hotel, paid him one hundred dollars.

I got out of the cab, walked around to Tatiana's side, and opened the door; I helped her out, feeling the cold rigidity of her body, and led her toward the entrance; but she, evidently revived by the long, peaceful cab ride, and now aware of her new surroundings, allowed the fight within her to surface again.

"No! No! No!" she screamed.

"Tatiana," I said, turning around to face her. "I'm *not* going to hurt you."

When she still tried to resist me, I looked around nervously, worried about drawing attention from others on the street, and then, without even thinking about it, picked Tatiana up and threw her over my shoulder. *I've lost it. I'm really fucking crazy for doing this.* I brought her into the hotel—she was flailing her arms and legs and screaming loudly, but, fortunately, the lobby was empty—and I quickly carried her down the hall, unlocked my door, brought her into my room, and set her gently on the bed.

"Tatiana," I said, as she began to hyperventilate, "everything's going to be OK."

She curled up into a ball and shielded her face from me with her hand.

Hoping I hadn't alarmed any of the staff or guests, I waited a few minutes, pacing back and forth in my room, before picking up the phone and dialing the hotel operator: "Can you please bring a cot to my room?"

I pulled back the sheets on the other side of the bed. "Tatiana, you should sleep under the covers," I said, gently touching her shoulder, which made her recoil in fear.

I heard a knock at the door, and, fearing that it was someone who'd heard all the commotion, I looked through the peephole and asked, "Who is it?"

"I have the cot here for you, sir," the middle-aged bellhop said. "I can go ahead and bring it in for you."

I opened the door and stepped out. "No, I'll take it from here," I said, handing him a greasy wad of one-dollar bills from my pocket.

"Are you sure, sir?"

"Yeah, it's fine. I can handle it, thanks," I said.

"Have a good night, then, sir," he said with a confused expression.

I waited for him to turn the corner at the end of the hallway before rolling the cot into the room and quickly shutting the door.

"See, I'm going to sleep on this thing. You can sleep in the bed," I said to Tatiana, who'd quieted down and was peeking at me through the little space between two of her fingers. "You," I said, pointing to the bed. "Me," I said, pointing to the cot. "Are you thirsty?" I asked, trying a different way to connect with her and show her that she was not in danger.

I filled a glass with water in the kitchen and brought it over to her. She lay still on top of the sheets and didn't acknowledge me; I set the water on the nightstand next to the bed, turned out the lights, and climbed onto my cot.

"Sleep well, Tatiana," I said.

I waited until her heavier breathing convinced me that she was asleep, before, careful not to wake her, I gently slid her over to the other side of the bed, took off her shoes, and pulled the covers over her.

I knew she'd be hungry at some point, so I quietly left the room—hoping Tatiana would stay where she was—and walked to a grocery store down the street that was open twenty-four hours. I grabbed a shopping cart in the parking lot, entered the store through the indiscriminately welcoming automatic glass doors, and loaded my cart with a variety of groceries. At the checkout counter, I asked the cashier for a few packs of cigarettes, and, after paying for everything, carried the bags back to my hotel. In the room, I noiselessly unloaded the groceries in the dark, putting some of them in the refrigerator and others in the pantry. I got beneath the sheets in my cot and tried to sleep, but it wouldn't come. *I'm in one hell of a messy situation here.*

A few hours later, when the light of the new day was just barely detectable, I bolted upright in terror as the terrifying sound of Tatiana's shrill screams knifed into the innocence of the early morning air. I rushed over to the bed and discovered that Tatiana was still asleep, but trembling violently, fully in the clutches of a horrific nightmare. She screamed again. I put my hand on her forehead, feeling her cold sweat, and when she screamed again, this time even louder, I shook her by the shoulders.

"Wake up, Tatiana!" I yelled.

She opened her eyes and lurched across the bed, away from my grasp.

"It's OK, Tatiana," I said, throwing my hands in the air in an act of surrender, trying again to convince her of my good-natured intentions. "You had a nightmare ... Here, take some water," I said, holding the glass in front of her.

Surprisingly, she accepted the glass, took two quick sips, and then finished the rest with a big, nourishing swallow. I took the glass from her, refilled it, and set it back on the nightstand. As she slipped back into her defensive pose, I pulled the sheets over her again.

For the next hour, I lay on my cot listening to Tatiana cry; her continuous, muffled whimpers, wet with tears, stirred me to uneasiness, because I wanted to help her, but didn't know what to do. Soon, thankfully, her breathing returned to a gentle rhythm, and I was relieved that she'd found sleep again.

Dawn was upon us, and a curious light trickled into the room to investigate my mysterious guest; I shut the curtains quickly, not willing to expose Tatiana to anyone or anything, and waited another hour before making breakfast. I fried two eggs, toasted bread, cut up a cantaloupe, and brewed a pot of coffee. On a plate, I put an egg on top of a piece of toast, added a few slices of cantaloupe, and brought it to her.

"Breakfast?" I said.

Her eyes peeled open and moved toward the plate, but then darted quickly back down to the sheets.

"I'll set it here for you if you want some later," I said, putting the plate on the nightstand next to the glass of water.

Her shaking hadn't stopped, and, seemingly trying to combat it, she curled up tighter under the sheets. I had my breakfast in the kitchen and sipped my coffee slowly, while Tatiana drifted back to sleep. I left the room, walked up to Melrose, found a barbershop, and had a shave and a haircut. Next, I went into a women's clothing store, and, guessing at Tatiana's size, picked out a few pairs of jeans and a few shirts.

I heard her screams as I walked down the hallway back to my room; I unlocked the door and hurried to wake her. Her body trembled more violently this time, and she also lurched away from me more intensely when she woke.

"Just another nightmare. It's OK," I said.

Her breakfast on the nightstand was still untouched. I handed her the glass of water. As she brought the glass to her lips, she tilted her head up, and I watched her eyes slowly elevate, pause on my face, as if to acquaint themselves with my unfamiliar, clean-cut look, and then land on my own eyes. She held her green-eyed gaze on me for the first time, and I smiled at her.

She handed the glass back to me, and I carried it into the kitchen to refill it, feeling pleased with our slight progress. After setting the glass back on the nightstand, I walked across the room to get the bag of new clothes, but decided against showing them to her when she started crying again. I pulled the sheets over her, snugging them around her body and up to her chin. I grabbed a book, left the room, read in the garden until noon, and then lunched at the restaurant, checking on her frequently throughout that period and always finding her in a deep sleep. When night fell, however, she unconsciously unleashed her screams of terror again. Sometimes I woke her, sometimes I let her scream through it. And, when she was awake, we connected with each other through a simple, intimate routine: I handed her a glass of water, she drank it, and then I refilled it for her.

The next morning was no different from the previous one, except that, after returning from a morning walk, I noticed that she'd nibbled a piece of fruit on the breakfast plate I'd set on the nightstand before leaving the room. She watched me curiously, as I put a clean towel at the foot of the bed and laid out her new clothes.

"In case you want to take a shower and change clothes," I said.

But when I returned from reading in the garden, she was asleep, and the clothes and towel were in the same spot I'd placed them. In the evening, I prepared a simple pasta dish, but she didn't touch it. Then the screams. Then the crying. Then the cold, eerie silence.

On our third day together, she ate half the plate of breakfast I cooked for her that morning, and, when I returned from lunch at the hotel restaurant, she was walking out of the bathroom, in a cloud of steam, her body wrapped in a white towel, her wet hair dripping down her back. She froze when she saw me.

"Hi," I said.

"*Hah-lo*," she said, staring down at the ground.

I walked over to the bed and showed her the clothes. "These are for you. I'll leave you so you can change," I said.

I had a beer in the bar and wondered, without any good ideas, what to do next. I paid the bill, returned to the room, and found Tatiana, barefoot, in a T-shirt and jeans, looking through a box of Henry's books.

Her jeans, perhaps a size too small, were tight against her legs, while her T-shirt, perhaps a size too big, hung loosely around her shoulders and chest, her hair still wet against the back of her neck.

At the dining table, I opened my laptop and searched for a map of the world. "Tatiana, show me where you're from," I said, pointing to the map on my screen.

She came over and looked at the map.

"Where are you from?" I said, again.

She pointed to a spot in northeastern Ukraine, near the border of Russia.

"You're Ukrainian?" I said, and she nodded her head. "Do you speak any English?" I said, and she shook her head.

I decided to make a pot of chicken soup for dinner. I removed a whole chicken from the refrigerator and washed it in cold water under the faucet. I put the chicken into a large pot of boiling water, brought it to a boil again, and then lowered the flame to let the chicken get tender. I cut up vegetables into large chunks, and, along with some garlic cloves, herbs, and a bit of salt and pepper, tossed it all into the pot and let it cook slowly. Tatiana lay on top of the covers on the bed, watching me while I worked. Sometimes I tried to catch her eyes, but she always led them away from mine when I looked at her. I let the soup cook on low heat for a while as I sat at the table pretending to read a book, but really sneaking peeks of Tatiana.

When the soup was done, I served her a bowl, and she joined me at the table; she brought a soup-filled spoon to her lips cautiously, and, after swallowing, looked into my eyes and smiled. I smiled back at her. No words passed between us, because we didn't have any words to share; instead, we communicated through the sounds of our spoons tapping on the bottom of our bowls and the sounds of the broth being sucked in through our lips and swallowed down. Our eyes danced away from each other like the eyes of two shy adolescents meeting for the first time. I felt the warmth of the broth within me, and with it came an unfamiliar sense of well-being. I finally felt good about helping her escape from that place. And here she is now, I thought, with me in my hotel room eating soup.

Maybe my progress with Tatiana was enough of a reason for me to believe that her screams would stay away, and that she could find peace in her dreams, but they came again that night, with as much terror fueling them as on previous nights. When they'd finally passed, the crying started and continued until she was drained of all her energy and could fall sleep again.

However, in the morning, I opened my eyes to Tatiana in the kitchen frying eggs; she'd already sliced some fruit on a plate and set it on the table. When I rose from my cot, she brought me a hot cup of coffee and smiled at me.

"Thank you," I said, and she nodded.

We ate in silence, until she pointed in the direction of my books and said something in Ukrainian. I gave her a confused look and shrugged my shoulders. She said something again, which, to me, sounded as if she'd simply repeated the words from before.

"I don't know ..." I said.

As I looked at her and then at the books, which seemed to interest her or, at the very least, arouse her curiosity about me, I got the idea that I should try to teach her English. After breakfast, I went online and ordered a Ukrainian-English dictionary and a series of instructional books (each of them with an increasing level of difficulty) that included both audio and written lessons for Ukrainian speakers trying to learn English. I paid the extra fee for my purchases to be delivered to my room at the hotel the next day.

I also searched the web for the most effective ways to teach English to a person who both knew very little of it and was learning it as a second language. I discovered the blog of a woman, in her early forties, who was, according to the description she'd written about herself, a first-grade English teacher with much experience in teaching young foreign students. In one of her posts, she stressed the importance of teaching the children two types of word groups: "sight words," which, given that they cannot be simply sounded out, give young readers the most trouble; and "high-frequency words," which are the most commonly used words in the English language. I bookmarked her blog, so that I could study up later.

"You need some more clothes," I said, while I was cleaning the dishes. "Let's go to the store and buy you some."

I toweled my hands dry and signaled Tatiana to follow me. We walked down the hallway and into the lobby, but when I grabbed her hand to lead her through the glass doors and out onto the street, she leaned back with all of her weight.

"No," she said.

"I'm just taking you down the street for some clothes," I said.

"No. No," she said again, as her gaze lowered to the floor and her hands started to shake.

"It's OK. We don't have to go," I said.

Back in the room, I clicked on Google's translation site, selected the option to translate English to Ukrainian, and typed: "Tatiana, I'm not going to hurt you. I'm only interested in helping you. I'm not sure how to help you, but somehow I believe you're better off with me than where you used to be. I'll take care of you. I have enough money for the two of us for a while. Are you OK with this?"

The Ukrainian characters appeared seamlessly on the right side of the page as I typed my English words on the left. I called Tatiana over and showed her the screen; the little green torch in each of her eyes lit up. She obviously knew how to read. I watched her eyes follow the words to the far right of the box and then track back to the left side, until she'd read my entire message. She looked into my eyes and nodded in agreement.

I started to type again, and, this time, she watched the words get translated in real time: "I can't offer much, but I can try to teach you English. Once you learn it, you'll be more empowered. You'll be able to protect yourself with it. Do you want me to try to teach you English, Tatiana?"

She nodded again. I opened one of my notebooks to a new page and handed her a pen.

"How old are you?" I typed on the screen.

She wrote "17" on the page and then pointed to me.

"How old am I?" I said to her, and she nodded.

I wrote "23" next to her "17."

She looked at me, and her eyes flashed green.

"How long have you been here in Los Angeles?" I typed.

She wrote "14."

"Jesus, you've been here for three years?" I said, as she looked at me confusedly. "It's OK. We can start over."

Her screams woke me again that night. I turned on the light, walked over to the bed, and gently shook her to consciousness; she jolted upright and breathed heavily. I grabbed my laptop from the table and brought it over to her. I loaded the translation site again and typed: "I know I'm not capable of understanding what you're going through. And we never have to talk about it if you don't want to. But I also know that when you're in it, it feels like it's never going to go away. Just remember that it can go away, that it will go away. It'll pass. It'll get better. I promise. But sometimes you need to will yourself out of it. Stay strong, Tatiana."

She finished reading and looked up at me. As her face crumpled, her eyes welled up slowly with tears, which then trickled halfway down her face before she wiped them away.

"It's going to be OK," I said, reaching out my hand to comfort her, but when she flinched, I pulled it back, returned to my cot, and listened to her cry until she fell asleep.

When the instructional-language books and dictionary arrived the next day, we started with the first lesson: learning the Roman alphabet. Right away, I ripped twenty-six pages from one of my notebooks and wrote one letter on each. We worked on the sounds of each letter individually over the next week, and then moved on to the sounds of some popular letter combinations. In my notebook, I also wrote down a long list of sight words, such as "is," "blue," "it," "pretty," "funny," "to," "could," "think," "so," and "together." Next, I made a list of high-frequency words, such as "the," "us," "which," "about," "said," "water," "each," "people," and "little." And we practiced all the words until Tatiana had committed them to memory.

When she was ready, we worked on some introductory phrases, like "Hello, my name is Tatiana," and "I am seventeen years old," and "I have green eyes," and "I am from the Ukraine, but I now live in Los Angeles." Soon, everything in our room had been labeled with English names; the bed had a sheet of paper taped to it with "bed" written on it—same for the window and the table and the refrigerator and the door and the sink and everything else around us, even everything in the bathroom. During the audio part of the lessons, Tatiana sat studiously and attentively in front of my laptop and repeated English words and phrases out loud, refining her pronunciation, until she was content with her progress. After I'd given her a pair of my headphones to use whenever she wanted, I awoke several times late in the night to see her nestled under a blanket at the foot of the bed—her face glowing in the laptop screen's light—wearing my headphones and whispering English phrases.

We worked every morning after breakfast, moving forward with the lessons in the books and often creating our own exercises. We continued until lunchtime, and then, because Tatiana was still nervous about leaving, cooked and ate in the room.

After lunch, I often took solo walks to get more groceries or cigarettes, or to just think about something to write. And, every day, I went to the only remaining bookstore in the area and bought Tatiana a children's book with a simple story and large, colorful pictures. When I returned to the room, Tatiana was usually immersed in the language books, repeating the lessons from the morning, but she always looked up, came over to me, graciously accepted the book I'd bought her, and flipped through it with a childlike excitement. She soon progressed beyond the simple children's books (she'd memorized every Dr. Seuss book, and her favorite was *One Fish Two Fish Red Fish Blue Fish*), so I began to buy her, feeling especially nostalgic when doing so, the works of Roald Dahl (Tatiana loved *Matilda* so much, she read it twice), the same ones I'd devoured as a young boy, and when she'd outgrown those, I began bringing her young-adult fiction. In no time, she was rapidly thumbing, with impressive fervor, through pages filled with adolescent angst and love and mystery.

Admittedly, I had no previous experience teaching a foreign language to anyone, but the pace at which Tatiana was learning English seemed inconceivable to me. Although she never, when speaking, used contractions of words or the colloquialisms used with absentminded ease by American-born speakers, and she sometimes omitted necessary words (often "a" or "the"), she was nearly conversationally fluent in three months. Sometimes she surprised me with her use of a more formal English word in a sentence, and I knew this to be a result of her unrelenting exploration of the Ukrainian-English dictionary. It was then that I realized I was never her teacher, just someone who'd allowed her the opportunity to discover her incredible aptitude for learning words. Still, I felt a bit of pride when I heard the soft, shaky intonation of Tatiana's repressed voice slowly blossom over the next few months into that of a confident, passionate, and intelligent student.

"You speak English very well," I complimented her one morning late into spring.

"I like English. In Ukrainian you have to say all this things. English is more simple because I do not know it much."

Her eagerness to learn was very apparent, so it was natural for the lessons to carry over into our daily conversations. One early afternoon,

I prepared two fresh trout for our lunch. She observed me as I chopped off the heads—just under the gills—the fins, and the tails, and then as I slid the knife along the bodies of the fish to remove the scales. She watched me rinse the fish in cold water, dab them dry with a paper towel, salt them, pepper them, massage them with oil, and stuff them with dill, butter, and a slice of lemon each. After a few minutes, when the fish had started to cook in the high heat of the oven, Tatiana, eager to make conversation, said, "It smells like fishes ..."

"Fish," I said.

"What?" she asked, curiosity emitting from her green eyes.

"It smells like fish. Fish, in this case, works for the plural, as well," I said, looking into her eyes.

"Fishes is not correct?"

"Well, it *is* a word. So you're not wrong. But I think fishes is correct when ... you're referring to a group of different kinds of fish," I said, speaking slowly enough for her to understand, but not too slow as to give her the impression that I was patronizing her. "So ... if a man caught a catfish and a trout, which are two different types of fish, I think he could say that he caught two fishes. But ... I'm cooking two trout, fish of the same kind."

"This is difficult, no? Too hard for me."

"It's difficult for anyone," I said. "Actually, now I'm confused. I'm not even sure if I'm right anymore."

She laughed and said, "Not something Dr. Seuss teaches us."

I laughed.

"OK ... it smells like fish in here," she said, smiling.

"Yeah, I think you're right," I said, smiling back at her.

As the days rolled by, much in the same rhythm, the sun strengthened, and the coolness of a waning spring lost the fight against the heat of an exuberant summer. The new season seemed to stir something within both of us, as we lounged in our room—after a full day of teaching and learning—with the sleeves of our shirts rolled up and beads of sweat on our brows. We began to enjoy wine together with dinner, and Tatiana, always very protective of her emotions when she could be, began to laugh with me.

One summer evening—after sharing a good meal and a bottle of red wine—as the dry, desert breeze wandered gently in through the open window and warmed our faces, Tatiana and I stared at each other across the table. She looked away first, and I got up to clean the table, brushing against her on my way into the kitchen. I turned on the faucet, let the cold water fall into my cupped hands, and then splashed my face with it. I took a deep breath and tried to calm myself down by listening to the sound of running water. *What is this feeling? It can't be right. Can it? But it feels right. So right.* I toweled dry, and, when I turned around, Tatiana was sitting at the end of the bed, wearing nothing but one of my white T-shirts; she'd rolled up the sleeves to her shoulders, and it hung down to the middle of her thighs.

"You must ... be very mad ... at that little bed," she said, speaking slowly, making sure to properly pronounce every word.

"It's not too bad," I said, walking toward her. "I'm used to it," I said, standing close to her, as she looked up at me.

I watched her swallow, as if she were trying to subdue her nervousness, and then close her eyes to concentrate on her words.

"Maybe ... you try ... this bed tonight," she said, opening her eyes.

She stood up slowly and looked up at me, waiting for me to do something. I walked around to the side of the bed, and she followed me. I pulled back the covers and looked at her. She got into the bed and turned to face me. I slid into the space next to her and slowly moved closer to her, until our faces rested inches apart.

"What are these?" I said, softly rubbing her hands and nervously seeking refuge in our teacher-student relationship.

"My hands," she said.

"Right. You have lovely hands. And these," I said, gently brushing over her closed eyelids with my fingers.

"My eyes," she said.

"I've always loved your eyes," I said.

She smiled with her eyes still closed.

"And that is your smile. The most beautiful thing about you."

She clutched my face with two hands and kissed me, and I felt the softness of her lips against mine.

I awoke first the next day. We'd slept in much later than we ever had; judging by the heat, it felt like early afternoon, but even the summer air was cooler than the heat from our intertwined bodies. She was still sleeping. Her head was resting on the inner part of my shoulder, one of her arms was draped over my chest, and the tips of her fingers were gently clinging to my collarbone. Under the covers, I felt her inner thigh lying across the fronts of both my thighs and one of her feet tucked under my calf. She woke up soon after me.

"That was the best sleep of my entire life," I said, as she kissed my chest twice and looked up at me.

"What about … the English lessons … today?" she said, now walking her fingers across my chest.

"Why don't we take the day off? I don't really want to leave the bed. Maybe … you can teach me something in Ukrainian, instead."

"OK. Say my words," she said.

"OK."

"*Dyakuyu*," she said and then pronounced it slowly for me, "Dya–koo–you."

"*Dyakuyu*," I repeated.

"This means, 'Thank you,'" she said. "Now something new. OK?"

I nodded.

"*Dlya zberezhennya meni*," she said and then sounded it out, "Dlya zbeh–rezh–enya meh–knee."

"*Dlya zberezhennya meni*," I said, as she laughed at my pronunciation. "Hey!" I said, playfully nudging her.

"This means, 'For saving me,'" she said. "OK, very difficult one now. *Ya budu lyubyty tebe na vikiy za tvoyu dopomogu*," she said. "Ya boo–doo lyoo–bih–tyh teh–beh nah vih–kiy za tvo–you do–po–mo–gu."

"My God, Tatiana. OK, here goes. *Ya budu lyubyty tebe na …*" I said, forgetting the rest and looking to her for help.

"*Vikiy za tvoyu dopomogu*," she said.

"*Vikiy za tvoyu dopomogu*," I repeated.

"This means, 'I will love you forever for helping me,'" she said, smiling and closing her eyes and turning her head away from me.

I pulled her back over to me and kissed her.

"What thoughts make you happy?" she said.

"Let me think about it," I said, giving her a look.

"Will you kiss me one time more?" she said.

"Yes," I said before kissing her.

"Now, come here," she said, turning her back to me, but pulling me closer with her hand.

I positioned my body like an outer shell to hers. She guided my arm around her body and held my hand tightly at the center of her chest. I lay behind her, feeling her warmth on my hand and my chest and the fronts of my thighs. My chin rested on the top of her head, and the bottoms of her bare feet rested on the tops of my bare feet, and everything was warm from the top to the bottom. It wasn't just warmth; it was a weighted warmth. Every night when I tried to fall asleep, I could bring myself more warmth by adding a blanket or turning on a heater, but a weighted warmth could never be attained without the intimate presence of another living being. It would be impossible to simulate the feeling. She lay in front of me, almost in me like books in a case, and I felt her warmth, but I also felt the light pressure of her weight, and it was so goddamn addictive. The addition of some weight besides my own made me feel connected to something far greater than myself, as if I were contributing to the world by carrying something beautiful through it.

I finally knew what Henry had been trying to tell me. I knew what he'd wanted me to feel. I wished I could talk to him about the feeling, about how an underprivileged girl, illegally trafficked in from the Ukraine, and a spoiled vagabond from Orange County, two irregular pieces in the world, had somehow found each other and dovetailed their existences.

Tatiana and I, listening to each other breathe and enjoying each other's weighted warmth, drifted back to sleep.

We awoke an hour later, intertwined in our cocoon of white sheets, to the summer-afternoon rays of yellow sunlight, tinged with a leafy green from filtering through the trees, streaming into our room. The bed had become part of us, and the sheets had become extensions of our nude bodies: they were Tatiana's wings and her bonnet and her dress; they were my cape and my hood and my jacket. Together, we went on white-sheet expeditions to the far corners of the bed, leaving imprints of our bodies along the way, and explored each new spot with the wide-eyed bewilderment of young travelers discovering beauty off the beaten path. Sometimes we talked, while I lay on my back and tossed a pillow into the air, and while she lay on her stomach and swung her foot down on the bed and raised it back up again.

"What kind of animal would you want to be?" I said.

"I think ... whale. They live in ocean and make pretty music," she said. "You?"

"Well, if you're living in the ocean, then I'll be a dolphin."

"If you are dolphin and I am whale, I take care of you instead."

"I'd be fast. You might not be able to catch me."

"Maybe one day you get tattoo of me as whale, and I get tattoo of you as dolphin. Then we never forget who we are."

Sometimes we rolled over to our own corners of the bed, curious about the experience of a solo journey, but soon we reached for each other and followed a path back toward the middle of the bed, until we were entwined again and as close as any young lovers in the world had ever been.

The distant, muffled sound of people lunching in the hotel restaurant—forks against plates, the clinking of glasses, people chatting—was soothing background music, mostly because it reminded us that whatever was happening in our world was far more intimate, as if we'd discovered something everyone else was searching for, but had not yet found; they were close, near to our paradise, but we'd surely have more time to revel in our togetherness before they discovered our secret.

It was an afternoon free of doubt and meaninglessness and screams and tears, not defined by the minutes and hours of the man-made clock, but by the soothing rhythm of the slow-swaying branches outside our window, their only mission to lull us to sleep and then gently wake us again. Only in the evening, when the thought of a meal began to rouse us, did we decide to leave our island and reacquaint ourselves with our feet on the mainland.

"Let's have dinner at the restaurant tonight," I said.

"OK," she said.

In the courtyard, I chose to sit at the table Henry and I used to sit at. As Tatiana and I took our seats across from each other, I thought about how it was my first time sitting at the table since Henry had died, and, surprisingly, I wasn't consumed with grief, but rather, happiness. "You need to understand that you can be happy being happy—just allow yourself the chance, Jake," Henry had told me. So it felt right to share the table with Tatiana. I only wished he was still around to join us: I knew Henry would like Tatiana, especially with her pure love of learning. The waiter came to our table, and I ordered an appetizer and a bottle of wine, while Tatiana watched a man fixing something in the garden.

"That man is farmer?" she said, pointing to him.

"Well, the word for him is gardener, I guess, or, maybe, groundskeeper."

"*Grounds ... keep ... er,*" she said, sounding out the word. "OK, I remember." She paused to gather her thoughts. "Jake, hotel name is

Farmer's Daughter Hotel?"

"That's right."

"I am farmer's daughter. I was farmer in Ukraine."

"They named the hotel after you. This is your hotel now."

"This would be nice."

"I want to be a farmer," I said.

"Jake!" she said. "You will hate it."

"I like the idea of small-town life. It seems peaceful to me."

"Jake! The word for this is not peace. You cannot read your books. We work whole day for little money."

"Tatiana, let's both go back to Ukraine and be farmers."

"No!" she said, laughing. "Maybe we switch. You be me, I be you."

"No. I like you ... as you."

And so began our relationship outside of the hotel room. We spent much more time in the courtyard—dining, playing card games, observing people—and in the garden, sunning ourselves on the grass under the trees, reading, sharing stories.

"We play chess today?" she asked me one afternoon at lunch in the courtyard, with two scraped-clean plates of what used to be paella on our table.

"Do you know how to play?"

"We can see," she said, smiling.

When the waiter came to refill our glasses with ice tea, I asked him to bring the chessboard, and, thirty minutes later, when each of our forces (she was white and I was black) had been diminished and only a handful of the pieces remained, Tatiana, on her turn, looked up at me with a mischievous smile.

"What is it?" I said, smiling back in confusion.

She moved her piece, still smiling, and said, "How you say this words in English?"

"What?" I said, then, following her gaze, looked down at the board and realized what she'd meant. "Oh, shit. Wow. Checkmate."

"Checkmate!" she repeated, smiling, raising her hands in the air.

"I didn't even see that coming—you sneak," I said, playfully sneering at her.

"*Sneak*? What is *sneak*?" she said, scrunching up her face and smiling in a way that suggested she was entertained by the sound of the word.

"It means ... like ... it's a person who—ugh!—let's just play again," I said.

"Jake, I play this game many times in Ukraine," she said, laughing at my apparent frustration. "My grandfather teach me when I was little girl."

"Your move," I said.

"Checkmate one more time," she said, this time only after fifteen minutes of playing.

"*What the*—how are you so damn good at this game, Tatiana?"

"I think it is not possible for you to beat me," she said, laughing again.

"God knows I'm trying."

"But God helps me, not you," she said.

One afternoon, on a weekday when the hotel was less crowded with tourists, Tatiana and I sat around the pool—in the same two chaise longues a robed Henry and I had relaxed on—and ordered fresh lemonade, and she told me about her youth in Ukraine: the small farming village she grew up in, her poor family, the laborious daily work forced upon her at a young age. She said that she'd always been interested in books, but that her parents would never allow them in the house, because there was always more important work to be done. She explained, in her own way, that her limitations had only fueled her thirst to discover something more about the world, to change her life, to travel and learn.

"I hear stories from people in my village about some people in my country with a lot of money—and they have *dacha,*" she said.

"*Dacha?*"

"Yes, how you say this ... for people that have two homes—one to live, one for a vacation."

"Oh, got it—like a vacation home," I said.

"Yes, I hear stories about vacation homes by the water—people go and have fun. I like those stories very much—maybe one day I have my own *dacha.*"

"Let's go see the ocean sometime, yeah? We can take a drive along the coast. Whenever you want."

"OK."

The waitress came by and refilled our glasses with lemonade. We then moved from the chairs and sat along the edge of the pool, with our feet dangling in the water, and Tatiana asked me questions, with wide-eyed curiosity, about the life of the young people in California, and, often, her face lit in fascination, excitedly interrupted me with, "Can you tell me this story again?" or "I cannot believe it," or "We are so opposites!" But never once did she speak about her time in Los Angeles before me, and I never asked her about it, or, because I sensed her fragility, about the thick scar that ran down the entire left side of her abdomen.

When Tatiana was ready to step outside the hotel, we explored near-by streets and found a haven in a small, cash-only, half-hut of a tea shop on Third Street, run by an old woman who stayed quiet, sipping from a mug at her table, unless we inquired about any of the hundreds of jars of tea that lined her walls from all over the world—and then she spoke knowledgeably and unremittingly about the finest details of the leaves and brewing techniques and blends and flavors and colors.

"Look at all this tea!" Tatiana leaned over and whispered to me. "I love to drink tea. But I drink only black tea."

But Tatiana loved it when the old woman told us, after I inquired about the best black teas, about a certain white tea instead—"Fresh from China," she said—that was wonderful to drink in the afternoon, and so, every other time we visited, Tatiana found a tea she liked along the wall and asked the old woman when it was best to drink it. Tatiana no longer drank only black tea.

"This is an herbal tea made with passion flowers, spearmint leaves, chamomile, and lemon peels. It's nice to drink in the nighttime after dinner," the old woman told Tatiana once. "It'll help you relax before bed."

"Jake," Tatiana said, turning toward me with the spark of adventure in her eyes. "Should we try tonight?"

"Sure."

We also began visiting the same vintage vinyl record store on Fairfax; each time we entered, we walked straight to the back of the store and thumbed through albums, often pausing to admire the exquisite cover art. Sometimes we bought a record and listened to it on Henry's player when we got home. I also took Tatiana to the bookstore in the neighbor-hood, the same one where I'd bought books for her, and, for hours, we leafed through the old, dusty pages of long-forgotten paperbacks.

Sometimes we treated ourselves at a self-serve yogurt place on Mel-rose—our first visit made particularly memorable by Tatiana's confu-sion.

"I do not understand," she said, staring at the variety of toppings.

"Just put everything you want on it," I said.

"Everything?"

"Yep."

"Anything?"

"Yep."

"What if they are angry?"

"No," I said, laughing. "We pay for it. They want us to do it like that."

One late afternoon, on my walk back to the hotel from getting a few groceries for dinner, I decided to go into a small flower shop that I'd passed by many times before. A sunburned old man, with a thick, white beard and a Panama hat, greeted me as I entered the store.

"It smells wonderful in here," I said to him.

"I've been in the flower business my whole life—so, for me, it just smells like regular air in here. But my customers always tell me it smells nice," he said with a raspy voice and a wink.

I smiled and said, "Well, I want to get some flowers."

"Have anything in mind?"

"No, I know nothing about flowers, but I trust your judgment—maybe just a good mix."

"For a special someone?"

"Well, for my home, but a special someone lives with me, so I want her to like them."

I continued back to the hotel, carrying the bag of groceries in one hand and a clear vase holding an arrangement of orange lilies and purple sea lavender in the other.

"I like them so much, Jake," Tatiana said, looking up from reading a book, as I walked into our room. She got up and walked toward me, as I placed the flowers on our table. "We can get new ones when they die, but we must try to keep them alive," she said.

The next time I visited the old man at the flower shop, he gave me a little leaflet with instructions on how to take care of different species of flowers, so that they would last longer. "For your special someone," he said, winking. I brought home, this time, some pink tulips in bud form, and gave Tatiana the leaflet.

"This book say the tulips are very thirsty. They must have a lot of water," she said, clipping the stems of the tulips, following the instructions, and then placing them in a vase with fresh water. "They will ..." she said, reading the words in the leaflet, "fully bloom in three or four days. I want to see them bloom," she said excitedly.

I enjoyed watching Tatiana try to "keep the flowers alive," as she liked to say, but, inevitably, usually after two weeks, the flowers began to wilt and droop and brown, and it was time for another arrangement. I made a game of surprising her with each new arrangement. "What ones today?" she would say excitedly, as I walked in the door. Once, when I brought home a bird-of-paradise, she laughed and said, "Wow. This is real bird!" Tatiana claimed to love all the flowers I brought home—although, judging from her reactions, I was sure that the lisianthus and the calla lily were her favorites—but her most memorable display of excitement came when I showed up with a vase filled with sunflowers.

"Yes!" she cheered. "I wait for this day!"

"Why? You love sunflowers?"

"Sunflower is flower of my country."

"Really? The national flower of Ukraine is the sunflower?"

"Yes! Jake, you did good job today."

One afternoon, during an after-lunch stroll, she tugged at my hand. "Many people hold those phones," she said. "You do not have phone?"

"I gave mine away to a friend."

"I want to see those phones ... in store. Can you show me?"

Tatiana did best in uncrowded areas; when too many people were around us on the street, she moved close to me, gripped my arm, and, with her eyes squeezed tightly shut against my shoulder, relied on my guidance through the crowd. So I was concerned when I took her to the Apple Store at The Grove, where, even on weekdays, hordes amassed outside popular eateries and coffee shops and stores. As we walked into the madness, I felt her recoil, but after I suggested that we turn around, she insisted on seeing where "those phones" came from.

Inside the store, I watched as she gazed in awe at the shiny, touch-screen world of technology. "This ... place is pretty. I never see something like this," she whispered, her eyes darting around frenetically, as if, right before my eyes, she'd traveled through time from her farm town in Ukraine to some futuristic era. But we had to leave when someone, pre-occupied with his handheld device, accidentally bumped into Tatiana. I felt her shake all the way home. Back in our room, I lay with her on the bed—her body cold and rigid—until she finally warmed up, unlocked, and came out of her paralyzed state.

Tatiana's bouts of depression, when it seemed all the sadness in the world was trapped behind the clear, green-glass walls of her eyes, continued to plague her, but her screams of terror in the night came less frequently, as did her crying. So we carried on, each new summer day giving her the added courage to try something new, and she gifted me the most intimate glimpses of her development. At first, she started making conversation with a waiter or the hotel "farmer."

"*Hah-lo,*" she would say. "The weather is nice today, yes?"

Then it was her eagerness to explore other parts of Los Angeles. One night, at her request, we drove to a nearby restaurant for dinner, and even stayed after for a nightcap of wine at the bar. The following afternoon, on a clear, sunny day, we took a drive on the Pacific Coast Highway, and, with the ocean on our left and our windows down to allow in the smell of the fresh ocean air, we cruised along the coast all the way to Malibu. For most of the ride, my left hand guided the wheel, while my right hand, interlocked with Tatiana's left, rested on the automatic shift. With her bare feet resting up on the dashboard and her honeyed hair blowing in the breeze, she watched, in wonderment, the unfamiliar scene passing by. When we got to Malibu, she didn't want to get out, so I found a place to park in front of the ocean, and we watched the waves roll in for a while. Then we drove home.

That night we took a fifteen-minute walk up Fairfax and had sandwiches at Canter's Deli, the place Henry had recommended to me. While we ate ham and cheese sandwiches, I thought again about how much I missed Henry, how I wished he could have met Tatiana.

Back on the street outside the restaurant, we decided to walk north another couple of blocks and then stopped, near the corner of Melrose, in front of a silent-movie theatre, appropriately named The Silent Movie Theatre. The board said that Charlie Chaplin's *City Lights* was playing for the month, and one show was starting in five minutes.

"Do you want to watch a film?" I asked Tatiana.

"Yes, OK," she said.

The theatre was empty, so we enjoyed the film, our bodies sprawled across two seats each, as if we were in the privacy of our own home. I'd already seen *City Lights*, though never in a silent-film theatre, but I was still struck by my reaction to the raw emotion of a film without any dialogue, as if the lack of it allowed me to really appreciate the music and the interaction between the characters—that is, of course, until Tatiana, who seemed to genuinely enjoy the comedy of Charlie Chaplin, began giggling, almost uncontrollably at times. At that point, I watched the film only through her eyes, stealing glances of her enjoyment, relishing the times when her hand brushed against mine, and growing more enamored of her with every passing minute.

When the film was over, we started our walk back to the hotel.

"I know why you show me this movie," Tatiana said, grabbing my hand.

"Why's that?"

"Remember that was us before we could talk to each other. You are that guy—the funny guy—and I am that girl with the flowers who you help."

I laughed and pulled her closer to me.

"Is this right?" she asked.

"Yes."

We still dedicated our mornings to the study of English, and the lessons became much more advanced, as she often requested that I read her part of a novel or some poetry from Henry's collection. As I read, she always interrupted me, her eyes flashing green with curiosity, to inquire about the meaning of certain lines. If I didn't produce an answer quickly enough, she relied on her own favorite assessment: "It means he must love her." She began reading the novels we had in our room, and our dinners became quite lively with conversations about plots and characters and themes. One night, she seemed particularly eager to discuss something with me

"I read book last night when you sleep. I read whole thing. I could not make myself stop. I like it because the people talk to each other a lot," she said. "But many things confuse me, also."

"Which book?"

"*The Sun Also Rises.*"

"Good one."

"But something bothers me for … whole day."

"Which part?"

"I do not understand … why it must end like this."

She left the table and retrieved the book from the place on the floor where she'd been reading it, the imprint of her small body still fresh from the night before, and sat back down at the table. She opened the book to the last page and read me the last line of the novel.

"'Isn't it pretty to think so?' What does this mean? Something is pretty to think?"

"Well, that was just his way of saying that their love could never work, even though they both wanted it to."

"Why?"

"Well, it's hard to know the first time you read it that ... well—he was wounded in the war in such a way that he couldn't love her as she wanted him to. She was also built in such a way that prevented her from giving him the love he wanted."

"But they *love* each other, no? Jake, you think they love each other, yes?"

"Yes, I do."

"I do not like this. It is so sad. They must stay together."

"I think so, too, but he's saying it sometimes doesn't work out the way we hope it will."

"The end of books should make me happy, or why do I have to read them? I think these sad endings are too difficult."

I laughed and said, "I think you're right. But, it's OK, Tatiana. It's just a story. It's fiction. Real life doesn't have to be that way."

And during one midsummer night in the half-light of a full moon, somewhere in the essence of Tatiana's passion for English words and the feeling of her skin against mine and the light in her green eyes and the far corner of her smile, I discovered my own words. Tatiana was lying on the bed reading a book, and I was sitting against the wall, under the window, smoking a cigarette, when the inspiration surged up within me, so profoundly that I felt submerged in it, almost choked by it. I hopped to my feet.

"What is wrong?" Tatiana said.

"I feel like writing something," I said, as I began rummaging through Henry's boxes until I found one of his more modern typewriters.

"You want to use this? You have computer!" she said, walking over to me.

"But, Tatiana, this inspires me," I said, setting the typewriter on the table and feeding it a sheet of paper from one of Henry's half-used reams.

"*Smith-Corona,*" she said, reading the label on the machine. "I like this. I let you write."

I pressed a key, the first letter, a capital "T"—my heart palpitated and my hands shook with excitement—and then, "a-t-i-a-n-a." *Tatiana.* I finished the sentence, "was a prostitute." And then, as if they were little motorists slowly coming around a curve to the start of a long straight-away on an abandoned country road, my fingers unleashed themselves onto the keyboard; I ferociously hammered at the keys, spawning words that leapfrogged across the page, misspelling many of them, but not caring, as they filled one page and bled onto another. I continued until my vision was blurry and my fingers were numb and then kept going after that, breaking only for sips of water, and, sometimes, to pace about the room when I was overwhelmed by my thoughts. *People are people. People. People. People. People need people. People need people. People need people! Meaninglessness. But ... must do something with our time. Hypocrisy. People just want to feel better. People are fallible. Not machines! Bound for fallibility from birth! Life. The veil over truth. People. People will fuck up. Nature. Conceal it or repackage it or justify it. Truth is haunting. Self-preservation. Religion. A chance to be forgiven! Eternal happiness. Relationships. Validation of self through another's love. Confusion. Death. Find a path with the least pain. Stay on that path.*

I worked all night and through the early morning, watching pages pile up at my side. When Tatiana opened her eyes, after a wake-up stretch to the sky, she said, "You are," pausing to yawn, "still writing?"

"Couldn't stop."

"What did you write?"

"I think I just started writing the beginning of a novel."

"I want to read it!"

"You'll be the first to read it."

"Your eyes are tired. Maybe you sleep?"

"No, it's time for you now. Let's get the coffee going. I just have to write one more sentence."

After I finished writing the last sentence of my first chapter, I quickly jotted down a few notes about my roommate, one year before, named Andrew, and how we'd come to live together. I was eager to get started on my second chapter, but more important to me in that moment was Tatiana.

"OK, Tatiana, ready?"

"Ready."

And so we added my writing to our routine; not much changed, except that, after dinner, I worked. I helped Tatiana in the morning; she helped me in the night. I noticed the pleasure she took in refilling my glass with water or bringing me a snack to eat, as I labored late into the night. But Tatiana helped me the most by keeping me company while I worked. Just knowing that she was in the room, in my peripheral vision, seemed to invigorate me, especially when I struggled to find the right word and could look at her and watch her smile. Sometimes I'd get up for a short break and lie next to her on the bed and cuddle up against her for a little while or tickle her, because I loved the sound of her laugh. Then, feeling refreshed, I'd sit back down at my desk and try again. She was also my source of comfort during my own frequent moments of weakness.

"Sometimes I don't know why I'm doing this. No one reads books anymore anyway," I said to Tatiana in frustration one night.

"I do. I want to read it. I promise to you," she said sincerely, which made me smile.

I began to experience spontaneous bouts of anxiety throughout the night, a feeling I never quite understood, while I battled through a medley of doubts about my writing (*This is the worst piece of shit ever written. Is that even a good sentence? Why the fuck am I wasting my time?*). But I stayed focused, and as the days shortened and cooled, reminding us of the arrival of autumn, the pile of my pages reached four inches in height.

When I returned to our room one night, after having a cigarette in the courtyard, Tatiana jumped on me, wrapping her legs around my hips, and smiled widely.

"Your book name is my name!" she shrieked with delight.

"Oh! Someone has been looking through my pages ..."

"I am sorry. You write so much. I want to see. Don't worry, I don't read much. Just the first page. I want your permission."

"I'm almost done. I can't wait for you to read it. But I want you to like it, so let me make sure it's just right."

"Jake, I will love it," she said.

"I hope so," I said.

"What is it about? Tell me one sentence."

"Love story."

"This is not full sentence!" she said.

I laughed and said, "You're right."

"It must be happy love story," she said, and then wrapped her arms around my neck and kissed me.

"We shall see. I'm still working on the ending," I said.

"OK ... Can you tell me who is Henry? You write 'To Henry' on it," she said.

"I thought you didn't read anything *else?*" I said, grabbing her face and kissing her.

"Jake! I read only two pages," she said with a guilty smile.

"Henry was my teacher and friend. The best man I've ever known, really. He died several months ago, not long before I found you."

"I wish I meet him," she said.

"He would've loved you," I said.

In bed late that night, feeling the warmth of Tatiana next to me and the joy that comes after a productive period of writing, I said, "Tatiana, I want to talk with you about something."

"We can talk about everything."

"I'm going to sell my car. We hardly use it, and we need the money. I've burned through most of mine over the last year. And I've been doing some thinking ..." I said, searching for the right words. "The money from the car should give us a few more months if we keep spending as we currently are."

I felt the muscles along her back tighten, so I held her close.

"Anyway, that should be enough time to figure things out. I have a condo by the beach about an hour south of here. Maybe we can stay there for a while, until I figure out a plan. I think you'll love waking up to the smell of the ocean ... It's much quieter there ... We could get out of the madness ... You could meet my parents," I said.

I felt the muscles along her back begin to tremble.

"I've been doing some research. You may not think so, but you have rights in this country. You're protected by something called the Trafficking Victims Protection Act," I said.

On breaks from writing, I'd researched and studied human trafficking, until I became conversant on the matter—one of the biggest criminal industries in the world, with nearly a million people (mostly women and children) trafficked across international borders each year, and billions of dollars made in profit. I also knew that only a small percentage of the trafficked victims lived long enough to get assistance from the government or find refuge from their assaulters. I'd read about how human trafficking had become a federal crime with the passage of the

Trafficking Victims Protection Act of 2000, that trafficked victims did indeed have protection (access to certain visas and witness protection), and that several state-level laws had been passed, including in California, for their protection, as well. I learned that the people most vulnerable to being trafficked into the United States came from impoverished areas in Eastern Europe, Southeast and East Asia, Latin America, and Africa. And I always kept myself well-informed about all the police raids of Los Angeles nightclubs, massage parlors, and brothels, secretly hoping to stumble upon some mention of the place where I'd found Tatiana.

"I ... want to stay here ... in hotel with you ... forever," she said, trembling harder.

"It's OK, Tatiana. Nothing will happen to you. I'll be right here with you, always," I said, holding her tighter to combat her shaking. "It might be good for both of us to get out of this place. I just need a little time to figure some things out. And I could help you get your GED. You have so much potential, Tatiana." But when she started to cry, I let it go. "I'm sorry. Let's not talk about it anymore. We still have plenty of time here in the hotel. Maybe I can find a job around here, and we can stay. Everything will be fine."

Tatiana's uneasiness was particularly unsettling for me that night, because it was another reminder that, even with her extraordinary progress, she was still susceptible to the crippling remembrance of her severe suffering, as if the well that her depression drew from was still full. Throughout our time together, I'd managed only to distract her from her own mind. I'd done nothing to drain the well. A simple conversation about a possible change in our lifestyle was enough to cause her body to tighten and tremble, bring her to tears, drain the life from her eyes. *She needs more help. I'll get her more help.*

Undoubtedly, the grimmest phase of my research involved reading about the profiles of common traffickers (often friends, neighbors, and even family members of the victims), and their strategies to entice their targets, one of them being the promise of a "better life" abroad; and even more unsettling were the ways the handlers maintained control over their victims once they reached the United States: beating, burning, gang rape, and threatening to kill family members back home. I'd read several gruesome testimonies of trafficked victims who, for the rest of their lives after being rescued, could never find peace, as they were often plagued by shame, diseases, constant nightmares, and post-traumatic stress disorder. All of this for a better life ... *Tatiana will find peace. I'll make sure of it.*

I lay awake that night, while she slept curled up next to me, in anticipation of her screams. In the beginning of our relationship, her screams had pierced the sheer silence of the room with such a haunting unworldliness, that I'd grown to dread their arrival, and, even more so, the look in Tatiana's eyes when I woke her; it was as if, during the few seconds after she'd opened eyes but before she'd regained consciousness, I had my own terrifying glimpse into her atrocious past. But over time, as my love for Tatiana grew, so did my frustration with the sound of her screams. They reminded me of her suffering, how prone she was to a setback, and how powerless I was to prevent it. I was no longer scared of the sounds, but, rather, enraged at them, as if they were predators of the night trying to steal Tatiana from me, and, like a mother bear with a cub, I stood watch over Tatiana, always ready to bare my teeth and fight when the predators came near. So when the screams came that night, I was ready for them, and woke her quickly.

"It's OK," I said, as she flinched within my grasp. "I'm right here."

I held her tight against me and felt her tears on my chest.

"It is in my head," she said. "It is always there. It is in there so much … I want to cry, but I can never cry it away. It always stays in my head."

"Someday it *will* go away. You have to believe that," I said.

"He tell me that … that he kill me if I look at other man in eyes. Many … rules. If I don't do what he say, he beat me until I cannot feel. Sometimes … he put me on bed in room with his friends. He tell to me how to be better at my job, better to please the customers. One time … he stab me and burn me. Every night, I don't know if I die or I live. Always, I hope I die," she said.

She moved closer to me until her hot, wet face was up against my neck.

"When my mother and father die, a woman come to me and say I can have good life in America. I didn't trusted her … but I want to leave my town. It is my problem what happened to me. It is because of me I am like this."

"No, Tatiana, you're wrong about that. Whichever way you look at it, in any case, what they've done to you has never been your fault. You *need* to know that."

"You cannot take care of me forever, Jake," she said.

"Yes, I can. And they will *never* hurt you again. I promise."

"I see how you look at me. Your eyes look at me as I am special," she said, crying harder. "It is not me. Inside me, I am ugly. Please stop looking at me this way."

Finally, after an hour or so, I felt the muscles in her body relax. After she was asleep, I let myself fall asleep, but woke up a few hours later, knowing something was wrong. Tatiana was sitting on the floor, in the dark, swallowing mouthfuls of wine from a previously unopened, now nearly empty, bottle.

"Tatiana, what the hell are you doing?" I said, rushing over to her and pulling the bottle away.

"Jake, I want to punch ... my head with my hand," she slurred, with a look in her eyes that frightened me. "I try to ... make it go away."

"Not like this," I said, trying to help her up and bring her back to bed.

"No—" she said, before vomiting all over herself.

I got the shower going, carried her into the bathroom, peeled off the white T-shirt she was wearing, and put her under the warm water. Despite her drunkenness (she could barely stand up), she still seemed concerned with trying to cover up, using both of her hands, the large scar on the side of her body, while I washed her.

After I had her dry and in a new shirt and in bed next to me, my mind drifted to a time when I lived with Andrew. We had a neighbor who loved to garden; he planted beautiful flowers on his balcony, so many that it was filled with an assortment of colors dripping over the railing, reminding me of an oil painting. It was quite magnificent to stare at from my window or from the street. One day, he invited me to join him on his balcony; we drank a beer while we sat on chairs and stared at the ocean. The balcony smelled lovely, as well; the whole package seemed heavenly.

"I planted some jasmine for that nice smell," he said.

"It really is beautiful. It feels like we're somewhere different. It feels like a vacation up here," I said.

I breathed in the fresh, flowery fragrances, as I ensconced myself in colorful beauty and fantasized about far-off, adventure-filled jungles and forests—places I hadn't thought about since early childhood. We sat in silence for a few minutes; I presumed that he was enjoying the experience as much as I was.

"Here's the interesting thing," he said, breaking the silence. "I've had many guests to my balcony, and just as you did, they always mention how beautiful it is up here. But after some time goes by, they all seem to have a similar reaction. You haven't had it yet, so I'm just going to tell you," he said and paused, waiting for me to come out of my trance. "After some minutes have passed, when they've had enough time to enjoy themselves, they start paying closer attention to the flowers. And when they do that, I've practically memorized the look on their faces that comes next. They start to notice that the deck is swarming with insects: bees, wasps, spiders, beetles. Their demeanor changes slightly. I notice them tighten up. I notice their smiles fade. I notice them looking around, paranoid, wondering if they're going to get bitten or stung. And right then, I know they want to be back inside, where it's safe."

I looked closely at the flowers and noticed them: bees and wasps buzzing about from flower to flower, some of them hovering close to our heads. I saw a spider walking along the balcony rail toward us. I had the sudden urge to smack my leg or frantically brush through my hair with my hands.

"See, at about this time with the others I suggest that we go back inside. I pretend that I didn't notice their faces. I don't want them to think that I'm offended. But for me, it's still beautiful here on this balcony every day. It's still beautiful to me, because I've learned to share the beauty with these bugs. And then I thought more about it. Beauty is not always as perfect as we imagine it to be, but it can be damn close if we learn to accept the scary parts or the ugly parts. We have to compromise a little bit. We have to share. But most people never come to visit my balcony again. I figured you'd be the type of guy to appreciate a story like that," he said, and I nodded as I watched the spider get closer to me.

I waited until Tatiana had slipped into the rhythm of a deep slumber, before detaching myself from her and walking over to the table. I opened one of my notebooks and started writing.

Tatiana,

You're sleeping right now. I'm looking at you, and you look so peaceful. I hope you're feeling as peaceful as you look. I wanted to write you something, so I'm sitting at the table now, writing you these words. I'm just going to write what comes to my head. I won't rip up this page and start over, because I want this letter to be unedited and pure and real. See, I don't think I've ever been very good at saying how I really feel, and the thought of you being a victim of this shortcoming of mine has driven me to try to make some sense of it all on a piece of my notebook paper—I'm going to try to write it out for you.

Have I told you that you're beautiful, Tatiana? Inside, too. I should tell you that more often. You asked me once what thoughts make me happy. In a past life, I would have told you that my happiness existed in the thought of the white foam that's created by blue waves beating against a cliff. The thought of a lonesome log cabin along a lake buried deep in the Rocky Mountains. Watching a hotel-room scene in a Sofia Coppola film. The sound of a harmonica in a song. The sunlight coming through a window.

I don't know if I'm making any sense. I guess what I'm trying to explain is that my happiness used to exist in the stillness of a perfect black-and-white photograph. When I was looking at it, I was happy, but the minute I looked away my happiness disappeared. It wasn't real happiness, Tatiana.

All these things I used to find happiness in were only distractions from the reality of my life—the life of someone just passing through. But when I'm with you, Tatiana, the thoughts that make me happy are not a distraction from my life, but proof that happiness exists in my reality—the reality of you waking up in my arms, the reality of your lips against mine, the reality of our weighted warmth under the white sheets. When I'm with you, for the first time in my life, I don't feel as if I'm just passing through.

People have always confused me, and, because of that, I'd given up on them. I saw in them only what I wanted to see, attributed my confusion to their flaws of character. But your strength, your passion, your willingness to defy the path set before you, are all indications that people are capable of truly remarkable things. That the potential for beauty lives within all of us. That it's not about unveiling the truth … Rather, it's about understanding that truth often comes with a veil.

I often think about the differences of our worlds—your tough life of poverty on the farm and my unappreciated life of opulence on the beach. But, when considering the differences, I'm drawn to the very wonderful similarity: we both sought something more in our lives and, in the race to find it on the other side of our worlds, we had the fortune of stumbling into each other somewhere in the middle. I know you think I saved you, Tatiana. But, really, you saved me.

I look forward to spending the rest of my life trying to figure out where to go next with you by my side. I love you, Tatiana.

—Jake

In the morning, I gave Tatiana the ripped-out pages from my notebook and told her that she should read when I wasn't around.

"A letter! No, I think I should read now!" she said in a way that suggested she was both truly excited and trying to show her appreciation.

As she read my letter, I watched in embarrassment, but still tried to imagine which words were making her smile. When she finished, she flashed me a radiant look. Then she read the letter again and smiled just as many times as she had during her first time through it.

"It is so nice, Jake. Really, the best thing for me to read," she said with a semi-restored light in her eyes. "I love it. I want to read it many times, over and over."

Over the next month, as the lingering heat from a worn-out summer dwindled to an autumn chill, Tatiana worked to find some peace again, while we focused on her studies and my novel. But I knew that she was struggling, that she was still being held hostage by the dark side of her mind, and often, out of the corner of my eye, I watched her turn to the letter I'd written her and read it over, until a half-smile fought its way onto her face.

Outwardly, for Tatiana's sake, I was as stoic and fearless as I could be, but, inwardly, I was consumed with a certain sadness for her, in that, even after so much progress, she seemed to be regressing, slipping back into her shaky state, losing her honeyed, healthy complexion. She started having trouble falling asleep, and when she was able to sleep, she was tormented by nightmares again. I continued to comfort her. I also worked tirelessly on my manuscript, with an inhuman determination, as if I believed that my finishing it would somehow save her, save us.

I went ahead with my plan to sell my car to bring in more money, and sold it to the first person who responded to my ad on the Internet— a young, cheery-eyed, college kid who agreed to meet me at the hotel.

"Wow. Incredible," he said, pacing around my car, turning the hat around on his head until the bill was backward. "Why are you selling it for such a good price?"

"Just need to sell it quickly."

"Yeah, I get it. Recession, huh?"

"Yeah, that's it."

"It's perfect. It's just what I've always wanted."

On a cool autumn Sunday morning, as we sat in the room sipping coffee that was still too hot to enjoy, I reached out and touched the top of Tatiana's hand.

"I finished my book last night. I want you to read it. I think you might like the ending," I said.

"Jake! I am so happy. Can I read it now? I will love it," she said, as she hopped one step over to me and jumped on my lap.

I put my hands on her bare thighs and gently slid them up under her T-shirt, where it was very warm and soft, and she kissed me as I closed my eyes.

"When can I read?" she whispered between kisses.

"Tomorrow, I'll take it to a store to make a copy of it, so I can make notes, and then the original is yours."

"I am very happy about this."

I stood up from the chair, holding her tight against me, walked us over to the bed, and set her down on it. I crawled over her, and she looked up at me through the hair that had fallen over her eyes. I slid her shirt off over her head, and then, as I lowered my body on top of hers, pulled the sheets over us. After it was over, we kicked off the sheets to cool down and catch our breath.

"Let's do nothing today. Only this," I said.

"OK. And tonight, we celebrate the book. Tonight I cook *you* dinner—a good Ukrainian dinner. Sound nice? We never leave the room," she said. "I never want to leave our room."

"Lovely."

"Can you kiss me again?"

"Yes."

In the early evening, Tatiana sent me to the market with a list of groceries to bring back, and, when I returned with everything, she said, "Can you go away for some hours? You can read books or write! I call you from window when food is ready."

I brought a book to the courtyard, ordered a coffee, and read until Tatiana poked her head out of our room window and said, "OK, ready."

When I came back into our room, the table was set for two with wineglasses, plates, bowls, little appetizer plates, and silverware.

"Sit down," she said, politely. "You ever eat *borscht* or *zharkoye?*"

"Never."

"Good. You can try real Ukrainian food for first time."

She brought a steaming pot from the kitchen to the table and ladled a very dark red soup into my bowl. "It has tomatoes and potatoes, and it is red from the beets," she said. Pointing to the sour cream in a little bowl on the table, she said, "Stir cream into soup." Then pointing to a plate of long, green onions, she said, "You can eat onions when you want, when you take break from eating *borscht.*"

"This looks great, Tatiana. Thank you."

"You must try first."

I stirred the sour cream into my *borscht* until its dark red color softened a bit and the consistency thickened. I dipped my spoon into the bowl and brought it to my mouth. Maybe it was my unfamiliarity with soup so red that made me doubt, before trying it, that I'd like it, but, as I tasted it, I was pleasantly surprised by its very soothing, hearty, rich taste.

"Tatiana, this is *fantastic,*" I said, truthfully. "Wow, really, really good."

"We also have bread," she said, handing me a piece from a plate with several slices. "Take garlic clove and rub bread. How you say name for this ... bread with garlic?"

"Garlic bread," I said, as I rubbed the clove on my piece and took a tasty bite. I finished the soup in a few minutes and had a second helping. She also made me try *salo*, white slices of cured and salted bacon fat on top of a piece of bread, and then some pickled tomatoes and pickles.

"Ukrainians usually have vodka to drink in little glasses when they eat pickles. But my parents drink vodka and say sad things about life every day when I was little girl. So we do wine instead. We have a lot of wine."

"Wine is fine with me."

"You drink vodka?"

"I haven't had hard liquor since I met you. I used to drink a little vodka, but mostly whiskey."

"We still have something more!" she said, excitedly, as if she'd forgotten about her other dish. "Now the meat." She left the table and came back with a pot filled with what looked to me like a beef stew. "This is *zharkoye*—beef and potatoes and onions," she said.

After I'd finished three helpings of the meat, and while we were sipping tea to end the feast, I looked into Tatiana's green eyes and said, "Tatiana, I'm blown away."

"What is ... blown away?"

"I mean, this was a lovely meal—just delicious."

"You are joking."

"No, I know how it sounds, but it was really good—one of the best meals I've ever had. I never knew that you were such a great cook."

"Then I did good!" she said, smiling.

Sluggish from the wine and the big meal, we relaxed on the bed right after dinner.

"You've gotten me curious about Ukraine tonight," I said.

"What you want to know?"

"Show me something that is, I don't know, very Ukrainian, something—"

"I know," she said. "You can search it on computer."

"OK, ready," I said, grabbing my laptop from the table and bringing it back to the bed.

"Look for *Cossacks*," she said, and when the screen showed the search results, she pointed and said, "There—you see these big, funny, red pants? This is very Ukraine."

"Maybe I should buy a pair," I said, as she smiled and curled up next to me.

I didn't remember falling asleep, but when I awoke later to Tatiana crying, I didn't say anything, just held her closer to me and waited for her to speak.

"We have to leave soon, yes?" she asked, nervously.

"Tatiana, you don't have to worry about it. I'll figure it out for both of us."

"But you think we should go?"

"Only when you're ready. We won't go anywhere until you're ready."

"But you want to go, yes?"

"I think we should move on at some point, yes. We can do anything we want. We can do so much together. But I won't go anywhere without you." *I'll get you help. I promise.*

Late the next morning, while Tatiana still slept, I quietly gathered my manuscript, and, before leaving our hotel room, checked my email; I saw an unread message from Andrew and decided to read it.

From: Andrew Martin
To: Jake Reed

Dear Jake,

I haven't heard from you in a while. Is everything okay? I have some incredible news. Tamarine and I are getting married! I proposed! SHE SAID YES!!! I know everything happened so quickly, but it seemed like the mature thing to do. My bosses are happy. Tamarine is happy. I'm happy. And guess what!? Tamarine will be able to stay in the country! It's a win/win for everyone. I couldn't be more excited, my friend. I wish we could celebrate together. Where are you? Are you coming home? I've tried calling you many times. Is your phone working? Anyway, I guess I'll just ask you now. I want you to be my best man! Will you accept? So exciting. Call me as soon as you get this. I hope you are okay. Things are looking up!

Cordially,
Andrew

From: <u>Jake Reed</u>
To: <u>Andrew Martin</u>

Congratulations! What incredible news, Andrew. I'm proud of you. I'm sorry I haven't been in touch. This past year has been a bit crazy for me. But I might be coming back soon. I still need to figure a few things out. I'll get in touch with you soon. Oh, and of course I accept the honor of being your best man. Can't wait to celebrate.

--Jake

I left the room, but a few seconds later, the door swung open, and Tatiana ran down the hall to catch up with me.

"You leave with no good-bye?" she said.

"I didn't want to wake you."

"I never went to sleep."

"Are you OK?"

"Yes."

"Tatiana, are you sure you're OK? I can stay with you."

"No, go. I'm OK. I wait for you here."

"OK. I'll be back soon."

"I love you."

"I love you, too," I said, as she kissed me and wrapped her arms around my neck. She leaned back, smiled at me, and then unhooked herself from my body and walked back toward the room, turning around again to look at me before she went inside.

Down in the lobby, I asked the concierge to call me a cab, and when it arrived, I told the driver to take me to Melrose and go east for a few blocks. He dropped me in front of a copy store, and I walked inside.

"Holy shit, man, is that a screenplay?" said a young kid with dreadlocks behind the counter.

"No, it's a novel—well, more like a novella, I guess. The first draft of one, anyway," I said.

"Congratulations, man."

"Thanks. It's probably nothing. Anyway, I need to make a copy of it."

"Shit, man, all those pages? Our machine's been acting up—could take a while."

Back outside, around two hours later, toting a bag with my original manuscript for Tatiana and a copy for me, I hailed another cab, but, when we began to slow in the midst of red brake lights and pedestrians on Melrose, about a mile away from my hotel, I told him to stop. *Tatiana is probably wondering where the hell I am. It'll be faster if I walk.*

"I'll walk from here," I said and paid him. "Keep it," I said, as he perfunctorily dug his hands into his pockets for my change. *A walk will be good. I need to come up with a plan for us, anyway.*

As I walked along Melrose, the smell of lunch saturated the air and the soft autumn sun warmed my face, and I suddenly became consumed with happiness. *A plan for us.* The thought of it injected a joyous burst into my step. I smiled at a group of middle-aged women passing me, and then at a delivery guy a few paces later. An organic pizza place, with its windows open to lure people in with the aroma of fresh, warm dough, had a live band playing folk rock in the direction of the street. The long-haired singer and his two acoustic-guitar-playing bandmates produced a melodious tale of summer love that compelled all the midday-strolling romantics to stop and listen. The sound of the harmonica, harmonizing with the soft chords of the guitar, resonated through the air to cheers from the gatherers, and I stood in the crowd, tapping my feet and thinking of Tatiana. *I'll get her help. She's so resilient. We'll be more than fine. She's so beautiful. Maybe I'll introduce her to my mother. Look, Mom, a nice girl. A beautiful girl. A smart girl. I'll help her with school. She'll help me with everything else. Later, she could take some classes at a local college. We could travel together. If she feels better, maybe I could bring her to Andrew's wedding. Only if she wants to go.*

After the song, I hurried down Melrose and turned left on Fairfax, feeling very excited for the next phase of my life. I walked down the hall to my room, and, in front of the door, set my bag down, and then, like a kid, jumped up to touch the ceiling, missing it only by a few inches. I took my original manuscript out of the bag to surprise Tatiana with it, unlocked the door, opened it, and, after taking one step into the room, came to a halt. The manuscript with Tatiana's name in big letters across the front fell from my grasp down to the floor, not far from where the real Tatiana lay. I bent down and picked her up, feeling her limpness, and turned her over. Red vomit lined the outside of her lips, and partly dissolved pills clung to the bottom of her chin like little white maggots. She wasn't breathing.

I ran to the phone, dialed the hotel operator, and screamed for an ambulance. I ran back over to Tatiana and carefully picked her up under the knees and behind her shoulder blades, as her head fell back lifelessly and her hair hung toward the floor. I carried her to the bed and wiped her face with the white bedsheet, which reddened with her vomit. Her left fist was still clenched tightly around the letter I'd written her, as if, in a final act of desperation, she'd tried to squeeze from its words a reason to keep fighting.

I looked down at the spot on the floor where she'd lain; two empty red-wine bottles and an empty bottle of prescription pills surrounded her imprint. I knew the label on the bottle of pills so well, that the words from it flashed in my head: "Jake Reed. Take one tablet by mouth every day as needed for anxiety."

The red lights flashed, and I stared at them, or stared through them, and didn't move. Other people, behind the yellow tape, gathered around, pointed, gawked, and took photos. When they pulled the sheet over Tatiana's face, I couldn't feel anything anymore. Someone was talking to me, but I didn't hear any words; then the person started to firmly shake my arm.

"Young man!"

I slowly turned my head and looked down into the eyes of a police officer holding a clipboard.

"Are you responsible for this girl?" he said.

"Yes."

"You are legally responsible for this girl?"

"No."

"Then we'll have to try to get in touch with the family."

"Her mother and father are dead. She's an only child. What will happen to her?"

"That'll be up to any remaining family members. It's not your problem. It's a next-of-kin issue."

He was still talking to me. I heard some of the things he was saying— "couldn't revive her" and "being a minor" and "more information from you" and "knew what she was doing with mixing both" and "nature of your relationship?" and "don't go too far"—but my gaze numbly drifted away from him and back toward the sheet over her body, as they moved her into an ambulance.

"Where do you want to go?" the man behind the ticket counter said.

"I don't know."

"Well, how am I supposed to sell you a ticket?"

"The next train out to wherever is fine," I said, staring blankly at him.

"Sir, let me try to help you out. See the map here? These are some popular routes. Anything of interest to you?"

The map had red-lined routes that snaked all over the United States. I pointed to one of them that started at the Los Angeles station and shot south to Tucson, Arizona, nearly grazing the tip of Mexico on its way through Texas, and ending up in New Orleans, Louisiana.

"The Sunset Limited line," he said. "Very beautiful ride."

I boarded the train, and, after being directed to the right section by an Amtrak employee, took my seat beside the window in the back corner of a coach-class car. I carried only a single bag and held it close, clutching the handle so tightly that the tips of my knuckles were white. An announcement was made over the train's loudspeaker to inform the passengers that departure time would be in fifteen minutes. The seats next to me remained vacant nearly all that time, until, minutes before departure, two slow-moving, loquacious old men, announcing their seat numbers to the whole car from far down the aisle, arrived next to me to claim their territory. One of them, with a cane, was being helped by the other. They spoke to each other with the excitement and forced con-geniality that comes with new friendships formed outside of comfort zones, like when two people strike up a conversation in the lobby of the doctor's office. Perhaps these two old men had met on the benches along the tracks while waiting for the train to arrive, and, as with many relationships formed in this manner, one of them had assumed a more agreeable disposition to accommodate for the pontifical nature of the other. I angled my body more toward the window, but couldn't force myself to ignore their conversation.

"I've had so many damn surgeries. They just can't seem to get it right. I'm taking eighteen pills a day right now, half of them for pain."

"Well, some of those pills lead to addiction, don't they?"

"I'm seventy-three years old—what do I care if I get addicted?"

"Well, I guess you might be right."

"If I ever get to the point where there is too much pain, I'll just find a way to end it."

"I've thought about that, too. It gives me comfort to know that I can just buy a gun and off myself if I need to."

"Yeah, I don't worry about none of that. I'm fine with death. Of course, the best way to go is in your sleep or on the operating table after they put you under."

"Yes, sir. We can only hope."

An awkward silence between them naturally ignited their curiosity about me, and I knew that they were desirous to make conversation with me, when I felt their curious eyes shift in my direction and their hot breath on my back. I stared inexpressively out the window.

"Young man," one of them said, "where're you headed?"

I held my gaze out the window, hoping he would forget about me.

"Young man?"

I turned my head in his direction, but kept my eyes toward the floor. "Nowhere. I'm just passing through," I said, clutching the strap of my bag tighter and turning my head back toward the window.

The train lurched forward unexpectedly, halted to compose itself, and then accelerated at a smooth pace out of the station. I reached into my bag, grabbed a tall bottle of whiskey, slowly unscrewed the cap, and took a large mouthful; I then pulled out the only other thing I'd brought with me, the copy I'd made of my manuscript, and traced, with my finger, the large, black letters of the title: T-a-t-i-a-n-a. *I know ... You never wanted to leave the hotel room. I should have realized that. It was my fault. So I left everything in the room for you. Everything. I left the original manuscript on the floor where you decided to leave me. It's our story. I think you would have loved the ending.*

Late into the night, when the car was dark and all the passengers were sleeping, I leaned my head against the window and found a little comfort in the hum of the train coasting along the tracks. Sometimes a train going in the other direction would appear alongside my window, and I got a faint glimpse of moonlit metal gliding past me. For as long as the trains were passing each other—never more than ten seconds—I heard a different tune emitting from the tracks, as if, in the excitement of their momentary closeness, the trains had collaborated on a new melody. I shut my eyes to listen, but reopened them immediately, for I was too afraid of what I might see behind the darkness of my eyelids. Then the tail of the other train whipped past the head of my train, and our togetherness was over, as we rode alone on the tracks again.

Later, the train came to a full stop in the middle of blackness, and I thought something might be wrong, but then I realized that we were only waiting for another train, coming our way, to cross over the tracks.

Waiting. I remembered something Henry had told me once about *waiting.*

"War, for me, was about *waiting*—waiting to take orders, waiting to give orders, waiting to go home, waiting to die, but mostly it was about helping the guys under my command deal with the anguish of all the waiting," he'd said.

I think I finally understood what he meant.

I stared into the heavy black night, until patches of velvety purple sprouted across the sky, and the tips of trees were made visible against the horizon; bits of orange began to attach themselves to the velvety purple patches, and, soon after, the tip of a rising sun appeared at the far end of the southwestern desert. Some of the passengers stirred in the light of the new day. The train looped around a bend, straightened out, and chugged on through small, dusty towns I'd never before thought to visit.

ACKNOWLEDGEMENTS

Thank you to Jesse Young, my longtime friend, business partner, and sharer of similar dreams.

Thank you to Courtney Rediger, my devoted editor and protector of Tatiana; Professor of English emeritus Thomas Mauch, my mentor; and Robin Harders, my copy editor and advisor, for their invaluable contributions to my work.

Thank you to my beautiful sisters, Mary and Ana, for their unceasing support, especially during my moments of neurosis.

Special thanks to: My readers and patrons, Mike Berman, Anthony Dedeaux, Deo Anunciado, Kevin Shalvey, Spencer Rinkus, Elizaveta Kholostenko, Duncan Jacobson, Elena de Sosa, Dr. Rossan Chen, Justin Rofel, Samy Mosher, Erin Benjamins, Larry Lantero, Adam Oesterle, Ashley Gottesman, Drew Todd, Kristin Ofria, Rebecca Lewis, Jayson Fox, Aaron Tumbry, Daniel Shapiro, Stephanie Pearson, Vinnie Pergola, Jillian Specter, Kim Litzius, Brady McCollum, Michael Murray, The Infamous H, Ryan Schissler, Otto Cedeno, Will Percy, Eric Maldin, Karlyn Byxbee, Christina Wakefield, Pat Cauley, Manuel Gomez, Janet Passanante, Anna Fine, Kaman Liang, Sarah Lherbier, Alejandro Perez, Magdalena Michalowicz, Nichole Delansky, Steve Hilferty, Scott Henderson, Phillip Butler, Taryn Ryder, Freya Waldern, Tyler Petersen, Paul Iskin, his mother, Geena Schneider, and his sister, Ashleigh Kay, for inviting me to have a delicious Ukrainian meal and allowing me to listen to their wonderful Ukrainian stories.

Thank you, all, for helping to make my dream possible.